MONTANA
Weddings

MONTANA
Weddings

LINDA
FORD

BARBOUR
PUBLISHING

Published by Barbour Publishing, Inc., P.O. Box 719, Uhrichsville, Ohio 44683, www.barbourbooks.com

Our mission is to publish and distribute inspirational products offering exceptional value and biblical encouragement to the masses.

ecpa Member of the
Evangelical Christian
Publishers Association

Printed in the United States of America.

Dear Readers,

I had so much fun with these stories—not just the writing but also the research. I live in Alberta, so when I decided to set this series in Montana, it provided a perfect excuse for some firsthand research. I packed up my sister and my live-in client and headed south (leaving my husband at home to hold down the fort). Visiting a place for the purpose of research gives one a unique, in-depth view they might overlook otherwise. And that's what I found on my visit. I asked questions, toured the streets of several towns, measured the distance from one place to another, and read and collected brochures. It was a great deal of fun. I found people so welcoming and helpful and the scenery wonderful. My goal was to make these stories as authentically Montana as possible. I hope I succeeded.

I also hope my stories convey hope and healing from God's almighty hand. That is always my goal. "To him who is able to do immeasurably more than all we ask or imagine, according to his power that is at work within us." Ephesians 3:20

I love to hear from readers. You may contact me through my Web site (where you can also find information on my other books): www.lindaford.org

Linda Ford

Cry of
My Heart

Dedication

To the Canadian Peacekeepers who risk their lives around the world,
and to their families who stay at home and wait for their return.
My prayers for your safety and peace of mind.

Chapter 1

She knew it was an answer to prayer—just not the one she'd expected. She hadn't seen Andrew Conners since she was ten and he twelve, and she had no desire to see him now. Not after the way he'd treated his aunt. Only God seemed to have sent this opportunity her way, so she marched down the alley and through the gate into the yard next door.

Standing on the step, facing the door, she smoothed her hands over the hips of her pink cotton pants and tugged at the hem of her matching floral blouse. Maybe she just thought it seemed like an answer to prayer because it fit her needs so perfectly.

God, if I'm mistaken, have him not be here.

She hadn't even said amen, hadn't even knocked, when the door jerked open, and she stared at a pair of arms clutching a large box. The box-carrying figure halted, turned, and regarded her with wide, startled hazel eyes. Slowly he lowered the box to the floor, and they stared at each other.

Her mouth fell open. She knew he wouldn't be the kid he'd been eighteen years ago, but somehow she hadn't thought he'd be so...so big. He had to be over six feet tall. Power and authority practically oozed from him. His blue jeans were faded, his black T-shirt smudged with patches of dust. His skin glowed golden; his brown hair shone with streaks.

She swallowed, her throat strangely stiff. This was Andrew? She remembered a scrawny, sometimes sad, sometimes angry boy. The only thing reminiscent of that person was his eyes. A smile flashed across his face, making those hazel eyes suddenly warm.

"Nicole Costello. I'd have known you anywhere."

Nicole tried to ignore the way her heart tripped over itself several times in her assessment of this man, leaving her as scatterbrained as her younger sister, Carrie, without the excuse of being seventeen years old.

"Hi, Andrew."

He quirked one eyebrow. "Make it Ace. I haven't gone by Andrew since—" He shrugged. "In a very long time."

"And it's Nicole Thomas now."

"You're married then?"

"No. My mom remarried. To Paul Thomas."

He snapped his fingers. "I remember. They got engaged that Christmas I was here, didn't they?"

She nodded, surprised he remembered. Surprised he even remembered how to get to small-town Reliance, Montana.

"So you've decided to come back?" She heard the way her voice grated with disapproval and hoped he wouldn't notice.

"You sound. . ." He paused before he said, "Surprised."

"It's too late, Andrew. Years and years too late." A tremor skated across her shoulders at the way his expression hardened. "You didn't even come for the funeral."

His eyes lost their warmth, and she knew if she'd hoped for an explanation she was going to be disappointed. But it was so sad. Aunt Millie wasn't even a relative of hers, only Gram's best friend for decades. She and Carrie and Gram were the closest thing to family Aunt Millie had in her declining years.

He fixed her with an assessing stare. "I remember you as a kid who said what she thought. I see you haven't changed."

She would like to tell him what she really thought, but it might not be conducive to the business she hoped to conduct. "I understand you're interested in selling the contents of the house." She handed him her business card. "I'd like to buy some things."

Not even glancing at it, he dropped the card in his breast pocket before he stepped aside and waved her in. "I'm anxious to be done and out of here. Anything in particular you're interested in?"

"Some of the antiques, if you're selling them."

"I'm getting rid of everything."

She wanted to protest the way he talked—like it was nothing more than stuff—instead of the remnants of his aunt's life. As she stepped inside the house a pang of emptiness touched her heart. She stood in the wide kitchen where she'd many times visited Aunt Millie.

Open-flapped boxes teetered along one wall. A cupboard over the sink stood ajar as if Andrew had been cleaning it out. The whole place smelled old and closed in.

She touched the chipped brown teapot on the table. "This was Aunt Millie's favorite."

"It's seen better days," he muttered.

"She said it made the best tea."

Andrew grunted impatiently. "It would make good landfill."

Nicole stopped smiling. It seemed every mention of Aunt Millie caused him to become increasingly defensive.

"And how are your parents?" he asked, as if hoping to divert her from the protest on her lips.

Nicole froze inside. It still hit her like a jolt. She stared at the label on a box. "They were killed in a car accident seven years ago. Carrie, Gram—Grandmother—and I are all that's left." If only they hadn't gone on that holiday. One minute they were full of excitement and joy. The next, gone, their lives destroyed by a swerving vehicle on a steep mountain grade. And in that moment, life for Nicole had taken a sharp turn. In her third year at university she'd quit to come home and help Gram raise Carrie. Only her faith in God sustained her.

"I'm sorry," he said. "Tough break."

Nicole relaxed, letting a gentle smile curve her lips. "It hasn't been too bad. I still have Gram and my sister, Carrie." Taking a deep breath, she faced him squarely. "What about you? I remember you and your mom were going to move in with Aunt Millie. You had such dreams. You were going to follow God and be a Christian soldier. I remember we talked about it for hours. And then nothing. As if you disappeared off the face of the earth."

His smile receded, but the quick masking of the expression in his eyes riveted her attention on his face. "Sometimes life interferes with our plans."

"For sure." What details had shaped his life since she'd last seen him? Not that anything could excuse his neglect of Aunt Millie. "Andrew, I—"

"Ace. Andrew's someone from my past." His hard tone made it clear he would tolerate no argument.

"All right. Ace then. Have you had a chance to go through the house?"

"Five bedrooms, a dining room, living room, pantry, and store room." He ticked off his fingers as he spoke. "Not to mention a basement I haven't dared venture into. All crammed with stuff."

She hoped she didn't look too pleased at his distress. "You've forgotten the garage and the attic."

"An attic?" He rolled his eyes and moaned.

She nodded. Maybe by the time he got through it all he'd have an inkling of what he'd missed in ignoring his aunt.

He lifted his arms in defeat. "Good thing I don't have anything urgent on my calendar." He sighed. "You're welcome to go through and pick out whatever you want."

"Oh, but not until you've had a chance to decide what you want to keep."

He shrugged. "I can't think I'd want anything. I'm not much for sentimentality."

"But Aunt Millie thought so much of you. Surely you want something to remember her by." Again that hard, closed look came to his eyes.

"Take whatever you want."

She curled her fingers. How could he be so unfeeling? As if nothing about Aunt Millie mattered?

"About the attic—I don't recall seeing an entrance."

Nicole nodded. "I'd better show you." She led the way through the living room, up the stairs to the back bedroom crowded with boxes, a huge wardrobe, an old-fashioned sewing machine, and other pieces of furniture. "You really do have your job cut out for you." For the first time she felt a touch of sympathy. "It can't be easy disposing of your aunt's things."

Again that sudden flash in his eyes. "It's only a job."

Her rush of sympathy flared into anger. "I heard your mother had died. I'm sorry. That left Aunt Millie as your last living relative. I'd think she deserved a little more regret or sorrow on your part."

"She was old and crippled even when I saw her last. I'm sure she'd suffered enough."

Against her will, Nicole was forced to agree. "I suppose I meant sorrow for what you've lost. Your family. That has to mean something."

The corners of his mouth drew down. "Family! What's that? Only people related by accident of birth."

She faced him squarely. "Family is a whole lot more than that." She realized her fists were planted on her hips and dropped her arms to her sides. " 'Course you only get out of family what you put into it." He'd put nothing into his. He'd get nothing back.

His scowl deepened. "Meaning?"

She slowed her breathing. "Some people don't value what they have." She felt the heat from his eyes as he stared at her without answering. She turned away. "Let me show you the attic."

◆

Ace watched Nicole yank open the double closet doors and flip a latch in the ceiling. He remembered her as an intense, skinny kid with a mane of long black hair. Her hair was no longer waist length, but she didn't seem to have lost any of her intensity. Her emotions vibrated from her. Sharp disapproval. Directed at him. Condemning him for what she saw as his failure to live up to her expectations. Huh! Fat lot she knew about it.

He shrugged. He'd learned to ignore all sorts of prejudice. He leaned against the wall where he could study her as she fiddled with a curl of rope.

An attractive bit of humanity. Small boned. Tiny stature. Ace let his gaze linger on her short, pixie-cut dark hair. He liked the way it emphasized her delicate features. Her olive skin, inherited from her Italian father, glowed with health.

No doubt she'd told him what happened to her father. But it was so long ago he couldn't remember. A freak accident or something. Then she'd lost both her mother and stepfather. Tough break for someone who valued family so much.

She tugged on the rope she'd managed to untangle. A patch of ceiling rolled back, and a set of stairs unfolded at her feet. She coughed at the cloud of dust sifting over her, brushed herself off, and faced him. "Ta da." She grinned and swept her arm up the steps. "The attic."

Ace's gaze lingered on her wide smile before he turned to stare into the dim overhead room. Why did he get the feeling she enjoyed his annoyance over the task ahead of him? She probably figured it served him right for not keeping in touch with Aunt Millie.

"Go ahead," she urged. "It's full of treasures."

"I'll bet." If the rest of the house were any indication, the attic would be crowded to the rafters.

She waited for him to lead the way and pointed to a pull chain for the light as he stepped to the board floor.

It was even worse than he'd imagined. Rows of old coats hung from wires. Boxes crowded under the eaves. Trunks, bookcases loaded with junk, and more boxes everywhere he looked.

"Great," he muttered. "A veritable gold mine."

Nicole stepped around him. "Before I grew up and left home, I used to come up here every year to help Aunt Millie get her Christmas decorations."

"Grew up? I don't think so." He held his hand out a little above waist height to indicate her short stature.

She sniffed and tilted her chin. "Gram says good things come in small packages."

"So does nitro."

Her chuckle rolled across his mind. "Let's hope the comparison doesn't mean anything." She turned to glance around the room. "There're the Christmas decorations. Right where she always had me put them." She picked her way around several boxes, an old leather trunk, and a crooked footstool with stuffing bulging out of ripped seams, to a stack of boxes marked C'MAS DECORATIONS. Kneeling, she pushed aside the boxes. "Look—here are the outdoor ones." She held up a wire frame shaped like an angel then turned to stare at a wooden crèche scene. "She loved decorating for the season."

Most Christmases passed without Ace even noticing, but watching the play of emotions on Nicole's face he could understand why it had been important, and probably enjoyable, for Aunt Millie. Seeing Nicole's pleasure, he could almost imagine himself liking the idea of stringing lights and decorating a tree. Then he jerked his thoughts into submission. He didn't need Christmas or lights or even neighbors like Nicole and her sister and grandmother. He was happy with things the way they were.

Nicole shoved aside the wise men and pulled out a life-size plastic reindeer.

"I'd forgotten about this." Turning to face Ace, she sat back on her heels. "Do you remember it?"

For one unguarded moment Ace recalled the excitement, the promise, the hope he'd felt when Aunt Millie bought that decoration, and then he snapped the gate shut on his memories. There would be no more wishing and wondering. No more false hopes. "Vaguely," he answered.

Nicole's expression sobered, and she studied him as if expecting more response. "Aunt Millie would never let me bring it down. She said it was yours and she was saving it for you. She told me when you came back you could put it up yourself." She tipped her head. "Ace, what happened to you? Why didn't you come back?"

Ace wished he'd never allowed her to show him the attic. "It's ancient history." But her pixie face screwed up, and he knew she wasn't going to accept his answer even before she shook her head and spoke.

"Not that ancient. Besides, I guess I want to"—she shook her head again as if troubled by her thoughts—"I want to understand what happened." She pushed the reindeer toward him.

He touched the red nose of the ornament and remembered how it had blinked off and on when the electric cord hanging from its neck was plugged in. He shoved the silly plastic animal aside and straightened until his head almost touched the low ceiling.

He'd succeeded in leaving behind that part of his life. He didn't need little Miss Nicole bringing it up. Crossing his arms over his chest, he said, "I doubt I could add anything to what Aunt Millie said."

"That's the strange thing. After you left, all she could talk about was you and your mother coming to stay. And then"—an enigmatic lift of one shoulder—"she just clammed up. Whenever I asked her what happened, she would get a real sad look on her face. Sometimes I caught a glimpse of tears in her eyes. I know she prayed for you, and I expect part of her prayers was for you to come back."

Ace stared past her. He focused on a broken coat tree, leaning drunkenly to the left. He had no intention whatsoever of delving into his past, revealing secrets, unveiling his heart. "I'll need to get a truck in here to haul this stuff away."

She shifted as she looked across the room. "I wondered if maybe your mother found a new boyfriend, and that's why. . ." Her voice trailed off as if she expected him to supply the answer.

He heard the invitation in her voice, and his chest tightened. *I'm not spilling my guts.*

"But you never came. I waited for you. I thought you'd come."

Her voice said it all. Her disappointment with him. Her opinion that he'd failed. She looked so concerned. He remembered this uncanny thing about her. How, even at ten, her frank, wide-eyed, caring look made him tell her things he'd thought were locked securely inside his heart. But now, older and wiser, he knew how to keep his secrets behind barred doors where they couldn't hurt him. He'd tell her only enough to relieve her misconceptions.

"No new boyfriend. My mother died that same year." She'd hit the bottle again and was ashamed to let Aunt Millie know. "When I was thirteen." What would she say if he told her how his mother had died? Downing one mickey after another until she passed out. Not an unusual occurrence by any means. But this time the blood alcohol was too much for her body to take.

"I heard she died. How awful. But then why didn't you come live with Aunt Millie? It would seem the natural thing to do."

"You'd think." He made no attempt to hide his sarcasm.

After the doctor's blunt announcement that his mother had drunk herself to death, Ace sat across a big mahogany desk and watched the doctor punch in the phone number that brought a social worker to the room.

For weeks, while he was shifted from the emergency shelter to a group home and then to the first of a series of foster homes, Ace clung to the hope that Aunt Millie would come for him. She'd promised they would live with her.

But she never came.

"I guess a teenage boy without his mother was more than she cared to deal with."

Nicole pinched her lips together briefly before she spoke. "No way. Aunt Millie wouldn't turn away anyone."

Except me. He pushed the pain back, behind a lifetime of walls.

"Why didn't you call her? Seems you could have at least let her know you were okay."

Her suggestion that he'd turned his back on Aunt Millie stung. "What makes you think I didn't? Fact is, I sent her a half dozen letters. I even managed to sneak in a few phone calls, but all she said was she'd get back to me." He shrugged, proving to himself it no longer mattered. "She never called, and she never came. And I quit bugging her." He'd shut Aunt Millie out of his life after that. Permanently.

Nicole rocked her head back and forth. "I just know there's more to it." Her eyes narrowed and darkened with intensity as she brought her gaze back to him.

He remained perfectly still, meeting her look steadily, knowing the least shifting of his eyes or even a fiddling of his fingers would provide clues to his emotional state he didn't wish her to see. Didn't even want to own.

She edged over to perch on an old trunk and, leaning her elbows on her knees, nodded. "Okay, tell me everything from when I last saw you."

"What?"

"Yup. Where you lived. How you felt. What was going through your mind? What you do now. How your relationship with God has grown—"

At her probing questions, tension grabbed the back of his head, making his scalp too tight. But he would not let her interest dent the protective shell he'd built around his emotions. He uncurled his fingers, rolled his head back and forth, then held up one hand. "Enough. You haven't changed a bit, have you?"

"Maybe. Maybe not. I guess I'm still curious."

"You think?" But even at ten it hadn't been idle curiosity. Even then she'd managed to get him to tell her his hope for a permanent home, his dreams for the future. Maybe her intense way of listening made him open up. Maybe her attitude said it mattered. Whatever. It held the same power today to unlock his thoughts. But today was different. He was different. He'd learned to guard his feelings. But knowing she wouldn't let him get away with saying nothing, he told her briefly of living in a steady stream of foster homes.

"I know I wasn't an easy kid."

"Umm. I can imagine your tough-guy act."

"How would you know?"

"You had a good start on it even back then."

"You saw that?"

She smiled. "Not really. But I remember my mom saying you thought you could protect yourself with what she called 'attitude.'"

"Yeah, well, my attitude was well honed by the time I was eighteen and out of the system."

"And then what?"

"I qualified for a scholarship, went to university, and took my degree in petroleum engineering. Worked on offshore drilling rigs for several years."

"And now?"

"Still in the petroleum industry. Only now I say when and where."

"And that's important, isn't it?"

"Saying when and where? You bet it is."

"Still. It's too bad."

"Too bad I'm more or less my own boss?"

"Not that. That's great if it's what you want. But you and Aunt Millie—the last of your family. Such a waste."

"I guess you don't miss what you never had."

She looked thoughtful. Was she as unconvinced as he? When her mouth made a little round shape and her eyes widened, he wondered what new idea darted across her mind.

"Here I am talking as if Aunt Millie was your only family. How stupid of me. You probably have a wife and kids by now."

"Not me. I've been far too busy."

She considered him unblinkingly for several seconds as if trying to discover what hidden message might lie behind his words. "And God?"

"You might say He's on the back burner." Way back. So far back he never thought of Him anymore. God, Aunt Millie, and hopes—all part of a childhood dream lasting one short Christmas season.

◆

Shock waves washed through Nicole's thoughts. How could he shove God away? Especially when he had no family. No one to love. As unthinkable as being at sea without a boat. She thanked God daily for His love and her family. "I can't imagine. To me, God and family are the most important things in the world."

"So I gathered." He pushed to his feet making it clear he didn't want to continue this discussion. "Come on. Let's get out of here."

She took a long, lingering look around the low room. She could almost see Aunt Millie bent over a box poking through the contents, her grumbling voice worrying over some item she couldn't locate. Nicole took a deep breath. Past the odor of mothballs and dust she caught a whiff of the rosewater and glycerin soap Aunt Millie used. Her throat tightened as she turned to follow Ace down the steep steps.

They came to a halt in the kitchen.

He took her business card from his breast pocket. "Grandpa's Attic. Nice name."

"It was my grandfather's store. Gram let me take it over and restore it."

He continued reading. " 'An eclectic art gallery. Something for everyone.' Sounds interesting. And you'd like to add antiques to your collection?"

She nodded. "I look for unusual and quality items. Aunt Millie had some wonderful things."

"Take whatever you can use," Ace said.

She licked at one corner of her mouth and tasted the dust from the attic. This was where things got difficult. What she wanted and what she could afford were two different things. She'd like to pack it all over to her storeroom. Every last dish, knickknack, and picture. Everything except what he should keep. But she'd spent the last of her savings on renovating the store and then on a buying trip to Great Falls.

Her business had proved moderately successful. She'd learned a lot. She understood she had three distinct demographics of buyers. The tourists who wanted something they could carry away in their purses or have shipped. Something reminiscent of the area. Then there were the decorators looking for signature feature pieces. For them the price was secondary to original, interesting, eye-catching appeal. The last group was the serious collectors who were willing to pay significant amounts for quality work. She knew the sort of thing that appealed to each group. If she could offer more stock—some truly unique and wonderful things—she could raise her profits significantly.

Right now she managed to pay the bills but with nothing left over. She couldn't continue at that level of income. There were always emergencies to plan for, like car repairs and family needs. And then Carrie would be graduating in a year. Their parents' life insurance had been meant for university, but with rising costs Carrie would require a whole lot more than the life insurance proceeds. First on her list of needs, though, was Gram's cataract surgery. The doctor had warned it would soon be necessary, and Nicole wanted the operation done at the best clinic available. She had to earn the funds.

If she could get some of Aunt Millie's things cleaned and on display, she would be able to take advantage of the busy tourist season.

"What's the matter? Have you changed your mind?"

"No. But there is a problem. I can't afford to pay what they're worth."

"So don't tell me what they're worth, and I won't know."

"That's just plain dumb." She glared at him. "I'll pay a reasonable price for whatever I take."

"Okay. What are you suggesting?"

"I'm hoping you'll agree to let me have them on consignment." She rushed ahead before he could refuse. "I'll give you a modest down payment. We'll make a thorough list of all the items I take and set a price for them. Then when I sell them I pay you. Okay?"

He shrugged. "Not a problem. I just want to get rid of it. I'm not worried about the money."

He said it like a man who didn't need to worry about where the next dollar came from. Of course he had no responsibilities. No family who depended on him.

She had Gram and Carrie.

"I *am* concerned about money," she said. Unlike him she couldn't afford to make decisions without considering the consequences.

"Suit yourself. I'm glad to let you have whatever you want. This stuff probably means something to you." He gave an encompassing wave around the room. "It means nothing to me except how to move it."

She stared at him with disbelief. "Some of Aunt Millie's stuff is priceless. You should at least make sure you get a fair deal."

He grinned. "You mean to say you antique dealers aren't above taking advantage of a person's ignorance?"

"I can't speak for anyone else, but I'd offer what I considered fair." Why did it all come down to money? So much more was at stake here. Family. Memories. Tradition. Aunt Millie had told her about things that had been in the family for generations. They should be kept there. "You need to go through and pick out what you'll want to keep. Like the collection of brass elephants that came from India with some ancestor of yours. Aunt Millie's great-uncle, I believe it was. And the cut-glass dishes, a wedding present to your great-great-grandparents. Aunt Millie said those dishes were the only thing to survive a tornado."

His expression had grown distant. "I'm sure some of the stuff has a fascinating history. And no doubt telling your customers will up your chances of a sale."

"But some are family heirlooms. You should keep the things that meant so much to Aunt Millie."

Again that hard, closed look to his eyes. "Don't you think we're a little past that?"

"But she was—"

"Family. I know. You've already mentioned it several times. But, honestly, don't you think family means more to you than it did to her?"

"How can you say that? As if Aunt Millie didn't care?" She shook her head.

"Come on, Nicole. If family was so important to her, don't you think she would have done things differently?"

"You mean she would have brought you here to live?"

He gave her a steady look. "What do you think?"

"I don't know what happened, but there has to be an explanation, because Aunt Millie did care about you. I'll prove it somehow. She deserves the truth, and so do you."

"Be careful that the truth isn't more than you want to know."

She returned look for look. No way was she afraid of the truth. "It's not me who's been running for eighteen years."

"Running? Who was running?"

"You, and I think you know it. The question is, what are you running from? Are you afraid of what you might find if you go back to the beginning? To the time before things fell apart for you?"

"Ah, I see you've been studying psychology. Or is that wisdom from a women's magazine?"

She smiled. It didn't take a psychology guru to put his disappointment and his long absence together and come up with avoidance. "Maybe you'll find the answers you need as you clean out the house."

He snorted. "I'm not looking for answers."

"I'm going to pray you'll find family and God again." She said it with the absolute conviction that grew out of having received God's answers time and again.

He looked at her with all the interest of having heard something spoken in a foreign language. "Would you like to start picking out the items you want?"

She glanced at the old red clock above the stove. "I have to go. Besides, I think you should sort out what's important to you first. How would it be if I come back tomorrow and see what you've uncovered?"

"Sounds like a plan." He held the door open for her.

As she went out the back gate and along the alley to her home next door, she thought about Ace's steadfast refusal to believe Aunt Millie cared about him.

God, it seems You've sent him here to find answers he doesn't even know he wants. If so, help him find them and find love at the same time—Your love.

Chapter 2

Nicole paused outside Aunt Millie's door to give herself a mental shake before she knocked. Sure, she was excited, but only because she wanted to get her hands on those antiques as soon as possible. Busloads of tourists were arriving daily. She couldn't afford to miss any sales. At the rate she was saving money, Gram would never get her cataracts removed.

It was *not* because she looked forward to seeing Ace again. She had to get it through her mind Ace was not Andrew, her friend of the past.

"It's open," Ace called.

Inside, he sat at the table, wearing a once-white T-shirt smudged with every shade of gray and black. He leaned back in his chair, crumbs and an empty coffee cup in front of him. Muddy sweat tracks trailed along his jaw. His mouth drew to a tight line. He looked hot, dirty, and discouraged.

Nicole's urgency over the antiques ground to a halt. Her heart went out to him. Perhaps it had finally hit him how much he'd missed. "Tough day?"

"Hot day. And dusty." He tipped his head from side to side as if easing a sore neck.

"Get lots done?" She'd noticed boxes filling the Dumpster. She hoped he hadn't thrown antiques out with the junk.

"Lots of nothing. I'm convinced Aunt Millie was a pack rat." He groaned as he stretched his neck.

"Sounds like you need some cheering up."

"What I need is a forklift to clean out this house."

"Would you settle for a fresh cup of coffee?"

"Just what I need. But I'll do it." He sprang to his feet, refilled the coffeepot, and turned it on.

They waited as the dark liquid dripped through, the aroma drowning out the dusty smell she'd noticed as she stepped into the house.

"You take cream or sugar?" he asked, pouring out two cupfuls when it finished.

"Milk, if you have it."

"I haven't, but I think I remember seeing some whitener." He opened the yellowed and chipped cupboards until he located the jar, screwed off the lid, and smelled the contents. "I don't know. It's probably a century old. But, hey, does a nonfood item perish?" He tipped the jar toward her.

When she saw the lumpy contents, she shuddered. "I suddenly feel like having it black."

"Wise choice."

He seemed lost in contemplation of the bubbles on his coffee as they sat across from each other.

She sipped her black coffee, her mouth protesting at the bitter taste.

"Ace?" But how could she tell him how desperately she needed to steal away his aunt's possessions when it looked as if it had finally hit home these things were all that remained of her life? Bits and pieces of a long life he could have shared if things had turned out differently.

He quirked an eyebrow. "What were you going to ask?"

She studied the contents of her cup. "Nothing."

"Hey, this is old Ace, remember? You told me all your secrets when we were young." He winked. "I haven't forgotten."

"Neither have I." He was flirting. But too many days and years had passed for her to react as if they were old friends. He was Ace, a stranger.

And yet not quite that either.

"You were the first girl who showed an interest in me." Her cheeks grew warm under his scrutiny. "I believe I was half in love with you back then." His deep chuckle bubbled down her spine.

"We were kids," she protested.

"Yeah." His teasing expression fled. "Kids. Too young and innocent to realize what lay ahead."

"I'm sorry. I know life hasn't been easy for you."

He shrugged.

She rushed on, anxious to use this opportunity. "But you're wrong about Aunt Millie."

He raised both eyebrows. "You mean she wasn't a pack rat?"

She giggled. "That part is true, but I mean she didn't forget about you."

"How comforting." His eyes glinted.

"Ace, I've been thinking about it. And it seems to me something happened. Something to explain why she didn't come for you."

His eyes had the glazed sheen of the pottery she'd bought at the art fair in Great Falls.

"Think," she urged. "There has to be some explanation."

"You mean like she lost my address and phone number and didn't realize she could get them from social services. Or maybe—" He snapped his fingers. "I know. Maybe she developed a case of selective amnesia. I'll bet that's it. Why didn't I think of it before?"

She scowled. "You're making fun of me."

"Sorry."

"Yeah, you sound sorry."

"Maybe you should accept that everything doesn't work out all neat and tidy just because it would fit nicely into your philosophy of families are forever."

She jerked to her feet, stung by his mocking tone. Planting her hands on the tabletop, she leaned over to glare at him. "Andrew Conners, we will find an explanation for why she didn't come for you."

He didn't edge back. Not a flicker of emotion in his eyes. In fact, she sensed that all feeling had been successfully quelled and only a hard, empty shell remained.

She sank back in her chair. "I believe God has brought you here for that very reason. So you can understand and open your heart to love."

He rolled his eyes toward the ceiling. "And all the time I thought I'd come to clean out my aunt's house. How could I be so mistaken?"

◆

Ace resisted the urge to rub the back of his neck. He didn't want Nicole to know how much her words affected him. He'd like to believe as she did, but it would take a miracle to convince him Aunt Millie loved him. Because if she had, why didn't she pluck him from those harsh homes? Homes where he'd been treated like free labor or where everything that mattered to him mysteriously disappeared or was denied him. But he could tell Nicole believed in miracles. She'd find out soon enough that only a few qualified for one.

If it weren't for the antiques spread out in the other room, he'd tell her to go home and mind her own business.

Okay, maybe something about her pulled at him. It was true he'd been half in love with her back then. Not as a man-woman thing—they'd been too young for that—but there'd been a sense of connection he'd never experienced before. And never again.

"I've picked out a few things you might be interested in." He led the way to the dining room where items he'd found during the day covered the big walnut table. Picking them out for Nicole had caused his thoughts to center on her way too much. How was he going to do this job and get out without any emotional stuff if he thought of her every minute of the day?

She rushed to the table and picked up the small brass elephant. "Wonderful. I haven't seen this for years." Her face glowed. "It's what I was telling you about. Where did you find it?"

"In a desk drawer among some old papers."

A tiny frown creased her forehead. "There were three of them."

"Maybe the others will turn up." When her forehead smoothed and her smile returned, the tension in his neck eased. He shook his head feeling suddenly as if they were kids again when he couldn't bear to see her unhappy. He'd gone out of his way to make her laugh then, even though they spent considerable time in serious discussion about things that mattered to kids. But he didn't want to go back to that time of his life. He wasn't the same person he was then.

She circled the table, her eyes measuring, lighting with pleasure. She wore a simple pale green dress. It made her look slender and vibrant as an olive branch. She picked up the items and examined them carefully. When she finished, she stood in front of him. "I'll have to start a list. Wouldn't want to cheat you."

"Or yourself."

Their gazes caught and held. He could sense her jolt as if she were seeing him in a new light. No longer the Andrew of her childhood, but Ace, a man, and she, a woman. Awareness flickered across her eyes, even as it stirred his own feelings. It was more than a physical thing. It was emotional. He felt safe with her. Just like when they were children. He knew he could tell her all his secrets and she would understand. The moment tingled with the promise of discovery. Yet a chasm as big as the Atlantic Ocean separated them. She had her dreams. He had his reality.

She looked away first.

He drew in a sharp breath. They were no longer children. He had no secrets he wanted to share. Life meant simply doing his job and doing it well. Then on to the next challenge.

She looked as if she wanted to say something. Knowing her directness, figuring she'd been as aware of the electricity between them as he, he decided to stop things before they got complicated.

"You can look after the details of pricing and all that."

She jerked back and stared at the table as if something was wrong.

"Yes?" he said.

She flashed the palms of her hands upward.

"What's the problem?"

"I hate to say this, but I hoped you'd have more stuff ready to go."

"Hah. When was the last time you looked in Aunt Millie's cupboards? She has everything mixed together like some sort of conglomerate. I don't dare dump anything without sorting through it piece by piece. Why, I found the deed to the house in a cupboard along with bits of string, unmatched gloves—with holes in them, no less—and some ratty old rags. It's pathetic. That's what it is."

"Whoa. Slow down." Nicole touched his arm to still his outburst.

Unexpected unfamiliar warmth leapt along his nerves.

"I'm sorry," she murmured. "I didn't mean to put on any pressure. It's just—"

When she seemed disinclined to finish, he said, "It's just what?"

She blinked at his impatience. "Really, it's none of your concern."

He growled. "Tell me."

She gave in with a little smile. "Oh, all right, if you insist. I need the money I'd get from selling these things."

He studied the worried expression she tried to hide beneath her tight smile. "How bad do you need this money?"

"It's nothing like that. My business is sound."

"So then what's your problem?"

She sighed. "It's not really a problem. I just have to generate more income to meet some family needs. I could make a tidy profit from selling these antiques." She paused to chew her lip. "Our busy season is about to start. Tourist buses and visitors, you know."

"I didn't realize there was an urgency. At least not on your part."

She grabbed his arm, rekindling warmth along his nerves. "Maybe I could help you." Her face turned up to him with a sweet, generous expression on her lips.

If only she didn't remind him of his past. A time when he'd allowed himself, under her intense concern, to admit how much he'd longed for things that couldn't be. When he'd felt so fiercely protective of her as she confessed her pain at her father's death and her excitement that her mother was going to marry again and make her dreams of family come true.

He ground the palm of his hand against his forehead. He had no intention of getting tangled up in an emotional mess that would leave him regretting this trip to Reliance.

No, he was going to dispose of all the memories of his aunt and leave town as fast as he could. Yet he couldn't resist her offer. If only to help him finish the job sooner. "Sounds like a plan."

◆

Next afternoon Ace wiped his arm across his brow. The heat in the house was unbearable, the job more difficult than he could have imagined. In and out with as few complications as possible had been his intention. Discovering the heaps of boxes and junk shot that theory in the foot. And running into Nicole again— seemed all she had to do was open her eyes wide to draw him almost into her soul, make him want to belong. But he'd stopped being a kid with childish yearnings. He'd become a man, capable of doing a job without getting emotionally involved. A secret weapon he'd learned to use to his advantage.

He carried a stack of boxes outside and deposited them on the back lawn. He lifted his head, letting the breeze cool his skin, then folded back the flaps of another box.

"How are you getting along over there?" At the voice to his right he looked up.

An old woman sat in an ancient rocker in the shade of the house, watching him. Nicole's grandmother. Older, grayer than he remembered. But what did he expect? Time took its toll on everything and everyone.

The old woman smiled. Still the same gentle, kind, welcoming smile of his memories.

He lifted his hand in greeting. "Just great."

"It's quite a task, this sorting out Millie's belongings." Gram struggled to her feet, groaning softly as she straightened. She limped to the board fence separating the two yards and leaned against the top. "Find anything useful or interesting?"

"Not much. Mainly old newspapers and worn-out clothes. I can't imagine why Aunt Millie didn't dispose of most of this junk ages ago."

"Millie liked to keep things. She always planned to do something with it."

"What did she plan to do with these?" He pulled out a nested stack of empty egg crates.

Gram laughed, a low gentle sound in the back of her throat. "I bet she planned to recycle them but never got around to it."

"What would you do with old clothes?" He held up a dress so worn the colors had faded into streaks.

"Rag rugs. Worth a fortune at a store like Nicole's. You ought to see what she has there."

"Her store must be crammed full of treasures." Imagine. More junk like he'd been uncovering all day. Though the idea of visiting Nicole at her store held a lot of appeal. With each new box he opened, every shelf he cleaned off, he thought of Nicole—her quick smile, her intense look. Not often life surprised him, but finding Nicole still here and once again experiencing a connection had been unexpected enough to put him a hair off balance. Momentarily. And he'd ended up telling more about himself and his past than he liked to tell anyone. But it wouldn't happen again.

Returning to the older woman's comment about Nicole's store, he said, "I'll have to drop in sometime."

"You do that, young man. My Nicole has done a wonderful job with it."

He grinned at her. " 'Course you wouldn't be the least bit prejudiced, would you?"

"I'm totally prejudiced when it comes to my granddaughters. That one in particular. She's more than a little special." She stared hard at him. "I imagine you noticed it, too."

He raised his eyebrows, saving himself the need of indicating yes or no, but he admired her directness. He shuffled through the remaining contents of the box and, finding nothing but old newspapers, carried the whole lot to the Dumpster.

Gram watched and waited as he returned and opened the next box. "It's a bit like dismantling her life, isn't it?"

Ace kept his eyes on his task as her words struck home. She'd nailed the feelings he'd struggled with all day. He felt like an intruder poking rudely through someone's life.

"I've never seen so much stuff." Going from foster home to foster home taught him not to become attached to things. More times than not, the foster family laid claim to anything he cared about.

And now lean living proved useful in his job. He could pack up everything he owned and be ready to move in minutes.

"This must be really difficult for you. Seeing so many bits and pieces of her life like this."

He shrugged, not caring to delve into it any further.

Nicole's grandmother ignored his hint. "Maybe Millie hoarded stuff because she could never forget she started with so little. In some ways she ended up the same—a houseful of belongings but alone except for a few close friends." She paused. "You were all the family she had left."

"Uh-huh." She didn't need to say anything more. He heard the accusation in her voice demanding to know why he hadn't been there for Aunt Millie. He wanted to tell her the truth; Aunt Millie hadn't been there for him. But what purpose would it serve except to add to the old woman's pain? Besides, he didn't want to talk about it.

He spoke without looking up. "I hadn't seen her in years."

"Why is that?"

He kept his attention on the contents of the box—more junk—and ignored the sharp, censorious tone of her voice.

"We lost contact."

"Didn't you want to keep in touch? You know, give her a phone call or send a Christmas card?"

What he wanted and what life offered were so far apart they didn't belong in the same world. "After a while you get used to being alone and don't think about how things might be different."

"So you're saying you wish they could have been different?"

He sneaked a look at her without turning his head. But her expression revealed only kindliness. Why was she being so persistent? Nicole and her grandmother both seemed bent on trying to change things. Or perhaps recapturing the past. But he didn't want to think about the past. It had no part of his present. His present consisted of short-term relationships that ended as soon as he moved on to a new job. It was the way he wanted it to be. "I'm happy with the status quo."

"I see."

Did he detect a note of disappointment in her voice? But what difference did it make to her?

He pushed the box aside—nothing but more junk—and attacked another box.

"I'd better go peel some potatoes for supper." But she didn't move.

Ace finally looked up to see why she lingered, mystified by the look on her face. As if she wanted something from him.

"Have a good evening," he said, not knowing what else she could want except a polite good-bye.

"Why don't you join us for supper? Say about six thirty?"

Ace hesitated. He didn't want to be a spectator at a sweet little family scene. Seeing the three of them all cozy and sure of where they belonged would only make him feel more isolated than sitting alone at Aunt Millie's table. But hungry and tired of his meager selection, he agreed. "Thanks. I'll be there."

She nodded, turned slowly, and made her way back to the house.

Ace sighed. No doubt she missed Millie. Friends for so many years. He pulled out more old clothes and tossed them into an empty box. Nothing even remotely useful. He picked up a faded chenille article. An old, threadbare housecoat unfolded across his knees, and a wave of memories engulfed him. The scent he'd been trying to ignore all day wafted over him—the flowery soap Aunt Millie used.

A boy of twelve. Too old for bedtime stories. But Aunt Millie didn't seem to realize it. So every evening during that long-ago Christmas season, he'd leaned against her shoulder, pressed his face into the chenille texture of this housecoat, breathed in the sweetness of her soap, inhaled the comfort of the routine, the security of her love—all things his alcoholic mother failed to provide. The fulfillment of his dreams and hopes.

He bundled the rag into a ball and threw it across the yard. It disappeared into the open Dumpster.

Chapter 3

Nicole hurried home. "Sorry to be late." She'd spent more time at the store than she realized, anxious to make room for items from Aunt Millie's house.

"Just in time, dear." Gram stood at the stove stirring a pan of gravy. "I've invited Ace to have supper with us."

Carrie and Nicole stared at her.

"You did?" Carrie's voice squeaked. "I wish you'd told me sooner." She rushed to the tiny mirror at the end of the cupboards and wailed at her reflection. "My hair." She raced from the room, and her footsteps thundered up the stairs.

Nicole sneaked a glance in the mirror as she passed and flicked her fingers through her hair to fluff it. The bright yellow sundress she'd worn to work would have to do. She would not go clattering up the stairs like teenage Carrie.

Gram turned back to the stove. "We need to make him feel welcome. Aunt Millie would be hurt if we didn't do all we could to help him."

As Gram talked, Nicole glanced around the kitchen. The white cupboards with red trim needed to be updated. The table where they took their meals, equally out-of-date—something Gram owned since Nicole could remember. The place felt homey and comfortable to Nicole, but perhaps Ace would fail to see beyond the surface of old and worn.

"Besides," Gram continued, "when I spoke to him a little while ago, he looked tired and discouraged."

Gram's words brought Nicole full circle to her vow to discover what had gone wrong. "Gram, why didn't Aunt Millie—"

A knock interrupted her question.

"It's Ace." Carrie dashed into the room and raced for the door. She grabbed his arm and practically dragged him to a chair. Nicole spared him a glance. Freshly showered, freshly shaved, his wet hair dark. A cotton short-sleeved shirt in soft blue. A pair of navy rugby shorts. She could smell his soap and aftershave. A masculine scent as foreign in this house as new chairs would have been.

"Do you want coffee or something?" Carrie asked.

"Coffee sounds good." Ace settled into the chair, a bemused expression on his face.

Gram held a full cup toward the younger girl who carried it carefully to Ace.

"Bet you're sick of cleaning out that old house."

Ace grinned. "I've thought of a few things I'd sooner be doing." He raised his gaze to Nicole and directed his question to her. "How did you spend your day?"

She poured herself a cup of coffee. Why should he care? But then who said he did? He was only making polite conversation. No need for her to turn it into anything else. "I'm making room to display Aunt Millie's things."

"You should see all the stuff Nicole has in the store," Carrie said, throwing her arms in a dramatic sweep. "Paintings and pottery and"—she turned to Nicole—"what did you call that other stuff?"

"You mean the fabric art?" Nicole studied Ace as she answered Carrie. If he showed the least annoyance with Carrie's turbo-charged enthusiasm, she would throw him bodily from the house, but he smiled at the younger girl.

She bit her lip to keep from telling her sister to stop looking so starstruck.

"That's it. Fabric art." Carrie leaned closer to Ace. "They're pictures but not paintings. More like—like—sculpting on a flat surface." She settled back, satisfied with her description. But only for a minute. "It's wonderful stuff. You should go see it."

"Must be quite a store. I'd like to see it sometime." His hazel eyes held surprising warmth and made Nicole remember how they'd shared dreams as kids. Before they'd both changed. Now all she wanted from him was Millie's antiques—and a chance to prove Aunt Millie wasn't the selfish, hard-hearted person he made her out to be. His aunt had been a sweet woman who baked casseroles for the sick right up until she was so crippled she had to have help herself. And for Nicole's high school graduation, Aunt Millie had crocheted a gossamer shawl Nicole cherished. Knowing how much pain it must have brought to the older woman's gnarled fingers to make such a delicate item, Nicole had used it only twice—for a friend's wedding and Aunt Millie's funeral.

Maybe God intended to use her family as a means of bringing Ace back to God and revealing the truth about Aunt Millie at the same time.

Gram spoke, pulling Nicole's attention back to the family dinner. "I told him what a fine job you've done on the store. Of course we were really discussing rag rugs."

Nicole's thoughts swirled. "Rag rugs?"

The amused sparkle in Ace's eyes made it impossible for Nicole to think straight. "Your grandmother told me how valuable all those old clothes of Aunt Millie's are if they're converted into rag rugs."

"That's right." She welcomed something concrete to discuss. "Didn't Aunt Millie make several?"

"I believe she did," Gram said. "Quite a few years ago. I'm surprised you remember, dear."

"I'm beginning to think Nicole doesn't forget very much." Ace's gaze held Nicole's.

She knew he referred to her memory of his confessions when they were so young.

"I believe everything is ready," Gram announced, pouring creamed peas into a bowl.

Nicole took the peas. "You sit down, Gram. I'll do that." She dished the mashed potatoes into a bowl, her movements stiff and unnatural as she felt Ace watching her.

She turned with the bowl and almost jammed it into his stomach. "Oh, I'm sorry." She hadn't heard him move across the room to stand behind her.

"Let me help." His lean fingers brushed against her hands.

She all but dropped the bowl into his grasp and spun around to pour the gravy into a server. This crackling awareness of him was totally senseless. She didn't want his presence to mean anything; yet her nerves quivered like wires taut with frost. She pulled the plate of sliced roast from the oven and hurried to the table, finding the only empty chair put her across from Ace. She took her place, pointedly looking everywhere but at the man facing her.

"Let us return thanks," Gram said.

She glanced at him then, wondering what he thought of their practice. His expression sober, he met her eyes briefly before he bowed his head. Foolishly she'd hoped he would show some amusement at Gram's lifelong habit. It would give her a reason to be angry with him. Instead she was left staring at the top of his head before she followed his example and bowed over her plate.

"Amen," Gram concluded. She picked up the tray of meat and offered it to Ace. "Help yourself." Gram waited until the food passed from hand to hand then said, "Ace, tell us about your work."

Nicole focused her attention on her plate, the salt and pepper in the center of the table, Carrie's excited expression—anywhere but Ace. His size overpowered the room. And his maleness. They didn't often share mealtimes with a man. Unless you counted the preacher. And she didn't. He was old and worn and comfortable like an old quilt.

Ace was hardly old. And comfortable? Anything but. His presence invaded her senses like a pounding rain.

Don't look. He's just a person sharing a meal. But her eyes developed a mind of their own and kept returning to his face. When his gaze touched hers, her throat tightened so she couldn't swallow.

Don't be so juvenile. You're acting like you've never before seen a man looking in your direction. With supreme effort she tore her gaze away and doused her mound of potatoes with gravy.

"I contract to a number of oil companies," he said, his expression bland.

It took a moment for Nicole to realize he'd answered Gram's question about his work.

"Mostly my job involves traveling around negotiating land deals. Helping nationals and oil companies find a middle ground."

"I heard you were a negotiator," Carrie said. "Like really scary stuff. It must be so exciting."

Ace chuckled. "Mostly I think of it as a job."

"It sounds really, really awesome. I want to know all about it," the younger girl persisted. "What was the scariest thing you ever did?"

"Can't say offhand."

"But there must be something."

"Carrie," Nicole warned.

"No. It's okay. I just have to think a minute." Ace paused. "I'd have to say the most tense situation was either when I helped with the oil well fires in Kuwait or negotiated a hostage situation in Brazil."

"How exciting." Carrie's eyes shone with admiration.

"Sounds risky," Gram said.

Ace shrugged. "Just my job."

Nicole's thoughts froze. She kept her gaze on her plate. Risks? Just part of a job? As if life had no meaning. As if it didn't matter who might be worried about him. Of course, pretending you didn't have family or they didn't care would ease any concern in that direction.

But how could he have forgotten Aunt Millie? Although maybe it was a good thing she didn't know what he was up to. Imagine how she would have worried. She would have spent twice as much time praying for him.

"You must have seen the whole world," Carrie said, her voice full of awe.

"Guess I've seen most of it all right."

"I wish my life wasn't so dull. But someday I'm going to do something really, really exciting." Carrie twirled her fork in the air.

A knot squeezed the back of Nicole's neck. "Carrie, don't be thinking about throwing away your life in search of excitement."

The younger girl looked stricken. "What's wrong with a little"—she waved her arm—"variety?"

"Nicole didn't mean any harm," Gram said. "She's always been a little cautious." Her kindly smile told Nicole she understood.

Nicole nodded, grateful for Gram's defense. "I've learned not to take risks. Too many people get hurt."

"People get hurt doing perfectly normal things," Carrie insisted. "Or they're busy minding their own business and someone else does something stupid."

Nicole knew she referred to the accident that took their parents.

"Seems to me," Carrie insisted with a little pout, "you might as well have a little fun while you're here."

"There's a difference between normal risks and doing something so thoughtless and risky it's bound to hurt someone." Nicole spoke slowly, even though her stomach burned to prove the point. "But I'm sure Ace doesn't want to listen to us argue."

Carrie instantly looked contrite. "I'm sorry. You're right. Besides, I'd sooner hear about his adventures. Tell us about the fires, Ace."

Nicole met his gaze briefly. "Yes, do." As he told of his experiences it grew clear he was everything she despised—a risk taker, delighting in adventure, someone who formed no emotional ties with anyone.

After the meal, she shooed Gram into the living room. Carrie hurried out to a babysitting job. Only Ace and Nicole remained in the kitchen. She wanted him to go. They'd done the neighborly thing. And now she wanted him out of her house. Out of her life before—

He gathered up a handful of dirty cutlery and carried it to the sink. "Why don't I help you clean up?"

"You don't need to do that."

"My pleasure."

She ran hot water and washed the dishes. He pulled the towel off the rack and dried them, the silence between them brittle and uneasy.

He nudged her with his shoulder and leaned close. "You have a nice family."

She relaxed; she could talk about her family anytime. "They're unique. But in a good way."

"You're very proud of them."

"I am." She smiled, trailing her fingertip through the soapsuds.

"You know"—his eyes darkened—"I think I envy you."

"I'm fortunate to have Gram and Carrie."

"Yes, you are. That isn't what I meant, though."

She sensed him struggling to find the words he wanted.

"I remember," he began slowly, "when we were kids and you talked about how excited you were to be getting a new father. I've forgotten a lot of it, but the one thing I do recall is how fiercely you wanted to be a whole family. And now, despite losing your parents, you're still a family unit. You got your dreams."

Sadness drifted through her like a whiff of smoke. She did have what she wanted. She thanked God for it every day. And she felt sorry for anyone who didn't enjoy the same thing. What harm would it do to be generous to the poor man who'd lost the last member of his family?

"Ace, I wish things had worked out for you. I'm still sure there's an explanation for why Aunt Millie didn't take you into her home. In fact, I was about to ask Gram about it when you came for supper. Why don't we do it together?"

The look on his face shifted through a range of emotions. She tried to read them. Fear? Hope? Then blank. As if he didn't care. But she'd seen enough to believe he needed assurance he hadn't been simply pushed aside and forgotten.

"Come on." She grabbed his arm and turned him toward the living room before he could refuse. Convinced he needed to feel the warmth of a family unit, wanting him to understand what it meant, she sat beside him on the couch. She kept thinking of the young boy who wanted so much to move in with his aunt Millie.

"Gram," she began, as the older woman glanced up. "Maybe you can help us."

Gram nodded slowly, as she looked from one to the other. "I'll do my best."

"Do you remember the Christmas Ace spent with Aunt Millie about eighteen years ago?"

"I recall it well." Her voice seemed cautious.

"Wasn't there talk about Ace and his mother moving in with Aunt Millie?"

"It was discussed."

"Well, why didn't it happen? Ace seems to think Aunt Millie couldn't be bothered with a teenager, but I'm certain there has to be some reasonable explanation. What do you know about it?"

Gram pushed the stitches to the back of the knitting needle and carefully wound the yarn into a tight ball. "Aunt Millie did intend to get you, Ace. Even after your mother died." She leaned closer to study him carefully. "She had her heart set on it."

Ace pushed back against the cushions, stiffening in silent disagreement.

Before he could speak, Gram sighed and continued. "Millie never would tell me exactly what happened. She kept saying what use is an old woman to anyone anyway. He's better off with younger people. Only I know she didn't believe it. The life sort of went out of her for a while. She never seemed to be as spunky after that." She again leaned over to stare into Ace's face. "Young man, I always wondered why you didn't come see her. She pined for you to her dying day."

A shudder tiptoed along Ace's arm, tingling against Nicole's skin where their elbows touched. *Do something, say something to ease his distress.* But before she could think of what to say, his muscles tightened and steel came to his voice. "I already told Nicole I tried to contact her. After a while you accept the obvious and quit trying to bang down cement walls with your head."

Gram shook her head. "Tsk, boy. You've grown into a fine specimen. Millie would be busting her buttons over you. But you need to develop some sense, as well. It wasn't Millie's reluctance to have you that got in the way. It was something else. I wondered if perhaps she ran into some rather obstinate authorities. For sure she wasn't young and was already crippled up with the arthritis." Gram picked up her knitting needles. "She was a prideful woman. She didn't want to bother people with her troubles. Wouldn't even confide in me, and after all we'd been through together. Best friends for all those years."

Ace jerked to his feet. "Thanks for the tasty meal."

"You're welcome, boy. Come again anytime."

Nicole followed him to the door. "Sorry it wasn't much help."

"Didn't expect it to be. I'm no longer bothered by the whole business." He grinned, driving the fierceness from his expression. "So don't you be bothering your pretty little head about it."

"I'm only looking for an answer."

"I know. You want everything to turn out nice and neat like your dreams. You want to defend your belief in forever families. All that sort of stuff."

He made her sound like an idealistic idiot. She opened her mouth to protest, but he grabbed her hand and pulled her outdoors.

"Are you coming to look at what I found today?"

"You think you can make me forget about defending Aunt Millie by dragging me over to look at her things?"

He screwed up one side of his face. "Nope. Don't think that would work." He pulled her down a step. "Maybe if we stand under that leafy maple tree and enjoy the evening, you'd forget."

Her cheeks warmed. He was flirting again. Or did the words fall out of his mouth without thought? Yet how long had it been since she'd known the pleasure of a man's company? Longer than she cared to remember. But now was not the time. Or the place.

And certainly not the man.

"I turned down a date so I could rescue Aunt Millie's antiques from being ignominiously relocated to the Dumpster, so let's go see what you've found." She pulled her hand away and tucked it safely against her side.

"Really? You turned down a hot date for me? I'm flattered."

"It wasn't all that hot. Just a schoolteacher friend who is going away for summer school."

"Man or woman friend?"

"A very nice woman." She could smell his aftershave. An exotic mixture of sea breezes and foreign spices.

"I suppose you have a long queue of admirers?"

Her mind slipped away to places fed by the scent—foreign, exciting shores with unfamiliar vegetation and the cry of strange birds.

"Still counting?" His deep voice shivered through her brain, becoming part of the jungle beat of her imagination.

"Huh?"

"I was wondering how many admirers."

She brought her thoughts back to Reliance, Montana.

Did he want to know if she had a romantic interest? "Seems to me there's no one here but you." Mentally she smacked her palm against her forehead. *Good move, Nicole. Bound to convince him you aren't interested in him. Yeah. Right.*

◆

He chuckled. From her pink cheeks and the way her gaze darted away from his, he guessed she'd flirted with him against her better judgment. He didn't want her to stop. "Just you and me. I think I might like that." In fact he flirted right back. What was the matter with him? He didn't want her to get the wrong idea. He was a loner. And she was family with a capital *F* bent on trying to make him believe in something similar.

He didn't want anything to do with it.

"Did you get some more sorting done in the house?" she asked.

Now would be the time to run as fast as he could in the opposite direction. Instead, he reached for her hand and led her through the back gate toward Aunt Millie's house. "Come and see." Was that hoarseness his voice?

As he reached around to open the door, she pulled away. He let his hand drift toward his side. Good thing one of them had some sense. But as he leaned close to turn the knob, his arm brushed her shoulder. He looked at her with more interest than he knew was wise in view of his decision to be in and out of this job without getting involved emotionally.

Her hair glistened in the slanting evening rays, trapping diamonds of gold and silver in the dark strands. She smelled like warm summer days and honey.

For one heartbeat he wondered what it would be like to be part of her world, and then he shoved aside the idea, pushed the door open, and followed her inside.

The heavy, hot air in the room crowded him. Pressed his foolish interest into deep crevices in his heart. He'd seen weird chemical reactions between rocks and acids in labs across the world—smoke, crackling noises, or a kaleidoscope of changing colors. Almost defying logic. But they were nothing compared to the chemistry pluming through him.

"Where are they?" she asked.

Reality check. Ignore the electricity crackling through the air. We're here to talk about antiques. He nodded toward the dining room and stuffed his fingers into his back pockets as she hurried through the door. He followed more slowly.

She'd have to be dead not to feel the attraction between them. Obviously she did and was uncomfortable with it. Which would explain her haste to escape to the other room.

The table was crowded with stuff he'd added since yesterday. The floor held its share, too, but she only glanced at the collection.

"Ace, I was sure Aunt Millie would have confided in Gram and told her what happened." Her dark eyes met his, and his heart kicked hard at the concern in them.

He sighed deeply. Would they ever get past this Aunt Millie thing? "Nicole, it really doesn't matter. I accepted the whole business a long time ago. I've learned to live with it. Fact is, I never think about it unless someone brings it up."

Her eyes flickered. Or perhaps only the light through the west window caught in them. "I think it matters."

"How so?"

"I think it's made you afraid of getting close to people."

"Who says I'm afraid?" He closed the distance between them. If she wanted proof to the contrary, he could provide it here and now. He brushed the back of his fingers along her cheek.

He shouldn't have done it.

The jolt that burned down his arm went straight to his heart, threatening locks on doors he didn't intend to open. The look in her eyes—intense, uncertain—twisted like a suddenly discovered key.

Forget the locks.

Forget the promises he'd made and kept these past dozen or more years.

Only one thing mattered: He wanted her in his arms.

He reached for her, but she stepped away, suddenly very interested in the framed sampler he'd leaned against the wall.

"Would you look at this? It's dated 1908. Aunt Millie's mother must have done it." She picked it up and held it to the light. "It's exquisite."

Her gaze slid past him.

His breath stuck in his throat.

"You'll be keeping it, of course. It's a family heirloom."

He had no family, didn't believe in it, and didn't want to go over the subject again.

She looked past him to the living room where he'd stacked boxes.

"Wow. You still have a lot of work ahead."

"I don't think there's any end to it. I'm sure they're multiplying. You don't suppose boxes breed like mice?"

She giggled, and he congratulated himself on erasing the tension from her shoulders.

"I can't imagine what's in all of them," she said. "I mean. . .one old lady. What would she have accumulated if she'd had a dozen kids?"

"You mean besides a gigantic headache?"

She grinned then glanced at the outer door.

He grasped at a reason to make her stay. "You want to open a couple and see if you unearth any treasures? Though I warn you I've spent all day at this, and what you see"—he waved at the items he'd carried to the dining room—"is the extent of my findings."

"And some very nice finds, too." But she crossed the room and knelt beside a large box. "Sure you don't mind?"

Mind? Could a man mind leaning against a wall watching a pretty girl sneeze as dust tickled her nose? Not likely. "Go ahead."

"It looks like letters and cards."

"I'll get a garbage bag." He returned and sat on the floor, close enough to breathe in her sweet scent. "Dump them in here."

"But don't you want to check and see what they are?" She pulled some yellowed, lined paper from an envelope.

"Probably from long dead relatives I never heard of." But if it kept Nicole at his side reading every word, he wasn't about to complain, and he grabbed a handful of letters and cards and skimmed through them.

After a half hour she sighed and tilted her head back. "I suppose these could be sorted in some fashion. Perhaps they'd make good research material."

He laughed. "Good try, but admit it. It's nothing but junk. Should have been burned four hundred years ago."

She giggled. "Maybe fifty years ago." She dug in and retrieved a box tied with grocery-store string. "Wait—look at this." She turned the box toward him. ANDREW was printed on the bottom in large letters.

"You better open it."

He shook his head. "She's only reused a box with my name on it. It doesn't mean a thing." But for one fraction of a second he'd hoped it did. When would he truly stop yearning for something more? "You go ahead."

Her gaze held his another heartbeat, and then she bowed over the box, broke the string, and lifted the lid. On the very top sat a chipped, faded ornament made of plaster of Paris.

His lungs wouldn't work. His eyes hurt. He stared at the cheap figure of a collie dog every bit as ugly as the day he bought it. Why had Aunt Millie kept it all these years?

Nicole turned it bottom up. Her brow wrinkled as she read the words he knew were scratched there.

"Aunt Millie from Andrew."

Her eyes widened as she stared at him. "You gave this to her." She sounded surprised. Even a bit amazed. "How special."

◆

Nicole could feel Ace's shock but watched his rigid control return quickly and firmly to his face.

"It was just a cheap gift." He grabbed the little dog from her and ground it into his palm. "Why would she keep it?"

"Maybe because she cared."

"Sure. Just like she cared about all these old rags." He swept away a pile. "And these old letters. She probably couldn't even remember who half these people were." When he moved to throw the ornament in the garbage, she stopped him.

"Why is it so hard to think she might have cared? Does it interfere with your theories of life or something?" She shook the box in his face. "Have you seen anything else labeled with a name? Anything?"

He only glowered fiercely at her.

"Of course you haven't. Everything else was just junk, and Aunt Millie would probably be the first to admit it. This"—she rattled the box—"meant enough for her to write your name on it."

He rolled his eyes. "Yeah, right. Next you'll be telling me she prayed for me every night."

"I'm certain she did." She pulled a letter from the box and studied the address. "How strange. This has your name on it." She checked the next envelope in the stack and then the next. "This is odd. These letters are addressed to you. They've been returned."

"Uh-huh. One for every Christmas, I suppose."

She frowned at him. "You're nothing but a skeptic. Here." She shoved them toward him. "See for yourself."

Sitting back, she watched him examine several returned letters. But when he made no move to open them, she grabbed one back and carefully opened it. "Afraid you might discover the truth?"

"Just not curious." But his gaze was riveted on her fingers as she unfolded the pages, brittle along the edges. "This one is dated years ago." She skimmed the words then slowly read them aloud.

"Dear Andrew, I have tried and tried to contact you to no avail. My letters are returned. I've been told not to phone, and when I tried, the number had been changed. Yet I will keep trying. My heart is aching. They won't let me see you or speak to you. They say it is best for you. They say it's what you want."

Nicole paused. "The words are blurred here." She gasped. "Aunt Millie must have cried as she wrote this."

Ace looked away, his face devoid of expression.

"Ace, don't you see? This proves she tried. It's like Gram said—someone wouldn't let her see you. Poor Aunt Millie."

He didn't move or acknowledge her words. Suddenly he thrust the box from her hands, letters fanning across the floor.

"It's a little late, wouldn't you say?"

Chapter 4

I t's too late for you and Aunt Millie to be a family, but now you know she cared. Doesn't it make a difference?" She wanted so much for him to allow love into his life. She couldn't imagine being so alone. No ties. No family.

Her thoughts blurred, and one idea blazoned across her mind—she wanted this for her sake as much as his. She wanted him whole. Ready to embrace family and love. Somewhere, deep in her heart, lived a connection between them. Something that had begun eighteen years ago and lay dormant until now. But before they could take a step toward each other, she silently warned herself, he had to return to his faith in God. She would never allow herself to care deeply for a man who, in his own words, had put God on the back burner.

This discovery of Aunt Millie's caring, an answer to her prayer, would surely begin the healing, restoration process for him.

He took her hands, held them so hard her fingers squished together as his gaze bored into hers. "Is that what you think?" His voice rasped. "A few old letters and I'm somehow magically all right in your eyes? Will everything that went wrong in my life be erased? I'll be fixed?"

She started to nod then changed her mind and shook her head. "I don't know."

"Let's find out." He grasped her shoulders and leaned toward her, his hazel eyes intense and demanding.

He meant to kiss her. Perhaps punish her for suggesting he needed to be fixed. She didn't want a harsh kiss. Yet she couldn't deny she was curious. What was this powerful connection between them? Nostalgia or something else? She had to find out. She leaned into his embrace.

His mouth, hard at first, softened, and he drew her closer.

Nicole relaxed into his arms. It was like returning home to a warm cup of chocolate after a cold winter outing. Like finding a long-lost friend. Ace, a friend she'd been missing for eighteen years.

"Umm," he murmured against her lips. "You taste good." He edged his back against the couch and cradled her head on his shoulder. "I've thought of you over the years and wondered how you were." He chuckled, the sound rumbling beneath her ear. "If I'd known you turned out so good, I might have come sooner."

She tipped her head and studied him. The tiny pale lines around his eyes from squinting into the sun. The streaked blond highlights from the same harsh sun. The dark shadow of his whiskers. The familiar face of long ago yet grown stronger, leaner, harder. And so very masculine. As was the scent of soap and spices.

She'd only been ten when he was here, but even then she'd glimpsed the man the boy would become. Was it possible she'd fallen in love with the boy/man even then? After all, both of them held the potential of who they would become. Maybe she'd been subconsciously waiting all these years for him to return.

"I wish you'd come back a long time ago. For Aunt Millie's sake. For yours." She paused then whispered, "And mine." And she wrapped her arms around him. This was where he belonged. Back where he'd first found the love of family, the love and grace of God. He'd finally found his way back. She thanked God for the return of the prodigal.

He rubbed his chin across the top of her head. "Admit it. I was your first love."

"I'll never give you the satisfaction of confessing such a thing." She stroked the plain white button of his cotton shirt. She wouldn't let him know she felt at home with him. Not yet. Not until he discovered for himself what she already knew—this was where he belonged. The place where he'd let go of the hard Ace and return to the faith-filled, gentler Andrew.

He tipped her chin up so he could kiss her again, softly.

She pressed her palm against his cheek. She could hardly wait to see his transformation. She only hoped it would be swift. She'd already waited a very long time.

The phone jangled.

She jerked back, expecting him to answer it.

"The machine will get it," he murmured.

It clicked on. "Ace here. You know what to do."

And then a voice boomed from the speaker. "Ace? Ace, are you there? It's Bruce. Just thought I should warn you. LaRue's on the prowl again. He's looking for you. Sounded as mad as all get out."

The caller paused, and Nicole sat up straight, pushing away from Ace's embrace.

"Sorry to say the new secretary told him you were in that neck of the woods. Best keep an eye out for him. Wouldn't want to see you dead or bleeding. Call me."

Dead? Bleeding? Icy tension twisted around Nicole's spine. Her heart beat erratically and far too fast, as if she'd had too many caffeine-loaded cups of coffee. She'd heard him talk about his job, heard him describe himself as a negotiator, but it had seemed unreal, too far away to touch her world.

She scooted along the floor putting a safe distance between them. "What was that all about?" she asked.

"Just a fella from the office."

"I mean the dead and bleeding part."

He laughed like it was a joke, but she gave him a hard look, silently demanding an answer.

"It's just one of those everyday sort of eco guys. Always got his shirt in a knot about gas wells and pipelines. I deal with his kind all the time."

"Then why did this—whatever his name is from the office—think he should warn you?"

"Precaution. Nicole, it's nothing I haven't dealt with a hundred times."

His words most certainly did not make her feel better. She took a deep breath. "I don't like—"

"Risks," he finished for her. "I know. But believe me, this is only some guy looking for free media coverage."

She wanted to believe him. Believe this wasn't anything out of the ordinary. She wanted it so bad she pushed aside the alarm skidding along her veins. Besides, she did have a habit of being overly cautious, and she admitted it.

"Come here, and I'll make you forget all your worries."

Amused at the way he waggled his eyebrows, she nevertheless shook her head and backed away. It was too soon. She needed to be sure of some things before she let her heart have its way. "I have to get home."

◆

Ace leaned over a box, his hands idle. He'd moved cartons around all morning but hadn't been able to sort their contents. Thoughts of Nicole filled his mind to the point that he couldn't concentrate on anything else.

She was everything he wanted.

Everything he couldn't have.

He'd learned his lesson a long time ago. And he wasn't about to forget it.

But he could barely hear his mental arguments over the pull of his emotions. Last night as they'd said good night under the golden glow from the light over the back door, she looked like an Egyptian goddess with her inky black hair and dark eyes.

He wanted to kiss her, but she again resisted. He felt her caution. Knew he didn't measure up to her standard.

Sure, they'd shared something eighteen years ago, but it wasn't possible to recapture it. He knew it wasn't. They were as far apart as the east was from the west. Yet—if they turned and faced each other—

What about his long-held vow: Never get involved in a relationship promising forever? Forever didn't exist.

He flipped open the lid of another box and stared into the contents. More old clothes and shoes. More worn-out appliances.

What was he doing here? Did he hope to find the belonging he'd never known?

He jerked to his feet, grabbed a cup of coffee, and went outside. He needed to think. He didn't belong in Nicole's world, and for sure he didn't belong in her life. He'd never fit. Not Ace Conners. He'd never been allowed to fit, and now it was too late. He was a loner. Dreaming of belonging, a family, a home—he must be out of his mind. Hadn't life taught him enough hard lessons?

He gulped his coffee. He needed to finish emptying out Aunt Millie's house and move on before Nicole got hurt.

About to head back indoors, Ace stopped. Every muscle in his body tensed. Had someone moaned? He glanced over the fence, saw nothing but the flower-filled yard and a book lying open on Gram's rocking chair. Yet the nerves along the back of his neck tingled. A sure sign of some sort of danger. He breathed quietly through parted lips as he assessed the situation. Slowly he turned, scanning the view. Nothing. He sighed. What did he expect? Snipers in the treetops? An armed ambush? Yet he couldn't shake the feeling something was wrong.

He eased toward the fence, poised for any possibility, and tensed when he saw a body on the ground next to the flowers. Then realized it wasn't an ambush.

"Gram." The old lady lay in the pathway between her sweet peas and azaleas. He vaulted the fence and knelt at her side. "What happened? Are you hurt?"

Gram groaned. "I stepped on a rock and twisted my foot."

The foot had already swollen like a ball. Ace untied the laces and pulled off her shoe.

"I tried to call out, but I couldn't. I prayed you'd hear me." Gram's voice thinned with pain.

"Let's get you inside and put some ice on that." He lifted her, surprised at how little she weighed.

Inside, he settled her in the big armchair, found ice, and packed it in a towel around her ankle.

"Maybe I should take you to the emergency room."

Gram waved the idea away. "It's feeling better already."

"Can I get you anything? Painkillers, coffee, something to eat?"

Gram laid her head back. "I could use a cup of tea if you don't mind."

Ace hurried to the kitchen, found the kettle, and put it to boil. He located acetaminophen tablets on a shelf next to the sink and poured out two. He carried the tea in and set a cup next to Gram's elbow. She took the pills without argument.

"You are a godsend," she said after a moment. Again she put her head back and closed her eyes.

Ace sat quietly at her side, waiting for her to fall asleep, but in a few minutes she lifted her head and shuffled backward in the chair. "My granddaughter has been spending a lot of time at your house." She studied him openly, quizzically.

"She's anxious to get her shelves stocked with Aunt Millie's antiques."

"There's more to it than that, young man. I've seen the look in her eyes when she doesn't know I'm watching."

Ace grinned. So Nicole wasn't as indifferent to him as she tried to make him think. Sort of made him feel good. Then steel vibrated along his spine. *No emotional involvement. Remember?*

"So where do you go from here?" Gram asked.

Did she mean between him and Nicole? Or his job? He decided he'd stick to talking about his job. "I'm planning to negotiate some lease problems in the Arctic."

Gram fixed him with a keen gaze. "And where does Nicole figure into this?"

"She belongs here with you and Carrie, her friends, and her store."

Gram leaned forward. "I don't want to see that girl hurt."

Ace considered her a moment. "No reason she should be."

Gram studied him so carefully he felt like a small, naughty boy. "You're a fine man, Andrew Conners. But you have to decide what it is you want."

What did he want? At one time it would have been exactly what he could have here—a family, love, and all the things that went with that. But he no longer knew if it was enough. Or maybe it was too much. He'd grown used to being alone.

And lonely.

But did he want to spend the rest of his life like that?

No. A thousand times, no.

Yet could he change?

"Is it possible to have what one wants?" he asked.

Gram nodded slowly. "If a person wants something badly enough, anything is possible. People can change. They do all the time. Sometimes without realizing it." She paused. "Andrew, how is your relationship with God?"

"God and I have lost touch."

She tsked. "That's where you need to start your journey. Get back in touch with God. Learn to believe in His love. You'll be surprised how easy it is to put the rest of your life together once you accept that."

If only things could be so simple. He knew they weren't. Wanting, needing, and getting didn't necessarily follow in logical sequence. Life had taught him not to expect miracles.

"Bring me that photo album, and I'll tell you about Nicole."

He did as she asked, settling the album across her knees and pulling a chair close so he could see the pages.

"Here she is at her high school graduation."

He studied the pictures of Nicole in a frothy red dress. He looked at poses of Nicole alone, gathered with classmates, surrounded by her parents and Carrie.

Gram tapped the book. "She was the prettiest girl there."

Ace agreed. She shone with excitement.

"Here she is getting ready to leave for university." Gram flipped a few pages. "She was always bringing friends home with her." There were pictures of Nicole with a variety of girls and boys at her side.

"Where did she go to school? What did she take? What were her plans?"

Gram laughed. "Sounds like you want to know everything."

He shrugged. He didn't intend to let the older woman guess how much he wanted to know. What made Nicole tick? Why did she cling so firmly to family? What scared her and why? What was responsible for that overdeveloped fear of risk?

"Very well. She went to the University of Montana. Started in business management then switched to history. She quit to come home when her parents died. I told her I could manage without her." Gram snorted. "But we both knew I couldn't. She always thought she'd wasted her time at university. Complains she never got a degree or anything useful from it. I remind her God knew what she needed. Her courses in business, history, and even art are exactly right to help her run the store." Gram tapped the page and seemed lost in thought. "Such a good girl. And so smart. She knew exactly what sort of business to start." She sighed and suddenly seemed to remember Ace sat at her side, fascinated with the insights Gram provided.

Nicole, intense and idealistic as a child, had grown into an idealistic young woman. She'd learned how to combine that with a wide streak of business acumen. *Way to go, Nicole.* He had no reason to be so proud of her. Just the same, he was.

"No special boyfriend?"

Gram grew thoughtful. "There was one I thought would last. But after Nicole came home to help raise Carrie, I never saw him again. Nicole only said they had different agendas." She sighed heavily. "I don't suppose too many young men would want to be burdened with an old lady and a teenage girl."

Ace studied the pictures. "Getting a family might seem like a bonus to some." It sounded mighty attractive to him, especially when the package came tied up with Nicole. Too bad it was too late for him.

Gram closed the album, her finger holding the page. She shifted so she could study Ace.

He sensed her measuring him, trying to decide if he met her approval, if he would be good or bad for her granddaughter. He smiled, calm and in control. Perhaps she'd share the answer with him when she figured it out.

She nodded slowly. "Let me tell you about my Nicole."

Ace leaned forward slightly, his interest on full alert. He wanted to hear everything.

"Nicole is. . .well, cautious, I guess. She feels doubly responsible to make sure both Carrie and I are safe. Why, that girl, even when I said the store was hers to do with as she wanted, she was so careful. Vowed she'd never go in debt. She's careful with everything she does. I don't think she's ever gotten over losing her father and then her mother and stepfather. Not that I'm complaining. As long as Nicole is in charge, I know we don't have to worry. But that said, I don't ever want to be a burden to her. She should think about what she needs and wants in life. Not always be thinking about what she thinks we need."

Gram shook her head. "Here I am rambling on. Probably doesn't make a lick of sense to you. But be warned." She shook her finger at Ace. "I would not stand by idly if someone hurt her."

He took her hand and squeezed it gently. "I think Nicole is far more resilient than you give her credit for. Sure, she's cautious. She has a lot of responsibility. She's had to make some sacrifices. But she's smart and knows what she wants." They studied each other. Gram's expression remained stern.

Finally, Ace grinned. "Gram, I'm not some monster. I would never intentionally hurt her." But as he thought about how good it felt to kiss her last night, her initial eager response then her caution, he wondered if it was already too late. But he reminded himself she was the one who had backed away. She was the one who knew when to put on the brakes. He, Ace Conners, known for his cool detachment, had been taken momentarily off guard by something from the past that reared its head and demanded equal time. It was true he'd been half in love with her when they were both much younger. She'd offered him something he'd never known before—a sincere interest in him, his hopes and dreams. With her and her alone, he had discovered a warm place deep inside his heart. A place now atrophied beyond redemption.

"See that you don't." With a quick nod as if she'd settled the matter to her satisfaction, Gram turned back to the album and continued to point out pictures of Nicole and tell Ace stories. Nicole was everything he'd imagined: fun, sensitive, feisty.

He rose to get more tea for Gram and fetch an older photo album. They were poring over the pictures of Nicole in grade school when Carrie burst through the door.

She took one look at Gram with her ankle packed in ice and squealed. "Gram!" She skidded across the floor and fell on her knees beside the older woman. "What happened?" And burying her face in Gram's lap, she burst into tears.

"Now, now, Carrie. Hush, child. It's nothing. Just a little bruise. I'm okay. Take more than a little rock to do me real harm." She patted Carrie's head as the young girl sobbed.

"Are you sure?" Carrie managed.

"I'll be just fine. Don't you worry."

Carrie hugged Gram and kissed her neck. "I don't know what I'd do if anything happened to you."

Ace saw the glint of tears in Gram's eyes as she rubbed Carrie's back. "You run and wash your face, and then we'll talk about supper."

Gram wiped at the corner of her eyes. "My girls are both so fragile." Her eyes held a silent warning.

But he got it. He understood. *Don't hurt my girls.*

He wouldn't. He'd be in and out of Reliance before anyone noticed. Nicole would take away the old things she wanted and forget him again—just another old thing from the past.

Even before he'd completed the thought, he knew Nicole wanted more. But what? Certainly to fix his past, which couldn't be done. He could not go back. But perhaps she hoped for even more than that. Did she hope to fit him into her life? Again, not possible.

He felt a tremor of danger. Her intensity, her ideals, spoke to his long-denied dreams. Both he and Nicole stood a very real chance of getting hurt if either of them let those childish wishes get in the way.

He turned away, unwilling to let Gram see his eyes. Knowing she would see more than he cared for her to see.

Chapter 5

Nicole stepped into the kitchen and stared. Gram sat in her rocking chair, her foot elevated and wrapped in icepacks. Carrie and Ace peered into a bubbling pot on the stove. Carrie held a spoon and licked her lips.

"A little more salt, maybe."

Ace nodded. "Agreed. Other than that, this is the best pot of clam chowder you could ask for."

Had she walked into the wrong house?

She savored the moment, knowing reality would erase it as soon as one of them saw her standing in the doorway.

Gram glanced up. "Nicole, don't look so surprised."

The two at the stove turned.

Carrie dropped the spoon and hurried toward her. "Gram hurt her foot. Ace found her and helped her, and now he's helping me make supper. Gram said she'd like some clam chowder, so Ace is showing me his way of making it." Carrie halted a few inches from Nicole and waved her arms. "Can you imagine him being such a good cook?"

Nicole's gaze locked with Ace's. All she could think of was last night. How good it had felt to be in his arms. To be kissed. He half winked. Was he remembering last night, too? Warmth surged up her neck. She was thankful no one but Ace paid her much attention.

His gaze remained unwaveringly on her. "I have a very limited knowledge of cooking. This is only something one of the camp cooks taught me because I requested it so often. Said if I liked it so much I might as well learn to make it." He carefully set the lid back on the pot.

Nicole hugged Carrie quickly before she hurried to Gram's side. "Tell me what happened."

Gram dismissed the whole thing with a wave. "It was nothing. A mean-natured rock thought it could get the best of me." She snorted. "Take a lot more than that to stop me."

Nicole raised her gaze to Ace. "Did she see a doctor?"

Gram flicked one hand, and Ace shook his head. "She refused. But the swelling is almost gone. However"—he gave Gram a hard look—"if it's still painful in the morning I'd suggest you push, pull, or drag her in."

Gram huffed. "There'll be no need, I tell you."

Nicole gently unwrapped the ankle. There was redness from the ice but little swelling. She touched the foot, and Gram flinched. "Tomorrow morning if it still hurts, we're off to the doctor."

"We'll see," Gram muttered.

"Thank you for coming to the rescue," Nicole said to Ace.

"No problem."

He wore the same old T-shirt he'd had on a couple of days ago and jeans with smudged patches of dirt. He'd obviously been going through dusty boxes. Had he found it annoying to have his work interrupted? She studied his expression. He didn't look upset as he handed placemats to Carrie and took a stack of soup bowls from the cupboard. In fact, he looked to be having the time of his life. It surprised her how easily he seemed to fit in.

"I'll be back as soon as I change." She slipped away to pull on white cotton shorts and a bright yellow tank top. As she skimmed a comb through her short hair she stared at herself in the mirror. Imagine coming home every day to Ace in the kitchen, Carrie and Gram happily at his side. She gently slapped one cheek. "Nicole Thomas. Give your head a shake. You and Ace are from opposite ends of the pole." Mentally she listed the reasons they could never belong together. He enjoyed the challenge of risks, downplayed them, lived happily without family. Or at least insisted he did. Most of all, he did not have a living faith.

She snorted, remembering one of Gram's acerbic comments about such people. *Good thing God didn't stop believing they existed.* She didn't know that Ace had stopped believing in God's existence, perhaps just His love and care.

Ace needed to learn to trust God again. Until he did, he was off limits to her. No more kissing. It was too tempting. She closed her eyes briefly. Even if he returned to faith, what made her think a cozy little family scene like the one downstairs was going to change who both she and Ace were? It wasn't possible. She scowled at herself for a second, trying to convince herself to stop hoping. But if he could admit Aunt Millie had loved him, if he were to stop hiding behind Ace and remember he was Andrew, if he stopped running from God. . .

She shook her head. It would take a miracle.

Her scowl fled, replaced by a wide grin. Miracles were God's business. She would pray for a miracle for Ace then sit back and watch God work.

She hurried downstairs and stopped outside the kitchen to watch.

"Why bother with forks?" Carrie insisted. "Just more to wash up."

Ace held up a spoon and then a fork. "I suppose you're right, though I never thought four tiny bits of hardware could make such a big difference in the cleanup. Wouldn't be a wee bit lazy, would you?" He waggled his eyebrows at Carrie, making her giggle.

"Just efficient," she said.

Gram smiled at the two of them. "We've spoiled Carrie."

Nicole wanted to protest but hung back watching the interaction between the other three.

Carrie bent to kiss Gram's cheek. "But look how good I turned out."

Tears sprang to Nicole's eyes. Family was meant to be like this—caring for each other despite differences in age and interests.

Ace turned and caught her dashing a tear from the corner of her eyes and smiled gently.

He fit in so well. As if he belonged right here with them. Did he ever imagine himself as part of a family? Or did his work satisfy even his deepest longings? She knew it couldn't, but he had been hurt and disappointed when Aunt Millie didn't come for him. He'd grown wary, calloused.

Yes, it would take a miracle. Hope found its way into her heart. God could reach into the most damaged, fearful soul. Ace would soon see how easy it was to belong and be loved. Dreams could come true.

"Soup's on," he said softly.

Ace helped Gram to the table, while Carrie ladled soup into each bowl. Nicole took the loaf of warm bread from the microwave, sliced it, and put it in a basket.

"Guess what I did today," Carrie said, after Gram said grace.

"Found a million bucks?" Nicole passed the bread to Ace. His finger slid along her thumb. She smiled quickly then ducked her head and concentrated on spreading butter on her slice of bread.

"Dug up buried treasure?" Gram suggested, as she tasted the soup. "This is delicious, Ace."

He tipped his head. "Thank you. From someone of your experience, I take that as a real compliment."

Carrie swept an annoyed look around the table. "You guys." To Ace she said, "They're always teasing me."

He grinned at her. "It's because they care."

"Well, sometimes they care too much." She shot Nicole another dark look, but Nicole knew she wasn't really offended. It was part of the game they played.

As if to prove her point, Carrie sprang forward on her chair. "I taught the twins to ride their bikes without their training wheels."

"Good for you. Carrie babysits the five-year-old twins across the street," Nicole explained to Ace.

Gram nodded approval.

Carrie turned to Ace. "Isn't that great?"

Ace gave Carrie a serious look. "If everyone is still in one piece."

"Yup. I probably have the most damage." She showed her bruised elbow.

Nicole glanced around the table. Such a simple meal, but the creamy chowder—full of vegetables and clams—and the yeasty warm bread satisfied in a comforting way. Good home-style food. It seemed to breathe family and togetherness. And Ace in the center. Passing food as if he belonged. Joining in the conversation as if he'd always been there. A golden glow filled Nicole. Her prayed-for miracle seemed so close.

Carrie suddenly looked at them all. "So what did everyone else do today?"

Gram's eyes twinkled as she answered. "I entertained a handsome visitor. Showed him the family photo albums."

Carrie and Nicole groaned.

"You didn't show him the one where I had my lips curled back to show my missing teeth, did you?" Carrie demanded.

Gram nodded. "Certainly I did."

Carrie wrinkled her nose then gave Nicole a mischievous look. "Did you show him the one with Nicole in that pouffy pink dress?"

Again Gram nodded.

Carrie hooted. "The Jolly Pink Pumpkin."

Nicole met Ace's gaze. He grinned widely. "I thought it was rather. . .rather. . ."

Carrie giggled. "Come on. I dare you to say what you really thought."

Her insides suddenly quivering, Nicole jerked her gaze away to stare at her soup bowl.

Ace took his time answering the question. "I just cannot think of the right word."

Carrie laughed. "I guess not."

Ace continued. "I told Gram I wish I could have been here to see it in person. Didn't I, Gram?"

"You couldn't quit looking, that's a fact."

Carrie laughed loudly. "Pretty unbelievable all right."

Nicole felt Ace's look and slowly lifted her head. At the glow in his hazel eyes, a jolt shot along her nerves. There was no mistaking his approval. He smiled slowly. "I enjoyed seeing her growing up."

Carrie sobered. "I should talk. I hate some of the pictures of me in those albums, but Gram has a fit every time I try to sneak them out."

"Family history," Gram said. "Lots of good memories in those pictures."

"Yeah." Nicole's voice was dry. "Most of the memories are from our knee-jerk reaction every time you bring them out."

Gram chuckled. "You ought to see yourselves."

Nicole looked at Carrie. "The album in the closet."

Carrie nodded. "I'll get it."

Gram pressed her hand to her chest. "Girls, you wouldn't."

But Carrie raced out of the room.

"This is a dirty trick," Gram protested. "She knows I can't chase her down."

Nicole stacked the dirty dishes and carried them to the counter. "How dignified would that be?"

Gram grunted. "Forget dignity."

Ace leaned back in his chair, watching the proceedings with a bemused look on his face.

Nicole felt she had to explain. "She has some dreaded photos, too."

"Poor Gram. What chance does she have against the two of you?"

Gram patted his hand, her face softening at his defense of her. "None whatsoever. I don't know how I put up with them." She sighed heavily. "It's been a trial as you can plainly see." The proud gleam in her eyes as she looked at Nicole dispelled any doubt about how she truly felt.

Nicole kissed the top of her head. "I love you, too, Gram."

Ace laughed.

Nicole wondered what he thought of the familiar, irreverent way they treated each other. It probably wasn't what he thought of when he pictured an ideal family. But then what did he imagine? For Ace, it seemed family meant disappointment, broken promises, all sorts of things that didn't fit in with their open, honest love for each other.

She leaned against Gram's shoulder. How grateful she was for the stability this dear grandmother had provided through the loss of two fathers and a mother. She and Carrie were so blessed. She sent a quick thank-you prayer heavenward.

Carrie skidded back into the room, swept her arm across the table to clear a spot in front of Ace, and plunked down a frail, black photo album. She opened it in the middle and pointed.

"This is Gram growing up."

The two heads bent over the pages, Carrie's bright golden one, Ace's darker, sun-streaked hair.

If only she could hold them all together just like this. For a moment she let herself dream. First, Ace would allow God's love into his life. It was her most fervent prayer. And then. . .

She pushed the thought away. Even if he did that, and she would pray earnestly he did, it didn't mean he'd want family. And even if he did, why would he want one consisting of an elderly woman and a teenage girl? He'd want his own family.

Ace finally looked up, his gaze resting on Gram. "These are beautiful photos."

Gram preened. "Thank you."

Carrie grimaced. "If you don't mind the funny clothes."

Gram sighed. "As I recall, Carrie, you were asking about our day." She turned to Ace. "I'm afraid I managed to make a mess of yours. I'm sorry, though I'm so grateful for your help."

Carrie and Nicole echoed her thanks. A shiver raced up Nicole's spine, but she refused to dwell on what might have happened if Ace hadn't heard Gram.

"An afternoon in your company was a pleasant reprieve," Ace said. "I didn't know if I could face another box of stuff. I've thought of simply dumping everything in one fell swoop, but I've found important papers and priceless antiques in with the junk, so I have to sort through it all." He smiled at Nicole. "I'm sure I wouldn't be forgiven if I tossed out things without due consideration."

Nicole drew about her the warmth his gaze lit inside her. "Tell Gram about the box we found with your name on it."

His gaze held hers another heartbeat, and then he turned to Gram. "Nicole is referring to a box of cards and letters. They were all addressed to me but had been returned."

"Returned?" Gram said. "I don't understand."

"It seems Aunt Millie tried to keep in touch with Ace after all, but her efforts had been refused."

Ace carefully closed the photo album and pushed it aside. "I found a letter that helps explain it." He cleared his throat.

Nicole could almost reach out and touch the brittleness coming from him. How she ached to be able to comfort him with her arms and her kiss. Except she wouldn't allow that to happen until he came back to his faith.

"From what I can piece together, it sounds as if Aunt Millie tried to gain custody of me. The letter said the authorities decided her health and age made it impossible. And in respect for the foster parents' wishes on my behalf"—his voice spiked with sarcasm and perhaps bitterness—"they asked that she not contact me anymore."

Shocked silence echoed through the room.

"Oh, Ace." Nicole didn't try to keep the sorrow from her voice.

"That's just so wrong," Carrie muttered.

Nicole took a look at Gram and, at the sight of tears trickling down her cheeks, sprang to her side. "Gram, don't cry."

Gram waved Nicole back to her seat. "Ace, I wish we could turn back the clock and save both you and Millie from such needless pain." She shook her head. "If only Millie had told us about it. Maybe we could have helped."

Ace folded his hand over Gram's. "Thank you for your concern, but don't be crying over me. Look at me. I turned out just fine, didn't I?"

Gram studied Ace carefully. "I suppose you did."

He smiled and began to turn away when Gram added, in a gentle voice, "At least on the outside. But it's the inside that counts, and I sense you felt abandoned, rejected, and hurt. How you've dealt with it I can't say, though it seems you've chosen a career where you don't have a chance to get close to people. Is that your way of protecting yourself from being hurt again?"

A visible shock raced through Ace's body. For a moment Nicole thought he would soften. Perhaps confess how much he longed for the things he'd been denied—family and security. But then he pushed himself against the back of the chair. His eyes revealed nothing.

◆

Ace banked his feelings. With Gram's injury and the pleasant afternoon then sharing a family meal, he'd let himself relax too much.

Okay, it had been a real shock to read that letter and have indisputable evidence Aunt Millie cared. But for whatever reasons, despite his desperate prayers to God for help, a home had been denied him. It no longer mattered. He'd given up his dreams. He'd stopped believing in miracles and a God who sent them.

He'd grown up. He'd learned to put aside his resentment and bitterness, but he could almost taste the poor-Ace feeling of the three females facing him. All pity and concern. But then they believed in forever families and happily ever after. He didn't. He believed in accepting the truth. Dealing with realities.

"I have a very good job because I worked hard and climbed to the top. I'm good at what I do." He had no intention of telling them the exact nature of some of the things he did, certain all three of them would consider a few of the situations he'd found himself in to be much too risky. They certainly had their reasons to worry about the safety of those they cared about, but he didn't fall into that category. They, at least, still had each other. What would it be like to have someone to care whether or not he took risks? He couldn't imagine.

Pretending to move the old photo album away from a speck of dirt on the table, he thought about Nicole. Would she ever consider accepting someone like him—a risk taker, a man with no experience of family? Not likely.

"I didn't mean to criticize what you do," Gram said. "I'm sure you're very good at your job. But then I expect you'd be good at whatever you set your mind to."

"Thank you." He had no intention of taking this conversation any further.

He turned to Nicole, narrowing his eyes with the cold distant look he'd perfected over a lifetime.

She met his look squarely, determination blaring from hers.

He got lost in the darkness of her gaze, swirling into unfamiliar territory filled with desires that were uniquely emotional rather than physical. He jerked a breath across his teeth and forced it into his gasping lungs. Time for reality.

"You coming to see what I found today?" His mind filled with thin cotton balls. He couldn't think. What treasures had he uncovered? The only thing he could remember was how her lips tasted like honey.

"Whose turn is it to do dishes?" Carrie demanded.

Nicole blinked and turned toward her younger sister.

Ace gave himself a mental shake. He could not let old photos, old memories, and old dreams put him off balance.

"I did them about four days in a row, so I'd say it was your turn," Nicole said.

"I guess." Carrie sighed.

"I'd offer to help, but I think I'll take advantage of my injury and watch the news." Gram pushed to her feet.

Ace helped her to the living room. When he returned, Nicole nodded toward the door, silently suggesting they leave, but seeing the disappointment in Carrie's expression he filled the sink with hot water and plunged in a stack of dishes.

"Many hands make short work," he said.

Nicole rolled her eyes but grabbed a cloth and dried the dishes as Carrie speedily finished clearing the table.

"This is great, Ace," Carrie said. "Thanks for helping."

Appreciation glistened in Nicole's eyes, and Ace smiled to himself. Seems doing a kindness for her sister or grandmother was a shortcut to earning Nicole's approval, although it hadn't been his motivation, nor would he ever allow it to be. He knew there was a reverse lesson to be heeded, as well. Neither would she forgive anyone who hurt them in any way. The whole family was fiercely protective of one another.

"Is that everything?" He glanced around before he pulled the plug and stood with his hands dripping over the sink. Nicole offered him a corner of her tea towel.

"Thank you," she whispered. "That was very kind."

He held her gaze. "I'm your ordinary, everyday, kind sort of guy."

Her eyes darkened. "Not so ordinary, I think." Her voice purred.

"Want to come see the stuff I've discovered?" He was talking about the antiques that kept springing from the corners of the house, but his thoughts were not on looking at antiques. He had his mind on discovering a different sort of treasure. Nicole. He wanted to know everything about her.

◆

Nicole hurried outside to the shelter of the summer dusk. She didn't know if she could trust the way she felt. She needed to examine her reactions and base her choices on what was best. Reality. Security. Not on how her heart did a happy dance against her rib cage.

She should never have allowed herself to dream of what would happen when—

All through dinner, every time she looked at him, her heart did a funny little jump that set her pulses racing. Fearing Carrie or Gram would read the longing in her expression, she allowed herself only glances. A short intense meeting of the eyes. Or a skimming glimpse of his face to study the appealing stern lines around his eyes. Several times she reminded herself not to stare.

She needed distance. But she couldn't say whom she needed it from—Ace or herself.

Ace followed her outside, grabbed her hand, and pulled her to a stop. "What's your hurry? Let's enjoy the weather."

They reached the shadows of the alley, and she allowed him to pull her into his arms. She'd been longing for this the whole evening. And all day. In fact, probably most of her life. She realized she'd subconsciously measured all her boyfriends against Ace and the way their hearts and minds seemed to knit together perfectly.

He murmured her name, turning her insides into cappuccino delight. Laughing, she ducked away from his kiss, allowing herself to stroke his cheek gently.

The lowering sun reflected in his eyes. Tenderness filled her. Of his own admission he'd never known love—the sort of love that endured. But one thing she was good at was loving. She would do her best to love him back to God and family. She took his hand and headed toward Aunt Millie's house. Reason must prevail. She had priorities. First, her faith. She would never love a man who didn't trust and serve God. And, second, her family. She would never jeopardize their security and happiness.

She stepped inside and hurried toward the dining room but barely noticed the additions, absently picking things up and turning them over without really seeing them.

Ace followed, stopping a thin inch behind her. She felt his warmth on her back. She closed her eyes and breathed in his scent. As he murmured her name, her heart opened up to him.

This was what God had intended when he created man and woman. This was how love was meant to be—connection to a man on one side and to family on the other.

Only God and family were not yet in Ace's vocabulary, and until they were, this love could not be.

Slowly she slipped from his grasp. "Let's see what you've uncovered today." She hurried to the collection on the table. "I need to start cataloguing and pricing things."

Chapter 6

The next day Nicole answered the phone as it rang in her store.

"Hi. It's me. Ace."

She recognized his voice immediately and smiled. "Hi." She turned her back to the shop, hoping no one noticed her far-from-businesslike tone.

"The reason I called is I found a whole stack of boxes in the basement, full of old dishes and stuff. I've no idea if they're worth anything or if I should pitch the whole lot in the Dumpster."

"Don't dump anything until I see it." She glanced around the store. The shop was quiet. Rachel, her capable assistant, dusted a display. She checked her watch. An hour and a half until closing time.

"I could come over right away and have a look." She'd rather spend the time exploring old boxes with him than trying to get rust stains out of tiny crevices of the cut-glass candy dish she'd been cleaning in the back room.

She'd spent most of the day telling herself repeatedly her attraction to him could mean nothing until she got her miracle. But she couldn't deny how much she enjoyed just being with him. They shared a connection as old and familiar as her childhood. She felt comfortable and complete. . .odd word choice, but it had been the same when they were kids.

"I'm going to check out some antiques," she told Rachel. "Close up for me, will you?"

Rachel turned and stared. "O–kay." She dragged out the word.

Nicole hurried away before Rachel could speculate about her leaving early. But, after all, it was work related. She was on a buying expedition.

She hurried along the streets keeping to the shady side, out of the hot sun. Heat waves shimmered off the pavement.

She knocked at Aunt Millie's back door and heard Ace's voice from deep inside the house.

"Come in."

She found him in the small room where Aunt Millie once slept. The bed had been dismantled several days ago and, along with several boxes of bedding, picked up by a charity. A dozen or more boxes stood in the middle of the room. Dust tickled her nose.

He stood, his hands on his hips staring down at a box with the flaps opened.

She chuckled softly, and he looked up, surprised.

"What?"

"You have dust on your nose."

He stuck his hand into the short sleeve of his grungy T-shirt and wiped his face. Done, he grinned at her. "Better?"

"Much." She'd given herself a good talking to on the way over. This thing between them had to be put on hold. But she couldn't help the way her heart caught halfway up her throat at the way he looked at her, his expression gentle, his eyes smiling.

She tore her gaze away and looked at the boxes. "What do we have here?"

"I don't know for sure. I've only opened a few. Old dishes, like I said. And bits and pieces of cloth and buttons. Looks like junk to me."

She knelt at the box with open flaps, flipped one side back and read OLD DISHES. "There you go. Just like you said. Let's have a look." The dishes had been neatly packed with layers of newspaper between that crumpled as she touched them. She gasped as she pulled a plate out. "It's a Willow." She turned it over. "A Dimmock."

He squatted beside her. "I take it that's good?"

"I'd have to check it out, but this plate is probably worth over two hundred dollars."

She put it aside and uncovered the next layer. Six small square plates followed by a rectangular tray with pierced side handles. Again she checked the back stamp. "These are authentic Burgess and Leigh. It's a sandwich set."

She dug further and uncovered more old Willow dishes. "Someone had quite a collection." She sat back on her heels, stunned at the discovery. "It's worth a lot of money."

She packed them back as carefully as she'd removed them and put the box out of the way. Then she turned and rubbed her hands with glee. "What else do we have?"

In the next box she uncovered a complete child's tea set in German china. "This is in perfect condition."

Ace opened the next box. "Old magazines." He sounded disappointed and began to shove the lot aside.

"Wait a minute." She checked the publication dates and condition. "These will sell well, too."

"This is the one full of buttons and junk."

Nicole wasn't about to disregard anything at this point. "Not just buttons and junk," she said, after looking through the contents. "Antique fabric and collectible buttons." They continued to open boxes. Each one had been carefully packed, cryptically labeled, and was full of treasures.

"This doesn't seem like Aunt Millie's stuff," she said. "I didn't see any of her boxes packed so carefully."

"It says Uncle Fred and Aunt Ina on a couple of boxes. I think she must have inherited this stuff. It doesn't look as if she ever unpacked it, though."

Nicole laughed. "She probably wondered where she'd put it." She sat comfortably on the floor surrounded by the now closed boxes, the smell of dust and old newspapers filling her nose. "This is quite a find. I'll do some research and see what it's worth. But I think both you and I stand to make a nice little profit from selling it."

He sat cross-legged a few inches from her and grinned. "Who'd have guessed such a dark, unfriendly place as the basement hid such treasures?"

"It's a miracle nothing's been damaged by dampness." She was grateful for the fact, but there was a miracle that would mean more to her than undamaged antiques or the profit they would generate. She leaned forward over her knees. "Ace, this house is full of treasures. And I don't mean the antiques. I'm thinking of Aunt Millie's letters to you and the letter to her explaining why she couldn't come and bring you home. But I'm also thinking of what else you had here." She offered a quick prayer that God would give her the words to say and Ace the heart to hear her. "I remember your faith in God. I remember how determined you were to be a Christian soldier." She locked eyes with him. His gaze cooled, grew distant, but she pressed on. "I know you figured your aunt abandoned you. And you were mistaken. Isn't it the same with God?"

She watched and waited, but his expression revealed only detachment. Then he smiled. A condescending little grimace.

"I waited for a miracle." His voice was soft but flat, emotionless. "I prayed that God would make sure Aunt Millie came and got me. It never happened." He shrugged. "I stopped hoping. I stopped praying." He paused. "I stopped believing."

"Believing what? In God? Family? Prayer? People? What?"

"All of the above, I suppose. I count on no one but myself."

She jerked back, hurt by his words. "You don't trust me?"

She sat perfectly still as he studied her, smiled self-consciously as his gaze came to rest on her face and prayed he would see his judgment was wrong.

"I guess if I trust anyone it would be you."

Her breath eased out of tight lungs. "Why would you choose to trust me?"

"Because you haven't changed." His smile lit his face, ignited an answering glow inside her. "You're just as enthusiastic, caring, intense, and idealistic as when you were a kid."

She nodded. "Because that's who I am." What a perfect opening to turn this subject toward God. *Oh Lord, help me use this. Give me the right words. Open his heart.* "And not changing is important to you?"

He considered it a moment. "Perhaps it's knowing I won't turn around and be surprised by something."

She wasn't sure she liked sounding about as interesting as an old standby chair, but right now that didn't matter. She wanted to explore how and what had shaped him into the man who sat before her, his expression half amused, half guarded. "Do you mean surprised in a bad way?"

"Yeah. Like finding out something that would make me wonder if I'd been mistaken in all the things I thought I understood about you." His voice deepened. "But as I said, you've grown up in a real good way. You're the same, only matured. I like what I see, what I'm discovering."

His words pleased her. Made her feel special. Not an old chair at all but something precious. Like one of these fine pieces of china. "Thank you. When Aunt Millie didn't rescue you, I guess you were disappointed and blamed God. But, Ace, God hasn't changed. He is the same yesterday, today, and forever. His promises never fail. He does not change His mind."

Ace's mouth set into a hard, unyielding line. "Then I know where I stand with Him."

She gasped. "You think He doesn't love you because of the bad things that happened." She shook her head hard. "You are so wrong."

"Yeah?"

"Yes. It isn't God who made the bad choices, but some humans with little compassion. And just as Aunt Millie didn't stop loving you, neither did God." She took a deep breath and plunged on even though she wondered if she might offend him. "Ace, you could have come back to Aunt Millie anytime after you were on your own. But you decided not to. You robbed yourself of the chance to know her love."

He sat as motionless as something made out of bronze. Not a flicker of motion in his face or sign of emotion in his eyes.

Praying again for wisdom, she rushed on. "You're doing the same with God. You're running from His love when you could return to it anytime you choose."

She stared into his gaze and waited. For several heartbeats she thought he was going to act as if he hadn't heard, and then he blinked. "You make it sound so easy."

"It is."

"Only for someone like you. Things have changed. I've changed. Aunt Millie is gone. It's too late."

"Ace, it's never too late."

But he pushed to his feet. "Want to look at the other stuff I unearthed today?"

She scrambled to her feet and glanced at her watch. "Look at the time. Gram will be wondering what happened to me." She headed for the door. "Maybe I can come back later?" Did she sound too eager?

"Sure. I'll be here."

"Better yet, join us for supper. Unless you have something planned." She glanced around the kitchen but saw only a can of coffee, a half-used loaf of bread, and an open jar of peanut butter. She nodded toward the fridge.

He grinned immediately. "It's empty except for butter and cheese. I haven't bothered much with food."

"Then come over. Gram will have supervised Carrie in preparing something."

"How's your grandmother today? Did you persuade her to see a doctor?"

Nicole laughed. "She said her ankle wasn't hurting very much so we compromised. She promised to stay off it if I didn't make her go to the doctor."

Ace chuckled. "Stubborn, is she?"

"She prefers to call it strong natured. You'll come?"

He nodded. "Give me time to shower."

◆

Ace tugged a clean shirt over his head, paused to check his hair, and decided he looked presentable enough to join the ladies for dinner. He might have refused if he wasn't so hungry and fed up with cheese.

He snorted. Sure he would have. He wanted to see Nicole every chance he got even though his instincts warned him he was playing with fire.

Normally he listened to his instincts. But not this time. This time his interest in one special little lady drowned out the voice of reason. She intrigued him with her fervent beliefs and loyalties.

Next door, Carrie and Gram greeted him warmly. Nicole stood back and smiled, happy to see him, or was she happy because her family brightened in his presence?

Whatever. He enjoyed the company of all three women. And if it made Nicole happy, it was good enough for him.

"I made porcupine meatballs for supper," Carrie announced. "With mashed potatoes and peas. It's my specialty."

Gram chuckled. "She makes it every time she has to make supper. Good thing we like it."

Ace turned to Gram. "How's your ankle?"

Gram darted a look at Nicole. "It's fine. I'm only keeping it up because I promised my granddaughter."

Nicole rolled her eyes.

Ace grinned, feeling amusement in the pit of his stomach.

"It's ready," Carrie announced. Gram allowed Ace to help her to the table, favoring her sore ankle more than she would ever admit.

After grace, they dug in.

Ace tried the meatballs. "Very good."

Carrie beamed, and Nicole sent Ace a grateful glance.

After the meal Carrie hurried out to a babysitting job. She paused at the door. "I got a new CD if you want to check it out."

Gram hobbled to the small sitting room off the kitchen to watch the news.

Nicole laughed. "Guess I'm stuck with dishes."

"I'll help."

"You don't have to. You're a guest."

Guest? The word echoed inside his chest making him aware of the dark, empty corners. If he allowed himself to be honest, he would be forced to admit he wanted to be more than a temporary guest. He shoved the idea away and started to stack dishes. "I want to help."

As they worked side by side, she told him of her plans to add more display shelves to her store and do a feature on the antiques. He enjoyed her enthusiasm.

They finished the dishes. He hung the towel neatly and leaned against the edge of the counter.

She stood in front of the sink, her back to the window, and watched him uncertainly.

He should go. But more dusty boxes held no appeal.

"You want to hear Carrie's CD?" she asked.

"Sure." That beat unpacking boxes any day. Especially with Nicole to keep him company. They went through the TV room where Gram sat with her head back, her eyes closed. Nicole held a finger to her lips as they tiptoed into the larger living room.

A huge old-fashioned stereo sat against one wall. An entertainment center next to it held a modern stereo with a collection of CDs in a stack. Ace bent, read the labels, not recognizing most of the names, then turned to the older machine and ran his fingers along the wooden cabinet. "This is beautiful."

"Gram's. I think she's had it since she got off the ark."

"Does it have a needle?"

Nicole struggled to get the plastic wrap off the CD. "Yup. She still plays the records."

"May I look?"

Nicole shrugged.

He lifted the lid. The phonograph looked to be in excellent condition. One side of the cabinet was full of records. He checked the labels. "Wow. What a collection. George Beverly Shea to Elvis." He read the Elvis titles. "I used to know all the Elvis songs." At one time he did a pretty fair Elvis imitation, and to prove it he sang a few bars from each song on the record he held.

She sat back and grinned at him.

"Sing with me," he said.

She shook her head. "I don't know the songs."

He lowered the record cover and stared at her. "You don't know them?" He did his Elvis voice. "Well, baby, there's no time like the present."

She giggled. "I thought we were going to listen to Carrie's CD."

He shrugged and returned the record to the cabinet and sadly said, "Elvis has left the building." He lingered at the stereo, loathe to put Elvis to rest, then sat on the couch.

Still laughing, Nicole pushed the CD into the modern machine then sank to the floor close to his knees. A drum solo began and then a female voice. Nicole sang along, her voice strong and clear, as beautiful and sweet as Nicole herself.

The song was unfamiliar, but the words were distinct. All about God and worship and peace and love. He tried to block the words from his mind so he could enjoy listening to Nicole.

The song ended.

"What do you think?" Nicole asked.

"It's not Elvis."

"No, but she has something Elvis couldn't seem to find—peace."

"You got me there."

Nicole tipped her head. "It's too bad. Seems like he knew about God, just didn't *know* Him. Not in a way that made a difference to how he felt."

"Guess it just didn't work for him. Not everyone can believe like you do—in family, God, miracles, and happily ever after. I can't."

She shifted to stare at him. "I don't understand. You have proof you were wrong about Aunt Millie. Isn't that enough?"

"It isn't just Aunt Millie. Or even the foster care system. Have you ever seen a child with his belly swollen to the point of pain, his eyes glazed as he slowly starves to death? Have you seen other children crying and alone because their parents have been killed by guerrillas? Or worse, by AIDS?"

"And that's God's fault?"

"He could stop it."

"I suppose He could. But how long before man found something more cruel, more devastating, to do? There's nothing worse than man's inhumanity toward man."

He didn't reply. If God was all-powerful, He could stop it.

Nicole pulled herself up to the couch and sat beside him, turning so she could face him as she talked. She practically vibrated with intensity. Her face glowed with enthusiasm; her eyes sparkled. "Ace, have you looked as hard for evidence of God's love?"

Only his years of practice at giving away nothing at negotiations enabled him to meet her look without flinching. Her question caught him off guard. He, the mediator of many tense situations, the one who tried to find a reasonable middle ground, who prided himself on being able to see both sides, had not once looked for a balanced view of God.

His whole life was built on believing he needed no one, wanted nothing. Bit by bit, brick by brick, Nicole was tearing down his resistance. Aunt Millie, Nicole and her family, perhaps even God if he let himself believe the things Nicole said—each doing their part to peel back the layers he'd built around his heart, exposing it to things he'd closed himself to for years. But where did that leave him? Who was he if he tore away everything he'd built his life on?

"Come to church with me," she whispered.

He nodded, unable to resist her gentle invitation. He inched forward, wanting to kiss her sweet mouth.

She edged away, just out of reach.

"Nicole," Gram called from the other room. "Are you there?"

"Yes, Gram."

"Can you help me to bed?"

Nicole sprang to her feet. "I'll be right there." She stopped and smiled at Ace. "Her ankle is bothering her even if she won't admit it."

He rose slowly. They stood a few inches apart. He searched her gaze, found a welcome there. And more. A belonging? A connection begun eighteen years ago? He wasn't sure. But whatever it was felt good and right.

"I'll be on my way," he said. "Are you coming over later?"

She hesitated, glanced at her watch. "Maybe not. It's already late."

Disappointed, he touched her cheek, wishing for more. But Gram called again.

"I'll see you tomorrow then?" His husky voice revealed how much he regretted having to end this evening so soon.

She nodded.

◆

Ace leaned closer to the mirror and adjusted his tie. The past few days had been wonderful. All he'd ever imagined life could be. For the first time since his visit to Aunt Millie one long ago Christmas season, he enjoyed a sense of belonging. The Thomas family, as fun as it was loving, opened up and drew him into their circle. Pulled him in and made him part of themselves without leaving any wrinkles or bulges to indicate his presence caused any disturbance.

He rearranged the knot of his tie, even though it already lay perfectly centered, then turned from side to side to check his reflection.

The short-sleeved white shirt would have to do. He hadn't come prepared with anything dressier. He flicked a strand of hair off his forehead and hurried across the yard to the Thomas house.

Nicole opened the door at his knock. "You're early." Pink stole across her cheeks. Pleased to see he'd caught her thinking of him, he brushed at the blush with his knuckles.

"Just couldn't wait another minute," he teased, though the words held nothing but truth. The daytime hours passed on snails' tails while she worked at the store and he pretended to sort out Aunt Millie's house. The task no longer demanded he hurry, because once he finished he would have to deal with his emotions, and right now he preferred to ride the current. So he whittled away the leaden hours until Nicole got home from work.

After supper, which he shared with the family, he and Nicole hurried to his house where the hours raced past like an Indy 500 event. They tried to concentrate on sorting and cataloguing Aunt Millie's valuables, but it took only minutes for them to be lost in conversation. He wanted more, but she always ducked away when he tried to kiss her.

He studied her now.

"Carrie, are you ready?" Gram called from the living room; then she and Carrie joined them.

Tightness gripped Ace's collarbone. Suddenly he was tense. Welcoming him in the privacy of her home was one thing. Going out in public quite another. He, of all people, knew that. How many times had foster families left him out of their activities? And yet she took his arm as they turned toward the door.

She felt exactly right at his side. As if she'd been born for that place next to his heart. He wanted to jump to the moon. Swing through the trees beating his chest. Warning lights flashed at the back of his mind reminding him of his vow to avoid the emotional quicksand this feeling signaled. He resolutely ignored the warning. For just now, while he cleaned out the house, he would allow himself to experience belonging and acceptance.

"Is everyone ready?" Gram beamed as she looked around. "Carrie, we'll walk together." Her ankle already better, she marched the girl out the door leaving Ace and Nicole to follow.

Nicole laughed softly. "Thank you, Gram."

Gram didn't turn around but nodded her head briskly.

For Ace, it was a walk to remember: the summer sun warm on his skin, the sky like a big blue tent, the birds an exuberant orchestra. A feeling in his heart as big as the whole outdoors. *So this is what it feels like to belong?*

He let the idea seep through his brain, ignoring the insistent warning accompanying it. *Better be prepared for disappointment.* He pressed Nicole's hand closer so he felt its reassuring warmth against his ribs and dismissed the uneasy little tremor in his brain.

Nicole waved at a family across the street but kept her other hand on his arm for all to see.

Life had finally turned around. All the things he'd ached for when he was a boy and put aside as a man now seemed within easy reach.

Trouble was, he didn't trust easily.

He didn't need a clout to the side of the head to know what bothered him. He and Nicole were as unlikely a match as anyone could imagine. She with her idealistic views of life and family, he with his jaded approach. Their lives had taken them in opposite directions. She was permanency, promises, safety—all things he wasn't. She believed finding a box of cards and letters proving Aunt Millie tried to keep in touch with him erased the years of feeling he didn't belong.

Sure, it felt good to know the old gal had tried. And suddenly a lot of things fell into place—the restrictions on the use of the telephone, the glances between the adults when he asked about mail. But it was only a part of what had gone into shaping him.

They reached the church steps. Nicole introduced him to those they met. Hands extended and welcomed Ace before they took their places in the polished wooden pews.

The muted light from the pebbled glass windows bathed Nicole in a warm glow. The room radiated with love. Or was it confined to Ace and the girl at his side? If love felt like this he ought to bottle the feeling and sell it.

Nicole's voice rang out clear and sweet as they sang hymns.

The pastor stood to the pulpit. "My text for today is John 15, verse 13, 'Greater love hath no man than this, that a man lay down his life for his friends.' God did more than that. He loved us and sacrificed His dear Son while we were enemies. His love knows no boundaries, no excuses, no limits. And yet how many of us run from this great love rather than opening our hearts to it? My question is, how far can you run from God and His love? Psalm 139 says, 'If I ascend up into heaven, thou art there. . .if I take the wings of the morning. . .'"

Ace sat back as if something heavy and hard had slammed into his chest. Was he running from God's love? The very thing he yearned for but feared to trust? Had God pursued him all these years waiting to pour love into his life? Had He brought him back to Reliance for that reason? To discover Aunt Millie had cared, Nicole and her family still cared? To find a place where he belonged? Was this what God had in mind for him? Something warm and fluid washed over his insides. Was this feeling of well-being for real?

He didn't hear a lot of the sermon; yet, as he left the church, he knew he'd never had such a deeply religious experience. His heart beat stronger than he could remember it beating before. As if it had been lovingly caressed.

The four of them retraced their steps toward home.

"You'll have dinner with us, won't you, Ace?" Gram said. "I have a casserole in the oven."

"Gram's famous Sunday dinner casserole," Carrie said. "Chicken and rice and peas. Umm, umm, good."

"Unless you've got something more appealing at home." Nicole gave him a wide-eyed innocent look that didn't fool him for a minute. She knew the meager extent of his supplies.

◆

Nicole knew how Gram's Sunday casserole tasted, but today it held none of the familiar comforting flavors. It could have been sawdust for all the enjoyment it gave her. Her whole being quivered with tension. Tears choked the back of her nose.

She'd been aware of Ace's startled reaction to the sermon. She knew it had touched his heart. Having Ace go to church with them and join them for dinner afterward felt so right. As if her whole life had shaped itself for this moment. She knew he was very close to believing in God's love.

"I'll do dishes," Carrie said, as they finished the apple crisp dessert.

Nicole's mouth dropped open at Carrie's uncharacteristic offer.

"Why don't you show Ace Mom and Dad's park?" Carrie added.

Nicole patted her sister's head. "Thank you, Carrie. That's so sweet."

She waited until Ace helped her step into his black SUV before she explained. "It's a public park, but Carrie likes to think it belongs to our family."

Following her directions, he turned left at the corner. The park lay on the outskirts of town. It had been a favorite place for campouts, wiener roasts, and picnics when her parents had been alive—her mother and second father. Since their deaths, she and Carrie and Gram made a yearly pilgrimage to remember the family they had once been.

"I have something special to show you." She pulled Ace toward the grove of trees close to the gurgling river. "See this?" She drew him to a tree and touched the carved initials. Inside a heart were the initials of her mother and stepfather. In two smaller hearts were her initials and Carrie's. "Our family tree." She laughed awkwardly.

Ace trailed his fingers along the letters and shapes, a thoughtful look on his face. His words were low. "A literal family tree. Neat."

"It was Dad's idea." She turned to study the circle of trees, the rusted fire pot, the burnt logs, and the green picnic table marked with years' worth of initials and shapes carved into its top. "We used to come here so often. It's where he proposed to my mother. We came here when they got back from their honeymoon and had a special family ceremony. That's when he carved my initials in my heart." She closed her eyes and waited for her throat to relax so she could talk. "We came when Carrie was six weeks old. Dad held my hand and helped me put the initials in her heart." She stopped again and steadied her breathing. "There were supposed to be more hearts, but it never happened."

Ace wrapped his arms around her and pulled her to the bench of the picnic table. He pressed her face into the hollow of his neck and held her tight, crooning her name as she let the tears flow. They lasted only a minute. She didn't often cry for her parents anymore, although she missed them at unexpected times and places—Carrie's ball games, the opening of her store, when Aunt Millie died.

She quieted and rested contentedly in his arms, comforted by his sympathy.

"I'm not sure which is worse," he murmured. "To never have known family life or to have known it and lost it."

"Even knowing how things would turn out, I wouldn't give up a minute of our time together."

He didn't answer, but she felt his doubt.

She pushed back so she could see into his face. "I had a whole family for a lot of years. I had a father who loved me." Her voice dropped to a whisper. "I needed that. It made up for what I lost when my own father died." Her smile felt wobbly. "And now I have Carrie and Gram. What more could a person ask for?"

He looked deep into her eyes, searching, she was certain, for answers to his own doubts, answers to questions he perhaps couldn't even voice.

"Nicole, what happened to your father?"

She knew he didn't mean Paul Thomas but Nicolas Costello. She sat up straight, twisting her hands into a tight knot. "I was five years old. He promised to bring me a special present for my birthday. I waited and waited, but he never came." Nicole steadied her voice. This was old news. She'd dealt with it and put it behind her. It no longer had the power to turn her inside out. "He died in a reckless skydiving accident." Her voice hardened. Pain iced her veins. "He didn't have to. He was a risk taker and a gambler. His gambling left the restaurant heavily in debt. Mom had to sell it and move back here to Reliance to live with Gram." Her eyes burned with memories of her hurt, her anger that her father gambled away his life on some thrill rather than be there for her. She faced Ace. "His decisions were selfish. He didn't think about us. How we would feel when things went wrong."

Ace nodded slowly, his expression guarded. "That's why you're afraid of taking risks."

"I will never do anything to jeopardize my family's stability."

He trailed his finger over her cheek. "Maybe we are more alike than we know."

"How can that be? We're as different as black and white. My family is the most important thing in my life. You don't even want to believe in family. I always take the safe route. Your job requires you to take risks. I believe fervently in God's love. You doubt it. How much more different can we be?" And yet between them lay a bond of velvety steel she couldn't overlook. Something in her reached out and found belonging with him.

It was the way he slid into her family. And how his practical common sense soothed away her worries. He seemed to match her emotionally. And there was no denying an attraction between them.

"Perhaps opposites attract," he said. "Perhaps our differences complete each other. Perhaps we share more than we know."

She waited for him to explain.

"You see, my mother, too, made choices that cost her her life and me my security."

She digested his statement. "How did she die?"

"She chose to die by the bottle."

"What do you mean?"

"She drank herself to death. Literally."

"Oh, Ace, I'm so sorry. I just assumed she had cancer or something."

Silently they held hands. Her heart actually hurt with every breath. They'd both lost so much. And paid such a price for choices made by other people.

"You've lost more than me," she said. "At least I've always had my family. You had no one except Aunt Millie, and she couldn't reach you. How awful."

"Perhaps good has come of it."

She clenched his hand tighter. "How?" She prayed he'd see God's hand in his life.

"It forced me to deal with my bad attitude. I learned to look ahead instead of back. Living in a series of foster homes taught me how to deal with all sorts of people. It's made me who I am." He pulled her against his chest. "And life has taught you to be loyal, kind, and—"

"Cautious," she finished for him.

"So where does that leave us?"

"I'm not sure." She sighed. "I don't want to think about it. Can't we simply enjoy this moment?"

He chuckled. "Sounds more like something I would say."

She nodded. But right now she wanted to rest in the comfort of what they shared. She knew he'd been touched by the sermon this morning. She knew God was at work. She would see her miracle. Of that she had no doubt.

Later they wandered among the trees, enjoying the birds and flowers and small children playing. She longed to ask him about his experience in church but knew she had to be quiet and let God work.

Chapter 7

D id you see this?" Rachel waved the newspaper in front of Nicole.
"Haven't looked at the news." She sat at her desk in the store, doodling on a slip of paper.

"Come on, girl. Get a grip. You've done nothing but moon around here for days. In fact"—Rachel leaned over to peer into Nicole's eyes—"I'd be inclined to say you were off in some dream world." She plucked the scrap of paper off the desk. "Ace. Oh ho. So that's it. Our elusive Nicole Thomas has fallen in love. And with a hard-eyed stranger at that."

Nicole snatched the paper back. "He's not a stranger. I've known him since I was ten." What possessed her to scribble his name in the margins?

Rachel perched on the desk. "Nope. It's love. Not that I blame you. He's quite the looker."

"I'm not in love." She wouldn't let herself think that. Even if he turned back to God, and she prayed he would, there was still his job to think about. She knew he encountered dangerous situations. Oil well fires, ecoterrorists, jungle fever, and who knew what else. Not the sort of risks she wanted to deal with or subject her family to.

"Nicole, sweetie, it's me you're talking to. Your best friend. Do you really think I haven't noticed the starry look in your eyes lately?" She chuckled. "I always knew you'd fall hard when you fell, but I never thought you'd go for a—well, what can I say? He's an adventurer. He'll drag you away from your safe little world. And about time, I'd say."

Rachel's words stung. She made it sound as if Nicole lived in a state of denial, locking herself in a padded cell or something. "I'm not about to leave my family, no matter what. I would never do that to them."

"Uh-huh." Rachel's look of resignation was the last straw.

"What's so interesting in the newspaper?" Conversation closed. End of subject.

Rachel sighed once then flipped the paper open to reveal an article. "That wonderful little woodcarver is selling out."

Nicole skimmed the article. Only a few lines in the back of the arts and entertainment section buried in a column about what's new and hot in the local galleries. But if anyone had seen his work, they'd be beating a path to his door.

She tapped her finger on the paper. "I've always wanted to get more of his work." She glanced around the store. "If I could buy him out—" Jumping to her feet, she circled the room. "Just picture his wild animal carvings on some shelves against this wall. I could hang Aunt Millie's linens on a rack over here and move the paintings to the stair wall." She raced up the steps, mentally measuring the space. "I have to get there before anyone else," she called over the wooden banister she'd sandpapered and polished inch by inch until it looked as good as the day her grandfather had installed it.

Rachel bounced off the desk and leaned against the banister watching. "I doubt any city dude will find the place. It took us hours to find that little log cabin. We would have driven right past it if we hadn't known what we were looking for."

Nicole ground to a halt and descended the stairs. "That's right. But I want those things so bad. They're exquisite." The elderly man did extraordinary work, everything from chain saw creations to tiny forest animals so delicate she held her breath so she wouldn't frighten them away. "What I wouldn't give to have some of those pieces right now." She didn't need a medical opinion to know Gram's cataract surgery needed to be done soon. She'd noticed how Gram counted the stitches on her knitting needle by feel rather than sight and how she opted to watch the news on TV rather than read the paper as had been her pleasure not so long ago. Nicole's income had increased with the addition of Aunt Millie's antiques, but her savings were growing too slowly for her liking. Getting the woodcarver's work would up her income substantially.

"Maybe you should go talk to him."

"You're right. I'm going to head out there this very minute." She studied the room again. "I want twice as much display space. Just think—I'll soon be making enough money for Gram's eye surgery and Carrie's university education." She grinned. "Maybe even new teeth for Gram."

"You go, girl. Grandpa's Attic is gonna be the best little art store in the West." She tilted her head and wrinkled her eyebrows. "Guess it isn't really an art store. Hmm. Not sure what to call it."

Nicole grinned. "I'll settle for your calling it 'best.'"

Just then the bell above the door jangled. Nicole turned to see who it was, and her knees weakened.

Ace stood framed in the door, his gaze searching the room until he found Nicole. Then a wide warm smile lit his face.

"Look at him," Rachel whispered out of the corner of her mouth. "He's got it as bad as you."

Nicole's pulse hammered in her throat as their gazes locked. It felt as if their hearts leapt across the room and collided. Sudden heat rushed up her neck, and she couldn't speak.

"I think I'll make myself scarce," Rachel muttered. "But if I were you, I'd be asking the hunk to take you to see the woodcarver. Nothing like a nice drive in the country."

Nicole barely noticed Rachel march away as Ace crossed the room and stood before her.

"Hi." She couldn't look away from his eyes. The hazel irises seemed almost iridescent. "What are you doing here?" She grimaced. What a way to greet a prospective customer. But somehow she didn't think he'd come to buy something. "I mean, I thought we were to meet after work." They planned to watch Carrie's ball game this evening.

"I couldn't wait. Besides, I've never been inside your store, and I keep hearing all these great things about it. Thought I'd have a look around." But his gaze never shifted from hers.

She swallowed hard and glanced around the room. It looked like a place she'd never been before. How dumb was that? She knew this building from the tiny attic hole to the damp basement. With effort she jerked her brain back into gear. "Let me show you around." Her words rote, she described various objects. What was he really doing here? She led him up the stairs to the second level.

She lifted one of the pottery mugs she'd brought from the show in Great Falls. "Isn't this beautiful? Look at the lines. And the glaze. Shelley Brash is the artist. I fell in love with her work as soon as I saw it. I knew it would be a big hit, and it has been."

He studied the mug and nodded. "I can see why people would want it."

His appreciation loosened her thoughts.

"This building belonged to my grandfather," she explained. "Since his death years ago, it went from being a hardware store to a grocery store and then a convenience store. I worked as a clerk here after I came back home. When the lease expired a year ago, Gram handed it to me and said to do what I wanted with it. And I did."

She told how she'd restored both the interior and exterior, discovered the plank floor under layers of carpet, linoleum, and paint, and polished it to a fine patina then created what she hoped were attractive displays.

His eyes widened with appreciation. "You've done a lot of work."

She sucked in warm air and grinned. "I don't mind the work. I love the beautiful things I've found. Some of them I hate to see go. But that's the whole deal. Buy beauty. Sell beauty. And hope to pay the bills." Right now she was barely breaking even, but that would change as she took in more and more stock. First, the lovely things from Aunt Millie's, and if she could get the woodcarvings. . .

If only she could scoop up the entire lot before anyone else discovered them.

What a draw that would be.

She pointed out the antiques she'd cleaned and displayed. "These are going over big as well. I love telling people how I knew Aunt Millie and little things I remember about each item. I hope the stories and memories will go home as well. Maybe keep a bit of Aunt Millie alive."

"That's important to you, isn't it?" His eyes looked far away as if trying to distance himself from that part of his life.

"Yes, it is." She tugged his arm and pulled him back to her. "Maybe someday you'll admit family is important to you, too."

His eyes narrowed, and then a slow smile widened his mouth. "I'm learning to appreciate family. Yours. Not mine. It's too late for me to have that."

She nodded, slowly, reluctantly. Aunt Millie was gone. They'd never had a chance. "I don't mind sharing my family with you."

He smiled. "So what's a smart businesswoman like you doing right now?"

She grabbed up the newspaper. "I was planning to head out to see this man." Remembering Rachel's words, she said, "Would you like to come along?"

"Woodcarver? Would I?"

She laughed. "No wood eyes, just wood animals."

He blinked, then laughed as he followed her outside. "Do you have directions?"

"Yup." She tapped her head, hoping she could find her way again.

"My vehicle's here. We'll take it." He'd driven his SUV to the store and hurried around to open the door for her. Following her directions, he turned his truck to the west and headed toward the mountains. She concentrated on the road, watching for some sign to indicate where to turn.

"North here," she said, hoping she was right. The road was barely a trail. Almost invisible. Just as she remembered it.

He slowed to make a corner.

She leaned forward to peer out the window. "Very few people have been able to find this place. Wait until you see the work the old man does. It's like nothing you've ever seen. If I can buy his entire business, not only will I stand to make a nice profit, I'll corner the market." She grinned at him. "It would be like a gift from heaven."

He shot her a puzzled look. "I never figured you to care so much about making money."

She concentrated on the road. "It's not for me. It's for Gram and Carrie." She told of their needs. "Carrie will make an excellent teacher."

"There it is." She pointed to a tiny weathered sign—LOST IN THE WOODS. The cabin was almost completely hidden among the trees.

"Appropriate name," he murmured. "This is really the back of beyond."

She nodded, eyes forward. "If it was any easier to get to, this man would have a worldwide reputation."

They pulled into a tiny clearing. A narrow log cabin faced them, weathered gray with age, flowers crowding up to the walls.

"Isn't it beautiful?" she whispered.

He agreed as they climbed the low verandah and pushed open the heavy door. A bell chimed overhead as they entered a narrow room. Along one wall stood large carvings of trees and bears and deer. Two of the other walls had sturdy shelves filled with smaller items. The nearest carving made Nicole hold her breath, and she touched Ace's arm to get his attention: A tiny deer poised under a spruce tree. She reached out, knowing it wasn't real yet needing to touch it to convince herself.

Nicole signaled Ace to wait, and they stood at the doorway not speaking until a tiny woman shuffled through the far door.

"I'm sorry." Her voice sounded like the wind sifting through the treetops. "We're no longer open for business."

"Mrs. Garnier, it's me, Nicole Thomas. I bought a set of birds from you earlier. Lovely work. I saw in the paper that you're selling out."

The old lady settled to a chair. "Hate to let it go but haven't got a choice. Arman's getting too old." She dabbed at her eyes. "He can barely see anymore. Forgets what he's doing. Almost cut his hand off t'other day."

"I'm sorry." Nicole spoke softly.

The older woman's cloudy eyes went around the room, lingering on item after item.

"Can't hardly bear to part with 'em but can't take 'em with us. Moving into a little place. What they call them places? Condos? No room. No room at all. But close to our daughter."

"I'm so sorry. Is the business still for sale?" Nicole hated to add to the woman's distress, but she didn't want some city fellow snatching the treasures from under her nose.

"One young man from the city came."

Nicole's breath jerked into her chest. Was she too late? She reached for Ace's hand, needing something to cling to.

The old woman shook her head. "He was so high and mighty. I hate to think of him taking our creatures. All he could talk about was how much money they'd make him. We didn't like that, did we, Arman?"

An old man shuffled through the door to his wife's side. He didn't respond to the question. Nicole was shocked to see how he'd deteriorated since her last visit.

"Are you still planning to sell them?" Nicole asked.

"Got to. Got to," the older woman muttered.

Nicole circled the room, picked up a bear here, a deer there, exclaimed over a squirrel holding a pinecone. She returned to the couple. Knowing she would never be able to afford the entire collection, she mentally picked out the pieces she'd like to have.

"I've always admired your work." She addressed the old man. "It's the most beautiful woodcarving I've ever seen. The animals almost seem to be alive, holding their breath, waiting for us to leave so they can get on with their work. I'd be honored to own some of your work."

The old woman took her husband's hand. "We want it to all go together. Wouldn't be right to separate them. We just want it over and done with. No hassling with a bunch of people."

"How much?"

The woman named a sum.

Nicole sighed. If only she hadn't depleted her savings at the Great Falls show. "It's a lot of money."

The old woman pushed to her feet and got a piece of paper from a desk in the corner. She handed the slip of paper to Nicole. Nicole studied it and nodded.

"Yes, I know. The price is more than fair. Would you consider letting me take it on consignment?"

The woman held her husband's hand. "You seem like the sort of person who would take proper care of our pets." She shook her head. "But we need the money. We have to pay for our condo."

Ace pulled his checkbook from his pocket. "I can see why you want this stuff. I'll lend you the money, and you can pay me the same as with Aunt Millie's stuff. As you sell it."

"No thanks." The look she gave him made him stuff the checkbook and pen back into his pocket.

The old man mumbled something. His wife looked long and hard at him then turned to Nicole. "We want you to have our pets. But we can't stay here much longer."

"I understand." She patted the old man on the shoulder.

"Arman wants me to give you two months to get the money."

Nicole nodded. "Thank you. I'll be back." She could barely make it out of the cabin. Two months? How could she hope to earn that much money in such a short time? It was impossible. Back at the truck she faced Ace. "If I planned to borrow money, I would go to the bank."

Without waiting for his help, she jumped into the truck and shut the door.

He climbed in. "I was only offering to help."

She sighed. "I know. I didn't mean to snap at you, but I really want that collection." She sighed again. "I just don't have the money. And I doubt if I can raise it in two months. Truth is, it's more than I expect to earn from the store in six months. I was hoping. . ." She shrugged. She'd hoped they'd consider consignment or perhaps a down payment and then monthly installments. It was the only way she could afford to go. "Guess I set my sights too high. Still, it's the peak of tourist season, and with Aunt Millie's things I just might. . ." It would take a miracle. Seemed as if she wanted more than her fair share of them lately.

"Where does this road go?" He nodded in the opposite direction from which they'd come.

"I'm not sure. Maybe the river."

"Want to go find out?"

She nodded, still distracted by the business at the cabin.

In a few minutes the road ended. They got out and clambered over the rocks to the edge of the bank overlooking the river several feet below them. Ace chose a spot, and they sat on the ground, their backs against a fallen tree.

Nicole stared down at the river. "They're the most exquisite things I've ever seen. If only they didn't insist I pay for it all at once."

"Are they asking a fair price?"

"More than fair. Some of his work would bring a thousand dollars or more from the right buyer. Whoever gets it will stand to profit."

"So you're saying it's a sound business investment?"

She nodded.

"I'd be more than willing to lend you the money."

She made a protesting noise, but before she could speak he went on.

"But, as you're opposed to that, why not borrow the money from the bank? That's what they're for, you know."

"I don't borrow money. I promised myself I never would." But if she didn't, she would lose a wonderful business opportunity.

He studied her carefully. "Is this about your father?"

She shrugged and picked up a twig. "Going into debt cost my mother and me our security." She snapped the twig between her fingers. "His risk taking cost him his life."

"You aren't your father, and there's a difference between foolish chances and an investment. To buy merchandise you know you can make a profit on is not a gamble. It's a business decision."

"I'd have to borrow against the store."

"You have nothing to lose, though. You buy the stuff. Sell it at a profit. Pay back the loan. In the meantime you have a unique and original collection drawing in customers so you sell even more—make more money. It isn't a gamble. It's a wise business choice."

She watched the water ripple past them.

"I don't know. I understand what you're saying but. . ." She sighed. "I just don't like to take risks."

"What risks?"

She grabbed another twig and twisted it round and round. "Borrowing money. What if. . . ?" She threw the twig into the water. "I would never do anything to hurt my family."

"And this would hurt them how?"

"I don't know." She flung herself down on her back and stared at the cloudless sky. "You're mixing me all up."

He leaned on one elbow, looking into her face. "It seems simple enough to me. Either you want the old man's carvings enough to get the money, or you decide it's easier to let them go."

"I want them."

"Then it's settled."

A mix of emotions played through her—uncertainty, fear.

She sighed. "You make it sound so simple."

"I'm not saying it's simple. Life is never simple. But sometimes it's necessary, and even healthy, to step away from old habits. Even if the first step is scary."

"I need to think about it."

"Yes, you do. But you make me wonder if your faith in God is as real as you say it is."

She sat upright and stared at him. "Of course it is."

"Then maybe it's time to put it into practice."

She knew what he meant. "Take the risk and let God be in charge of whether it succeeds or fails?"

He settled back, as relaxed as could be while she felt ready to explode.

"Isn't that what trust is all about?"

"Not exactly. I think we're expected to make wise choices." This conversation filled her with confusion.

"Borrowing money is sometimes a wise choice. It certainly is here. If you don't get the money in a matter of weeks, someone else is going to buy that stuff, corner the market, and make a nice profit. I think"—he kept his voice soft and low—"you're afraid of risks. So afraid you can't even trust God."

She stared at him. "You're wrong." But even to her own ears she sounded uncertain. "I do trust God. In fact, I'm going to trust Him to help me raise the money in the next two months."

"By selling your merchandise?"

She nodded slowly. "I know it will take a miracle, but God is a God of miracles."

He plucked a feathery head of grass and brushed it across her arm. "So you prefer to make God do the work?"

She jerked away from the tickle of the grass. "Believe me, I'll be working."

"But if you don't get the money, it's God who failed to provide a miracle, rather than you who passed up a business opportunity God sent your way?"

"No. Hey, aren't I supposed to be trying to convince you to trust God, not the other way around?"

"Maybe you've done such a good job I've passed you."

He brushed the head of grass up her other arm. She snatched it from him and tossed it away.

"What did you say?" she demanded.

"I'm a quick learner?"

She leaned over, pinning his eyes with her gaze. "Tell me, Ace Conners— have you decided to trust God?"

His eyes reflected the dark pines around him. She sensed his uncertainty as he hesitated. "Almost," he whispered.

She cupped his cheek in her palm and laughed. "I truly believe in miracles. You are proof."

He quirked an eyebrow. "How so?"

"Since you came, I've been praying you would find your way back to faith."

"I said *almost*."

She let herself enjoy the feel of his warm skin, the roughness of his whiskers beneath her hand, then drew away. "At least you're headed in the right direction. And I'm going to trust Him for a miracle to buy Arman's collection, as well. That way I don't have to take any risks." She ignored the knowing look in Ace's eyes. Sure, to him it sounded like a cop-out, but no way would she borrow money and risk losing the store. Even if it looked like a certain thing. She knew better than to think anything was certain. She quickly amended her thought: except God's faithfulness.

Ace got up and pulled her to her feet. "We're going to be late for Carrie's game."

"No way. She'd never forgive us."

Chapter 8

Ace led her back to the SUV, and they made it to town just in time for the start of Carrie's game. He cheered and whistled each time Carrie caught the ball or batted.

Carrie waved and bowed and blew him kisses. Nicole grinned at the two of them.

But Ace's thoughts were busy elsewhere. Nicole couldn't have made it clearer that he didn't belong in her world. She didn't take risks. Period. Not even safe ones. And he was a risk. His job, his past, his views on life and living. Even his tentative trust in God. All constituted risks. Bad risks. If he had a lick of sense he would walk away this minute and never look back. Let a moving company come in and dispose of the rest of Aunt Millie's stuff.

But he didn't have the sense of a grasshopper.

Or maybe because he *was* a risk taker he didn't move on. He intended to hang around and see what happened—to his interest in Nicole, to her business, to his fledgling trust in God. Still too fragile to be called "trust," he wanted to see where things went. Not quite ready to commit himself to faith, he wanted proof. He wanted to see if God really cared about him, Ace Conners.

◆

"I've decided to call in a dump truck to clean out the garage," Ace said days later. "I don't feel like tackling another stack of boxes."

Nicole jerked back from washing dishes. "You can't do that. The place is full of wonderful antiques."

Ace shrugged. "I'm sick of poking through garbage for something that might be worth a few bucks." The whole business held no pleasure when he had to do it on his own. Set on raising money to buy Arman's collection, something he knew was impossible in the time frame allowed, Nicole spent every minute at the shop. She'd decided to stay open late and, rather than pay for help, stayed herself. The only way he got to see her at all was to invite himself over for the evening meal. And accompany them to church on Sunday. Not that either activity proved a hardship. The ladies were good company, and he eagerly listened to every word the preacher delivered. The consistent message seemed to be God's love and faithfulness. Ace found it easier and easier to believe it was true. Still, he wasn't one hundred percent convinced it applied to him.

Nicole sighed deeply. "Would it help if I lent a hand?"

He held back a smile. He figured she would go for the bait, but he wasn't about to let her know he'd set her up. "You don't have time."

"Rachel is always saying she'll put in a few more hours at the store. I could probably get her to stay until closing time a few nights."

He dried the last pot and stowed it in the cupboard before he answered. "I guess I could put off arranging a truck for another day."

A little frown hovering between her eyes, she grabbed the towel from him and wiped her hands. That tension hadn't existed before her visit to the wood-carver's cottage.

He touched her shoulders, bringing her gaze upward to his. "Nicole, when are you going to stop pushing yourself so hard? You can't possibly raise enough money in two months. Go to the bank and borrow what you need. It's not a risk."

She clung to his gaze. He felt her determination. Her desperation. Heard it in her voice when she said, "It's only six weeks now."

"Which means you should have raised a quarter of the money. Have you?"

She looked panicked. "Not even an eighth. But something will happen. I just need to make some big sales."

"Nicole, you'd need to sell most of the stuff in your store."

Her eyes glistened with tears. "I need more stock."

"You need to stop trying to do this yourself. Let me help you. Or borrow the money from the bank."

She rocked her head back and forth. "I just can't take the risk."

The same old story. Nicole would never do anything she perceived to be risky. That included him. He would never really belong. Yet he couldn't walk away. He closed his eyes. Here in Reliance, in the warmth of her family and the belonging he felt with her and, yes, the way his heart opened toward God, he admitted he wanted to belong like he'd never wanted anything before.

Not true, he realized. He'd wanted it since he was a kid. He'd wanted a home. He'd wanted a family.

He'd been denied it by some nameless, faceless authority. And in his disappointment he'd shut God and love out of his life.

He headed for a repeat of the same disappointment if he kept hanging around waiting for Nicole to accept his devotion.

But he couldn't leave her struggling to live her safe little life. Perhaps losing the things she really cared about. Like Arman's work.

He pulled her into his arms, cradling her against his chest. He ached for her to belong there. He wanted to kiss away all her fears. But even though she pressed her face into his shirt and wrapped her arms around him like she was afraid to let go, she never allowed him to do anything more than give her a friendly kiss.

He kissed the top of her head and breathed in the smell of lemon and lilac from her hair.

She pushed away. "We better get at that garage."

Reluctantly he let her go.

❖

"Wanna come to Great Falls with me?" Ace asked Nicole as they examined the boxes in the garage. So far they'd found nothing she deemed of value. He could feel her discouragement and wanted to do something to ease it. Perhaps a trip away would help her regain her perspective.

"I have to go to the office for a few minutes," he said. "Then we could do something fun."

She sat back, a stunned look on her face. "You have an office in Great Falls? You've been less than an hour away all this time and we've never seen you?"

He chuckled. "Hardly. But I couldn't continue to ignore my work so I rented office space, and my secretary, Martha, has set up quarters so I can handle a few details."

She looked appeased then sighed. "I can't go. I have too much to do."

"When did work become the most important thing in your life?"

She made a protesting noise as she flipped open a box; then her interest shifted away from Ace's question while she pulled out old bottles and examined them. "Finally something of value. These are in mint condition." She glanced up and met his gaze, looking thoughtful. "I know a gallery owner in Great Falls. I could see if he'd take some stuff on consignment. If I could double my sales. . ."

"So it's a yes?"

She shifted, scanned the remaining boxes, and sighed. "I'll have to get a bunch of stuff ready." She finger-brushed her hair. "But I don't know where I'll find the time."

"Could I help?"

She looked at him, right through him—he suspected to a mental view of her work—wondering perhaps if she dared accept his offer.

He nodded at the greenish jar in her hand. "I'm sure I can wash old bottles without breaking them."

Her gaze shifted back to focus on his eyes. A smile curved her lips. How he wanted to wipe that hint of anxiety from her expression. He wanted to hold her, take care of her, be here for her every day—

He jerked his thoughts back to reality. Just as he couldn't deny this sense of rightness between them nor how much he cared, neither could he build a future filled with nothing but dreams.

"I thought you were anxious to get this stuff cleaned out." She nodded to the unopened boxes and unexamined piles of stuff.

"A few more days won't make a world of difference. Let's go to your work-room right now, and I'll show you how handy I can be."

She put the green jar back in the box and closed the lid. "Let's take this."

He grabbed the box and headed for his SUV.

At the store Rachel, busy with an older couple studying one of the fabric art paintings, nodded hello to Nicole, her eyebrows shooting up when she saw Ace.

He followed Nicole into the back room and glanced around. "I see you've been busy."

"Every spare minute." She brushed past him to clear a space on her worktable.

He set the box on a nearby shelf and rubbed his hands together. "Show me what to do."

"I need to get everything ready to display, but it's time-consuming clean-ing and polishing. And if I'm going to put some stock on consignment with my friend in Great Falls. . ." She shook her head and murmured, "I need a miracle."

"Will I do?" he asked gently.

She straightened, blinked, and suddenly grinned. "Miracles come in all shapes and sizes." She handed him a pot of cleaning compound and a soft rag. "This lantern will sell well as soon as it's polished."

They polished brass and scrubbed glass. They brushed and patched. They catalogued and priced. And they talked.

"You're going to gloat when I tell you this." He worked on a brass bed lamp. "I was really hurt when Aunt Millie didn't come for me." It was the first time he'd freely admitted it.

She didn't smile. He'd give her credit for that. She didn't even look happy about it. "Ace, I am so sorry. It was so unnecessary. I mean, if they wouldn't let you live with her, they could have least let you visit."

"Or told me what happened." He couldn't keep the bitterness from his voice.

"I know. All those years of thinking she didn't care." She lifted a cut-glass vase to the light. "That looks better." She picked up its mate and began meticu-lously cleaning every line. "I'm so glad you found the truth." Pausing, she studied him. "It helps, doesn't it?"

"It does." But not half as much as the way Nicole and her family welcomed him into their hearts. In fact, the whole community seemed set on drawing him into its midst. At ball games people talked to him as if he'd lived there all his life. Many came up to him and offered condolences on Aunt Millie's passing. Often they shared a fond memory of his aunt, making her seem more alive than he'd thought of her since he'd been abandoned. Strange. A few weeks ago he would have considered the whole business invasive, but now he discovered it consoled like a healing balm. He thought he'd put the bitterness and anger behind him years ago, but now he realized it had gone underground like a boil below the surface. The kindness of Nicole, her family, and a community of strangers had excised the infection. And something happened deep inside his soul—he wasn't ready to call it faith or trust or acceptance of God, but it was something as real as the greetings of Aunt Millie's friends.

They worked late into the night. Nicole was determined to get ready as much as she could to take to Great Falls. They arranged to leave right after breakfast the next morning.

◆

Nicole studied Ace's strong yet gentle hands on the steering wheel. He'd been a good friend these past few weeks when her insides felt shaky. Mentally she clung to his support. She knotted her fingers together to stop herself from reaching out to touch his hands, seeking comfort from a physical contact.

Ace drove with casual concentration on the narrow, quiet road. She shifted her gaze away and looked out the window at the green grain fields and golden pastures. Rough rock-banded buttes rose from the fields. Dark green trees lined the river in the distance and always the serene, blue mountains as a backdrop. She settled back, soothed by the calm beauty of the landscape.

Ace made his way through traffic past the statue of Charlie Russell and his horse to the brass doors of the Montana Building in the heart of historic downtown Great Falls and pulled to a stop. "I get off here. You take the truck and visit your gallery friend. Meet me back here in two hours."

He touched her chin, dropped a quick kiss on her cheek, and hurried away, briefcase in hand.

She slid behind the wheel and headed around the block to the Western Gallery, owned by her friend Brian.

Brian agreed to take most of what she'd brought. They settled on prices and commissions. He signed the papers then shoved them across the desk to her and leaned back. "There're a lot of rumblings about a woodcarver out your way. Seems he has a real treasure trove of goodies and might be selling lock, stock, and barrel. Know anything about it?"

Nicole signed the last of the papers before she answered. "Read something about it in the arts column a few weeks ago." She wasn't about to say more.

"Have you seen any of his work?"

She couldn't lie. "I have."

"Is it as good as they say?"

She rose and looked over the half wall to the store below. "Depends on what they say."

"Maybe I should pay this place a visit. Might be worth getting the whole kit and caboodle. You know how it is—if you have sole rights to someone's work, you corner a large portion of the market."

"I know how it is." She wanted to corner that market. But time was running out, and she didn't have a quarter of the money she needed. Her whole insides ached at her quandary. She wanted to believe God would provide the funds but realized how selfish it sounded. Not that she didn't think He cared. She knew He did. But wasn't she always telling Carrie that God gave her a brain to use? And Nicole's brain told her she was avoiding the obvious answer—borrow from the bank.

But her fears were stronger than her common sense. "I appreciate your taking these things for me."

He picked up a cranberry carnival glass bowl and held it to the light. "We'll both benefit. This stuff sells like hotcakes."

She glanced at her watch. "I have to go."

On the way back, she considered her options. If someone from the city drove out and offered Arman and his wife cash on the spot, would they feel obligated to wait for Nicole? Would it make any difference if they did? She didn't have the slightest chance of raising the money in time.

Ace stepped out of the doors as she stopped at the curb. She slid over, and he got in.

"Finished your work?" he asked.

"Yes." She couldn't keep the worry from her voice.

"You don't sound very pleased. What's wrong?"

She explained it to him.

"You know what I think."

"I know. Borrow from the bank. I can't bring myself to do it."

They stopped at a red light, and he slanted her a look.

"What?" she asked at his probing stare.

"I'm just wondering what it would take for you to see it isn't a risk—"

"Borrowing money is always a risk."

"Okay. Maybe what I mean is it's an acceptable risk."

His look was rife with meaning. Her thoughts swirled. Was he talking about the shop or something more? The traffic began to move, and he turned his attention away. She looked out the window, but her thoughts took a journey of their own. No doubt he noticed how she kept him at arm's length. She told herself he had to turn to God before she would allow herself to be interested. But even after he'd confessed he was learning to trust God again, she kept him at bay. Although part of her yearned to be comforted in his arms, she held back. His job, his love of adventure, all the things he had become were foreign and frightening. She wouldn't let herself consider him as more than an old friend on a quick visit.

He stopped again at a red light, looked across at a nearby car, and stiffened. Nicole peered past him but didn't know the driver of the other vehicle.

Ace suddenly switched lanes and made the next right turn.

She laughed at his sudden burst of speed. "Where are we going?"

He shrugged. "It's a surprise." He kept glancing in the rearview mirror. She turned around to see what held his interest.

"What is it?" She saw only traffic—nothing out of the ordinary.

"I thought someone was following too close."

She looked again. Of course they were close. They were in downtown Great Falls.

He turned again, heading back the way they'd come. "Did you forget something?"

He shook his head. "Changed my mind about where we're going. On second thought, where would you like to go? What would you like to do?"

She wanted to go home and get more pieces ready to display, but she owed Ace a few minutes of free time. Suddenly the idea of some quiet appealed. "I'd love to go to Gibson Park and wander around. It always refreshes me."

He made his way to the park and stopped, glanced over his shoulder as he pushed open his door, then took a long look to his right and left. "Ace, who are you looking for?"

"Nobody."

They wandered past the stained-glass display depicting the park, meandered through the brightly colored, scented flower display. She led him toward the duck pond, sat down, closed her eyes, and let the splash of the fountains and the noisy gabble of the geese and gulls ease away the tension that had become her constant companion.

Ace took her hand. She let herself relax against him, her head on his shoulder. He pressed his chin to the top of her head. "This is nice."

"Umm." She didn't know if he meant the pond or sitting so close, quiet and content. For now she didn't care. She let peace fill her.

Suddenly Ace leapt to his feet, grabbed her hand, and strode away so fast she had to trot to keep up. "Ace, what on earth?"

"Come on." He didn't slow down until they were back at the parking lot. He gave a long look over his shoulder then practically ran toward the car.

She jerked her hand from his and stopped. "What is this all about?"

He looked past her and relaxed. "Sorry." He laughed. "I thought I saw someone I didn't want to talk to. He's gone now."

"So much for a peaceful interlude," she murmured.

"Sorry." He reached for her hand. "Do you want to go home?"

Oddly she no longer did, but she nodded and followed him to the vehicle.

Chapter 9

Weary to the marrow of her bones, Nicole locked up the store. It had been a good day. Two busloads of tourists practically cleaned off the shelves. She barely got them restocked before a carload of seniors came. They weren't interested in antiques but bought one of her more pricey paintings.

It had been a productive day. And a profitable one. She'd done a quick tally before she left the store. But she knew without totaling that by the time she paid her bills and Rachel's salary and gave Ace what she owed him from the sale of Aunt Millie's stuff, she'd barely made a dent in what she needed.

When was she going to get her miracle?

She plodded home, too tired to care that it was a beautiful evening. She crossed the street, took the walkway around the side of the house, and paused when she saw Ace playing catch with Carrie.

"You're a great ballplayer." Ace tossed the ball to her.

Nicole groaned. She'd missed Carrie's game tonight.

"Put your body into it more," Ace said. "Follow through." Carrie tossed the ball. Ace caught it. "Good job."

"I've had enough." Carrie ran toward the deck, plopped down next to Gram's old chair where Gram sat with a book open on her lap, watching the other two. Nicole had noticed before that more and more of Gram's books remained on her lap; she felt a stab of guilt. She needed money for Gram's surgery. She needed money for Arman's carvings. In theory, buying the latter would bring the former within easier reach. In reality, neither seemed accessible anymore.

Ace dropped the ball and glove into the storage chest on the patio and sat beside Carrie. "Your flowers are nice," he said to Gram.

"Thank you. I find them cheerful."

Nicole hung back, watching her family, feeling distant from them. She'd been putting in such long hours at the store that she'd barely had time to eat with them for days. But Ace seemed to spend every evening with them. The irony of the situation didn't escape her.

She was about to join them when Carrie turned to Gram. "Gram, did you ever wish you'd lived someplace besides here?"

Gram stroked Carrie's blond hair. "No. This is where I found love."

"You might have found love somewhere else."

Gram chuckled. "Then I would have gone there and been happy."

"But didn't you ever want to travel? Wasn't there something you wanted to see? Like Egypt or Paris or Australia?"

Gram didn't answer right away, and Nicole waited for her reply. "Child, life offers us all sorts of options and challenges. The trick is to know which ones to pursue and then be content with our choices. God promises to guide us. And no matter what we decide, His love is ever present."

Carrie sighed. "I want to see the world."

Nicole remembered she'd once dreamed of seeing Italy. Finding her father's family. Visiting the places Mom talked about, stories she'd repeated from Nicole's father. But Nicole grew up, took on helping Gram raise Carrie, and now she had so many responsibilities she no longer had room for dreams. No, she amended. She now had different dreams.

"Ace, you know what I mean, don't you?" Carrie said. "There's so much out there to see for yourself."

Ace nodded. "There's lots to see all right, but don't think it can take the place of family and home and being part of a community like you have here."

The heat of the earlier part of the day seemed to pool inside Nicole's chest where it crowded her lungs so they couldn't work. This was Ace talking, defending family and home? She wanted to grab his arm, pull him around until she could peer in his face, and demand an explanation. A trickle of caution made her take a deep breath. Just because he defended family didn't give her reason to think he planned to stay. And when he left, could they again be happy being just the three of them? Could she?

Carrie bounced to her feet. "I never thought I'd hear you talking like Gram and Nicole." She spun around. "Oh, hi, Nicole. You're just in time to join in a home-is-everything discussion. Count me out." She swung away in disgust and went indoors.

Ace got to his feet and smiled down at Nicole. "Here's the workaholic."

"Glad you're home." Gram pushed to her feet. "I think I'll go inside, too. I need to put my feet up."

Ace took Nicole's hand and led her toward Gram's chair. When she sat down, he pulled another chair close. "You look tired."

Nicole laid her head back. "I am tired. The shop was busy."

"So you're making money hand over fist?"

She didn't want to talk about work. It discouraged her. She wanted to know his plans. She had to make sure no one in her family got hurt. "Ace, you fit into our family so well. Both Gram and Carrie enjoy your company." She sat up and fixed him with a demanding look. "But what happens when you leave? How will we pick up the pieces?"

Ace took her hands between his and studied her face before he answered. "Like Gram says, there are options."

"Like what?" She wouldn't allow herself to dream up options to her liking.

He tapped the back of her hands with his thumbs and smiled. "Remember what the preacher said a few weeks ago about running from God's love?"

She nodded, though she wasn't sure what Sunday or which sermon he referred to.

"He asked us how far could we run from love. He meant God's love, but I think it also applies to other kinds of love." His hazel eyes serious, he looked at her chin, her mouth, and then into her eyes, holding her gaze with the power of a steel shaft. "I feel God pulling me. I want what He offers. I'm tired of running. I want to be home."

Nicole couldn't think. Home? Love? God? "You're planning to stay here?"

He nodded slowly, thoughtfully. "It sounds like a good idea."

"What about your work?"

"I could travel, use this as a home base, or I could do consulting here." He held up his hand. "Actually I haven't really thought it out, but the idea has been growing slowly."

"I don't know what to say."

He tucked a strand of hair behind her ear, his touch making it even more difficult to think. "Don't you want me to stay?"

"Of course I do. It's just—well, so sudden. So unexpected." Which wasn't entirely true. She'd prayed for a miracle. That he'd—what? Let God back into his life? Stop running, as he said? Then she could—she closed her eyes. She could allow herself to love him?

But loving a man like Ace carried far too many risks to her family. He'd come and go, doing dangerous things. They'd worry. He could get hurt or worse. She wanted Andrew back. But he was no longer Andrew. He'd grown up into Ace, who lived a life that frightened her.

"Nicole, I want to be part of what you have here."

She looked hard into his gaze, his irises like shadowed forest ponds.

"Let me help you with the store. I want to invest in it."

"You already have with Aunt Millie's antiques."

"I want to lend you the money for Arman's woodcarvings."

"I can't let you."

He jerked back and frowned. "It's a sound business deal."

"Nothing is sure."

He studied her intensely, his expression hard, withdrawn, a striking contrast to the softness and gentleness of a few seconds ago. "Exactly. Nothing is for sure. Doing something is a risk. But not doing anything is also a risk."

"No, it's not."

"If you borrow the money, either from me or a bank, you risk having to pay it back even if the business fails. Which it's not going to. But"—he held up his hand to emphasize his point—"if you don't borrow the money and buy Arman's stock, you run a very real risk of someone else's buying it and cornering the market. And then you'll lose out on the money you could have made." He sat back obviously pleased with his argument. "See—risks on both sides. It's always like that. Risks if you act. Risks if you don't. Everything has risks. You just have to decide which ones are worth taking."

"I stand to lose a great deal if someone else buys his stock."

He leaned forward, cupped her face in his hands. "I was hoping I might be a risk you'd consider." He didn't wait for her to argue or reason or accept. Gently he stroked his thumbs along her jawline. "Think about it. And here's something to help you decide." He kissed her so sweetly, so gently, tears welled up at the back of her eyes.

◆

Two days later at supper, Nicole jumped up from the table for no apparent reason, stared at the counter then sat down again. Only to jump up again. Gram had to ask her twice how work had gone.

"Fine. Busy. Okay." She twisted her fork as she talked.

Ace studied the tension on Nicole's face. It was his fault. He shouldn't have said anything about his fledgling plans. Not until the details were worked out. But the idea had been growing with each meal he shared with the Thomas family, every hour he spent with Nicole, every time he stepped inside the church. He was tired of running, tired of being homeless, fed up with denying his belief in God, a belief that survived years of pretending it didn't exist.

But it didn't change who he was and the fact he had nothing to offer Nicole except his love. And she deserved so much more. He could offer her money to buy Arman's woodcarvings but not the security she longed for. Security for Nicole meant an absence of risks. He didn't think such a thing existed.

Carrie, oblivious to the edginess gripping at least two people sharing the evening meal, told a story about the twins trying to catch a butterfly.

Nicole stirred her salad then pushed her fork away and faced Gram. "I've decided to go ahead with the purchase of Arman's carvings." She sucked in a deep breath and rushed on. "It means I have to borrow some money. But I feel it's a wise investment."

Ace's hand stopped halfway to his mouth with a load of salad on his fork, and he stared at her. Had she decided to let him lend her the money? To trust him? Had she decided he was a risk worth taking?

"I talked to Marian at the bank today. She seemed enthusiastic about it."

Nicole gave a tremulous smile.

Ace understood this was a giant step for her and buried his disappointment she hadn't come to him, accepted his offer, trusted him. But the very fact she'd taken a step involving the risk of action, rather than inaction, thrilled him. He could hardly wait to be alone with her and ask what she'd decided about him. He loved her; he wanted to share his life with her. He wanted to be here in Reliance, part of her family, for as long as God gave him. He just didn't know what shape the belonging would take. Or if Nicole would allow him to be part of what she had.

Nicole leaned toward Gram. "I'd like to use the store as collateral, but I wouldn't do it without your approval."

Gram patted Nicole's hand. "It's yours now. I trust you to make the right choices concerning it." She turned to Ace. "My Nicole has quite a head for business."

Nicole groaned. "Gram, it's not as if I run a multimillion-dollar business."

Her eyes, full of purpose and determination, met Ace's. He gave her a thumbs-up sign. Her answering smile sent ripples of pride and pleasure through him. He knew this represented a major step for her. It signified in a concrete way she'd confronted her fear of risks.

But did she see him as an acceptable risk?

◆

She'd done it. She'd flown into the mists, taken a risk. Nicole restrained the bubbling feeling in the pit of her stomach until she and Ace stood in Aunt Millie's house; then she spun around in a circle, laughing. "I'm excited and scared at the same time." She hugged him and chuckled at his amused expression. "I have you to thank for all this."

He quirked an eyebrow. "All this?" He indicated the boxes waiting to be hauled to the Dumpster and the latest batch of things he'd sorted out for her. "It's Aunt Millie you should be thanking, not me."

"Not this stuff, silly." Her insides hummed with the adventure of it. "I, Nicole Thomas, have done something I've always refused to do. I have actually gone to the bank and asked to borrow money." Her smile felt too wide for her face. "I feel as if I've stepped into a brave, new, scary future. And I have you to thank for pushing me out of my safe little world."

"And how did I do that?"

She looked up into the warmth of his hazel eyes. "You're teasing me. You know what you did. You made me see that everything involves a risk. You choose the ones worth taking." She held his gaze, searching for answers in both herself and him. He'd asked if she would consider taking a risk on him. She'd thought of it between business talk all day long. Was she brave enough to take this giant step— trusting her future to a man like Ace? Trouble was, she still couldn't separate Ace from Andrew in her thoughts. She knew Andrew. She'd loved Andrew most of her life. But Ace wasn't Andrew.

"It doesn't change who I am, Nicole."

The question haunted her every thought. "Who are you, Ace?"

He strode to the window and stared out. He returned and took her by the arms, holding her close yet not touching anywhere but the warm spots on her shoulders. He looked deep into her eyes. "Nicole, I am a man who has known little about family. I'm a loner, a risk taker. I am probably the worst person in the world for you."

Their gazes caught and held in a look that went back eighteen years. They'd shared something special then. A connection, a bond surviving years of separation, growing and thriving in the past few weeks. She felt something with this man she'd never known with another human being. Connection? Yes. Belonging, too. But more. So much more. She couldn't even find the words to describe it, except it felt as if he completed her world.

Was he a risk worth taking?

She delved deep inside her heart for the answer and came up with a handful of fluttering butterflies. "I didn't ask who you were, but who you are. Who is Ace?" What did she want him to say? What would it take to convince her to allow her love expression? She waited for his answer, hoping it would erase her fears.

"I'm tired of running from God. I'm tired of pretending I don't want to love and be loved. I want to belong, but trusting this whole belonging business—family, community—I don't know. It's completely foreign to me."

"But isn't that what families are? Belonging, community, forever?"

He tipped his head back and stared away. His jaw hardened. "That's not been my experience."

Her throat hurt so she could hardly talk. She wanted him to believe in family and happily ever after. With her? Until he could really believe, she could not let go of her tightly held protectiveness of her family. With a jolt she realized she was protecting herself as well. From disappointment and hurt. It wasn't that she didn't know who Ace was; the problem was she did. A man who strode into dangerous situations, who commanded respect and probably fear in opponents, a man who would turn her world upside down.

He looked deep into her eyes. His gaze shivered with hazel depths.

Not until she'd somehow put to rest the remnants of fear refusing to leave the pit of her stomach could she know what she truly wanted.

Chapter 10

Nicole filled out papers for the bank loan, worked on marketing plans, and forecast expenses and income. Figuring it out on paper increased her sense of rightness in doing this.

She crowded in a visit from the local carpenter and had more display shelves built along one wall in anticipation of the carvings soon to arrive.

She bounced in and out of the office area, excitement giving her life fresh color.

Every evening Ace joined them for supper, adding an undercurrent of enjoyment to the meal. It seemed Gram and Carrie vied with each other to tell him about their day and get his comments. He always found something to joke about, or he pointed out the silliness of some of their conclusions. But especially he gave a sense of solidness to their gatherings.

Nicole smiled as she watched his kindness with Gram and his patient humor with Carrie even when she spilled a jug of water over his shirtfront. He simply grabbed a towel and sponged the moisture off and said, "Nothing so refreshing as a cool shower on a hot day." When Carrie looked as if she'd burst into tears, he flicked drops of water at her until she relaxed and giggled.

Nicole glanced around the kitchen—as familiar to her as her own skin—but no longer did the walls shut the world out. No more did she want to pull them around her and protect herself and Gram and Carrie. She had taken a step that moved her beyond the safe walls, to boldly embrace challenges and walk out into the world with strong motives. Every day she felt more confidence in her move.

She ran a comb through her hair and dabbed some perfume behind her ears. The sun shone through her bedroom window with exuberant brightness. The sky glistened with midsummer blue. A beautiful Sunday. And Ace would be walking to church with them again.

She didn't want to think any further ahead than that. She refused to acknowledge the thread of worry in the back of her mind. A couple of times Ace had mentioned he would soon be finished cleaning out the house and the word "work" came up. He hadn't said what he intended to do, and she hadn't asked. She wasn't ready to deal with his real life. She knew she wasn't being fair to Ace.

Lord, show me what to do. Help me deal with these fears.

It had become a daily, fervent prayer.

Ace accompanied them to church and gave the sermon his undivided attention.

Nicole wished she could do the same, but her thoughts kept hopping from one thing to another. Ace's growing faith. Her insurmountable caution. His work and lifestyle. Her determination to protect her family from being hurt.

She caught enough of the sermon to know it had been about God's unfailing love and care. The pastor closed his talk by asking them all to stand and read together Psalm 23. Knowing the words, she didn't need to read from the overhead. Ace's deep voice joined her, saying the words with bold confidence. She caught his gaze as they said the psalm together.

" 'The Lord is my shepherd; I shall not want. He maketh me to lie down in green pastures: he leadeth me beside the still waters. He restoreth my soul: he leadeth me in the paths of righteousness for his name's sake. Yea, though I walk through the valley of the shadow of death, I will fear no evil: for thou art with me; thy rod and thy staff they comfort me. Thou preparest a table before me in the presence of mine enemies: thou anointest my head with oil; my cup runneth over. Surely goodness and mercy shall follow me all the days of my life: and I will dwell in the house of the Lord for ever.'"

The words sank deep into her soul, erasing her fears, giving her a holy assurance. God was in control of her past, her present, and her future. She could rest in His blessed unfailing love and care.

She smiled at Ace after the words died away, let herself love him wholly.

Church over and their neighbors greeted and visited with, Nicole, Ace, Gram, and Carrie headed home, laughing and talking. She could hardly wait to be alone with Ace and tell him her decision. She loved him. He was a risk well worth taking.

As they rounded the last corner, a man blocked their path. A man with a wicked looking knife in his hand.

"Conners," he growled. "I've been waiting for you."

Nicole felt a shock race down Ace's arm. He took her hand from where it rested in the crook of his elbow and gently pushed her behind him.

"Hello, LaRue. How are you?"

There was no mistaking the cautious, almost weary note in Ace's voice. The name LaRue sounded familiar, but Nicole couldn't remember where she'd heard it.

LaRue spat on the ground beside him. "How do you think I am? You and your friends keep messing around with me, thinking I can't do anything about it. Well, you've got yourself another think coming."

Hearing the anger in his voice, Nicole peeked around Ace to have a look at this man.

His dark blond hair hung past his ears and pushed out at wild angles from the ring of his ball cap. He looked as if he hadn't shaved in days. But it was his eyes that frightened Nicole. Wide. Wild. Darting from Ace to the women standing behind him.

"There's more than one way to deal with oil men." LaRue's gaze met Nicole's. Something evil flickered through his eyes. She caught her breath between her gritted teeth and ducked back behind Ace. LaRue! The man the telephone call had warned Ace about. An ecoterrorist, Ace had said.

Ace crossed his arms over his chest.

"LaRue, why haven't you contacted my office? We've agreed to do the tests you wanted and pay for any damages you feel you've incurred."

The man grunted. "You think you can put me off, but it didn't take me long to track you down. I saw you in Great Falls with your pretty lady."

Nicole's eyes widened. That's what had made Ace so nervous, always checking over his shoulder, rushing her out of the park.

LaRue gave a bitter laugh. "Nice bunch of women you got there. I wonder what you'd do if old LaRue happened to run into one of them some night and sort of took a little drive with them." He chortled mirthlessly. "Maybe I'd arrange to have a little knife in my pocket. Just think what I could do to that old lady."

Nicole didn't have to look at Gram or Carrie to feel their shock. Her blood pooled in the soles of her feet as cold sweaty anger flooded through her veins. She squeezed her hands into hard fists. How dare that despicable man threaten Gram?

"I'll bet ya that pretty young one would squeal like a stuck pig if old LaRue so much as threatened to have a little fun with his knife. Sort of payback time, if you know what I mean. For all the hassles you guys put me through." The man gave a wicked snort of laughter. "And what about that dark-headed beauty hiding behind yer back? Bet you'd do anything to protect her. Hey? What about it, Conners?"

Nicole felt, as much as heard, Ace's angry grunt. Without moving he said, "Nicole, take your grandmother and sister home. Go through the yard behind me."

Nicole hesitated. Did she dare leave him to face this man alone?

"Do it now," Ace ordered.

She spun around and grabbed Gram with one hand, Carrie with the other. "Come on—let's get out of here."

Carrie hung back. "What about Ace?"

"I can look after myself," Ace said.

Nicole rushed them through the nearest yard and around the house, not caring if anyone saw them and wondered what they were doing. She raced out the gate and down the alley toward home. By the time she pushed the back door open, Gram struggled for breath. Nicole helped her to a chair.

"Carrie, call the police then make Gram some tea."

Nicole headed for the door.

"Where are you going?" Carrie asked.

"To see if Ace is okay. You look after Gram." She retraced her steps, halting behind the hedge, hoping LaRue hadn't noticed her return.

Through the twisted branches she could see Ace standing with legs slightly spread, his arms still crossed and a look of indifference on his face. Nicole was certain it was only a pose. She couldn't imagine he felt as cool and detached as he looked.

Careful not to make any noise, she watched and listened.

"LaRue, I wish you'd called the office as we agreed. I'm sure you'd be pleased with the concessions we've offered."

LaRue grunted. "You'd like to think so, I'm sure, but the only thing that would make me happy is for you people to get off my land. And be forced to stop all the underhanded things you do."

"We've done everything we could to ensure no harm has occurred to you or your property."

LaRue spat again. "Talk is cheap. But I know about all sorts of things no one reports. No one accepts responsibilities for. This stuff has to stop. One of these days you guys will push me too much and then—" He flicked his knife in the air and made an explosive sound.

The sound reverberated up Nicole's spine. She dropped back on her heels, her limbs quivering. How long did it take for the police to answer an emergency call? Ace could be dead before they got there.

Ace's voice, calm and detached, reached her. "I don't think you want this to go any further. Why don't you meet me in Great Falls tomorrow afternoon, and we'll work out something?"

Nicole's breath shuddered over her tense nerves. She jerked her head up at the sound of sirens and leaned forward to peer again through the leaves as a cruiser skidded to a halt and a young police officer threw the door open and stood behind it, his gun leveled at LaRue. "Drop it."

LaRue dropped the knife and shot his arms over his head. The policeman edged forward, kicked the knife out of the way, slapped on handcuffs, and then ran his hands up and down LaRue's body searching for hidden weapons before escorting the man to the back of the car.

"I'll be back!" LaRue hollered. "Perhaps I'll pay a visit to those sweet little gals you've been hanging around with."

Ace strode after him and leaned over to growl through the window. "You leave them out of this. Or you'll regret the day you were born."

LaRue snorted. "Finally found something you care about, eh, Conners? Maybe now you'll understand how I feel when I see my animals dying. My babies getting sick."

"Leave them alone," Ace warned him again.

LaRue stared at Ace another moment then turned away.

Weakness shivered up Nicole's limbs, and she sank to the ground.

LaRue had threatened Gram and Carrie because of her involvement with Ace. She loved Ace.

But her love for him had brought danger to her family. She couldn't be responsible for putting them at risk.

◆

Ace opened the door and looked around the kitchen.

Gram gave a shaky smile. "Glad to see you're still in one piece," she said. "I hope you sent that man packing."

"The police have taken him away."

Carrie sprang to her feet. "What a horrid person." She shuddered. "What did he want anyway?" She looked past him. "Where's Nicole?"

"Isn't she here?" The hair on the back of his neck tingled when Carrie shook her head.

"She went to see if you were okay."

Carefully masking his expression, he said, "I'll go get her." He waited until the door shut him from their view before he broke into a run, sweat beading his brow. Had LaRue escaped and found her?

He skidded to a stop on the sidewalk and looked around. Nothing. No vehicle, save those normally parked along the street. Not a sound that didn't belong.

He took a slow deep breath. *Think, man. Where is she? Don't let LaRue's threats get to you. He's in jail right now. He can't do anything. Besides, he just wants a few thousand bucks to add to his bank account. He'd never harm anyone. He doesn't have the guts to face the consequences.*

He continued silently trying to convince himself as he strode down the sidewalk. But his mind conjured up images of LaRue's knife with a drop of blood on the tip. Nicole's blood.

"Nicole," he called. Nothing he'd faced to this moment prepared him for the panic shafting through his heart. If she had been hurt—

A soft moan to his left. He spun toward the sound.

"Where are you?" He crashed into the yard, saw her, and raced to her side.

Tears streaked her face. Her eyes had a tortured look.

"Are you okay? What's the matter?" He knelt at her side and reached for her, but she pushed his arms away.

"That man threatened my family."

"I know. He's in custody right now. He'll never hurt you." He sat back on his heels waiting for her to calm.

Her expression grew fierce. "Can you guarantee that?"

"Of course I can't guarantee it."

"Exactly." She pushed to her feet, shoving aside the hand he extended to help her.

His insides felt like cold glass as their eyes met and he felt her shattering anger.

"I'm not willing to gamble my family against a crazy man."

He held his ground in front of her. "What are you saying?"

A shudder raced across her shoulders. "I will not put Gram and Carrie at risk. For anything."

He crossed his arms over his chest as he continued to block her escape. She'd been understandably frightened by the encounter with LaRue, but there'd never been any real danger. He had to convince her of it. "I'll talk to LaRue. I'm certain he'll be adequately mollified by the concessions we're prepared to offer him."

She lifted her chin and met his look squarely. "How nice for him."

Her response confused him. What did she want? "I don't believe he ever constituted a risk to any of us." Then why was he so afraid when he didn't know where Nicole was?

"As you yourself said, you can't guarantee it."

Anger and frustration drowned out caution and calm. "Life doesn't come with a fail-proof guarantee. Bad things happen all the time. A tree could fall on you. A fire burn down your house." At her look of fear he wished he had found another example. "But it's not likely. You can't walk around trying to anticipate and avoid any eventuality."

Her eyes blazing, she tilted her chin higher. "I know I can't predict the future. I know I'll have to deal with difficult situations. I've done so in the past. But"—she blinked hard—"I will not knowingly take risks that threaten my family's security."

He should have seen it coming. He should have known better than to open up his heart. Fool that he was. Fool.

"And I'm too great a risk? Is that what you mean?"

For a moment she hesitated then nodded. "You have enemies. You do dangerous work. It's too great a gamble."

"*I'm* too great a gamble, you mean." He'd known it all his life, so why did it sting like acid? He silenced the crying of his heart and bolted back the feelings he'd allowed to surface after a lifetime of holding them at bay.

She faced him squarely, uncertainty flickering across her face. He hesitated, willing her to change her mind. Then her expression hardened, and he knew her decision before she uttered the words that stopped the blood flowing to his heart.

"I'm sorry. I can't make any other choice."

He lifted his hand, wanting to touch her one more time; but she drew back, and he dropped his arm to his side. It was over. Big surprise. He allowed himself one more lingering look at her sad face and dark eyes then quelled any regrets.

"Good-bye then. Nice knowing you and all that stuff." He had his job. He'd keep busy. Life would go on. He spun on his heels and marched away, rigid self-control stiffening his spine.

He slammed into the house and poured himself a cup of cold coffee.

◆

Nicole couldn't remember returning home. Her world had turned black and empty.

"Where's Ace?" Carrie demanded, as Nicole closed the door behind her.

"Where have you been?" Gram asked then, after a look at Nicole's face, added, "What's happened? You look terrible."

"Where's Ace?" Carrie asked again. "I'm starving."

"We'll go ahead without him," Nicole said, her voice quivering noticeably.

"I can wait. I'm not that hungry," Carrie said.

Nicole dropped to a chair. "He's not coming."

"Not coming?" Carrie looked as if Nicole had said the sun wouldn't rise tomorrow. "Why not?" She gasped. "Oh no. He's been hurt, hasn't he? Where is he?" She had her hand on the doorknob before Nicole's words stopped her.

"He's not hurt. He's fine. Probably having lunch right now over at Aunt Millie's house."

Gram leaned forward. "Child, what's happened?"

The kindness of Gram's voice almost undid Nicole's rigid control of her emotions. She took a shuddering breath before she could speak. "Ace won't be coming over anymore."

Carrie bristled. "Why not?"

"I don't want to see him anymore." *Please, please don't make me say more. My insides are bleeding out through my pores. I don't know if I can remain sane long enough to deal with this.*

Give it up, Nicole, she scolded herself. *You've made the right choice. Family first. These are the two most important people in the world. This is what matters.*

"Are you crazy?" Carrie demanded. "After he saves us from that man. After all he's done, you don't want to see him?" She glared at Nicole. "You are crazy."

Nicole couldn't look at her sister. She couldn't answer her accusations.

"Well, I don't care. I want to see him again, and I will." She flounced from the room.

Nicole continued to stare at the tabletop, aware of a waiting silence. Finally she faced Gram.

"What really happened?" Gram asked.

"Things would never work out for us."

"You aren't overreacting to that little scene out there, are you? I think Ace handled himself and that man very well."

Nicole hid the guilt she felt as she shook her head. "I'm just facing reality."

"As long as you're being fair to Ace." Gram studied her carefully. "And yourself."

"I'm doing what I know is right." Her own aching desires didn't count when she knew they put Gram and Carrie in danger.

Carrie refused to join them for dinner. Nicole had little appetite and mostly rearranged the food on her plate.

She was thankful Gram ate a little and refrained from saying more about the situation.

◆

Sweat soaked Ace's shirt. He yanked it over his head and snatched a clean one off the bed.

Racing up and down two flights of stairs and out to the Dumpster all day left him tired. Dust settled on his skin. Cobwebs tangled in his hair. Amazing how much stuff Aunt Millie had packed under the eaves. But he'd managed to clean it out.

He wiped at his face and arms with his drenched shirt. Too bad his frantic efforts hadn't succeeded in keeping his thoughts at bay.

Three days since Nicole had informed him he didn't fit into her tidy little life. Three torturous days of trying to convince himself it was over and he didn't care.

He slipped his hand under his shirt and rubbed the scar on his right side. A souvenir of the one time he hadn't talked his way out of a confrontation without incurring a little damage. He pressed his fingers into the soft flesh and wondered what Nicole would think if she saw the spider-shaped scar.

He knew her reaction.

Too risky. Too risky.

The words chanted through his brain with the sound of a hundred school-boys taunting him. All his own voice.

He curled his hand into a fist and ground it into his side.

Seems all his life he had ached for love and belonging. A family like the one Nicole cherished.

But who could blame her for not wanting a man like him?

The house was stifling. He spun on his heels and hurried outside.

The evening air was blessedly cool and fragrant from Gram's flowers next door. He settled on the wooden steps, leaning his elbows on his knees. Quiet fell around him.

He jerked his head up. "Nicole?" He couldn't see her. Or hear her. But he sensed her presence.

Only the fluttering of a bird in the branches answered his call, but he knew she was close by.

"Can we talk?" he asked softly.

For a moment he thought she would refuse; then he heard the soft padding of her footsteps coming in the back gate. He rose slowly. She stopped a few feet from him. It was too dark for him to read her expression, so he led her inside.

At the sight of her beautiful eyes he forgot he'd decided he didn't care. With aching arms he reached for her.

She shook her head and moved away.

He dropped his hands to his side. His words slow, he said, "You're the one who made me believe I could be loved. Until you did, I was happy enough making my way through life without love."

Seeing the flicker of regret in her eyes, he allowed himself to think she could change her mind.

"I love you, Ace. But—"

He didn't let her finish. Steely fingers dug at his heart, snatching away hope. "But? I've heard it all my life. We love you, but. You're too old. You're too difficult. You're too big." As if he could help that he'd grown early but awkwardly. All hands and feet that tangled themselves together making him clumsy. "I thought you were different. I thought you'd be the sort of person who could love regardless. Regardless of flaws and imperfections." He clamped his teeth together. He would not say more. He would not turn this into a pity party.

"Ace, I do love you." Her eyes were wide and dark, begging for him to understand.

All his life he'd ached to hear those words. But especially these last few weeks. And even more so since he'd opened up his heart to loving her.

He didn't understand her resistance, and he would not let her off so easily. "Yeah, right. If there's one thing I've learned, it's that words are easy." If she wanted absolution she'd have to find it at church.

"I can't think only of myself," she insisted. "I have to consider what's best for my family."

"You're not thinking about what's best for anyone. Not Gram, not Carrie, and especially not yourself. Your father acted foolishly when you were a child, and you've never gotten over it. You think you can insulate yourself from anything that threatens the narrow little walls you've built around yourself." He saw the shock in her face, but he couldn't stop. The words poured out as if they had a life of their own. "Sooner or later your walls will come tumbling down."

Her hand pressed to her mouth, she turned to the door.

"And I'm not your father. I would never carelessly do something to hurt you. Or your family."

The door shut behind her.

"I am not your father," he muttered then whispered softly, "I love you." But in the silence, something inside him died.

He poured a cup of coffee, not even flinching when the hot liquid overflowed on his thumb.

He would not allow regrets. He would not waste time wishing for what might have been.

Nicole was right. Family should count above everything else. For one brief, delicious, stupid moment he'd allowed himself to think he could belong to that elusive, elite group—those people who joined arms in unity. Family. Love. Belonging.

He slammed his cup down.

It was time to get on with his life.

He reached for the phone and made several calls.

Chapter 11

Gal, you've been sitting there doodling for an hour." Rachel's voice startled Nicole from her thoughts. "Why don't you just go find that man and say you're sorry?"

"I was thinking about the store," Nicole said. She wasn't thinking about Ace. She'd put him out of her mind.

"Yeah." Rachel snorted. "And I'm the cat's whiskers." She tapped her fingertip on the paper before Nicole. The word "Ace" had mysteriously been scribbled all over it. Nicole snatched the paper away and crumpled it into the garbage.

"It's not what you think."

Rachel perched on the corner of the desk. "And what do I think?"

Nicole shot her friend a look dripping with disdain. "I know you. You think a person should plunge into life without thinking about the consequences."

"Nope. Wrong. But I do think a person can be just a wee bit too concerned with 'what if.'"

Nicole rose to her feet. "What if I tell you to butt out?"

Rachel shrugged and followed Nicole up the stairs to stand in front of a display. "Oh, I'd listen real good. Like I always do."

Nicole grunted. Rachel had never in her whole life listened to a thing Nicole said if it disagreed with her own direction of thinking. "Guess I'd be expecting a bit much, wouldn't I?"

The day finally ended, and Nicole plodded home determinedly keeping her gaze on the cement cracks in the sidewalk as she passed Aunt Millie's house. It should be getting easier to slip by without listening for sounds of Ace inside. Without holding her breath so she wouldn't catch the scent of his maleness. Pretending she didn't strain to hear if he sang his favorite Elvis songs or played the radio. Telling herself repeatedly she would get over him.

Out of the corner of her eye a fresh post caught her attention, and she gaped at a For Sale sign. She stared at the words as if hoping they'd disappear. Then she spun about and looked at the blank windows. The house stood forlorn and empty. She knew he was gone.

She gasped for breath, wrapped her arms across her chest, and moaned. It was over. She sucked in trembling breaths and waited for the sickness in her stomach to end. Her knees wobbly as cooked spaghetti, she shivered toward home.

It was over. Really over. Time to get on with her life. Now she could settle back to normal without the constant temptation of knowing he was close.

"He's gone." Carrie didn't wait for Nicole to close the door before facing her with accusations. "It's all your fault. You chased him away." She turned her back but not before Nicole caught the glint of tears in her eyes.

"I'm sorry, Carrie, but I can hardly go out with a guy just because you like him, now can I?" She squeezed the younger girl's shoulders hoping to make her laugh, but Carrie shrugged away.

"Don't pretend you didn't like him, too." She glared at her sister. "You're just scared."

Nicole laughed. "Scared? Of what?"

Carrie's eyes narrowed. "You don't want to grow up. In fact, sometimes I think I'm more grown up than you are. I'm ready to accept change, but you want to keep everything nice and safe and predictable."

Nicole stared at her, startled Carrie could so easily misinterpret Nicole's motives.

"That's why you dumped Ace." Carrie nodded. "He wouldn't be part of your nice little world." She looked satisfied with her assessment. "Maybe you should grow up."

The phone rang. Carrie glared at Nicole a second longer then hurried to pick it up.

Nicole took a deep, settling breath before she faced Gram who'd silently watched the whole scene.

Nicole laughed gently. "She'll discover far too soon that life isn't as simple as she'd like it to be."

Gram's expression didn't change. "I expect she's already discovered that. Life hasn't been easy for her either."

Nicole turned away, feeling she'd been attacked by both Gram and Carrie when she'd expected support and approval.

But what did it matter as long as she did what was best for them all?

◆

Several days later Marian called from the bank to let Nicole know the papers were ready to sign for her loan.

After she hung up the phone, Nicole sat staring at the top of her desk.

Rachel hurried past to collect some brochures to hand out to the departing busload of seniors. She paused. "Bad news?"

Nicole sighed. "No. The loan papers are ready."

"Well, then, I guess it's good news. You can get those lovely carvings in before the tourist season peters out."

"I can hardly wait."

She knew from the puzzled look Rachel gave her as she hastened back to the counter that her voice lacked enthusiasm. Enthusiasm seemed a thing of the past.

Truth was, Ace had persuaded her to seek a bank loan for the merchandise. Something she'd vowed she'd never do. Now that the loan had been approved, did she want to go ahead with borrowing the money?

Nicole rested her forehead in her palms. She'd told herself over and over she'd get used to the emptiness Ace's departure left. Again and again she recited it was for the best.

But life had lost its flavor, and she didn't know how to get it back.

Reaching into her pocket, she fingered the key Gram had given to her with instructions from Ace to clean out the antiques he'd left. She hadn't done it yet. Suddenly she made up her mind.

"Rach," she called as she hurried out, "I'll be back later."

At Aunt Millie's house she was almost overwhelmed with the smell of stale coffee and dust. And although she tried to pretend it wasn't so, the scent of Ace's aftershave lingered in every corner, triggering memories she wanted forgotten. . . had to forget if she was to get on with her life.

She hurried to the dining room to attend to business. But as she examined the antiques, memories flooded her mind. Ace leaning against the doorway watching her. The expression on his face when he found the little ceramic dog. The dawning of hope when they discovered the letters and cards from Aunt Millie. The night they'd kissed for the first time.

Tears stinging her eyes, she gathered up an armload of stuff and hurried out to the car to set the lovely lamps, the fine bone china teapot, and the pair of figurine bookends on the backseat of the car.

She leaned her head against the top of the car and forced back the pain shafting through her limbs.

She missed Ace.

She'd been missing him all her life.

Straightening, she forced a deep breath into her aching lungs.

Somehow she'd managed to survive quite comfortably all these years. She just had to focus on the right things. Like taking care of Gram and Carrie. Running her store efficiently. Finding the right things to stock her shelves with.

Right now she had these beautiful antiques of Aunt Millie's to clean and display. Life would go on. In a few days she could have Arman's woodcarvings if she went ahead with the loan.

She would learn to put these few weeks with Ace in proper perspective. A childhood dream with no place in her adult reality.

Gathering calmness about her like a cloak, she marched back to the house to collect more things. But the memories of Ace were too overpowering. She clutched a cubical paperweight in one hand and a brass candelabra in the other and hurried out, locking the door behind her.

At the store she carried the items into the back room and set them on her worktable then stepped away to admire them. She pulled a wide ledger toward her and began to catalogue each item, noting what she considered a fair purchasing price then what she hoped to be the selling price.

That done, she got cloths and polish from a shelf and set to work cleaning the brass.

Rachel entered the room. She picked up each item and exclaimed over it then sat on a stool and watched Nicole work.

Nicole concentrated on her job. She had almost forgotten the other woman's presence until Rachel said, "You can't scrub out memories, you know."

"Just bringing out the best in this lovely old brass." She held it up to the light. "It takes a lot of work to get the tarnish from around these little grape leaves." She found a toothbrush and bent over to work on the design.

"Oh, come on, Nicole. You're so focused you're driving me nuts. Talk to me, gal. What's going on?"

Nicole shot her a startled look. "I'm cleaning brass. What's the problem?"

"You might fool some of the people all of the time and all of the people some of the time, but you can't fool me. I can practically read your mind."

Knowing it was true, Nicole didn't take her eyes off the candlestick holder. If Rachel so much as glimpsed her face she'd know Nicole's thoughts had slid back to Aunt Millie's house and the man who'd resided there so recently.

"Okay. Don't look at me. It doesn't matter. So you've told this man to get out of your life. Now what are you going to do?"

"What else could I do?" She scrubbed at a corner so vigorously she sprayed cleaning compound all over the tabletop. "You know what happened. That man threatened Gram and Carrie."

"Wasn't there. Can't argue with that. But, hey. We hear about random acts of violence every day."

"Not in Reliance." She wiped the spots off the table and continued more slowly.

"Maybe not. But it seems to me you're punishing Ace for something that wasn't his fault."

"It's not that simple."

Rachel leaned her back against the shelves and planted her feet on the table.

"Huh. Life never is. It throws you curve balls all the time. But sometimes it's better to catch one of those curve balls than to keep ducking."

Nicole shuddered. "Sounds dangerous. Guess that's why I never got into playing baseball."

"It isn't just playing ball you've avoided for fear of getting hurt." Rachel dropped her feet to the floor and planted her hands on her thighs as she leaned close to Nicole. "You avoid everything that hints of risk."

Nicole kept her attention on the candelabra even though she'd practically polished it to death.

"And this is bad because?"

Rachel leaned back again. "Because, dear girl, you won't let yourself see the possibilities—the adventure. The thrill of a fuller life."

"You sound like a pop psychology major. What would you have me do? Live life in the fast lane?"

"Nothing as rash as that. But what would be wrong with grabbing and enjoying all the goodness and beauty that come your way?" She paused then added, "Even if the whole idea frightens you."

"You're saying I'm scared?" Nicole glared at Rachel.

"Aren't you?"

Her friend's soft words annoyed her even more than her insinuations. "Not at all. Besides, what's there to be scared of?"

Rachel narrowed her eyes and gave Nicole a stern look. "Maybe of trusting someone. Letting yourself care enough about them even when their choices could hurt you." She held up her hand stopping the words Nicole had been about to release. "And I'm not talking about Gram and Carrie." She paused and gave Nicole another hard look. "It's time you came to grips with your feelings about your father."

Nicole's head jerked up. "What are you talking about?" What was it with everyone thinking this had to do with her father?

"Think about it. You should be able to connect the dots."

The bell over the door sounded, signaling a customer.

Rachel headed for the door. "I'll get it." She paused. "Nicole, sometimes it seems you're so afraid of being hurt you're going to miss out on the best life has to offer. Just think about it. Okay?"

Nicole scrubbed at the brass. She didn't want to think about it. But Rachel's words upset her carefully constructed arguments. She set aside the candelabra and stared at her blackened fingers.

She always considered family when making decisions. Doing what was best for them was her first concern.

Wasn't it?

This wasn't about her father.

It was about family.

Her only concern had been to save Gram and Carrie from the disappointment and pain she'd felt when her father abandoned her to pursue other interests.

Okay, so strictly speaking, that wasn't what happened. He hadn't abandoned her. He died. Doing something he didn't have to, taking an unnecessary risk. It felt like abandonment.

And I never want to feel that way again.

Her thoughts twirled in knots. Jumping to her feet, she scrubbed her hands clean then called to Rachel, "Close up if I'm not back in time."

She drove around town growing more and more confused. Finally, in desperation, she headed home. Maybe she would find the peace she ached for in the shelter of its four walls.

Gram looked up from her TV program and checked the time on the clock over the door as Nicole entered. "You're early today."

Nicole nodded. "Can I make you some tea?"

"That would be nice."

Gram made small talk as Nicole filled the kettle and waited for it to boil.

"What really brings you home in the middle of the afternoon?" Gram asked when Nicole settled beside her with a cup of tea for each of them.

Nicole smiled. "Can't fool you, can I?"

Gram patted Nicole's hand. "Growing old has some advantages, and one of them is that I've learned to see when someone I love is troubled. It's Ace, isn't it?"

"I'm so confused."

Gram waited patiently as Nicole sorted through her thoughts, trying to verbalize her turmoil.

"Rach thinks I'm afraid to let myself love someone because I feel my father abandoned me."

Gram nodded, her expression thoughtful. "Rachel has known you a long time."

Nicole nodded. "Almost forever." But did that give her the right to evaluate Nicole's thoughts?

Gram continued. "No doubt you've shared lots of secrets."

"Like maybe she can see things about me I can't see for myself?"

"What do you think?"

Nicole shook her head. "I don't know what to think. I vowed I would never do anything to hurt you or Carrie."

"Child, you have been such a comfort to me, but don't you realize if you throw away your own happiness on my account it would hurt me very deeply? Carrie wouldn't want it either."

"I know." Gram's words didn't ease the tension eating at Nicole's nerves.

"You know Ace isn't a risk to our happiness, don't you, child?"

She nodded even though she wasn't sure she agreed.

Gram squeezed Nicole's hand. "This isn't about us. It's about you. What do you want? What do you need? Allow yourself to be happy."

Nicole hugged Gram. "Thanks." She glanced at the clock. "You sit and watch TV while I make supper for a change."

She made everyone's favorites. Fried chicken for Carrie, mashed potatoes and gravy for Gram. And apple crisp for dessert—a favorite for all of them.

Carrie gave her a suspicious look, but she must have seen something in Nicole's expression that kept her from reiterating the words she'd spoken every meal since Ace had left. Words of accusation about driving Ace away.

Nicole barely spoke throughout the meal, trying to sort out her feelings. And later, as she lay in bed, she tried to make sense of the confusion in her heart and mind.

Did her happiness matter? Wasn't that selfish? Or was she using Gram and Carrie as protection against getting hurt?

Pain stabbed through her. A reminder of the pain she'd felt when her father died. She'd loved him so much. She used to wait at the door for his return. He'd scoop her into a bear hug then toss her in the air.

"I love you, baby," he'd say as he rumpled her hair.

She still ached for his hugs and words of love.

Why did it hurt so much more to lose him than Mom and Dad?

Because they couldn't help it. Mom and Dad had been hit by a careless driver. It wasn't their fault.

Her father had a choice. He didn't have to go skydiving.

She shook her head in the dark.

It wasn't as if he'd done it on purpose.

All sorts of people did daredevil things. He'd done it lots of times.

In fact—she sat bolt upright in bed, remembering something she'd blocked from her mind for years. He was an instructor at the skydiving school. Her mother had told her he'd died trying to save a student who panicked.

She fell back against the pillows.

How had she forgotten that?

Turning her face into the pillow, she muffled her groan. She'd blocked it from her mind because it was easier to blame him than to accept the finality of her loss.

For the first time ever, without anger or resentment, she allowed herself to weep for the loss of her beloved parent, the one she looked like, the one she'd been named for, the one she missed with an ache that would never leave.

Her pillow was soaked with healing tears when she made up her mind what she had to do. Spent from her emotional cleansing, she fell asleep.

◆

Ace stared at the flickering screen of his laptop perched on the top of the wide mahogany desk in the spacious office.

Martha, who'd been buzzing in and out of his office all morning, hovered in the doorway. "Sorry to interrupt, sir, but I have Mervin calling from Kuwait. Do you want to talk to him?"

Ace shook his head. "I still haven't decided. Tell him I'll call him as soon as I know." Kuwait. The Yukon. Offshore. Everyone seemed to want him at once.

He sank back into the leather chair. It was good to be back to work. It was where he belonged. Where he fit. That little interlude at Reliance served one worthwhile purpose—to reinforce the fact he would never love or be loved.

Through his mind flashed the memory of a shoebox with his name on it, filled with cards and letters from Aunt Millie.

It hurt to know she'd wanted him but had been denied access.

He couldn't think of Aunt Millie without picturing a dark-haired, sweet-faced little elf. But for all her talk, Nicole's belief in love and family did not extend to anyone but Carrie and Gram.

She didn't even have Aunt Millie's excuse. No one had denied her the freedom to love Ace.

He sighed. This was for the best. For his own good. Some things were just not meant to be. Not for him. Love and family were not in the works for Ace Conners.

He opened the top drawer of his desk where he'd stashed that stupid little dog he'd given Aunt Millie one dream-filled Christmas when he'd still believed love and family were possible for him.

Why had he brought it with him?

Because he couldn't bear to throw it out. He planned to pack it in his luggage to accompany him on his travels. He'd never packed one ounce more than necessary in all his years of moving and traveling, so why this pathetic ornament?

He fingered the chipped ears of the misshapen dog.

Most of his life he'd carried around the conviction no one cared. He'd blamed Aunt Millie for deserting him. A convenient excuse for the hardening of his heart.

He'd shut out God, blaming Him for not answering his prayers.

A startling, unforgiving truth faced him.

He could no longer blame someone else for the way his life had turned out.

He could no longer pretend he didn't bear some responsibility. Why hadn't he bothered to look up Aunt Millie? He could have returned to Reliance any-time in the years since he reached adulthood. He could have gone to see her.

But he hadn't.

Because, he admitted, he preferred to run away. Blaming others for what he lacked in his life had become a convenient habit.

Pushing the laptop away, he set the little dog in front of him and stared at it.

So now it came down to another choice, similar in so many ways.

He could either continue to run, or he could commit himself to the cause of finding love. Finding out if it was real and enduring. Running seemed the safest thing to do. The most familiar. Change was difficult and scary.

He stared at the dog for a long time, slowly accepting things he knew to be true.

God's love was real. He could run from it, but he couldn't deny it.

His love for Nicole was real. He could ignore that, too. Or he could be there for her, stand by until she was ready to trust his love.

He reached for the intercom. "Martha, call Mervin. I've made up my mind."

◆

Nicole hurried from the bank. She paused outside her shop and looked up at the sign.

"Grandpa's Attic has taken a big step," she whispered.

Inside, she waved the papers at Rachel. "I did it. I signed the papers for the loan."

Rachel gave her a puzzled look. "I thought it was a done deal."

"I could have changed my mind right up until this morning when I signed the papers."

Rachel shook her head. "Why would you change your mind?"

"Because it's a risk. What if I can't pay it back? What if they foreclose on the store or something?" She laughed. "Forget it." It no longer mattered. She was finished with living in a cocoon of safety. "By the way, can you look after the store by yourself a couple of days?"

Rachel's expression grew more puzzled. "I can call in one of the high school girls if I need help. Why? What are you up to?"

"I'm off to Great Falls."

"Why?"

"To find Ace."

"Why?"

"To tell him I love him. Beg him to believe me and give me another chance."

Rachel hugged her, and they laughed together.

"Good for you," Rachel said.

Nicole got to the city midafternoon. "Please still be here," she whispered. It took her several minutes to locate a parking spot. Her insides quivered with anticipation. And dread. What if he'd packed up the temporary office and moved elsewhere? What if he wouldn't talk to her? After all the disappointments and failures of love in his life she could hardly blame him if he didn't trust her now. *Lord, please let him hear me out. Forgive me for not trusting You sooner. Because You are the One who holds the future.*

Her footsteps quickened as she entered the building and headed for the stairs. She panted by the time she reached the second floor. The butterflies below her heart multiplied and fluttered rapidly. She forced herself to take slow, deep breaths.

A woman with dark-rimmed glasses, in the process of pulling a door closed behind her, glanced at Nicole. "May I help you?"

"May I speak to Ace Conners, please?"

"I'm sorry—he's not here."

Her insides froze. The butterflies died. "Can I make an appointment to see him in the morning?"

"He's closed this office. He won't be returning."

Nicole hoped her legs wouldn't let her down. "Where has he gone?"

"I'm sorry. I'm not at liberty to say."

Nicole didn't know how she managed to stumble away without collapsing. Down on the street she leaned against the wall, moaning, her shock too deep for words or tears.

It was too late. Her foolish fears had cost her the one thing she'd wanted all her life. Love. Overwhelming love.

Somehow she made her way back to her car and sat for a long while without turning the key.

It was dark by the time she pulled herself together enough to make her way out of the city.

She was thankful Gram and Carrie were in bed when she dragged herself into the house, too weary to think. Her mind numb, she fell onto her bed without removing her clothes.

She woke late the next morning with a raging headache and covered her head with the pillow.

Then it hit her. She had one more chance. The house. He must have left instructions for the real estate agent to contact him.

She jumped from bed, caught a glimpse of herself in the mirror, and shuddered. Yuk! It was enough to make her sick. She stripped off her wrinkled clothes and showered until her skin tingled. Hurrying now, anxious to get on with locating Ace, she pulled on a pair of faded jeans and a bright yellow T-shirt, pausing only long enough to smooth her hair with a brush before she raced outside and around the house to the front. She'd been afraid Gram would demand to know what she was up to, but she saw no sign of her; then Nicole remembered it was

Gram's day to have tea with a bunch of her cronies.

She skidded to a halt in front of Aunt Millie's house and stared.

The FOR SALE sign was gone.

She stared at the empty spot. It must have fallen. She searched under the trees and through the tall grass. Nothing. No missing sign.

She made her way to the backyard before she collapsed in a sobbing heap on Gram's rocking chair. Why, oh, why had she been so slow to recognize what mattered in her life? Holding on to her tight-fisted security seemed vastly shortsighted now. And so empty without the one thing that mattered. Ace. She groaned his name and wrapped her arms across her stomach as if she could somehow stop the pain. But the pain ate at her until it consumed her. How would she ever survive? *Ace. Oh, Ace. How could I be so blind? I'd give anything to have another chance.*

"Nicole?"

His voice came from her agonized longings. She closed her eyes and rolled forward over her stomach to block the sound.

"Nicole, look at me."

She felt a touch. Oh, that it were real and not her tortured wishes. Pressure on her shoulder turned her. A finger tipped up her chin.

"Look at me."

She opened her eyes, squinting against the brightness of the azure blue sky.

"Ace?" She bounded from the chair, practically knocking him off his feet.

He staggered back, grinning. "Hi."

"Hi." She leaned forward trying to bring him into focus. He seemed real enough. She sniffed. It was the same trade-mark mixture of scents. "Where did you come from?"

He laughed. "I decided to come back."

"The FOR SALE sign?"

"I took it down. Thought I'd fix up the old house." He sobered. "Nicole, I've spent a lifetime throwing love away when all the time it was the cry of my heart. Suddenly I saw I had to grab it if I was ever to have it. I've decided to stop running. And I'm hoping I can persuade you it's safe to love me."

"You're going to find your job pretty easy."

His eyes lit with an inner glow. "What do you mean?"

"I've done some serious thinking, too. I've been hiding. Afraid to let myself love anyone as I did my father. Afraid I might be hurt again. But no more. I wouldn't want to miss the best of life because of childish fears."

He opened his arms, and she flung herself into them. It was like coming home.

The need for words was silenced by his kiss.

He tucked her into the warmth of his shoulder and turned her toward Aunt Millie's house.

"I've been busy this morning." He lifted her chin with a firm fingertip and pointed to the roof.

There, with its red nose blinking off and on, perched the reindeer that had spent so many years in the attic.

"You've come home to stay."

"This is where I found what my heart needs. I'm going to let my associates do the fieldwork. I'll do consulting work out of the house."

Epilogue

Nicole stood at the door, her snow-white dress a perfect princess line. The sun shone bright and golden. Gram's flowers bloomed with joy. And waiting for her at the end of the path stood Ace, so handsome in his black tux that for a moment her knees wobbled. Carrie made her way down the path, stood across from Ace, and turned to smile at Nicole.

Rachel followed Carrie, their yellow dresses bright as the sunshine.

Two of Ace's friends stood at his side. All of them watched the door, waiting for Nicole.

She stepped out and saw no one but Ace as she slowly closed the distance between them.

"I love you," he whispered, as she took his arm and faced the preacher.

"I love you, too," she whispered back. And then they listened as the preacher exhorted them to love and trust and be true.

They had written their own vows.

Ace turned and, his voice husky, said, "Nicole, I will love you until death. I will never let anything come between us or knowingly separate us. 'Thy people shall be my people, and thy God my God.' Nothing but death shall part you and me."

Nicole smiled through her tears. They'd kept their promises secret until this moment, and the fact he'd quoted from Ruth, the same passage she'd chosen, thrilled her. She took a deep breath and, her voice quavering, said, "Andrew, Ace, I love you with my heart and life. I will trust you throughout our lives together." Her voice grew stronger as she quoted the verse she had chosen. " 'Whither thou goest, I will go; and where thou lodgest, I will lodge. Till death do us part.'"

They kissed for the first time as man and wife, and the friends and neighbors who'd gathered to share this moment cheered.

Later, much later, they slipped into Aunt Millie's house, now their home. Gram and Carrie would continue to live next door until Carrie left for university next year. Nicole would be close enough to help Gram as she grew older. Ace had already set up his consulting business. But wherever he went or whatever he did in the future Nicole would be at his side.

Ace looked down at her. "I never thought this would happen. I have really and truly come home."

"I will thank God every day for bringing you back."

"Amen."

They smiled at each other, and then he lowered his head and kissed her. They had both found what their hearts desired.

Darcy's Inheritance

Chapter 1

Late. Again. Blake Thompson rushed into the house and headed for his bedroom. How long did it take to read a will? How long to settle things amicably and shake hands all around so he could get back to his chores? Cows and calves to look after. The tractor to service. He didn't have time for this, but he had too much at stake to avoid it. He breathed a silent prayer: *Lord, let this be short and sweet.*

He grabbed his wallet and headed down the hall, his six-year-old half sister, Amy, dogging his heels.

"How long you going to be gone?"

"Not a minute longer than I have to."

"I wish I could go. There's nothin' to do here."

He paused at the living room. "Aunt Betty!" he called to the older woman sitting across the room. "I'm on my way to town. Anything you need?" She shook her head as she concentrated on her knitting.

"I wanna go with you," Amy persisted.

"You'd just have to sit in the truck. Besides, don't you have twelve cats waiting to play with you?" The cats were a nuisance, always underfoot in the supply room, but he wouldn't deny his sister the pleasure she got from her pets.

"Can you get me more cat food?"

"Hey, aren't you afraid they'll get fat and lazy?" He grinned down at her. "And then they wouldn't do their job."

Her gorgeous blue eyes could be dark and moody one moment, and the next, guileless and sky bright, like now. "Uh-uh." She shook her head until her blond hair sprayed around her face. "Bullet caught a mouse yesterday. He's real fast, you know." She stuck out her bottom lip. "You never take me with you."

Ignoring her whining, he held out his arms. "Come on. Give your big brother a hug and kiss." He braced himself as she launched into his arms, squeezing her arms around his neck until he could hardly breathe.

He slowly released her, letting her land on his boots. She clung to him, giggling when he swung her high with each step until he reached the truck. "Gotta go, squirt. Behave yourself while I'm gone."

Twenty minutes later he jerked to a halt on the main street of Blissdale, Montana, population 786. For a moment he rested his forearms on the steering wheel. His own father had died when he was thirteen, and his mother four years ago. He still missed them. Sure, he didn't think about them all the time; but when he least expected it, *pow*—a sucker punch jerked his breath away. He knew it wouldn't be any different with Rob.

He straightened, rolled up his sleeves, hung his sunglasses from his breast pocket, and slid from his truck. He dusted the seat of his jeans and strode past the sign—Eugene Smart, Barrister and Solicitor—and into the office. Gene's receptionist ushered him into the inner room.

She sat across the desk from the lawyer—the woman who'd refused to visit Rob as he lay dying.

But she sure had no trouble making it to the reading of the will.

He'd seen Rob's photo of her as a kid and knew she bore a resemblance to Amy. He just wasn't prepared for how strong the likeness was. Clear blue eyes like his little sister's. And right now they were cool and steady. In fact, if he didn't miss his guess, he would say they were challenging. As if daring him to object to her presence. Fiery, red-hot lights burst in his head. He objected, all right.

He stared hard, intending to let her know what he thought about her dereliction of duty. The way he looked at it, if a person didn't have normal affection, he or she still had duty. This woman had neither. She deserved nothing of Rob's.

She wore a denim skirt and black high-heeled boots. He focused for a moment on the boots. On any other woman he might have thought them attractive.

Gene stood. "Miss Hagen, let me introduce Blake Thompson."

The woman held out her hand. "Hello."

Tall and slender with a voice of pure music. Too bad the music didn't go any deeper than her voice box.

Blake hesitated, then took her cool, smooth fingers. He resisted an urge to jerk back and shove his large, rough hands in his pockets. He withdrew slowly and faced Gene. "Let's get this finished. I have things to do."

Gene nodded him toward a chair, then looked at her. "Are you ready to proceed, Miss Hagen?"

"Yes, let's get this over with." She settled back and crossed her legs.

Blake stared at the books crowding the shelves behind Gene. He caught a whiff of orange. Wasn't much chance it came from Gene's dusty books and stacks of papers.

The lawyer rustled the papers before him. "Rob was very clear and specific about the terms of his will." He gave Blake a steady look, then ducked his head and read, "I hereby bequeath to Blake Thompson my share of the land and all farm-type assets." The lawyer glanced up. "He knew the ranch morally belonged to you even though your mother had made him joint owner when they married."

Blake nodded. Better than what he'd expected. He crossed one ankle over his knee and tried not to think of the chores left to do.

"Exclusive," Gene read, "of what is known as the 'old property' consisting of five acres and a house, which I bequeath to my daughter Darcy Hagen." He smiled at Darcy. "There are two houses on the ranch. The older one has its own title, and it's now yours."

Blake dropped both feet to the floor and faced *Miss Hagen*. "I knew Rob would leave you something. Just wasn't sure what. I've already made arrangements for the necessary funds to purchase the property from you. We can sign the papers now, and I'll transfer the money to your account as soon as everything clears."

She looked remote, as if none of this meant anything to her. But of course it didn't. She hadn't wanted anything to do with the ranch or its inhabitants when her father was alive. And he, Blake Thompson, now owner of the entire spread except for a few acres, didn't want anything to do with her. She had no part of his home, his life, or his thoughts.

She returned his stare with clear blue eyes, not flinching before his displeasure. He always got a kick out of the way Amy fearlessly tried to stare him down when she was in trouble, but the same look from this woman made his neck muscles twitch.

"How much money are we talking about?" she asked.

"Fair market value."

She slid her gaze away but not before he saw her silent accusation and the quirk of her eyebrows, her message as plain as the barlike rays of sunshine slanting through the blinds beside Gene's desk. *As if I'd trust you.* He resisted the urge to grind his teeth.

"I'll let you handle the details of the sale," she told *his* lawyer, then uncrossed her legs and leaned back. "I have no interest in anything my father left me. We've had no contact for years. How long will it take? I have obligations back home."

Gene rattled some papers. "I think you'd both better listen to the rest of the will before you make any decisions." He took a deep breath. "Your father named you both as joint guardians of Amy."

Blake's mouth dropped open. He clamped it shut, swallowed hard, and found a croaky imitation of his voice. "No way."

Gene ignored his protest as he focused on *that* woman.

Darcy leaned forward. He was sure he could hear the gears turning in her head. *Is this going to interfere with my plans to take the money and run?* "Who is Amy?"

Gene ricocheted a glance off Blake, then kept his gaze on Darcy. "Amy is your half sister. Your father and Blake's mother had a child. Your father's wife passed away four years ago, so Amy is now without parents. Luckily she has two half-siblings. You and Blake."

"I have a sister?" Her voice spiraled upward. She spun around and glared at Blake. "Why didn't anyone tell me?"

He let her see his scorn. "In this part of the country, the telephone lines run both ways."

Her Amy-blue eyes turned icy. "In my part of the country, so do the mail, the airplanes, and the roads."

Gene sighed loudly. "Can we get back to the business at hand? There are decisions to be made."

Blake corralled his desire to yank the will from the lawyer's hands and shred it. "What decisions? Nothing's changed as far as I'm concerned. I'll pay her for the piece of land she inherited, and she can get back to her life."

"You'll have to sign custody agreement documents. You'll need to—"

Blake slapped his hand against his thigh. "I won't be signing any such thing. Gene, make out the papers for the purchase of the land. Call me when everything's in order." He strode across the room.

"This changes everything." Her words stopped him as if he'd run into a fence. "I want to meet my little sister."

He slowly turned around. "Over my dead body."

Gene stood. "Blake, she has a right—"

Blake scowled at Gene. "As far as I'm concerned, she has no right." He glowered at the woman, his eyes burning.

She pressed the tips of her fingers together in a tent. "It wouldn't have hurt anyone to tell me about her. Does she know about me?"

Blake shook his head. "Rob thought it would only confuse her."

The coldhearted woman planted both feet on the floor. "I'd like to see this house I've inherited and my little sister."

"What happened to your obligations?"

Her triumphant smile grated up his spine. "Your lawyer warned me I might need a few days to take care of business, so I took some time off. I meant to spend it touring the mountains, but I can delay my trip for a few days."

Gene must have noticed the way Blake clenched and unclenched his jaw and curled his fists into knots. "Blake, what's the harm? Take her out to the ranch. Show her the house. Introduce Amy." He paused. "I'm sorry, but you really don't have a choice."

Frustration gnawed at Blake's throat. He prayed for patience, knowing he was going to need more than the usual amount. "How many are a few days?"

She shrugged and smiled. "I'm free for the next two weeks."

He didn't welcome two days. Not even two hours. Two weeks? No way. "What about your vacation in the mountains?"

"I'm uncommitted."

"No kidding."

"To a schedule."

"Then it's settled." Gene tidied the papers on his desk in obvious relief. "I'm sure Blake will be glad to show you to the ranch."

Blake choked back a growl. He'd be glad to show her the way out of town. *Lord, where is that patience I ordered?*

"I'm sure I can get directions from Gene," she said in a smooth, cool voice.

Gene shot him a warning look.

Blake knew when he was over a barrel. "Forget it. I'll show you the way."

◆

Darcy didn't get to her feet right away. Not that she wasn't ready and willing—except for her legs. They quivered as if she'd run all day. She ignored Blake waiting at the door, ready to take off. She wasn't about to chance falling on her face at the feet of this overbearing man who remained oblivious to her shock at his appearance.

This...this fully grown man was the boy who'd stolen her father's affections? She'd excused her father all these years by imagining the boy he'd chosen to raise as his own when he married his second wife was a cute little toddler while Darcy was already a gangly adolescent. That neatly explained why her father didn't want anything to do with her. But this man had to be older than she. It shot her theory to the mountain peaks and back.

And for no one to let her know she had a little sister? To hide the fact of Darcy's existence from the girl as if she—Darcy—could be erased from all of their lives?

It was unforgivable. Her stomach coiled and twisted. She couldn't believe no one had said anything. Not one word. It couldn't be more obvious that she'd intentionally been shut out.

What did she expect? It had always been the same. Her father never thought of her. Even this inheritance promised to be one colossal headache. She hadn't wanted to come to this meeting. In fact, she'd sooner have stood on hot coals in her bare feet, thank you very much. But the lawyer hadn't given her an option, so she'd driven almost a thousand miles to be here.

Blake rattled the doorknob. "Ready?"

"You bet." She picked up her tiny purse. While pretending to adjust the straps, she gave her limbs a desperate command. *Don't fail me now.* She could do this. It was like preparing for a race. She took a deep breath and held it until oxygen flowed to her muscles. "Thank you, Mr. Smart." She could spare the time to be polite to the lawyer. And use the delay to steady herself.

She pushed from the chair and tested her legs, breathing easier when they held her weight. But she reached for the edge of the lawyer's desk as quivering trembled up her body and settled in her stomach. She wasn't going to throw up, was she?

"What are you driving?"

"A car." When he sighed, she added, "The little red one at the curb." He didn't need to look at her as if she'd left her brain in storage. Her state of shock was his fault, after all. His and her father's. It required a miracle for her to walk after the information dumped on her.

She followed the glowering man outside. It didn't take a genius to see Blake Thompson wasn't pleased with the way the reading of the will had gone.

Ha! He ought to try being in her shoes. She glanced down at her footwear. Or boots. She stood at the curb, staring at her car. "I have a little sister." She thought she wouldn't talk to him at all, but the words slipped out. In fact, a whole crowd of words rushed to her mouth. "Her name's Amy?"

Blake faced her, his expression hard. "Listen to me. Amy doesn't need you. She's well cared for and happy. And you don't need her. You've made that obvious."

She planted her booted feet several inches apart and stuck her face close to his, raising to her tiptoes to help equalize their height. "You know nothing about me, so you can stop judging me. And you can just accept the fact that I am going to see my house and meet my sister." She settled back on her heels. "Like it or live with it. I don't care."

He muttered something nasty under his breath.

Like that hurt. "I've never owned a house. Never lived in one of our own growing up. I might like it so much I'll decide to stay." She enjoyed goading him, especially when his eyes turned thunderous. "I'm really looking forward to meeting Amy. How old did you say she was?"

His long legs ate up the distance to a big black truck complete with dual wheels and roll bar. "I didn't."

And you don't intend to. "Fine. I like surprises." Nice surprises like a party, a great sale, a new flavor of coffee that purred across her tongue. She could well do without the sort of surprise Blake Thompson was turning out to be. Seeing him had shaken her far worse than she cared to think possible. Why had her father chosen him over her? She shook her head and shoved back the anger tearing at her throat. And a little sister? Not only had she been robbed of her father, but she'd also been robbed of a sister. She closed her eyes. *Lord, help me remember the past is forgiven. Help me not let it steal away my joy.* She opened her eyes and smiled into the blue sky.

"Get in your car if you want to follow me to the ranch."

She jerked her heels together and saluted. "Yes, sir." At the look of outrage darkening his face before he yanked open the truck door, she laughed. No way was she going to let him get on her nerves. Even as she thought it, a pain shafted up the side of her face, and she reminded herself to relax her jaw.

"I have to stop at the grocery store." His tone indicated she could follow him or rot in the sunshine. And she knew which he preferred.

"Good idea. I'll need some supplies if I'm going to enjoy living in *my* house."

The slam of his door shook the truck. The motor growled to life, and he roared away from the curb.

She followed him down the dusty little street, her mind spinning as fast as the wheels under her car. "I have a little sister." Over and over she repeated the words, trying to get her head around the idea. Shivers raced up her arms. A sister. She tried to picture her, but not knowing if the child was big or little or somewhere in between made it impossible. She did some quick mental arithmetic. Her sister had to be at least four given the fact Blake's mother died that long ago. When had she last spoken to her father? She pretended to think about the answer. But she remembered very well. Seven years ago after he'd failed to show up for her high school graduation.

So many times she'd built fantasies of his return. After his marriage to Blake's mom, she had dreamed of visits. She waited for him on her birthdays even though she had no reason to think he'd come. No reason but her own need. Each time he failed to show, she made excuses for him. Too far. Too busy. Forgot.

But missing her graduation hurt. This time he had promised. She'd counted on it, planned on it for weeks. And then for every one of her friends to witness her disappointment...

That's when she'd made the decision she wouldn't give him the opportunity to disappoint her again.

Had she had a little sister then? Would her father have bothered to tell her if she had?

Fifteen years ago he'd married Blake's mother. Maybe her father chose this family over her because Amy was on the way. Not because Blake was a cute toddler.

That meant Amy would be fifteen.

Or not. No one had ever said a word about it. Not even Mom. She gripped the steering wheel so hard her fingers cramped. A combination of surprise and anger—fresh and hot—stung her insides, uncovering an old, old sense of being so unimportant in her father's eyes she became invisible.

Blake pulled to a stop in front of a building with a plain brown face of aluminum siding and a bold black and white sign across the entire front: BROWN'S GENERAL STORE.

Darcy parked beside Blake's truck. She took a moment to push away the turmoil inside her and whispered another prayer. "Please, God. I've dealt with those feelings. With Your help I've put them to rest. Please help me concentrate on all the good things You've given me." She smiled hard. *Like a sister.* She couldn't wait to meet this surprise person. It was the most incredible thing—she had a sister. She *was* a sister. They were about to meet for the first time. A little thrill skittered up her spine. All her life she'd felt isolated by her father's leaving. Sure, she had Mom, but somehow it never seemed she had family. But a sister made her part of a nuclear family unit. Sort of. She could hardly wait to meet her.

No way Darcy could express to her sister how much it meant to have someone, but she'd take a gift of welcome and gratitude.

Oh yeah, and she'd see the house her father willed her. What would it look like? The old property, the lawyer said. Probably a decrepit building. Probably short in modernization. She wrinkled her nose. Would there be an outhouse?

Unless the toilet stood white—or any color but wood—and flushable in a room with a tub and a sink, she'd be heading straight back to town and the comfort of a motel. She glanced around. She didn't see a motel, but she'd find one.

Not that she planned to stay long. She'd meet her little sister, decide what to do about her guardianship responsibilities, and sell the house as Blake had suggested. She snorted. His "suggestion" sounded more like an order. Not that it mattered. She wanted nothing to do with the hurtful emotions she associated with her father or Blake's obvious displeasure.

Blake disappeared into the store, and she hurried after him, catching him just inside the door.

"I'd like to take Amy a gift." She spoke to the man's back because he left her no choice.

He seemed bent on putting as much distance between them as possible. "It would help to know how old she is and what she likes."

A young man with a nose too big for his face stood behind the counter. He glanced up from reading a magazine. "Hey, Blake!" he called. "How's it going?"

"Hi, Joe. Things are just great." Darcy knew she didn't imagine the sarcasm in his voice. He turned to her. "Listen to me. Amy doesn't need anything. Get it? Nothing."

Darcy hoped she revealed only her stubbornness. "I'd have to be as stupid as this cart"—she yanked one toward her—"not to 'get it.' You want me to know Amy doesn't need me." As if he had to say it. How much more obvious could it be than to keep Amy's existence a secret? "But need I remind you that apparently my father thought differently?" A little late in the game, but at least he'd remembered her in death, if not in life.

Blake spun around and strode down an aisle.

She headed in a different direction. Halfway down the length of the store she remembered to look at the shelves for supplies. Suddenly she stared ahead. The modern grocery store at the front had become an old-fashioned hardware store with coffee-colored wooden shelves and creaky oiled wood floors complete with the scent of lemon oil, twine, and leather. She wanted to linger, poke through the shelves and touch pieces of history, but she heard Blake back at the cash register. She grabbed items off the shelves. She'd need some food if she meant to stay at the house, and she selected fresh produce.

Blake stood at the checkout with a super-big bag of cat food. She wondered if he had a super-big cat to match.

She stood in front of the household section, shamelessly listening to the conversation between Blake and the clerk as she decided what she needed. Definitely some cleaners and a good strong bug killer. She put an extra-large, industrial-strength can of it in her cart.

The young man at the counter chuckled. "More food for Amy's cats?"

Blake laughed, too. "Gonna have to take on a part-time job just to pay for cat food."

Cats, huh? She detoured down the next aisle and selected a handful of cat toys. Not exactly her top choice for the first gift for a new sister. But better than twine and nails.

As she unloaded her cart to ring her selections through, Blake waited at the door, glancing frequently at his watch and casting a look toward his truck as if trying to decide if he should wait or leave her to find her own way to the ranch.

"What brings you to our part of the country?" the clerk asked.

She ignored Blake's impatient sigh. "I've come to see the house I inherited."

The young man raised his eyebrows and glanced at Blake, who said in a voice thick with resignation, "Rob's daughter, Darcy. She inherited the old house."

She certainly didn't like the way they kept saying "old house" and shuddered at visions of huge spiders. Fat, lazy mice. Spooky sounds in the walls. Maybe she should get another can of bug killer.

The young man leaned over the counter. "Welcome to your new home. My name's Joe Brown."

She smiled at the eager clerk as she scooped up the bagged groceries and rushed after Blake. "Wait. How far is it? When can I meet Amy? We need to talk."

He brushed at his face as if she were a pesky mosquito. "If you follow me, I'll take you to your house." He headed for the truck as if a national emergency required his immediate attention.

Darcy called after him, again talking to the man's back. "I *will* be meeting my sister," she said, her voice hard with determination. "You don't have the right to refuse it."

He yanked the door open and spun around. "The way I see it, a piece of paper written by a dying man doesn't give you the right to march in here and start making demands."

She took a step toward him. "That piece of paper gives me as much right as you. And I will not be denied it." She'd been pushed out, left in the dark, excluded from her rights as a daughter all her life. She would not let anyone, including Blake Thompson, keep her away from her sister.

Blake yanked his truck door shut, effectively shutting out any more discussion.

Darcy clenched her teeth as she crawled into her car, depositing her purchases on the seat beside her. No way was he going to deny her access to her sister.

Chapter 2

Darcy followed Blake down the highway. As the road flashed under her wheels, she looked about. The Rockies rose in the west like uneven dinosaur teeth. She'd loved the drive through the mountains, the sun shining off them so gloriously. She imagined herself running down the highway, breathing in the rare air, waving to the deer in the trees. By the time she got back to Seattle she'd be in such great condition she'd easily win the charity challenge run. She, Darcy Hagen, the winner, pumping her arms over her head in a victory cheer and everyone from her office yelling and congratulating her. As the winner, her office would present the funds raised by the event to the charity of its choice—the homeless shelter.

She smiled at the thought. Maybe the homeless wouldn't be off the streets, but at least they'd have a place to sleep.

Now she didn't know if she'd be spending much time in the mountains. She wanted to meet Amy and get to know her. Anger spurted to the surface again. How would she ever make up for the missed years, be they four or fifteen?

She sucked in a deep steadying breath and prayed for peace in her heart. Slowly her anger abated, and she returned her attention to the sights outside the car.

Grassy fields spread out like thick, pale gold corduroy. Other fields seemed thin, as if they'd been washed too often—some kind of crop residue from the last growing season, she guessed. But what she knew about farming or ranching wouldn't fill the cap of her pen. Cows she recognized and knew they came in various colors, mostly brown and black.

The brake lights flashed in the monster truck ahead of her, and she slowed as Blake turned onto a gravel road. His dust forced her to drop back, but she didn't have to worry about getting lost. The swirling gray cloud shouted the way.

A few minutes later the air cleared as Blake pulled to a stop. She glanced at her watch. Twenty minutes from town. Unbelievable. She couldn't imagine not being able to run across the street for a magazine or to the corner for a mocha.

As she parked next to his truck, her gaze riveted on the small house behind him. Her house? She couldn't imagine owning a house. Too bad it was out in the middle of Nowhere, Montana. She leaned over the steering wheel and peered through the window. It didn't look *that* old. Sure, the trim needed painting, and a curtain hung crookedly in one window. But it had a sunporch. Just like a summer home. A place where a person could come and forget her troubles. Her insides ping-ponged around. A haven.

Not that she needed a physical haven. Years ago she'd found what she needed in her faith. One of her favorite verses caressed her thoughts. It was from Deuteronomy—chapter thirty-three, if she remembered correctly. *"The eternal God is your refuge, and underneath are the everlasting arms."* Her faith had sustained her for years and would continue to do so into the future. She took a deep breath and let peace fill her mind.

Her attention turned to Blake, shifting from foot to foot and frowning so deeply he drove gouges into his forehead. She sighed. Looks as if she might need a haven, after all—someplace to get away from him. She gave him a little wave and laughed at his curt nod, refusing to let his bad temper steal away her stubborn peace.

She studied him. How would she describe him to the girls at the office? Rude.

And physically? She examined him closely, building a word picture. Lean, like a runner. All muscle. Long legs and broad shoulders. She studied his face. Wide forehead. Nicely shaped brows. Short brown hair brushed back. Highlighted with blond streaks, straight from sunny Mother Nature, if she didn't miss her guess. Irene would sigh dramatically if she could see his eyes. Dark brown and intense. In fact, to be honest, if he were anyone but her father's stepson, she'd be just a tiny bit interested in him.

He crossed his arms and glowered at her.

She blinked. How long had she been staring at the poor guy? She hurried to get out of the car. As she straightened, she plastered on a smile. "This is my house?" A bouquet of strange scents greeted her—pungent animal smells, the aroma of damp, sweet hay, and the hint of something sharp and spicy.

He nodded. "Give me a couple of minutes to clean out some stuff." He pulled a box from the truck and headed to the door.

Darcy bounced after him. "Listen—we have to discuss Amy. When am I going to meet her?"

He threw open the door without answering.

"It wasn't locked?" She hesitated, glancing around nervously. They stood in an entryway large enough for a washer and dryer and a row of hooks holding an assortment of Goodwill coats. "What if someone's in here?"

"There's a key on the nail by the door if you want to keep it locked."

A sigh released her lungs. "That's good." But he'd already stepped into the next room. She hurried after him to a large, airy kitchen. A wooden table and mismatched chairs stood in one corner next to patio doors with a view of the sunroom. She could almost imagine settling in, stretched out on a chaise lounge, reading and enjoying the sunshine. Her skin warmed. She could hardly wait. She even had a recent fashion magazine. This could be enjoyable if she didn't have to contend with Blake and his lack of cooperation.

"You can't keep ignoring me. I have a right—"

Blake picked up a shirt and a clock and dumped them in the box.

"Someone's living here?" In her shock and excitement she hadn't thought she might be putting someone out of their home. "Who?"

"No one lives here." He crossed to the next room.

Darcy followed him into what was the living room—a fireplace at one end, dusty bookshelves across another wall. It looked and felt occupied. "Sure looks like someone lives here." She faltered. "I wouldn't make them leave. I can always go back to town and stay in a motel."

"I said no one lives here. Besides, it's yours. Remember?" As he talked he carefully took some framed photos off the shelves.

Peering past him, she saw a serene-looking woman standing beside a familiar figure. "That's my father."

He dropped the photo into the box.

"Was that your mother with him?" she asked.

"Uh-huh."

"Did they live here?" Getting words out of this man was like trying to gain an extra minute in an hour.

"No. They lived in the new house."

"Then why is their picture here?"

He picked up a trophy of a man swinging a rope and set it in the box before he faced her. "I lived here until. . ." He turned away but not before she'd seen the tightness around his eyes. "Until Rob got sick and I moved in with them to help."

Darcy's thoughts stuttered. She didn't want to think about her father.

"Rob lived here before he and Mom married," Blake said.

Something cold dribbled down Darcy's spine. Her father lived here at a time when she still hoped he'd come back to her and her mother. When she still believed things would work out. She spun away and stared out the window, forcing herself to see the view. Mountains far to the west. Dark brooding pines to the right. Scraggy-fingered poplars to the left. "How long was he sick?" She hadn't meant to say the words. She hadn't even meant to think them. No way was she going to give the past any power in her life.

"Almost a year."

"I'm sorry. Truly I am. It must have been a difficult time for you."

His gaze scorched her.

Instinctively she stepped back and raised her hands to protect her face from the heat.

"How can it mean nothing to you?"

"Look. I said I'm sorry about your loss. I know it's recent and still hurts like mad. I got over my loss years ago."

He made a choking sound as he grabbed his box and strode into the next room. She sighed deeply. Maybe she should turn around and go back to town. Only she had a little sister she was truly curious about. So she followed Blake into a sunny room he'd obviously used as an office. The large oak desk would have held his computer. There remained a stack of paper in a tray and mugs filled with pens and pencils.

He stood in the middle of the room. "I slept here as a kid. Before my parents built the new house." He wandered over to the window and stared out.

His silence made Darcy uncomfortable. She didn't want to be dragged into his grief.

Suddenly he faced her, his expression dark. "He was a wonderful father to me."

Her heart clenched. Pain shot through her chest. His words stung. But it wasn't as if she'd never before thought what it meant that her father raised someone else's child.

She could deal with her unexpected reaction. It was no different from running. You hit a spot where you wanted to give up. Your muscles hurt. Your lungs screamed for air. But you pushed past that hurdle, and suddenly it eased. Your lungs learned to expand. Your muscles got the required oxygen, and you settled into a rhythm you could maintain for miles. She just had to focus on her breathing until it leveled. She sucked in air and eased it out slowly.

His expression had softened as if he'd read her reaction, but she didn't want to hear another word about her father. Giving him a curt nod, she said, "How nice for you." The room suddenly crowded in on her, and she hurried away.

She peeked into the last room. A rumpled bed. This was where Blake had slept. Had her father slept there, too?

She stepped back and crashed into Blake. He cupped her shoulders to steady her. Embarrassment filled every pore, and she pushed past him, heading for fresh air.

Blake followed her outside. "What're you so upset about?"

Arggh. How could he be so dense? "Nothing."

"I saw—" He waved toward the far room where she'd let herself react to the surroundings.

"It was a long trip. I'm tired."

"Right. I'll just get the rest of my stuff." He headed for the bedroom.

She lowered her shoulders. This wasn't going to be easy. But then why should she be surprised? Nothing to do with her father had ever been easy. She followed Blake and prayed for wisdom to deal with him. "Blake, I want to meet Amy. As soon as possible." She'd been shut out of her sister's life far too long. Well, no more.

He halted, his back to her. "Don't you think you should give me a chance to prepare her?"

Although she didn't care for his harsh tone, she saw the sense in what he said. "Fine. But when?"

She refused to allow him to use it as a delaying technique. She suspected he might try to delay it forever.

"As soon as I get a chance."

Ha. She recognized *that* as a deliberate attempt to delay. "Today then?"

He shrugged and concentrated on pulling things off the desk and dropping them into his bag.

"So I can meet her tonight?"

He turned slowly, his expression fierce. "First let's see how she reacts."

She gave him a hard look. This all had a familiar feel to it. Empty promises. Having her feelings shoved aside by a man's excuses. *Well, not this time, buddy.* She wouldn't allow it. "I will not wait forever."

They did silent battle with their eyes, and then he strode from the room.

She grabbed an empty plastic bag off the counter and headed for the bathroom to collect Blake's stuff and help him on his way. In the medicine cupboard she found a collection of men's cologne and aftershave and began to clean the shelves. One bottle looked weirdly familiar. Red, with a white sailing ship. She smelled the bottle. Why did it send little shivers across her shoulders? The sounds of laughter through her thoughts? A distant memory of a little girl on a swing, arcing skyward, giggling? Her throat tightened. How odd.

"You found Rob's Old Spice."

Blake's voice behind her startled her, and she dropped the bottle. It broke, and the scent almost choked her.

"I'll get a rag."

She was still staring at the mess at her feet when he returned with paper towels and swiped up the mess.

"Sorry," she mumbled, backing out of the room.

"You'll be stuck with the smell."

She coughed. Why was she letting a little bottle of outdated aftershave upset her equilibrium? A truly stupid reaction. She swung her gaze to the outdoors. "There's lots of fresh air."

He dropped the paper towels and broken glass into a bag and tied it shut. "I'll get rid of this." He tossed it in the back of his truck, then returned for the box. "I'm out of here."

She couldn't blame him for the bitter note in his voice. After all, this house meant a lot to him. To her, it was more like a guilt offering. One she didn't want and wouldn't accept. Only one thing made her stay. Amy. "I'll expect to see my sister very soon."

He didn't even glance back as he climbed into his truck and drove out of the yard.

◆

Blake drove away from the old house and its memories, his frustration burning like a spray of battery acid. Why had Rob involved his older daughter? Now he was stuck with a woman who would march into his life—and Amy's—then leave. If her past were any indication, the visit would never be repeated. In the meantime, he had to pretend to be nice. And everything in him rebelled at the idea.

He remembered the passage they'd been discussing at Bible study. Something to the effect of forgiving those who have sinned against you. He couldn't remember the exact wording because at the time he didn't see how it applied to him. He didn't hold grudges. Didn't need to forgive anyone.

He gripped the steering wheel, arms and shoulders tight with frustration. And wasn't that just the point? Darcy hadn't hurt him—she'd hurt Rob. And now he carried a grudge on behalf of his stepfather. For years after Rob moved to the ranch, there was no contact between Darcy and Rob. Blake wondered about it occasionally, but they were all busy and content. Except for the picture on the bookshelf, Rob seemed to have erased his previous life from his thoughts. Blake accepted the situation with a certain amount of gratitude. Perhaps a little self-righteous pride that Rob seemed to prefer his present circumstances over anything from the past.

And then suddenly, out of the blue, Darcy had sent Rob an invitation to her high school graduation. His mom was included. Rob had been cautiously happy about it. Mom kept saying it was the beginning of reconciliation. Rob could face his past and deal with it instead of ignoring it. Rob always answered by kissing Blake's mom and saying he preferred to enjoy what he'd found here.

Blake pressed his lips together and let the pain pass.

But the visit never happened. Mom ended up in the hospital. Her unexpected pregnancy with Amy revealed her weak heart. She tried to persuade Rob to go alone, assuring him she'd be well taken care of in the hospital, but Rob refused to leave her side. He called to explain, but Darcy never gave him a chance. She said she never wanted to hear from him again. Rob shrugged and said perhaps it was best to leave things as they were.

Blake couldn't agree more. He'd attempted to talk Rob out of trying to find Darcy when he got sick. Just a few days before he died, Rob expressed regret that he'd failed. Blake's jaw clenched. He had to prevent Amy from going through the same disappointment Rob had with Darcy. He pulled up to the barn and hoisted the bag of cat food to his shoulder. The supply room door swung open, Amy riding it, her toes jammed against the board on the bottom.

"Did you get the food?" she called.

He studied this little sister who meant the world to him. Dirt smudged her cheeks. Cat hair clung to her ragged jeans. He guessed she'd been out here playing with her pets since he left. He tried not to see the likeness between the sisters. "Cat food and a present from your boyfriend."

She gave him a disdainful look, her lips pursed like a big kiss. "I don't have a boyfriend."

"Then I guess you don't want this sucker Joe sent you?" He held up the red candy.

"Oh, Joe. He's not a boyfriend. He's old. Maybe as old as you." She reached for the sucker, yanked the paper off, and popped the candy into her mouth.

"Joe said to say hi." Blake shook his head and pretended to be puzzled. "He seems to think a lot of you. Sure you won't break his heart by saying he's not your boyfriend?"

She shrugged. "Maybe when I'm older."

He chuckled as he set the cat food in the corner.

She dropped off the door and followed him. "Whatcha going to do now?"

"I've got some cows and calves to look after."

"Can I come?"

"Not this time, pumpkin." One of the cows was unpredictable. No place for a little girl.

"Aw." The kid could pack a whole world of emotion into that little sound. "I got nothing to do."

"Why don't you go up to the house and put together one of your jigsaw puzzles?"

Amy drooped her shoulders and hung her head in a way that would win her an Oscar if she were playing a kid in one of London's eighteenth-century orphanages. "Already did my puzzles today."

"Then play with your stuffed animals."

She sighed long and loud. "Don't want to."

"It's almost suppertime. Maybe you should go clean up."

She ignored his suggestion.

"Come on—get on my back, and I'll give you a ride to the house." He had to change his boots before he headed into the corrals.

She climbed the fence and jumped on his back. He trotted to the house, bouncing her until she giggled. "I have to go to the bathroom."

He jerked to a halt. "Not on my back." But when he tried to shake her off, she clung like a stubborn cowboy set on winning the day's purse at a rodeo.

He leaned over his knees, pretending to be exhausted. "Okay, you win, but don't have an accident on me."

She giggled. A sound that made him grin. He felt like a superhero to be the one who made her forget to be sad for a minute. They'd both lost so much; yet they could still enjoy each other.

He continued his journey toward the house, his steps slow and measured. Where was Darcy when Amy had been born? Where was she when Amy and Blake's mother died and Rob was too grief stricken to deal with Amy? The task had fallen on Blake. And where was Darcy when Rob got sick and Blake became more and more responsible for Amy? Why had Rob involved Darcy in Amy's care? He had trusted Rob since before the man married Blake's mom. Yet he had to wonder at this decision.

At the house he dropped Amy to the ground and shooed her upstairs to change her clothes. "Wouldn't hurt you to have a bath either."

Amy shrugged. Blake promised himself to supervise bath time tonight.

He changed his boots and headed out to tackle his work. He sighed wearily and rubbed at his neck. No way he'd finish everything today, which meant that much more to do tomorrow. He was beginning to think he'd never catch up. And now one more thing to deal with. Darcy Hagen and her joint guardianship of Amy.

He'd keep her from seeing Amy if he thought he could, but all he could realistically hope to do was delay it as long as possible. Maybe Darcy would get tired of hanging around and take herself off on her planned vacation.

Except she'd made it plain that wasn't going to happen, and if she were anywhere near as stubborn as Amy. . .

Well, he knew she wouldn't leave until she got what she wanted. About all he could do was try to protect Amy from being hurt because it seemed Darcy didn't get it—Amy had been through more than her share of loss in her six years. She didn't need a sister who blew into her life and out again.

He suddenly remembered his mother. After his father died, Blake had struggled with anger and resentment. Looking back, he understood there was a lot of fear as to how they would cope. Even then, at thirteen, he saw his mother's pain. But she remained serene and confident, explaining they had a choice—wallow in their sorrow and fret about the "what-ifs"—or trust God. She had quoted a passage in Isaiah so often the words were blazed in his memory.

"But now, this is what the LORD says—he who created you, O Jacob,
he who formed you, O Israel: 'Fear not, for I have redeemed you; I have
summoned you by name; you are mine. When you pass through the waters,

I will be with you; and when you pass through the rivers, they will not sweep over you. When you walk through the fire, you will not be burned; the flames will not set you ablaze. For I am the LORD, your God, the Holy One of Israel, your Savior.'"

He didn't know if Darcy was a river threatening to drown him or a fire waiting to burn him, but who and what she was didn't change God's care and protection. He would follow his mother's advice and choose to trust God in this.

Which meant he had to prepare Amy to meet her sister.

Chapter 3

Darcy scrubbed the floor vehemently—a wonderful catharsis for her anger and frustration. She'd waited hours last night for Blake to bring Amy over. She'd practically glued herself to the doorframe, looking toward the two-story house across the yard. A nice comfortable distance for country neighbors, she guessed. Close enough to be able to see a person walking around outside, yet far enough you couldn't see in the windows.

She'd memorized her view of the house. White siding, green shingles, three sets of windows facing her on the upstairs. Downstairs, four big windows on one side of the wide front doors and three smaller ones on the other side. She guessed most of the traffic went in and out of the back of the house, toward the barns and fences. And where she couldn't see.

She'd stared at the house for hours, waiting for Blake to appear with a girl at his side. She tried to picture the girl. Would she come up to Blake's shoulder, or was she still knee-high?

But Blake failed to show. Finally, as darkness closed in around her, she gave up, changed into an old, familiar pair of jeans, and turned her energies toward scrubbing the house until it squeaked a protest. She worked late into the night and again this morning, all the time fuming.

Blake might have bought himself a few more hours, but that was all. Only concern for her little sister kept her from marching up to the other house and demanding entrance. In all fairness someone should prepare Amy. But if Blake didn't, Darcy would. She just had to figure out the best way.

She prayed for wisdom as she scoured the dirt off every shelf, cleaned every cupboard, and polished the windowpanes.

She finished washing the floor, sat back on her heels to admire her job, and grimaced at her red, wrinkled hands. She'd have to slather on lotion and give herself a manicure tonight, but it was worth it to see *her* house cleaned. Despite her anger and frustration over Blake not doing what she expected, as she scrubbed she experienced the foreign emotion of belonging. For every speck of dust she captured, every smudge she removed, every retreating bit of dirt she swept up, her joy grew. She *owned* this house, unlike every other landlord-owned, temporary home she'd known. She never guessed having her name on a title would make such a difference. She snorted, mocking her fanciful thoughts. Of course, she'd sell it and return to Seattle. But it was hers. Hers to keep or sell.

"What're you doing in Blake's house?"

The clear sound of a child's voice jerked Darcy's attention to the door where a small face pressed against the screen, lips bubbled into graph paper squares.

Darcy's heart knocked at her chest as wave after wave of emotion swept through her. Surprise. Regret. Disbelief. And a hundred things she couldn't identify. She couldn't breathe. It was like the air had been vacuumed from the room. She couldn't move. She couldn't hear or smell or think. An intense feeling of loss crashed over her. Tears stung her eyes.

She stared at the little girl. Blond hair tangled around her head like a bad case of bed head. Blue eyes wide, she regarded Darcy with a familiar expression. She might have been looking at a picture of herself as a child. Except this girl had blond hair.

Slowly she rose, setting the pail of dirty water in the sink.

"This is Blake's house," the girl said, her tone challenging.

"Didn't Blake tell you about me?"

The girl shook her head.

Humph. How like a man to promise to do something and then not do it. "Do you want to come in?"

She hesitated, then jerked the door open and slipped in to stand just inside the room, her expression cautious.

Darcy took a step closer, but as the child's shoulders tensed she stopped and studied the tiny girl in front of her. She wore dirty jeans, torn at the knees and frayed at the bottom, and a T-shirt too wide at the bottom and sagging at the neck.

"You're Amy, aren't you?" Her words caught in her tight throat.

Amy nodded. "Who are you?"

Darcy smiled at the way Amy hid her fear behind a demanding tone. "I'm Darcy. How old are you?"

"Six. Whatcha doing in Blake's house?"

"I'm cleaning it." And scrambling mentally to figure out what to tell her. Should she confess she was an older sister? And then how to explain why Amy had never seen her before? Or even heard of her. And what did she say about the guardianship issue? Would you tell a child this small such things? She didn't have a clue. About all she could remember about being that size was her disappointment when her daddy left. If only he had explained it to her, made sure she didn't blame herself. Ah. So she'd answered her own questions. Even a tiny child deserved honesty.

"How come? Is Blake going to live here now?" Darcy heard the tremor of fear in Amy's voice that even her belligerence didn't disguise.

"No. I am."

"You can't. It's Blake's. You can't change things."

"Doesn't Blake live with you?"

Amy nodded.

"You wouldn't want to change that, would you?"

"No." Amy crossed her arms over her chest and stuck out her chin as if daring anyone to try.

"Then he doesn't need this house anymore."

"Didja buy it?"

"Not exactly."

"Then you can't have it."

Darcy laughed. She loved the stubborn streak she glimpsed in her little sister. One thing she admired was someone who stuck to her beliefs. "Someone gave it to me."

"Who? Blake?"

"No. Your father."

For just a moment Amy's expression crumpled; then she widened her eyes. "My daddy's gone to heaven."

Darcy squatted to eye level and touched Amy's shoulder. "I know. I'm sorry. You must miss him a lot."

Tears washed Amy's eyes as she nodded. "My mommy and daddy both went to heaven so they could be together."

"Ah, sweetie. I'm so sorry." She opened her arms. Amy hesitated a moment, then threw herself against Darcy. Darcy staggered back under her assault and landed on her bottom. She sat on the floor holding the crying child.

After a minute the tears stopped, but Amy remained with her face cradled against Darcy's neck.

"How come he gave you the house?" Amy's breath was warm.

Darcy held back her anger at Blake for putting her in this position and tried to think how and what she should tell Amy. About all she could do was answer her questions as honestly as possible. If Blake didn't approve, he should have taken care of it himself. But she didn't know Amy and didn't know how she'd react. She silently prayed for wisdom. She inhaled slowly, then spoke softly. "Because he was my daddy, too."

Amy leaned back and stared into Darcy's face, her eyes narrowed in concentration. "He wasn't Blake's daddy."

"I know."

"Then how come he's your daddy?"

"He was my daddy before he married your mommy."

"Is Blake your brother?"

"No." She explained as simply as possible how she could be Amy's sister, yet not be Blake's sister.

Amy settled back on her heels and looked Darcy up and down. Twice. She squinted into Darcy's eyes.

Darcy hardly dared breathe as she let Amy study her. She knew from Amy's look of concentration that she was assessing the information she'd just received. Darcy wondered what her reaction would be.

"Were you his little girl?" Amy asked.

The words clawed at Darcy. She pressed her hand to her chest to ease the pain. "Once upon a time I was."

"You look like the little girl in the picture."

"What picture is that?"

Amy shrugged. "Just a little girl in a picture." Her eyes misted with sadness. "My daddy's gone forever."

Darcy pulled Amy toward her. "I know how much you miss him." She remembered the feeling well. Waiting day after day, desperately hoping. Endlessly wanting. Until she'd made the decision to stop torturing herself. At least Amy would be spared the uncertainty and continual disappointment. Her parting was complete and explainable.

"But you know he's in heaven now." Darcy couldn't go on. Had her father become a Christian? He wasn't when she knew him. Her mother had only become one a few years ago.

Amy nodded. "He's with my mommy. He promised me I would see him when I go to heaven."

"That's good then, isn't it?"

"I miss my daddy so much." Amy started to cry. "But I don't want to die."

"Oh, honey." She hugged Amy fiercely, her heart bleeding at Amy's pain. "I'm certain your daddy doesn't mind waiting. He knows you have so many things to discover yet and so much stuff to do. The world is just waiting for Amy Hagen to do the things only Amy can do."

Amy leaned back. "Really?"

"Of course. That's why God made you. So you could do the Amy things in the world."

"Like what?"

Please, Lord. Give me the right words. She thought of when she'd started going to church. "I remember when my mom and I moved to a new house. I was about thirteen. There was a nice lady living next door, Mrs. Roland, and she invited me to go to church with her. She taught a class of girls my age and encouraged us to learn Bible verses we could use as guidelines for life. She gave us really neat rewards if we learned all the ones she chose." Even though Amy listened closely, Darcy was sure she didn't want to hear about the sleepovers and camping trips Mrs. R took them on. Nor that it was through Mrs. R's love and gentleness that Darcy found her way to God. "I think some of those verses might help you see what I mean. 'Whatever your hand finds to do, do it with all your might.' Rejoice in everything you have put your hand to.'"

She smiled into the eyes that were so much like the ones she saw in the mirror every day. "That means whatever is in front of you to do, that's your job. You should do it well and be happy."

"Like feeding my cats?"

Darcy nodded.

"I like feeding my cats."

"There are Amy jobs everywhere. Going to school, being kind to your friends, giving out free smiles."

Amy giggled, then sobered so suddenly Darcy knew she'd been surprised by a thought. "How come I never heard of you?"

Darcy's throat tightened, and she rocked her head back and forth, and breathed slowly before she could speak. "I don't know."

Amy jerked to her feet. "You're my big sister."

Darcy nodded.

Amy stared openmouthed and then smiled so wide it must have hurt. In fact, Darcy knew it did because her smile matched Amy's.

They grinned into each other's eyes for a full, sweet minute; then Darcy got to her feet. "I have a present for you." Amy followed Darcy as she padded barefoot into the bedroom and retrieved the parcel she'd brought from the store. "It's a welcome-sister present."

Amy tore the bag open and pulled out the catnip balls and bell toys. "For my cats. Goody. They love toys." She looked uncertain. "I don't have a welcome present for you."

"But you do." She was the best present one could ever expect, but Darcy knew that wasn't what Amy meant.

"What?"

"A big hug and kiss."

"Aww. That's nothing."

"It means a lot to me." Darcy sat on the edge of the bed and opened her arms. Amy planted a warm, generous kiss on her cheek and hugged her so tight Darcy almost choked.

◆

Blake finished the barn chores and headed straight for the house. He'd planned to sit down with Amy last night and tell her about Darcy, but the yearling steers had broken down the fence and gotten in with the cows and calves. It was a mess and totally preventable. He'd noticed the loose planks on the fence days ago but kept running out of daylight before he could fix it. In the long run it would have saved him time to get to it somehow.

It had taken him three hot and frustrating hours to fix the fence, then separate out the steers and put them back in their own pen.

And then the maternity pen demanded attention.

By the time he'd cleaned it all up and headed for the house, it was long past Amy's bedtime. Aunt Betty had bathed her and put her to bed, and then had gone to bed herself.

Aunt Betty, bless her heart, had left food out for him. She wasn't the world's best cook. She favored macaroni cooked to the consistency of glue, colored with processed cheese. Sometimes she varied her menus with scrambled eggs, fried hamburger, and canned vegetables, but she seldom bothered with the grade-A steaks and roasts in the freezer. To make up for Aunt Betty's lack of culinary skills, Blake kept the fridge stocked with fresh fruit and other healthy treats for Amy to snack on. Their diet was adequate despite his craving for a good meat-and-potatoes meal.

The cold food Aunt Betty left held no appeal. He scraped what remained into the garbage and built a thick peanut butter-jelly sandwich. The nutrition-deprived white bread stuck to the roof of his mouth as he chowed down on it. He could vaguely remember thick slices of homemade bread, nutty rich with freshly ground whole wheat flour. His mother had made the best bread in the world before she got too weak to do anything but care for Amy. He chased the sandwich with a tall glass of milk, rubbed a weary hand over his aching eyes, and thanked God for the temporary reprieve in dealing with the elder Hagen daughter.

But things were under control this morning—for a few hours—and he hurried to the house to find Amy. He'd tried to decide how to tell her about Darcy. But how did he explain why she'd suddenly shown up? Why she'd never contacted any of them? It was due to her own neglect she didn't know about Amy, but he had no idea how to put a positive spin on it for his little sister.

"Aunt Betty, where's Amy?"

The woman was mixing up the special diet she prepared for her old, ailing cat named Missy. The cat had seen better days and elicited more affection and attention from Aunt Betty than he understood. He was, nevertheless, grateful for the older woman's help. Her idiosyncrasies seemed minor in comparison to what some of the other nannies had inflicted on him. He'd endured everything from hot pursuit to huge long-distance charges on his telephone.

Aunt Betty paused a moment to answer him. "She was playing next to the house."

"I'll see what she's up to." Amy wasn't next to the house. He checked upstairs, but she wasn't among the scattered stuffed animals or on the rumpled bed. He picked her dirty sneakers off the pillow and carried them down to the back entryway where he dropped them on the floor. "I'll have another look in the barn."

He searched the supply room and wandered through the machine shed, calling her name. Nothing. She wasn't on the swing set in the backyard. She wasn't under the tree where she often played. He stood in the middle of the yard, rubbing his chin. Where had she disappeared to this time? His gaze shifted to the low house half hidden in the trees not more than five hundred yards away.

It wouldn't have taken more than a few minutes for her to discover the unfamiliar car parked over there, and knowing her curiosity. . .

His neck went into full-out spasm. What was he thinking not to tell her about Darcy before this? As he jogged toward the house, he uttered a desperate prayer he would get there before Amy made any unpleasant discoveries. Why had Rob brought this on them? What was God thinking to allow it?

He headed for the back door. His boots echoed across the wooden deck. He caught a whiff of something that made his taste buds spring to life with a vengeance. Then he heard Amy laughing and skidded to a halt. Battered by so many losses, Amy never laughed with anyone but him. Not since Rob's death. Hot protectiveness scorched up his throat. He would not let his fragile little sister be hurt by this woman.

Through the screen door he heard Amy's voice. "Do I put them in now?" she asked.

"Yes. And now you have to stir it." A pause. "Gently."

Blake smiled. Amy didn't do anything gently. He knocked.

"It's open!" Darcy called.

Blake stepped into the kitchen and stared. The two of them stood before the stove, Amy on a chair as she stirred a pot. The similarity between the two was unmistakable. Both wore old jeans and baggy T-shirts. They smiled at each other with the same pleasure-filled expression. The same wide blue eyes. Due to the difference in their ages, the sisters looked like mother and daughter.

Memories fired across his brain. When his mother was alive, he'd lived with scenes like this—domestic scenes full of food and love and warmth. Mom flipping pancakes. Her pride in her homemade spaghetti sauce. The special smile she reserved for him. He always felt so warm and welcomed in her presence. Would he ever know that homey feeling again? Did Amy remember standing on a stool next to their mother, chattering away like a bird?

An ache as wide as the blue Montana sky swallowed up his insides. The "what-ifs" and "if-onlys" that haunted him late at night when he couldn't sleep rushed forward for attention, but only in the depths of the darkness did he admit he longed for a home such as he'd known. A woman who smiled at him and greeted him as if her world revolved around him. Instead he had Aunt Betty and the responsibility of his precious little sister.

He pushed aside the memories, shoved the pain into hiding. He had Amy to take care of now. He wouldn't let anything—anyone—hurt her. He had neither room nor time for more. The hole in his life would never be filled.

He focused on Amy. She looked different. It took a moment for him to realize her hair had been brushed back into a ponytail matching Darcy's hairdo.

The delicious aromas made Blake's stomach growl.

"Amy," he said. "You shouldn't be here."

Two pairs of blue eyes looked at him with scorn.

"Why not?" Amy demanded.

Even though Darcy didn't speak, he read her silent echo of the words. "Aunt Betty's worried about you."

"Why?" Amy's question was blunt. "I can look after myself."

Both pairs of eyes turned back toward the bubbling pot from which came aromas of tomato and garlic. The smell was enough to drive a man mad.

"We're making chicken ziti," Amy said. "Right, Darcy?"

"That's right." Darcy flicked a glance toward Blake. "There's plenty. You're welcome to stay for lunch." She looked at Amy as she spoke, her gaze filled with such hunger Blake immediately forgot his appetite.

"Can we, please, Blake? Please?" Amy would have bounced off the chair if Darcy hadn't caught her.

When the two sisters looked at each other and giggled, Blake's insides filled with fire. He didn't want Amy to be hurt. "Aunt Betty will expect us. We have to go."

Amy pushed her bottom lip out so far he could have hung his hat on it. "I don't like what Aunt Betty cooks." She made a gagging sound.

Blake's stomach threatened to revolt at the thought of choking down another meal of unappetizing food. But staying here was not an option. "The food is perfectly adequate."

Darcy lifted Amy down. "You'd better go home. Thanks for your help."

Amy hugged Darcy. "I want to stay here."

Darcy hugged her back and laughed. "You just want to eat my food." But Blake saw the sheen of tears.

"Run along, pumpkin," he told Amy. "I'll be right there."

Amy slammed out of the door.

Blake waited until he heard her footsteps pounding away before he faced Darcy. "She shouldn't have been here."

Darcy gave him the same defiant stare Amy had. Great. This was going to be fun, dealing with two of them.

"Why not? She's my sister, and I have, need I remind you, joint guardianship of her."

"I can't imagine what Rob was thinking when he did that."

"Me either. Unless it was guilt."

"Guilt for what?"

"You'd never understand."

"Listen to me. Amy is going through a difficult time, and I don't want anything to make it worse. Besides, she didn't have permission to come here. I've been looking all over for her."

"So tell her to ask permission before she comes back."

"You just don't get it, do you? I don't want her visiting here."

Darcy succeeded in looking as if he'd slapped her. "No, *you* don't get it." She jerked her gaze away, turned the burners off, and wiped her hands on a towel. "I think we need to talk." Her eyes were as hard as her tone. "Why don't we sit at the table?"

He hesitated. He didn't want to spend any more time in this house than he had to. It was too full of memories—memories he couldn't afford to think about. He had far too many responsibilities to linger on the past. But she was right. They needed to settle this. The sooner the better. Then she could return to her vacation schedule, and he could get on with his work.

He crossed the floor and parked himself on the chair next to the patio doors.

"Coffee?" She began to pour a cup.

"No, thanks." He regretted his answer as she poured the coffee down the drain and sat across from him.

She studied her hands clasped in her lap, then slowly brought her gaze upward. Her generous smile caught him off guard. Maybe he'd misjudged her.

"You said you would tell Amy about me."

He shrugged. "Something came up."

As did her eyebrows at his excuse. "I see. No, actually, I don't. But it doesn't matter. I told her we were sisters."

He couldn't get rid of the churning, burning bile taste in his stomach. He had prayed for strength to deal with this. He was intent on trusting God. But all he had to do was sit across the table from her, look into her determined face, and his good resolutions fled like snow in a heat wave.

"I've left it to you to tell Amy about the guardianship order." She made it sound as if she'd done him a favor.

"I don't mean to tell her." Now when had he decided that? Why did this woman make him put his brain in park and drive with his errant emotions? He gave himself a mental shake. Nothing about this woman could be allowed to distract him from what really mattered—protecting Amy.

She stared at him. "Why not? Kids deserve the truth."

"What would be the point? Don't you see how stupid and useless it would be? You're leaving again in"—he glanced at his watch, hoping she would get the none-too-subtle hint that he hoped it would be very soon—"how long, did you say?"

"I didn't."

"What's to keep you here?" No need to remind her she wasn't interested in visiting when her father was alive. When she might have had a reason.

"Amy."

He planted his fists on the table as he leaned toward her. "What are you trying to do? Mess her up? She's had enough to deal with. She doesn't need a sister"—he sneered the word—"who is here today, gone tomorrow. Just leave her alone." He leaned back. "Leave us all alone."

She looked hurt and confused. *Nice touch,* he thought. *Try to make me feel sympathetic. But it's not going to work.* He relaxed as stubbornness set into her features. This emotion he understood.

"I want to get to know her better."

"Don't mess with her. She's just a kid."

"I'm not going to hurt her, if that's what concerns you. I know what it's like to be a kid and be disappointed by adults you care about."

The skin around his eyes tightened. "You keep suggesting you were a poor, helpless victim of some injustice. Sorry. I don't buy it. And I won't let you blame Rob, especially when he's not here to defend himself. You could have visited him anytime you wanted, but you didn't. How am I supposed to think you won't treat Amy the same way?" He pushed back from the table and stood over her. "Don't you think it would be best for everyone concerned if you let the lawyer look after arranging the sale of this house so you can get on with your vacation?"

She grabbed his wrist before he could escape. "Wait." An electric shock raced up his nerves at her cool touch. "I've decided to stay for a few days, so can't we be civil about this?"

He jerked away. "There is no room in my life for anything but my work and Amy. So if you're going to stay, I suggest you keep out of my way."

She huffed. "Like that's going to be a problem. But what about Amy?"

"What about her?"

"Is she going to be allowed to visit me?"

He glowered at her, matching her look for look. "Are you the least bit concerned with what's best for her?"

Again he caught a fleeting look of pain that made him feel like a heartless bully. Then she lifted her chin, and he wondered if he'd imagined it.

"Yes, I am. I see a little girl who's hurting from the death of her parents. I think I can help her." She didn't blink under his stare.

He felt himself dragged into the significance of what she said. As if she knew how to deal with loss. As if she knew the shape of pain. He stared out the window. If she did she had no one to blame but herself, and he was getting thoroughly sick of her suggesting it was Rob's fault. No disrespect to his own father, but Rob had been the best father a man could ask for.

"Unless you're afraid." Her soft voice rang with challenge.

"What would I be afraid of?"

She lifted one shoulder. "Are you sure it's Amy you're trying to protect? Or yourself? Maybe you can't handle the possibility she might find someone besides you to care about."

Anger stomped through him, indignant and hot. How dare she assign her motives to him? But he'd let her accusation go unchallenged if it gained him an advantage. And he knew exactly what he hoped to gain by ignoring her words. "I'll let Amy visit on one condition."

"Name it."

"When you leave you give up your guardianship."

She stepped back. "You can't be serious."

He had her cornered. "Aren't we talking about what's best for Amy?" He kept his voice soft, pressing his advantage. "You live in Seattle. How can you begin to think you could have input into her daily life?"

She turned her back to him, stirred the savory-smelling concoction. "You're right, of course." Her words were soft. "But I'm afraid I can't agree to your one condition." She swung around to face him, her expression fierce. "I will not lose my little sister. Not when I've just found her. And I won't let you keep us from enjoying each other."

He blinked and tried not to admire her guts in challenging him, even as anger chewed through his insides at her failure to agree to his very good plan. He closed his eyes for a moment and prayed for patience. Tons of it. Immediately.

"You have two weeks off?"

She nodded.

In two weeks she'd be gone and out of their lives. And if her past was any indication, they'd probably never hear from her again.

She suddenly grinned. "Do you realize I might be doing you a favor?"

He snorted. "How's that?"

"She's on spring break, right?" She barely waited for his nod. "Seems she could use a little more supervision." He started to protest even though he knew it was true. He just didn't need an outsider coming in and pointing it out. But she went on steadily, not giving him a chance to pull his thoughts into a coherent argument. "I can help keep her entertained." She shrugged as if to suggest the advantages were obvious. And even though he didn't want to agree, he knew she was right.

They stared at each other. He wouldn't blink first. Finally she smiled, a conciliatory gesture. Her eyes turned sunny blue. She was nothing like he'd expected. And it wasn't just her resemblance to Amy. It was the quickening of emotions that danced through her eyes before she could hide it. She seemed almost normally human with regular emotions, which he wouldn't have thought possible twenty-four hours ago. Something inside him yielded. He put it down to God showing him it was okay to give in on this.

"Two weeks, and then you'll be gone." It was more of an order than a question. Her smile fled, and he instantly regretted his harshness.

"I have to return to my job."

"I'll tell Aunt Betty that Amy has permission to come whenever she wants."

Darcy's eyes brightened. "Thank you."

He snickered. "You might not be thanking me in a few days, after you've had Amy barging in here like a runaway freight train whenever she feels like it."

Darcy shook her head, smiling widely. "You're wrong. I'll still be thanking you."

He wondered if her voice trembled just a tiny bit.

Chapter 4

Darcy pressed her arms across her stomach and stared out the window until she could no longer hear Blake's receding footsteps. Only then did she let the intermingling waves of pain, shock, rage, and grief wash over her. It was tempting to cry. To scream and rail against *her* loss.

She pulled herself together. She'd forgiven the past, her father's abandonment. She'd learned to lean on God as her strength and healer. But right now she couldn't seem to separate her faith from her feelings.

She hurried to the bedroom, pulled her cell phone from her purse, and punched in a familiar number. It rang twice before someone answered.

"Mrs. R. I'm so glad you're home. I hope I'm not bothering you. I need to talk to someone," she wailed.

The older woman chuckled. "You are never a bother."

Darcy smiled. Mrs. R always said the same thing, and Darcy always liked to hear it.

"How are you?" Mrs. R asked. "Or should I ask, where are you?"

"At the ranch where my father lived." She explained the events of the past day to her longtime friend and mentor, imagining her sitting in her big armchair, her salt-and-pepper hair in a wild disarray of curls, her Bible next to her, a notebook open on her lap as she made notes for her Sunday school class. Her gray eyes always so watchful and kind, as if every word Darcy uttered, even as an eager new Christian, mattered more than the next breath.

"Sounds like God has a purpose for your visit beyond the reading of a will."

"You mean Amy, don't you?" Darcy sighed. "She's a sweetie, for sure. And hurting."

"I don't just mean Amy, though I'm sure you'll be a real comfort to her. I mean you, dear. This can be a time of healing for you."

Darcy gripped the phone so hard it beeped a protest. "I thought I'd dealt with all this stuff about my father." At first she hated him and resented the new family, but it was a destructive emotion. Through Mrs. R's counseling and pointing Darcy toward God's love, she'd let all that go. "But being here and listening to Blake tell what a wonderful father he was—" She couldn't go on as pain pierced her soul.

"Forgiveness is a choice; healing takes time."

Darcy rocked back and forth. "I don't want to go back to all that stuff. I just want to move forward."

"That stuff, as you call it, will always be part of who you are, how you feel and react."

"You know what really hurts?"

"What, dear?"

"Blake thinks I should stay away from Amy." She repeated Blake's ultimatum. As she talked, she wandered into the kitchen and faced the slanting rays of the sun coming through the sunporch. "Amy and I clicked. To think I missed six years of her life. I will never forg—" She made herself stop as she realized the mistake of what she'd been about to say. Of course she forgave everyone concerned. She had long ago learned the futility of anything less. "I've missed enough of her life. I intend to enjoy every minute of my vacation with her."

"What happens when you have to go back to work?" Mrs. R asked softly.

Ahh. Something twisted in Darcy's gut as her friend's words echoed Blake's concern. "I guess we'll make some sort of arrangement." Perhaps both Blake and Mrs. R were right. Maybe she should move on now. After all, they didn't need her. They had each other. She had her life. But telling herself so didn't change how she felt. She wanted to be part of Amy's life. She needed to feel she mattered to Amy.

"I'll be praying for you to have wisdom and strength to deal with this situation." Mrs. R's words smoothed Darcy's emotions.

"Thank you. I don't know what will happen. I just know I won't walk away. I've been deprived of my little sister too long."

"And she's been deprived of you."

"Yes." Mrs. R made it sound like an equal loss. "I suppose you're right." Despite Blake's objections, Darcy knew there was something important about being a big sister. "I'll do my best for her while I'm here, and then we'll decide where to go from there." She took a deep breath. "Thanks as always, Mrs. R."

The older woman laughed. "When are you going to start calling me Olive?"

Darcy laughed, too. It was a long-standing joke between them. "When I'm older than you." She paused. "You know I like calling you Mrs. R."

The woman laughed. "You just like making me aware of my age."

Darcy chuckled. "You haven't aged a year in all the time I've known you. Nope, I just like you being Mrs. R, the woman who saw past my anger as a teenager and loved me into God's family."

"You were easy to love. Still are."

"Thank you." She hung up a few minutes later, feeling refreshed. She knew why she was here. Because of Amy. Not even Blake's resistance would make her leave.

She dragged a chair out to the sunroom and called Irene to bring her up to speed.

"He sounds like a nice man," Irene said after Darcy finished telling her all the news.

"Probably is, except he doesn't like me. In fact, he's made it clear he'd like nothing better than for me to leave ASAP. Or sooner."

"Want me to come out and persuade him otherwise?"

Darcy imagined Irene flexing her arms and laughed. "I'll call you if I need some muscle."

"Promise? He sounds like my sort of man."

Darcy made a choking noise.

"Don't say it," Irene warned.

Darcy took a deep breath and tried to sound bewildered. "What is it I'm not supposed to say?"

Irene sighed dramatically. "That I never met a man I didn't like."

They laughed together and chatted a few minutes longer. Darcy felt tons better after talking to two of her closest friends. With God's help she would find the grace to deal with this situation.

◆

Blake didn't go directly to the house. He was too upset to risk meeting Amy or Aunt Betty. Instead he went to the shop and began repairing the cultivator. Bad enough he was stuck with Darcy for two weeks. Now he had to sit back and let his little sister spend as much time as she wanted with the woman. How was Amy supposed to deal with all this? But his loyalty to Rob caused him the most confusion. He'd loved the man. He'd also trusted Rob totally and completely. A niggling doubt skidded over his thoughts. Until now. Yet, knowing Rob, he knew the man must have had a reason for bringing Darcy into their lives. Something more than the misguided guilt Darcy suggested.

He heard a shuffling sound and turned to see Amy in the doorway, her face folded into a scowl. He could no longer put off talking to her about Darcy. He leaned the hammer against the cupboard and wiped his hands on a rag. "Let's go see your cats."

She followed him without a word, although her mutinous expression spoke volumes. She was going to have some hard questions for him.

At the supply room he waited while Amy filled the cat dishes and murmured to the animals. He wasn't surprised to be excluded from her conversation.

When he and Amy were both sprawled comfortably on the floor, he asked, "What did Darcy tell you?"

She crossed her arms and plunked them over her chest. "She's my sister."

"Uh-huh."

"The house is hers."

"That's right."

She scooted away several inches. Blake told himself it was only Amy showing her displeasure, but the little gesture made it clear that no matter what Darcy did or said, it was going to affect the rest of them.

"How come you never told me about her?"

"There didn't seem to be any point. I never expected she'd ever come. She's never been here before."

"How come?"

"I really can't say." Though he had his own opinions. Too self-centered. Full of bitter unforgiveness. Jealous. Any or all of the above.

"How come Daddy didn't tell me about her?"

"I don't know." In hindsight he, too, wondered. But then Darcy had never given any of them any reason to include her in their lives.

Amy studied him hard, her expression thoughtful. "Is she your sister?"

"No. She's your half sister. Just like I'm your half brother." He tried to explain the convoluted relationship but wondered if it made sense to Amy.

She giggled. "You're half a brother."

He growled low in his throat. "I'm all here, thank you very much."

She tipped her head and looked serious. "How come you didn't want to see her before?"

He shrugged. He could hardly tell her his personal opinion of the woman—without natural affection or a normal sense of duty. "Guess I was too busy to think about it."

Amy harrumphed. "I don't think so."

He chuckled. "Like any of us have had time to run out to Seattle to look for her." He didn't expect Amy to understand how swamped he'd been. For years. Even before Rob got sick, his mother needed help. Seems there had been more work than they could catch up with for a long time.

"I would have gone to see her."

He knew Amy thought she was old enough to tackle anything in her path, but the idea of his little sister on her own made him smile.

"I would have," she insisted.

He ruffled her hair. "Good thing you won't have to. She's here for two weeks. You'll get plenty of chances to visit her." He hesitated. He had to prepare Amy for the inevitable. *Lord, give me wisdom. This situation is more than I know how to deal with.* He gave Amy a gentle look. "Just remember it's only a visit. Then she's leaving again. She lives a long ways away. You might not see her again"—he couldn't leave her without a speck of hope—"for a long time."

Amy sat back and stroked several of the cats who'd finished eating and wrapped themselves around her, purring. "Why can't she stay here?"

Already the regrets and shattered dreams. What would it be like after two weeks? He knew it wasn't going to be pretty. He leaned closer. "Listen to me, Amy. She's only here for a visit and then gone again. Don't start to think she will stay, or you're going to get hurt, and I don't want that."

Amy's eyes clouded. "But why can't she stay? She's my sister."

Blake rubbed the back of his neck. "She can't. She's got a job back in the city. She lives there. That's all." She couldn't live here. She wouldn't. And she'd likely forget Amy as soon as she left. Poor Amy. He was thankful there was no need to mention the guardianship thing. Darcy would probably forget it once she was back in Seattle. He was counting on it.

"Come on. Let's go have lunch." He stood and pulled her to her feet. "Want a horsey ride?"

She nodded soberly and climbed to his back. By the time he bounced her halfway across the yard, she was giggling. And he could breathe easy again.

His stomach rumbled as they went into the house. Aunt Betty's idea of lunch was canned tomato soup and grilled cheese sandwiches made with processed cheese between slices of anemic white bread. Sometimes they got a treat and had vegetable soup. Not that he was complaining. It was a perfectly good combination. But every day? It got a little tiresome. He'd bought other things, suggested a few alternatives, but Aunt Betty said she'd grown up with that menu every day and she saw no reason to change it.

Aunt Betty had the food out. She plopped her cat in the blanket-padded box at her feet.

Amy looked at Blake and rolled her eyes, then scowled at the cat who returned her glare with such a disdainful look that Blake shook his head. Amy and the cat hated each other.

Aunt Betty sat down and nodded at Blake to say grace. He had to pause a moment to feel thankful. After his prayer, he turned to his aunt. "Rob left the other house to his older daughter. She's there now."

Aunt Betty nodded. "Thought I saw someone down there."

"Amy has permission to visit her while she's here."

"I do?" Amy asked around her mouthful of sandwich.

Blake nodded. "As long as you don't make a nuisance of yourself. And remember what I told you. She's leaving in two weeks."

"Oh goody, goody, goody. We are going to have so much fun."

Aunt Betty sighed. "Can't say as I mind. Maybe it'll keep her out of trouble."

Blake wasn't sure Amy wasn't substituting one set of "trouble" for another.

"Amy, I'm going to take the four-wheeler and check the pasture fences this afternoon. Want to come along?" He probably wasn't playing fair. Riding the quad was one of Amy's greatest pleasures.

Amy shook her head.

He plunked his fists on the table and stared. Maybe she hadn't heard him. "You can come with me."

"I know." She stared at him, eyes wide.

"You never turn down a chance to ride with me."

"Can't I stay and see Darcy?"

He thought of saying no, but if he forced her to go with him she'd be miserable the whole time. "Sure. But remember. . ."

"I know." She sighed. "Two weeks."

◆

Blake didn't stay out as long as he'd originally planned. Normally he would have bummed a meal somewhere rather than return for supper. Any one of his neighbors would have welcomed him. Especially Norma Shaw, who'd been trying to get Blake interested in her daughter, Jeannie, since Jeannie came back to teach at the school. He might have been more interested if he wasn't already so busy he hardly had time to scrape the crud off his boots.

But Mrs. Shaw and her lovely daughter would have to wait. He was worried about Amy, restless at the thought of her being with Darcy all afternoon.

"Amy!" he called as he barreled into the house. "Ame, where are you?"

Aunt Betty came from her room, straight pins between her teeth. She removed them so she could speak. "No need to shout down the house. She's over with her sister." She waved the pins at him. "About time I had some peace so I could get these quilts done. Those children in Romania have nothing." She hurried back to her room and her quilting.

Blake wondered if it wouldn't be more charitable for Aunt Betty to give Amy as much of her time as she gave those nameless orphans she knitted and sewed for and for whom she attended endless meetings. He stood in the middle of the room and tried to decide what to do. He had no excuse to run over to the other house. Besides, he probably wouldn't fool Darcy. She'd know he was checking on her.

He had lots of work to choose from, but used to Amy hanging around demanding attention, he felt restless. It seemed he wasn't indispensable anymore. He reluctantly headed for the office. He was in a bad mood anyway; he might as well pay bills.

The box Blake had brought from the other house sat in the middle of the desk. It seemed like a good enough reason to put off the loathsome job of paying bills, but he'd already put it off far too long. He grabbed the box. Smiling up at him from among the books and his roping trophy was the photo of his mother and Rob. They'd all been so happy back then. He put the box in the closet, picked up the picture, and let the missing fill him. He swallowed hard, his eyes burning. He waited for the hurricane of emotions to pass. He looked around for a place to put the picture, saw the old photo of Darcy that Rob always kept on the shelf by the desk, grabbed it, and shoved it in the bottom drawer—an appropriate spot for it. She had no place on this ranch. He put up the picture of Rob and Mom, smiled at them, and sat down to pay bills, comforted by their presence.

Chapter 5

Suppertime approached. Blake welcomed the excuse to leave the desk, the bills, and the record keeping, almost as much as he welcomed the legitimate reason to take Amy from Darcy's house.

He stood in the afternoon sunshine and stretched. Spring was his favorite time of year. His fingertips hooked in the front pocket of his jeans, he headed across the yard. He heard them before he saw them, recognized Amy's throaty giggle. Then he heard an echoing giggle, sweet as a bird's song. Why did her voice tickle across his senses like music?

At the outside corner of the sunroom, he came to an abrupt halt.

Amy and Darcy sat cross-legged on a black and red blanket he recognized from the closet of the old house. Darcy looked like a flash of sunlight in a bright yellow T-shirt and matching striped pants that ended at her knees. Both the girls wore dandelion chains, piled on their heads like golden crowns and hanging around their necks like happy Hawaiian greetings.

Amy grasped a handful of yellow flowers and reached for Darcy, trying to brush the dandelion butter on her already-painted face.

Blake leaned against the wall and watched Darcy bat Amy's hands away, each time swiping a yellow streak across Amy's already very yellow cheeks.

Darcy ducked out of Amy's reach, laughing as she tumbled over. Amy rolled into Darcy's arms. She hiccupped and giggled. Darcy echoed her, and they exploded into louder giggles, punctuated firmly by more hiccups. Darcy wiped tears away, smudging the yellow into war paint.

As the sisters rolled around like playful puppies, giggling and hiccupping, he let a deep laugh boom out. *"A cheerful heart is good medicine."* Another of his mother's often-quoted Bible verses. How long since he'd enjoyed a belly laugh?

Darcy sat up, pushed Amy to her side, and met his gaze across the greening yard. Her eyes were as blue as summer skies, bright as the flash of running water in the sun, full of magic and fun and welcome and living. Life shared, blessed with the sharing.

Amy saw him, bounced over, and tackled his knees. He grunted and steadied himself without breaking eye contact with Darcy.

"Come play with us!" Amy demanded.

"What are you playing?" He couldn't pull his gaze from Darcy. He didn't want to. His heart bundled up inside his chest and demanded more. He wanted to discover the secret behind her flashing eyes.

Amy shook his legs to get his attention. "We're playing spring."

"With dandelions?" He couldn't help but smile at the amusement in Darcy's face.

She turned her expression suitably sober, but her eyes continued to remind him of all life offered to the brave and free. To someone who hadn't vowed to guard his heart against more loss and pain.

Darcy nodded seriously. "Dandelions are the official badge of spring. Proves it's finally here to stay."

"Funny," he murmured, still stuck in the spell of her gaze. "I always thought it was the meadowlark." As if on cue, a bird trilled from a nearby fence post, and they turned toward the sound.

"Can't be. Not everyone gets to enjoy a lark. But everyone gets dandelions."

He chuckled. "Glad you didn't say enjoy them or I'd have to argue."

She flashed him a quick smile. "I believe we've proven they can be enjoyed." She waved a bouquet of yellow blossoms. "If the world hands you dandelions, make crowns and celebrate."

Blake again fell into the promise of her gaze, the promise of enjoyment found in ordinary things, ordinary events turned into celebrations. Amy diverted his attention as she lifted a dandelion wreath from her head and offered it to him.

"Bend over and I'll give you a dandelion crown."

He hesitated.

"Aren't you glad for spring?" Amy said, disappointment thinning her voice.

He saw the challenge and curiosity in Darcy's look.

"New life, new hope, new beginnings." She spoke softly, her musical voice reminding him of the meadowlark's song. "The Lord's mercies are new every morning," she said. "I never feel it more true than on a fine spring day like this."

To disagree seemed heretical after that. He bent and let Amy place the yellow crown on his head, then sat on the corner of the blanket. Again he met Darcy's look. "I'm not doubting what you say about new life. . .or God's new mercies, but. . ." He struggled to find the words to explain a fragile thought just out of his reach. Slowly he formed it into words. "New doesn't mean you're free of the past."

She turned toward the bird, singing his heart out. "Look at him. He's sitting on an old, splintered post surrounded by a mud puddle. But his surroundings haven't quenched his spirit or muted his song."

"I guess not. Is that your philosophy? Ignore the past. Sing and dance and pretend it doesn't exist?"

She twirled a limp dandelion for a moment, then met his gaze.

He allowed himself a fleeting sense of disappointment that the warmth and fun in her eyes had fled, replaced by cool detachment, cautious defense.

"Some things a person can change. Others you just have to accept and move on or"—she paused—"or let them destroy you. I don't believe in letting the past and things I can't change or control rob me of the joy of the present." Her gaze turned to Amy.

Blake did not like the possessive look in her eyes.

She jerked back to face him. "Are we so different, really? Don't you have to move on from your loss and, dare I say, disappointment? Don't you have to choose to trust God for both the past and the future?"

He hadn't known she was a Christian, and despite himself he again fell into her gaze, knowing a click of instant connection based on their shared faith. He nodded slowly, his tongue thick and uncooperative. "I daily choose to trust God."

"Me, too." Her voice was soft as the dandelion Amy brushed against his chin.

She smiled, and he smiled back. A sense of something sweet and wonderful passed between them.

Amy hugged him, practically throttled him. "This is the happiest day of my life." She spun around and gave Darcy an equally exuberant hug.

Blake wanted to grab Amy and hold her on his lap. He wanted to keep her from Darcy. Keep her from being hurt. Yet he also wanted to capture the joy of this moment and lock it inside Amy's heart where she could pull it out after Darcy left and find comfort in it.

He stared at the green blades of grass poking up through the straw carpet of winter. He couldn't trust moments like this. They were too soon replaced by sorrow, loss, and regret. He pushed to his feet. "Come on, Amy. It's time to go home."

"Aww," Amy protested.

"You can come back anytime," Darcy assured her, and apparently cheered by that thought, Amy raced across the yard.

Blake felt Darcy's gaze on his back as he strode away. He felt as if he had been on a wild bull ride of emotions. For one exciting moment he'd let himself feel things he hadn't allowed in a long time—joy, connection, anticipation. But reality was the thump when the bull landed on all four feet, the thud jarring up his spine into the base of his head. Reality was the workload that threatened to become a living avalanche, the care of Amy, and protecting her from further hurt.

Amy waited for him at the house. He swiped at the yellow dandelion butter on her cheeks. "You'll have to scrub really good to get that off."

She nodded. "I don't mind."

"Amy—" How did he voice his fears without robbing her of the temporary joy? "Amy, remember. Two weeks and then she's gone."

Amy sighed dramatically. "She's the best sister in the whole world."

Blake's neck spasmed. Amy was going to be heartbroken. And he seemed powerless to prevent it.

◆

Darcy pulled on her running shorts and a wicking T-shirt. She laced up her running shoes and headed out. She pounded down the dirt trail. So far she'd run three directions from the ranch. To the north she'd discovered a field of pale purple crocuses. South, she passed three home sites. One with a beautiful cedar log house, one with a sprawling ranch-style house, and the third with a tiny two-story box of a house badly in need of painting with a rusting collection of machinery filling the yard.

Today she ran west and found a wide river. She dipped her fingers in the water and discovered it icy cold from the spring thaw.

She turned down the road toward the ranch and laughed again at the sign over the gate. BAR T RANCH. Did anyone stop to think *Bar T* sounded like "party"? And no one here seemed to know how to have fun. Work was the defining quality as far as she could tell. She ran early in the morning so she could spend the rest of the day with Amy. Despite being nineteen years older, Darcy couldn't remember ever knowing such joy in another person. Daily she thanked God for bringing Amy into her life.

But no matter how early she went for her run, she saw Blake either out in the fields or hurrying across the corrals in long strides as if he had no time to waste. Except for Sunday. She'd slipped into the service late, not wanting to encounter Blake's unfriendliness. She'd slipped out during the closing song.

She looked around now. Yup. There he was. Climbing onto a tractor. Already hard at work.

He saw her and waved her over.

She hesitated. She didn't have to be overly brilliant to realize he'd been avoiding her the past few days—since the day he'd found her and Amy making dandelion wreaths. And to think she'd felt there had been a little connection between them, had been certain they'd shared something warm and sweet. A touching of the spirit and soul. Acknowledgment of a similar faith.

But it just showed how wrong she could be. About all they shared were his dark looks. She'd had her fill of his scowling at her or watching her as if he expected her to steal the land out from under his feet. She could pretend she hadn't seen him, but he waved again and called something. No way she could escape. She changed direction and jogged across the field toward him.

"Can you drive a truck?" he asked as soon as she was close enough to hear him.

"Sure. Why?"

"With standard transmission?"

"I've done it a time or two. Not very often," she added hastily in case he thought she was an expert.

"Would you mind helping me?"

She blinked and suddenly grinned. "Me?" She pressed her palm to her chest. "You're asking me—the girl most likely to annoy you—to do you a favor?" She laughed at the expressions of frustration and resignation crossing his face and wondered at the incredible lightening of her heart that he should turn to her for help. "Clearly you wouldn't be asking if you weren't stuck, but still it feels good." She gave a wide look around. "You sure there isn't someone else you'd rather ask?" It was a lot of fun teasing him, especially when he rolled his eyes and looked pained. And incredibly handsome, framed against the sun-bright sky, his brown hair haloed with sunshine. He wore faded blue jeans and a white T-shirt.

"Rub it in. But I'm stuck."

She planted her fists on her hips and grinned widely. "I will be so pleased to help you." She knew her tone conveyed just how happy she was to have him at her mercy—if only briefly.

"Why do I get the feeling you're enjoying this way too much?" He stood on the tractor step, grinning down at her.

"It's just nice to be needed." She stared up at him, caught by the warmth in his dark eyes. He enjoyed the teasing as much as she! She realized how long they'd been grinning at each other and jerked her gaze away. "What do you want me to do?"

"Can you follow me in the truck? I have to bring home some bales."

"Done." She jogged over to the vehicle and started the motor. She managed to remember how to clutch. She found the gear and jackrabbited forward.

Blake sat behind the steering wheel of the tractor, shaking his head and grinning.

She flashed him an okay sign, then followed him across the field and along a muddy trail until they reached a field with big round bales on it. He stopped the tractor and held up his hands to signal her to stop, pretending to be afraid. At least she thought he pretended. Yup. He grinned as she jerked to a stop.

He jumped down and pulled her door open. "Been awhile, has it?" His voice rolled with mirth.

"You have no idea." She jumped out and hurried around to the passenger side while he slid behind the wheel.

Just then his cell phone rang. He pulled it from his breast pocket, flipped it open, and said, "Hello." Darcy could hear a shrill voice. "Hey, squirt. What's wrong?"

Amy. Even from across the cab of the truck she sounded upset. Darcy shamelessly listened to the conversation. As if she had a choice. She couldn't make out the words, but obviously Amy didn't like something.

"Amy, just do what she says."

More shrill sounds from the phone.

"You know you can't do that. Behave yourself." He listened, murmuring, "Uh-huh," several times.

The shrill sounds diminished, so Darcy heard only a drone.

"I can't come home right now. You be good, and I'll see you later." He broke the connection.

"Problems?" Darcy asked.

He kept his attention on the trail as they bounced back to the farm. At first she thought he wasn't going to answer; then he sighed deeply and rubbed his palm along the steering wheel. "Amy doesn't like obeying Aunt Betty. It's been hard on her having so many changes in her life."

"I—" She'd been about to suggest she could take over more of her care. But, as he said, Amy had dealt with enough changes. She could understand his concern about how her visit would impact Amy. How could she assure him it wouldn't when it was a fear she shared? How could she ever say good-bye to her little sister? Yet she didn't belong here. She wouldn't be able to stay once her vacation was over. "I've enjoyed getting to know her," she said instead. "She's a spunky little thing."

Blake laughed. "She's been like that from day one. Maybe even before. She came two weeks late. Mom said we should have known then that she would do things her own way in her own time."

Darcy leaned back, watching the pleasure on Blake's face and wishing she could have been part of this charming little girl's life from the beginning. She chomped down on the bitterness rising in her throat. It was pointless to blame people now dead. She knew the past could destroy her enjoyment of the present if she let it. And she wasn't going to.

Blake slanted her a look full of warmth and humor. She knew it was because his thoughts were on Amy, but she enjoyed the way it made her feel part of something special. "When she was too young to talk, she still made us all understand she had her likes and dislikes. The bottle had to be just the right temperature or she'd give us an annoyed look and refuse it." He shook his head and laughed. "She was never afraid to try things. She was so determined to walk she was fearless. No matter how hard she fell, up she got and right back at it. She had bruises from head to toe. We used to worry someone would report us to the authorities."

"You sound as if you were very involved with her from the beginning."

His smile fled. "Mom was sick. She didn't know until after she got pregnant that her heart wasn't up to it. I guess she'd had some sort of virus infection that damaged it."

Darcy saw him stiffen and knew he was dealing with his private pain.

"She never recovered from having Amy. Yeah, I was there a lot, trying to make things easier for her."

Darcy stared out the window, trying not to imagine an attentive, supportive Blake. Trying not to think how her life had been the opposite. She'd learned early to stand on her own two feet and not expect anyone to be there to help her. Her mom was too busy working, too restless.

They moved so often she had no close friends.

Her father had conveniently forgotten her. She had no siblings. Except now she did. She had Amy.

Blake sighed deeply. "Rob once said Amy reminded him of you. He said you were ornery as a child, too."

As a child. He remembered her as a little girl, but he didn't know her as an adolescent, an adult. And now he never would.

They stopped beside the machinery shed. He leaned his left arm on the steering wheel and studied her, his expression faintly amused. "I guess I should have been prepared that you would resist everything I suggested."

She ducked her head, unable to face his look without feeling disoriented. She didn't know if it was regret, unfulfilled wishes, or something else, but a deep longing created a hole in her thoughts. "I hope I've learned to pick my battles," she murmured.

Blake laughed, and she looked up to see his face creased with amusement. "I think you mean that to sound mature and reassuring, but I get the feeling it could also be a warning. If you want something bad enough, you're prepared to fight for it. Right?"

Surprised by the approval in his eyes, she could only nod.

He squeezed her shoulder. "You and Amy are a lot alike."

Her lungs tightened at the warmth of his big, work-hardened hand on her. Blood pulsed in her cheeks. Just when she thought she'd pass out from lack of oxygen, he pulled his hand away.

"Thanks for your help." He jumped from the truck and headed around to her side.

She shoved the door open and slid out before he could help. With a muttered good-bye she headed for her safe little house.

Chapter 6

Blake watched her jog across the yard. The first time he'd seen her running, he thought it was an animal. He'd stared at her loping across the landscape, as smooth and graceful as any deer he'd seen. Her long legs ate up the miles. He tried to calculate how far she went every morning, but it didn't seem possible she ran more than five miles before breakfast.

But right now he didn't have time to watch Darcy. He had a ton of work to do. Some of it should have been done last fall, but with Rob sick and... Well, it just hadn't been done, and now he was playing catch-up.

He hooked up the flat deck and drove back to the tractor. He spent the morning loading bales and hauling them home. Normally he lost himself in the rhythm of work, finding a soothing release from worries and concerns, but not today. Each time he drove into the yard, he glimpsed Darcy. First washing the windows of the old house, polishing the place like a diamond. Didn't she realize it would probably be left uninhabited when she left? Unless he rented it out. Might not be a bad idea.

Next trip she sprawled on a new chaise lounge, a small table at her elbow, a book propped in her hands. The life of luxury. A word he hardly recognized. She disappeared from his line of vision, and he pushed away the weary ache behind his eyes.

Next time he passed, Amy sat beside her. They seemed to be busy looking at Amy's feet. Had she hurt herself? He almost braked. But then the sisters looked at each other and laughed. What were they up to? He wanted to stop and see, but he'd never get these bales home if he didn't keep at it. He studied Darcy's face. She always looked so happy, so cheerful. Even when he came down hard on her, she maintained her sense of humor. Driving by, he suddenly felt old and sour. Where was the mindless calm he usually got from working?

His stomach rumbled as the noon hour approached. But he didn't have time to stop for a regular meal. He snorted. When was the last time he'd enjoyed such a thing? He grabbed his cell phone. "Aunt Betty. I'll just pick up a couple of sandwiches when I go through the yard."

She didn't offer any opinion about his decision. Probably busy taking care of that ragged old cat of hers. The poor thing should have been put out of its misery years ago, but Aunt Betty nursed Missy along, giving her regular shots for diabetes and fixing her a special diet. The cat was fed better than he and Amy. Small wonder Amy hated the animal.

He blew out his lips. Life used to be so easy. Do his work. Enjoy his little sister. Enjoy meals his mom cooked or the ones he cooked in the house Darcy now owned.

He stopped to pick up his lunch. Darcy and Amy sat under the sprawling elm tree where Amy liked to play. A circle of stuffed animals surrounded them, and they giggled as Darcy made a tiny bear dance and talk.

Amy saw him and raced to his side. "Blake, see how pretty my toes are." She rocked back on her heels and tipped her toes upward, every nail painted a different color.

Blake laughed. "Rainbow feet."

"Yup. And now we're having a tea party with my animals."

"So I see. Have you eaten?"

She nodded solemnly. "Every bite."

"What was it today—tomato or vegetable?"

"Tomato." She raced back to Darcy and plunked down cross-legged in front of her. "Make Tiny Tim again."

Hesitating, Darcy shot Blake a wary look.

"Go ahead." Blake grinned. "I'd like to see Tiny Tim."

She huffed. "You just want to mock me."

He pressed his hand to his chest. "Me? I promise I won't mock you. A Tiny Tim imitation is quite a challenge."

She raised her eyebrows, then turned and picked up a red, loose-limbed bear. Her voice high and quivering, she swayed the animal back and forth and sang "Tiptoe Through the Tulips." Amy giggled and held up a brown bear.

"What's wrong with your voice?" she said in her best gruff bear voice.

Tiny Tim stopped dancing and squeaked, "What's wrong with *your* voice? Can't you talk normal, like me?"

Amy struggled to control her giggles, then moved her bear face-to-face with Tiny Tim. "You're very sick. You should see a doctor."

Darcy laughed and ruffled Amy's hair. "You're way too smart for Tiny Tim. He doesn't know what to say about that." Her eyes glistening with amusement, she shot a look toward Blake.

Grinning back, he felt a jolt of shared enjoyment of Amy.

Amy scooted over and climbed into Darcy's lap. "Was Tiny Tim really real?"

"He sure was. My mom used to sing his song when she was happy."

Blake needed to get back to work, but he couldn't tear himself from this cozy scene. Much as he hated to admit it, Darcy was good with Amy. Perhaps even good *for* Amy. She'd stopped moping about the house, complaining she had nothing to do. Of course, Darcy kept her amused with painting toenails and playing make-believe. But even he, despite his reluctance, could see the two shared a special connection. He spun away.

"What made her happy?" Amy's question stopped him. He turned back to the homey scene, wanting to hear Darcy's answer. He wanted to know why her expression had suddenly grown sad.

"Moving. She loved to move."

Amy shifted, getting more comfortable. "I never want to move."

Darcy laughed. "I might get tired of sitting like this."

"No. You won't."

Darcy looked at Blake and shook her head. "If Amy doesn't want it, it just isn't going to happen." They shared a secret smile.

Amy jumped to her feet and waved her arms in a big circle. "This is where I live. I'll never leave." She raced up to Blake. "Right, Blake? We'll always live here."

"That's right." He watched the way Darcy's gaze turned toward the house she now owned, her expression surprised. "This ranch has belonged to the Thompsons for four generations," he added for good measure.

"Am I a Thompson?" Amy demanded.

"You're a Hagen," he said.

"I want to be a Thompson."

"I guess, seeing as you're my sister, you're almost a Thompson."

Darcy brought her dark blue gaze back to him. "I've never had a house of my own."

"Enjoy it while you can." His voice was brittle. No way could she even think of changing her mind about the way things were going to be settled. "Gotta go, squirt." He hurried inside, grabbed the now-cold grilled sandwiches wrapped in plastic and headed back to work, mentally listing the number of trips left to make in order to clear the field, then planning the spring work. Stuff that kept him from thinking about anything else, especially emotional stuff.

But that nasty little feeling of impending danger wouldn't leave him.

Amy was going to be hurt when Darcy left. They just didn't need any more pain around here. He meant Amy, of course. No one else would be hurt when Darcy disappeared again as he was sure she would. *Lord, keep Amy from being hurt. Help me know how to protect her.*

◆

"I like to do jigsaw puzzles," Amy said in response to Darcy's questions about the things she did. Darcy yearned to know everything about her little sister. Much would remain hidden in the years she'd missed, but she discovered that Amy, in first grade, could already read very well. She loved make-believe and had a whole bunch of cats, but she couldn't have one in the house because of "Aunt Betty's stupid old cat."

"You want to do a puzzle with me?" Amy asked.

"I'd love to."

Amy grabbed her hand. "Come on. I have to keep them in my bedroom 'cause Aunt Betty says they're too messy."

Darcy hesitated. She'd never been invited into the other house but was dying to see where Amy and Blake lived—no, she scolded herself, she only wanted to see where Amy lived. She had no interest in Blake. Never mind that she could inventory his entire outfit: a faded blue plaid shirt with the sleeves torn off, giving her lots of opportunity to admire work-muscled, sun-bronzed arms. Equally faded blue jeans, worn almost white across the knees. A wide leather-banded watch drawing attention to his masculine wrists. Cowboy boots, originally tan in color, she guessed, now scuffed to the color of dirt. Maybe the boots gave him the rolling gait. To top off the picture, he wore a black cap, the bill curled into a trough. It sat back on his head at a jaunty angle. The girls in the office would drool so bad they'd need bibs. If someone chose him as the poster boy for a tourism ad, Montana would be overrun with women of every age.

"Come on, Darcy." Amy tugged at her hand.

"I'm coming." She let Amy lead her into the house. Darcy stared in disbelief as she stepped into an open area that appeared to serve as cloakroom, back entry, and general storage. Aunt Betty considered jigsaw puzzles to be too messy? Darcy would have been more concerned Amy would lose pieces in the jumble. Of course, it was the back entrance on a busy ranch. Maybe the rest of the house was neater. Cleaner.

Amy tugged her into a big modern kitchen. Darcy had to strain to imagine the black granite counter beneath the clutter and struggled to picture the stainless steel appliances gleaming.

A woman stood next to the fridge—no doubt Aunt Betty in the flesh. Darcy had managed to glean a bit of information about the older woman. Blake's mother's aunt, she had apparently left her little house in town to help Blake with Amy when Darcy's father became ill—after what, Darcy guessed from Amy's comments, was a succession of unsatisfactory nannies.

◆

Aunt Betty opened a can of something that smelled decidedly fishy. Without glancing in their direction, she scooped the contents into a thick china bowl and bent to offer it to an animal. Darcy shuddered as she saw Aunt Betty's cat. The animal had long, shaggy hair.

Amy tried to drag Darcy from the room, but Darcy cleared her throat, determined to greet the woman who had the responsibility of caring for Amy.

"Hello. You must be Amy's aunt Betty. I'm Darcy."

Finally the woman turned and nodded. "I've heard about you." She studied Darcy frankly.

Didn't that sound friendly? Darcy returned the stare, seeing a woman far older than she'd imagined. Probably in her seventies. Steely gray hair cut in a short no-nonsense, no-fuss hairdo. No makeup. Did women that age even use the stuff? Eyes, dark like Blake's. Suddenly the woman smiled, and the sternness fled.

"About time we had someone younger and more energetic around the place. I don't mind admitting I'm not up to running after a six-year-old. The way I look at it is I've done my share of child rearing. And now I have my own interests." She dropped her gaze to Amy. "Did you bring your laundry down?"

"Forgot," Amy mumbled.

"Well, remember." Aunt Betty nodded briskly and turned back to stroking the cat.

This time Darcy allowed Amy to drag her away. She managed a glimpse into the living room as they passed. Cluttered with books, papers, and pieces of mismatched furniture. Upstairs, Amy's bedroom was as messy as the rest of the house.

Amy rushed over to a table and spread out a half-dozen puzzles. "Which one you want to do?"

"Let's get your laundry before you forget again." There seemed to be plenty of it, lying limply on the floor and bed. Darcy began to gather up the soiled clothes, piling them at the doorway as Amy groaned her protest.

"Let's make your bed. Are there clean sheets somewhere?"

"In the closet."

"Can you show me?"

With Amy's help she found the linen closet in the hall, just beyond a room with an open door. She glanced in. Black jeans hung over the back of a brown wooden chair, and a pair of shiny black leather cowboy boots stood as if Blake had just stepped out of them. His room smelled like grass and lemons and leather. Darcy could picture him pulling on jeans, brushing his hair with the brown-handled brush on the long dresser. She jerked away and selected a set of clean sheets.

Another door, closed, stood at the end of the hall. "Who sleeps there?"

Amy went to the door and opened it, hovering at the threshold. "Mommy and Daddy did. But I don't remember Mommy."

Darcy, curious, joined her at the doorway. It was a simple room, the bed neatly made with a forest green duvet, an earthy-colored area rug in the middle of the hardwood floor. A large framed photo of the farm hung next to the closet.

Over the bed was a picture of the four of them—her father, Amy's mother, Amy, and Blake—looking like the perfect family. Amy must have been about two. Darcy could see the older woman already showed evidence of her failing heart in the dark shadows under her eyes. And Blake's look of adoration and determination showed he'd already shouldered his protective stance. She tried not to see how her father leaned over them, obviously loving them so much he could forget he had another daughter somewhere. One who'd been forced to grow up without that sort of love and acceptance. She looked into his blue eyes so much like her own and Amy's. She didn't realize they shared that with their father. Or had she pushed away the knowledge? She crushed the pile of linen to her chest and pushed resolve deep into her being. She'd learned a long time ago how to survive without her father. The only thing he'd ever given her was Amy.

She smiled down at her sister rocking back and forth on her heels, studying her painted toenails. "Let's go make your bed."

Amy talked as Darcy stripped the soiled sheets from the bed and remade it. The laundry pile grew larger as she added the sheets and socks she'd found tangled in the bedclothes.

"My favorite is the kitty puzzle. Do you want to put it together with me?" Amy asked, impatient with the delay.

"I'll make you a deal."

Amy looked wary. Darcy laughed. The kid had already figured out Darcy wouldn't be happy until the room was clean. She decided to sweeten the offer. "I'll do two puzzles with you if you help me pick up all these toys."

Amy gave her an annoyed look that made Darcy laugh again; then she screwed her face into an equally annoyed look, silently challenging her little sister. Amy pulled her lips down even harder, and then she laughed. "Okay."

Soon the room was neat, the shelves filled with books and toys, and the stuffed animals piled in the hammock attached to the wall. Darcy would have liked to dust and vacuum, as well, but a deal was a deal. Amy had done as agreed. So would she.

Two hours later they had finished all six of Amy's puzzles. Amy yawned. "Want to see my cats? They're lots prettier than Aunt Betty's ugly old thing."

"Sure." She scooped up the heap of laundry as she followed Amy downstairs. "Show me where the laundry room is, and I'll dump this stuff."

Amy led her to a bright sunshine-yellow room off the kitchen, and Darcy dropped her armload on the floor next to another pile. Seemed Aunt Betty wasn't in a big hurry to tackle the job. "I'll put a load in before we go outside," she told Amy.

The washer was full, and so was the dryer. She pulled out four pairs of Blake's jeans. Her face felt hot and prickly as she folded them and stacked them on the dryer, then blindly emptied the washer. By the time she sorted out the whites and dropped them in the machine, she'd convinced herself just how foolish it was to think about doing this on a daily basis.

◆

They stepped into the barn, and Amy turned left into a room. Darcy breathed the strange smells—a combination of mushroom, ammonia, and some kind of disinfectant.

Cats sprang from every corner and raced in from the rest of the barn, meowing and wrapping around Amy, who plunked to the floor so they could crawl over her. She made sure to pet each one.

Darcy stopped at the doorway, reluctant to enter what was obviously Blake's domain. The whole room bore signs of his labors, carried hints of his scent, and gave her a warm, cozy feeling. She pictured him coiling ropes with his strong hands, hanging the leather halters on hooks, and smiling the secret pleased smile she'd glimpsed a time or two.

"Fatty isn't here," Amy said. She pushed the cats away and hurried to a wooden box. "She's had her babies. Look!" Amy almost screamed in her excitement.

Avoiding the cats tangling around her feet, Darcy hurried to see. "Ohh. They're so little. I've never seen brand-new kittens. Can I hold one?"

Amy looked deadly serious. "You better let me get one. Fatty knows me and won't mind if I touch her babies."

The mother cat meowed a warning as Amy lifted out a tiny black kitten and carefully transferred it to Darcy's cupped hands. The kitten nuzzled about, helpless and blind. Such tenderness engulfed Darcy that tears stung her eyes. "It's so tiny. I never imagined." She'd never seen a kitten that wasn't bouncing around playfully.

A cow in the barn lowed. A deep voice spoke soothingly.

"It's Blake." Amy raced to the door and yelled, "Blake! Blake! Fatty had her kittens! Come and see!"

Darcy didn't want Blake to witness how a tiny kitten made her feel mushy and protective. And helplessly vulnerable. Her reaction to the kitten was mixed up with regret at so many things—an odd emptiness she couldn't explain but which had been growing steadily the last few days. It sucked at her insides like a hungry yawn. She couldn't let herself be swallowed into that chasm. It frightened her. It mocked her. It made her want to run back to her own house, curl up under a fuzzy blanket, and pull it over her head until she felt warm and secure. *Lord, please give me Your peace.*

"Let's have a look." Blake saw Darcy and smiled. She pulled in a gulp of musty air and found calmness. The world righted itself.

He crowded close to her and bent over the box, murmuring soft words to the mother cat, telling her what a fine job she'd done. "Five of them. Amy, if this keeps up, you'll have to get a job to pay for their feed."

Darcy recognized his teasing, but Amy took him seriously. "I can help you, and you could pay me just like you do Cory when he comes over."

Blake chuckled and ruffled her hair. "I was kidding. I think we can afford a bag or two of cat food." He picked up a mottled kitten, cupped it in his palm, and held it at eye level, chuckling when the tiny thing snuffled at his thumb.

Darcy thought she would choke at the sight of his large hands holding the kitten so gently. She turned away, pretending to study the kitten she still held. How silly to let five animals, each no bigger than a mouse, trigger so many emotions.

Blake returned the kitten to the box, murmuring reassurances to the mother cat, and then he stroked the one Darcy held, his fingers brushing hers. Her heart danced with a hundred different reactions. A longing for the tenderness he revealed. An ache to be protected the way he protected his loved ones. The need to belong to her father's heart as Blake had. She tightened her muscles to keep from jerking away, offering a silent prayer that she'd keep things straight in her head.

"All healthy and strong," he said. "Guess we'll have to keep them all, won't we, squirt?"

Amy nodded. "I'll take good care of them. I promise."

Brother and sister studied each other intently. A silent understanding flashed between them. Blake grinned. "I know you will." He glanced at his watch. "You'd better go get washed up for supper. I'll be there as soon as I look after a cow." He flashed Darcy a grin as he headed out of the room.

It wasn't until he disappeared from sight that Darcy could get enough air into her lungs to stop the dizzy feeling that descended at the way the casual brush of his fingers on hers had started a storm of emotions.

A few minutes later she and Amy parted ways, and Darcy headed for her house. She dropped to the old sofa and pulled around her a beige afghan she'd found in the narrow linen closet.

Her insides felt jumbled. She didn't like it. She had long ago learned some emotions were best ignored. Maybe she'd become too efficient at turning them off because it scared her to see the tip of so many unexplained feelings poking through the edges of her carefully constructed life. Part of her demanded she pack her bag and continue with her vacation right now before something erupted she didn't want to deal with. Another part, one she hardly recognized, demanded she stay and find out what lay beneath the surface. Truthfully, giving up her vacation didn't seem like a hardship. Not in the least. The ranch was a nice place to spend her time. The scenery superb. She pretended she meant the rolling hills and the distant mountains and the glorious sunsets, but all she pictured was Blake striding across the yard, adjusting his cap against the sun, hunkering down to touch the kittens, or ruffling Amy's hair.

Her chest felt as if something hot and heavy descended on it, making it almost impossible to breathe.

Okay, sure, she'd admit Blake was good-looking. In fact, she ought to buy one of those disposable cameras and take some pictures for the girls back at the office. But she wasn't interested in him that way. She couldn't be because of the wall of resentment that he'd been the one her father chose. She'd seen the look on her father's face in the picture hanging over his bed.

She'd also seen the look of tenderness in Blake's expression as he held the tiny kitten and ruffled Amy's hair.

She threw aside the afghan and jumped to her feet. This was ridiculous. There was no room for her here.

◆

The next morning, as Darcy tied her running shoes, she watched Blake drive away. She spent the day with Amy, admiring the new kittens and playing pretend under the trees. After Amy reluctantly returned to her house for supper, Darcy headed for town.

She got enough supplies for the next few days and bought herself a large pot of flowers to put in the sunroom. If she were staying longer, she'd be tempted to redecorate it like an Italian villa with lots of wrought-iron furniture, some big pots of plants, and a few statues. She poked through the display in the hardware section. But she wasn't staying, so what was the point?

She would hate to sell her house. Perhaps she'd change her mind and keep it. She could use it for a vacation home. The girls at the office would be thrilled to share it with her. They could admire Blake firsthand.

Her insides knotted at the idea. She didn't want any of them drooling over him. She blinked. Was that jealousy? How absurd. How primitive. How infantile. She didn't even know how she felt about him. She'd enjoyed some fun moments with him. She'd been touched by the evidence of his soft side, but it was all mixed up with the thought he was the one her father chose while she was the one left out.

As she drove back toward her house, she saw a boxy gray car parked in front. She grabbed the wheel with both hands. She didn't know anyone who'd be visiting. Had she locked the door when she left? She'd been getting careless about it. Had Blake seen the car drive up?

A quick glance toward the barn and she knew Blake hadn't returned. Her shoulders sagged when she saw Aunt Betty drumming her fingers on the wheel, Amy bouncing up and down on the seat beside her. What was going on? She barely turned off the motor of her vehicle before Amy burst from the gray car and headed toward her. Darcy opened the door so she could hear her.

"Aunt Betty wants to know if I can stay with you."

"Of course." She grabbed her bags and headed toward the older woman, who rolled down her window.

"Blake was supposed to be back ages ago. He knows I have my sewing circle tonight. I told him from the beginning I wasn't going to give up my own interests, and he assured me I wouldn't have to. Now look what's happened. I'm going to be late, and he's nowhere to be seen." Aunt Betty frowned so deeply her face turned into a topographical map. "Seems like all he can think about is his work. Men can be so blind sometimes." She gave a mirthless smile. "If you don't mind watching Amy until he gets home. . ."

"Not at all." But she doubted Aunt Betty heard her as she shoved the car into gear and drove away.

Darcy laughed. "Can't imagine getting that excited about sewing."

Amy crowded to her side. "She made me go with her once. It's a bunch of old ladies sitting around talking. B–o–r–i–n–g. Then she got mad when I found some old books. I didn't mean to upset them on the floor."

"Of course you didn't." But Darcy could guess Aunt Betty wouldn't be anxious to take a restless child with her again. "Come on. You can help me put away groceries, and then I have to make my dinner. You can help if you want."

Amy ran ahead and threw open the door. Darcy promised herself she'd be more careful to lock it in the future. She set the groceries on the counter. Amy peered into the bags.

"Vegetables. Didn't you get any good stuff?"

"You'd be surprised how good vegetables taste when I'm finished with them."

Amy turned big eyes toward Darcy. "Whatcha gonna have?"

"Stir-fry steak. Have you eaten?"

Amy made a gagging sound.

Darcy leaned down to eye level. "Why do you do that?"

" 'Cause I hate macaroni."

Darcy hated to pump Amy for information about what went on in the other house, but she wondered about this unusual reaction every time Amy was asked about dinner. "Why do you hate macaroni?"

Again that gagging sound and Amy covered her mouth. Darcy got the distinct impression Amy's reaction wasn't fake. "It's all sticky. It tastes like—" She pressed her fingers to her mouth again.

"But surely there's something else to eat? What about potatoes or rice, vegetables or meat?"

"Aunt Betty says she doesn't like cooking."

The picture Darcy got was distressing. "How often do you get macaroni?"

"All the time."

Darcy made up her mind. "Why don't you help me cook my dinner, and then you can share it with me."

Amy looked doubtful. "Is it only vegetables?"

"And steak and rice. Has Blake eaten?"

"He didn't come home yet."

Darcy decided then and there to save some of the meal for Blake, ignoring the tremor of excitement the thought gave her.

But hours later Amy slept on Darcy's bed, and Blake still hadn't shown up. Darcy worked up a good head of steam as she waited. Finally the truck drove up to the other house. Blake went inside, emerged a few minutes later, and headed toward her place. Before he reached the steps, she had the steak strips frying. She could at least feed him before she tore a chunk out of his flesh.

◆

At Darcy's invitation Blake stepped into the kitchen, his taste buds shifting into overdrive at the aroma of frying steak. Seeing her tight smile, he paused. Why did he get the feeling she was displeased? She couldn't possibly have a reason. He hadn't even seen her since yesterday in the supply room. He'd been far too busy.

First a cow had needed to be moved home so he could doctor her. He didn't like how thin she'd grown. Then he'd spent the better part of the day fixing fences. Some idiot cut the wires in several places—probably for the pleasure of snowmobiling last winter. Little did they care about the work and the dangers they caused. If he missed a spot, his cows could wander away. Even onto a road.

He and Rob had built that fence together, and as he repaired it memories assaulted him. Good memories, but still hard to deal with. It was one of those days when he missed the man so much it felt like a giant toothache.

And then Matt, the neighbor to the south, called to say someone left a gate down and their herds were mixed up. They'd worked until dark to part the cows into the right pastures.

On his drive home he'd been aching for a soft place to stretch out. He'd decided he was too tired to eat. Leftover macaroni had all the appeal of. . .

But as Darcy stirred the meat, his stomach gnawed at his backbone. He was hungry enough to eat anything. He quickly amended that. Anything but macaroni.

"You have Amy here?"

"She's sleeping on my bed. I've saved you some supper."

He swallowed hard. He couldn't tear his gaze away from the pan on the burner. "Sounds good, but I have to warn you I'm starving."

"There's lots." She scooped out the meat and dropped in a colorful array of vegetables. "Have a chair." She tilted her head toward the table.

He sat where he could watch Darcy. She moved with a smoothness reminding him of her grace when she ran. She was a woman easy on the eyes. He leaned forward, his forearms on the table. When had his feelings toward her shifted from antagonism to admiration? Perhaps when she'd been such a good sport about helping him? Or when she made him laugh as she played with Amy? Or seeing the gentle way she held the newborn kitten? When she'd shared bits about her faith? The jolt when his fingers had brushed hers as he stroked the kitten in her hand, the awareness of something far more than physical? To be honest, all of them made him open his eyes a little wider.

She pulled a bowl of fluffy rice from the microwave and put it in front of him, handed him a plate, waited until he'd scooped out a generous portion of the rice, and then slid the stir-fry mixture on top. He could barely swallow the saliva back fast enough.

"Go ahead. I hope you enjoy it."

His mouth was already too full to answer.

"Can I make you coffee or tea?"

"I'll take a glass of water if you don't mind."

She filled a tall glass with ice water and set it before him.

"Sit with me and talk."

"Okay." She sounded wary.

He gave her a good hard look. Did his presence remind her of all that wrong stuff she believed about Rob? He longed to clear up her misunderstanding. "I couldn't stop thinking of Rob today."

"Strange. I never thought of him once."

She obviously hadn't thought of him in years, but he didn't voice his thoughts. They'd been over that territory already. He needed to come at it from a different angle. "How come your mother and Rob got divorced?"

She blinked with surprise. "Because he left us."

"But why? There must have been some reason."

"Yeah. He didn't care about us."

Blake shook his head. "I don't buy that. That wasn't Rob. He was a devoted father."

"Huh. Try being a little kid wanting to understand." She leaned back into her chair and looked disinterested.

Blake couldn't tell if she pretended the look or if it was real, honed from years of believing what she said. "You need to get over your prejudice. It keeps you from seeing the truth."

Her eyes narrowed. "The truth about what?"

"About Rob."

"Blake, the truth is it appears he was a good father to you and Amy. But you have to accept he walked out when I was five and never once came to see me."

"It's a long ways from here to Seattle, and he was busy getting the ranch back on solid ground."

"A convenient excuse."

He hated to admit the reality of her words. Why hadn't Rob visited his elder daughter? He couldn't imagine treating Amy that way. "Why didn't you visit him?"

"Because I couldn't face any more rejection."

Did he detect her lips trembling? She clasped her hands together on the table, squeezing them hard enough to turn her fingertips red. He ached for the pain she constantly denied. He wrapped his hand around her cold fists.

"I'm sorry," he said.

She gaped at their hands, then slowly lifted her gaze to his face, her expression guarded, questioning.

"Sorry you've been hurt."

Her eyes turned cloudy. She looked so vulnerable he wanted to kiss her. Drive away all that uncertainty about being loved. This woman was made for loving. He'd seen it in the way she touched Amy, making her laugh, cuddling her at every opportunity. She was a woman full of grace and beauty. He saw it every time he watched her run. He saw it now in her trembling lips and the catch in her breath. He swallowed hard. "I'm sorry you missed having Rob as a father." His voice turned husky. "Sorry it's now too late to change things." He leaned forward, intent on capturing her mouth and kissing away all her hurt.

She jerked her hands away and sat up straight. Her eyes went from wide and warm to narrow and hard in a blink. "You're right. I can't undo the past. But I can speak to the present. You can't keep running from reality, burying yourself in your work."

Feeling as if he'd been thrown into an icy stream, Blake jerked back. "What are you talking about?"

"You're always working. Like a man possessed." She paused. "Or trying to outrun something."

"What? We were talking about you," he said. "Besides, I'm not running from anything. The pure and simple fact, for your enlightenment, is the ranch has been neglected for the better part of a year. I don't know what it's like in the city. Out here, if someone doesn't do the work—meaning me—it doesn't go away." He was on a roll. She'd hear all the hard realities of his life before he stopped. "It sits there waiting until I do it. So with a little imagination you can see I have twice as much work to do as normal." He glowered at her in angry defiance. "You make it sound as if I'm making excuses to be away from the house." Not for the world would he admit, even to himself, that he did prefer to be out working to being around the house, dealing with the constant reminder of the death and dying of the past several months. "The work has to be done. I have no choice." He told himself those words daily.

"I have no idea how much work you have to do or how long it takes." She shrugged as if it didn't matter. "But I do know a couple of things. First, you can't bury your emotions forever."

"You didn't hear a word I said. Listen to me: I am not burying myself in work. In fact, if anything, the work is about to bury me."

She barely flicked an eyelid as she waited for him to finish, then went on as if he hadn't spoken. "Second, you have busied yourself almost out of Amy's life."

"You don't know—"

She held her palm toward him, ignoring his interruption. "Who would be spending time with her if I weren't here? You say she's well provided for, but"—Darcy leaned close, her eyes bright and challenging—"she needs more from you than a roof over her head. She needs your time and attention."

"You met Amy only a few days ago. What do you know about her needs?"

She returned him stare for stare. "I know what it feels like not to matter enough for someone important in my life to give me a few hours of his time."

They glared into each other's eyes, both breathing hard.

He shook his head. How had this deteriorated from wanting to kiss her to feeling an urge to strangle her?

He pushed to his feet. "Where's Amy? I'm taking her home."

She led him into the bedroom. He scooped his little sister into his arms. She smacked her lips twice, then burrowed her face against his chest. Fierce protectiveness burned through his veins. Darcy didn't know zip about his baby sister. Where was she when Amy was born? Where was she when Amy ran a high fever and had them all worried to death? Where was she when he and Rob explained over and over to Amy why her mommy was never coming home again? Where was Darcy when Rob died? She should have been at his side.

He strode out the door. "Thanks for supper and baby-sitting." Just before the screen slapped shut, he heard Darcy's soft words.

"You can't run forever, Blake."

Long after he'd tucked Amy into her bed and turned out all the lights and gone to his own bed, Blake lay staring into the darkness, mulling over the events of the evening. How had his attempt to help Darcy understand Rob gone wrong so fast? He dug his toes into the covers and jerked them down so they weren't bundled under his chin.

Sure, he was busy. Everyone understood that. Except, it seemed, Darcy. He had cows to move. Calves to process. Bales to haul. Fields to work. On top of that he had to go to a couple of auction sales, trying to find a good used rake.

That didn't even take into account the paperwork waiting in the office, which he'd been putting off because it involved sorting Rob's personal stuff and clearing it from the office. Ahh. The paperwork. He could take care of two things at the same time. He flipped to his side and fell asleep.

Chapter 7

Darcy ran toward home. She'd added a couple of miles to her daily workout, building her endurance without undue effort. It surprised her how much she enjoyed running in the country. Today the fields were velvet carpets of brown and gold and silver. The sun shone in a satiny blue sky, unseasonably warm for April. She'd heard Blake muttering about a spring storm.

Blake. Last night ended in an argument. Not that she expected he'd be happy about her interference.

A swirl of dust down the road signaled a vehicle. It looked like Blake's. The truck pulled to the edge of the road and stopped. Blake swung out of the door. He leaned against the fender, his fingers tucked into the front pocket of his jeans, his cap shoved back as he watched her approach. At the warmth in his brown eyes her heart rate zoomed into the red zone.

She slowed her pace. What did he want? She'd seen the way he'd looked at her lips last night, knew he'd meant to kiss her. She'd stopped him by talking about Amy. Did he still want to kiss her? She faltered. Or argue some more?

He didn't speak until she drew abreast. "You're going farther every day."

She nodded, surprised he'd noticed. "I'm training for a race when I get back."

"I've been thinking about what you said. You know, about me being too busy. As I tried to tell you, I can't help it. There's just too much to do."

"Maybe you should think about getting help."

He nodded. "I've thought of it. Unfortunately, some of the stuff can't be handled by strangers. You're family. Maybe you could help."

"Me?" she squeaked. When had he ever considered her family?

"Sure. You could sort the stuff in the office. Would you consider doing that?"

He'd invited her into his family? His house? What next? His heart? She pushed back the lurch of emotions at the idea. She allowed no dreams leading to futile hopes. Wasn't that the lesson she'd learned from her father? But there was no harm, no risk in helping Blake, giving him more time to spend with Amy. She wouldn't allow herself to think *she* might like to spend more time with him. *Lord, I trust You to help me protect my heart.* "Sure. I'll help if I can." She wiped her hand across her forehead.

He grinned, reaching out and brushing his fingers along her jaw. His gaze followed the path of his fingers. His hands had a roughness that caused her skin to tingle.

She couldn't breathe. Without conscious thought she leaned forward.

She let him tip her chin toward him, held her breath as he lowered his head. She allowed one flicker of hesitation, knowing this might change things between them in a way she couldn't control, and then she welcomed his kiss. She brought her hands up to his arms, reveling in the strength of his biceps. She admired a man with well-defined muscles.

He pulled back.

She swayed toward him. The touch of his mouth had warmed her lips, started a wash of emotions surging through her. She felt keenly the loneliness and longing she'd lived with all her life, wanting what she couldn't have, followed by a tidal wave of something warm and sheltering like finding a safe harbor. Blake. Her safe harbor? He was all she could hope for, a good man who loved his family. Uncertainty edged in. What did Blake mean by this kiss? Was she a safe harbor for him? Or was it gratitude for her offer to help? Appreciation for the way she kept Amy amused?

She settled back on her heels. Forced her emotions back into a calm sea. She wasn't ready to ride the crest of that wave. She wasn't ready to open herself to the possibility of rejection.

He looked as surprised by the kiss as she was by her reaction.

They stood inches apart, gazing deeply into each other's eyes, searching, exploring, wondering. He smiled. "I'm off to town, but when I get back meet me at the house, and I'll show you what you can do."

"Okay." She watched his mouth as he talked, liking the way his lips flashed a smile.

He hesitated then climbed into the truck.

She waved at him in his rearview mirror. Without turning, he lifted his hand. She jogged slowly back to the ranch, grinning at a crow flapping by. Blake had kissed her. She liked it. Liked the feeling of being wanted. Her steps slowed. Was she playing house? Looking for something her father had denied her? Belonging. Home. Family. *Lord, Blake seems like such a good man, but I don't want to be substituting one ache for another. Give me wisdom to see clearly what I should do.*

She lengthened her stride, promising herself to be cautious.

By the time she showered and dressed in a pair of cool cotton shorts, a T-shirt, and a pair of matching flip-flops, all in teal blue, Amy was at her door.

She spent time with Amy, braiding her hair and reading her a book. At Amy's interest in Darcy's flip-flops, Darcy promised herself to buy her sister a pair next time she went to town. And maybe some new bright short sets.

Usually when she played with Amy, the little girl had her undivided attention, but this morning Darcy strained to hear Blake's return. It was almost noon before he drove into the yard and parked by the big house.

"Let's go see what Blake's doing," she suggested to Amy.

Amy bounced out of the door and raced toward her brother. Blake braced himself and caught the little girl as she launched into his arms.

Darcy squeezed the bridge of her nose. The affection between the two was touching. She envied Amy her assurance of Blake's love. She slowed her steps. It was only because Blake was Amy's father figure. She was wondering what it would be like to feel such assurance of love from Blake as a man. *Be careful,* she reminded herself.

Blake smiled over Amy's shoulder as the little girl clung to him. "It took me longer than I planned. Seemed everyone picked today to go to town."

She nodded, her eyes feeling too bright. "I wasn't waiting." She was only curious about what he wanted her to do.

He unpeeled Amy and set her on the ground. "You can take these into the kitchen." He gave the girl two grocery bags. "You want to help?" he asked Darcy, holding out two more bags, one in each hand.

"Sure." She slipped her fingers into the handles, brushing her knuckles on his. The bags hung suspended between them. The moment froze as she looked into his eyes, a tiny pulse making itself felt high in her chest. She wondered if he felt the same disorientation she did.

"Got ice cream," he murmured. "It needs to go in the freezer."

So much for him being as bewildered as she. Obviously, he was not. It was only her unrelenting need to belong that made her think he might be. She took the bags and headed for the house, dropping them on the counter. Blake came in behind her, opened the side-by-side freezer, and stashed the ice cream.

"Where's Aunt Betty?" he asked Amy, who shrugged. "Aunt Betty!" he called, striding into the living room.

Darcy heard a sharp response, and then Blake returned. "She's on the phone with one of her cronies. Said she doesn't have time to make lunch today. She has to go into town and have lunch with a friend who's only here for a few hours. So. . ." He rubbed his hands together and looked gleeful. "We're on our own."

Darcy backed away. "I'll be back later then." She didn't wish to intrude.

Blake grabbed her wrist. "I'm hoping you'll have mercy on us and cook up a meal like last night."

Amy bounced up and down. "Please, Darcy. Cook us something."

"Anything but. . ." Blake grinned at Amy, and together they whispered, "Macaroni."

Darcy snapped her fingers. "That's exactly what I had in mind. Thick, gluey, yummy macaroni."

Amy gagged, Blake frowned, and Darcy laughed. "Just teasing. Seriously, what do you have in the house?"

"There's a whole freezer full of meat downstairs. Come on—I'll show you."

She followed him down to a large storeroom. Not only was the freezer full, but the shelves were well stocked, and a narrow door opened to a cold room with a solitary bag of potatoes.

"You have tons of food here."

Blake shrugged. "It's an old tradition on farms and ranches to keep in a good supply. I suppose it has its roots in pioneer days when you stocked up for the winter, but I know Mom always said we had to be prepared for a storm."

"I guess it's too late now to worry about that."

"We often get late snowstorms. We can be shut off from civilization for days at a time."

"You certainly wouldn't starve to death if you were. Why doesn't Aunt Betty use this?"

"She doesn't like cooking. She made that plain from the beginning."

Darcy poked through the contents of the freezer. "What do you want?"

"What can you do?"

From the supplies here she could cook up almost anything a person could dream of. But she knew he wouldn't want something four hours later. Something quick would have to do. "Hamburgers. Steak. Something with chicken breast?"

"Did I hear the word *steak*?"

"Steak it is. You want potatoes?"

"Yes."

A few minutes later they climbed the stairs again, carrying supplies. She had the impression the man was starving for a good old-fashioned meat-and-potatoes meal. So while Aunt Betty fussed about, gathering up her things and complaining she never had enough time in the day, Darcy peeled potatoes, thawed the steak, and prepared an apple crisp using a can of pie filling.

Both Amy and Blake hung about, drooling.

"Mom used to cook like that," Blake said.

Amy perked up. "She did?"

Blake nodded, his expression sad as he regarded his little sister. "You were too young to remember, but Mom loved to cook."

Amy tipped her head toward her brother. "Did I like what she made?"

Blake laughed. "You loved her mashed potatoes and gravy."

Darcy decided then and there she would make the creamiest mashed potatoes and richest gravy she could. With no fixings for a salad and no fresh vegetables, she chose three varieties of frozen vegetables and hoped they would pass the taste test.

Forty-five minutes later they sat down at the dining nook surrounded by a huge bay window providing them a panoramic view of the rolling fields and distant mountains. Blake uttered a hurried grace.

Amy tasted everything tentatively, her eyes growing wider with each mouthful. Blake, not nearly as cautious, filled his plate and dug in like a condemned man at his last meal.

Darcy accepted their words of praise. "I love cooking," she admitted.

"Like my mom," Amy said. She turned to Blake. "Did I like her potatoes and gravy better'n this?"

Blake chuckled. "I don't think so." He sent a warm glance to Darcy as if sharing secret enjoyment of this little girl. As far as Darcy was concerned, it wasn't a bit secret the way she felt about her sister. Amy meant more to her than she could have ever guessed. And Blake? Her gaze shot back to him. The jury was still out on that. Her feelings had certainly shifted toward him, but it was way too early to contemplate what that meant.

Everything was gone but little puddles of vegetables in the bottom of the bowls. Darcy took away the plates and serving bowls, and dished up generous portions of hot apple crisp with ice cream melting down the edges.

Blake sighed loud and appreciatively when she slid the bowl in front of him.

Amy glanced toward the adults. "Do I like this?"

Blake turned serious and shook his head. "I don't think so. You'll have to let me eat it for you."

Amy narrowed her eyes and studied him. "I'll try it first." She took a spoonful. Her eyes widened as she chewed. She smacked her lips and sighed, then leaned forward and wrapped her arms protectively around her dessert. "You can't have any of mine."

Darcy's gaze met Blake's as they laughed together. Enjoyment and peace slipped deep into her heart. She'd never been part of a warm family unit like this. Mom had always been busy and restless. Always heading for the next opportunity, the next great plan. Darcy knew this situation was temporary. She'd very soon—far too soon—have to go back to her real life. But just for a few minutes she let herself enjoy it, accepted it as one of God's generous gifts.

Blake finished his dessert first and poked Amy's elbow. "Looks like you need help." He winked at Darcy. Was he flirting with her? What was with that? It made her feel noticed. Special, even. After last night she'd expected disinterest, or anger. Did this mean her words made sense to him and he was grateful?

Amy tightened her grasp on her bowl and continued to eat.

Sending Blake a teasing grin, Darcy leaned forward and touched Amy's hand. "I gave you a large serving. You don't have to eat it all, you know."

Amy hunkered closer over her bowl. "I want to."

Blake leaned back, his arms crossed over his chest and watched. "You're going to explode."

Amy shrugged his comment away and plowed onward. Several minutes later, her bowl scraped clean and licked, she leaned back, patting her stomach. "I'm full."

Darcy looked at Blake, and they laughed.

He gathered up dirty dishes and carried them to the dishwasher. He stood close to Darcy as she washed the pots; then he took each item from her soapy hands and dried it. She finished and turned away, uncertain where to go, what to do next.

He dropped his hand to her shoulder, turning her toward the living room. "We have an appointment; did you forget?"

What appointment?

He led her down the hall and into a large room. A big oak desk sat in the center, a computer on one corner. Shelves lined two walls, filled with books and mementos. Large windows gave a view of the outbuildings and a glimpse of her house.

"The farm office," he said, dropping his hand to his side. "A lot of Rob's stuff is here. I haven't had time to sort it. That's where you come in. It would be a great help if you tackled the job." His voice sounded strained. "Maybe if his stuff was gone, I could face coming in here to do the farm books."

He wanted her to sort her father's stuff? No way. She didn't want anything to do with—

"It really makes more sense for you to do it than me. He was your father, so that gives you the right. And I'm sure you can do it with less emotional attachment than I could."

"Of course." Hadn't she told him often enough she had no feelings about the past? Why then did this suggestion bother her so much?

"Good." He jerked several boxes out of a closet and put them on the desk. "Most of his stuff is here."

"What am I supposed to do with it?"

He shrugged. "Whatever you think best. Anything to do with business, pile on the desk. Anything you think someone might want to keep, set aside for him or her. I guess you dump the rest."

She peeked in one box. It was filled with clippings and odds and ends. Nothing she couldn't handle. Yet her heart quivered, and she silently prayed for strength.

Chapter 8

For the first time since Rob died, the demands of work didn't keep Blake from returning to the house. He tried to tell himself he wasn't curious to see how Darcy was doing. As he stepped into the house, the aroma of freshly brewed coffee greeted him. Darcy stood at the pot, waiting for the amber liquid to drip through. Amy hovered beside her, chattering away about a card she held.

"Smells good in here."

The sisters spun around to face him. Amy rushed over, waving the card. "Look what Darcy found. A card I gave Daddy when he went to the hospital. I made it before I even started school." He bent to examine the homemade card she shoved at him. "Do you think Daddy liked this?" She twisted it around, appraising it. "It's not very good. Look how I spelled my name."

He took the card. "I remember when he got this. He was so proud of you. He thought you did a fine job for being only five."

Amy nodded. "I think I'll keep it."

"I suggested she frame it or put it in a scrapbook," Darcy said.

Amy looked serious. "We got any frames, Blake?"

"You can pick out one the next time we're in town."

She skipped away, her gaze on her treasure.

"I found the card in my father's things," Darcy said.

"I'm glad you thought to give it to her. It's made her happy." They regarded each other.

Blake sensed her wariness. Whenever the discussion turned to Rob, she pulled back into herself, cautious, guarded. He'd hoped sorting Rob's things would help her see the good side of the man.

"How is it going?" he asked.

"It's slow. I feel like I have to check every item carefully to make sure I'm not throwing away something valuable."

He didn't ask if she meant valuable in a monetary sense or emotional. It encouraged him she'd seen the value of hanging on to Amy's card. She'd treasure it in the coming years.

"Coffee?" Darcy offered him a cup.

Normally he didn't bother with the stuff, but it smelled so good he couldn't bring himself to refuse. He took the cup from her, wiped a streak of dust from her cheek, felt her tense. Her gaze lifted to him, and he read the wonder. He edged forward until they almost touched.

"Blake! Blake!" Amy called. "Can we go to town now?"

He jerked back. "Sorry, squirt! Not today!" He gulped his coffee.

"Do you want to see what I've done?" Darcy asked.

He followed her to the office where neat piles covered the desk. A big green garbage bag squatted beside the desk.

"I threw out the old sale catalogues and flyers. This pile"—she pointed toward the desktop—"looks as if it might be farm stuff. I'll let you decide whether or not to keep it." She touched the box on the desk. "I think the first box was the easiest. There wasn't anything personal in it." She took a deep breath. "This box, however, seems to be mostly personal stuff." She lifted her gaze to him. "You sure you don't want to go through it?"

He shuddered. He couldn't face the painful reminders of the man he missed so much. "I'd sooner wrestle a bear."

She nodded, her expression troubled. "It's a lot harder than I thought it would be."

That's what he wanted. Wasn't it? For her to mourn the man who'd been her father? Acknowledge he'd meant just a little to her?

She pulled out a picture and smiled widely, her eyes sparkling like sunshine on water.

He gave his cup of coffee a hard look. The caffeine had shot his heart into overdrive.

"I believe this must be you." She held the picture toward him.

He took it and groaned. "Naked as a baby."

She giggled. "You were a baby."

He read the inscription on the back. " 'Rob. This is Blake at six months. Cute or what? Love ya. Kathy.'" He flipped the picture to the desk. "Why would Mom give him this?"

She patted his shoulder. "Probably so they could have a good laugh. After all, what were you when she gave him this? Thirteen? Fourteen? And maybe a bit rebellious?"

"Not me. I didn't have time for that. My dad died when I was thirteen. By the time I was fourteen I was doing a man's work."

"I guess you must have been glad when my father came along."

He heard the brittleness in her voice. "I was relieved to have someone else share the responsibility. I was happy he made Mom laugh again. But, Darcy, he didn't choose me over you. You have to believe that."

She stared hard at him. "Why?"

"Because—"

"It eases your conscience?"

"I don't need my conscience eased. I loved Rob and miss him like crazy."

"As I've said before, I'm sorry for your loss." She moved back to the desk and pulled out a handful of pictures.

"I'm no psychiatrist," he said, to which she arched her eyebrows. "But I think it's you who are running. Afraid to acknowledge the pain of losing him."

She smiled. "Nope. Because you see, I was forced to deal with losing him fifteen years ago."

"Surely you have some questions."

"Like what?"

How could she act as if nothing about Rob mattered to her? He wanted to force her to admit it did. "Like why he never came back?"

She nodded. "So now you're willing to acknowledge it wasn't my fault?"

He tossed his hands in the air. "You could have visited him anytime you wanted. No one would have chased you away."

"The same could be said for him."

"I give up. We just go round in circles."

"So why keep trying to convince me? Or yourself? The past is over and done with. I don't want to dwell on it. Or be stuck in it. I gave it to God a long time ago, and I don't intend to take it back."

◆

The next day was Sunday, and she gladly turned her thoughts to church, thankful for a way to avoid thinking about the house across the yard, the office inside the house, the man who once occupied the office, and the younger man who now had all the responsibility of running the place. Her feelings toward her father and Blake had tangled inside her head. Going to church would help her get back on center.

The church building was as traditional as one could imagine, white siding with a tall spire. Darcy stood back to admire it, felt welcomed, her heart filled with peace. She'd declined an invitation to go with Blake, Aunt Betty, and Amy. She wanted to be alone and able to concentrate. She waited until just before the service to slip into a back pew. She saw Blake's back toward the front. Amy squirmed around and looked for her, lifted her hand in a quick wave when she spotted Darcy, and then, obeying Aunt Betty's warning look, faced forward and sat quietly.

Darcy had a quick look around. Easter Sunday and the front of the church overflowed with lilies. The worship leader greeted the congregation warmly, then announced the first song, one Darcy knew. She joined in the enthusiastic singing, her heart filling with praise and joy as she focused on God's love and provision. Bible verses Mrs. R had taught her came to mind as she sang. *"Never will I leave you; never will I forsake you. . . . The Lord is my helper; I will not be afraid. What can man do to me?"* Her confidence returned. Whatever she faced while on this visit, God stood at her side and would guide and direct her.

The pastor spoke further words of encouragement, reminding them of God's power in raising Jesus from the dead and what that power meant for each of them living a life of obedience to God.

She slipped out at the end, refreshed and renewed. She'd intended to leave without speaking to anyone, wanting nothing to shatter her newly regained sense of peace. Many stopped and welcomed her, however, and then Amy was at her side, Blake only a few steps away.

"How did you enjoy the service?" he asked as they left the building.

"Very much. Both the music and the sermon. And the people are so friendly."

"Will you be over later to tackle the office again?"

She quickly made up her mind. If he didn't work on Sunday, this would be a day for him to spend alone with Amy. "Not today." Due to Amy's teachers taking a couple of professional days following the vacation time, Darcy still had a few more days to spend with Amy before she had to return to school.

She spent the afternoon enjoying the sunshine, phoning Mrs. R and Irene, and missing Amy's enthusiasm and Blake's steadiness. How would she go back to the city and not see them every day? *Stop worrying about the future. Leave it in God's hands.*

◆

On Monday she returned to the task of sorting her father's papers and facing the evidence that he'd had another life—one that hadn't included her. There was nothing new about that. She'd accepted the fact years ago. But pulling out picture after picture, letter after letter, memento after memento was like poking at a scabbed-over sore.

She hadn't seen Blake since yesterday at church. Somehow she'd let herself think he might hang around the house just to see her. As if. She pressed the heel of her hand to her forehead. Hiding out in this office, burrowing through papers, was getting to her. She'd again lost her mental equilibrium. *Lord, You are my strength and guide.*

Amy bounced into the room, upsetting a stack of calendars filled with notes. Darcy wanted Blake to decide whether or not to keep them. "Wanna play house?" Amy asked.

Darcy sighed. In her mind she'd been doing exactly that, imagining making meals for Amy and Blake, doing their laundry. She glanced out at the sunshine. She had to get out of here. "Why don't we go on a picnic?"

Amy danced up and down. "Goody, goody, goody."

Darcy guided her to the door. "Go tell Aunt Betty; then we'll go to my house and get ready." She'd make a simple lunch and take a blanket and some toys.

As they crossed the yard, Blake drove up.

"We're going on a picnic," Amy announced.

Blake smiled at his sister, then lifted his gaze to Darcy. "Where are you going?"

Darcy answered, "To the river west of here."

"Sounds like fun."

"Why don't you come with us?"

He shook his head. "Can't."

"Aww," Amy said. "You never play with me anymore."

"You have Darcy."

Amy nodded. "We'll have lots of fun, won't we, Darcy?"

"We sure will." She flashed Blake a tight smile. She hadn't honestly thought he'd tear himself from his work for an afternoon of fun and games, and she hid her disappointment. "Too bad you'll have to miss it." As she and Amy walked away, Darcy clamped her lips together to keep from pointing out that Blake was going to miss more than just a picnic if he kept it up. He was going to miss the most delightful years of Amy's life.

When their picnic was ready, Darcy drove down the road as far as she could; then they walked to the river.

Amy looked around. "Let's play pretend."

"Okay." Darcy realized she was getting pretty good at pretend. And not just with Amy. She'd allowed herself a few delicious moments of pretending she belonged here. Welcomed by Blake.

"Let's make a house." Amy directed her toward a shaded area surrounded by trees. Darcy draped the thick blanket she'd brought from home over a low branch, creating a tent, and they settled under it. Amy sat cross-legged, her hands resting on her thighs. "I think we're the first ladies to come here."

"Right. How did we get here?"

Amy spun a tale of a horseback ride away from home to a new area. Darcy smiled at her imagination.

The noise of a heavy animal sent a shiver across Darcy's shoulders. "Shh. Do you hear something?"

Amy's eyes grew round.

The sound came again. Closer. Heavy thuds on the gravelly ground. Darcy reached for Amy's hand, prepared to— She didn't know if they should remain motionless and silent or run for their lives.

The sound grew closer. Something brushed the blanket. Amy let out a squeak. A bulky shadow fell across the opening. Darcy screamed, then laughed in relief as Blake ducked down.

"Hi," he said.

Darcy giggled nervously. "You scared us half to death."

Amy, her eyes much too large, whispered, "I thought it was a bear."

"Sorry," Blake said, bending nearly in half to slip under the blanket and wedge himself between them.

He filled more than the space in the tent. He filled Darcy's thoughts, her emotions.

"So what are we doing in here?" he asked.

"We're pioneer women," Darcy explained, and Amy repeated her story. Darcy heard very little of the tale, thinking instead about how his arm behind her felt so warm and protective. He was a big man; yet he hunkered down around her like they belonged together. Which was too stupid for words. She scrambled out from under the blanket and sprang to her feet. "Let's go out in the sunshine."

Blake untangled himself until he stood. "It *was* a little too tight in there." He pulled the blanket off the tree, spread it close to the river, and stretched out, patting a spot beside him.

She eyed the narrow space and finally perched beside him, watching Amy spin around, chasing sunbeams.

"This reminds me of some books I read when I was a kid," Darcy said. "Something about a giggling brook and laughing trees. I liked pretending the things of nature were human."

Amy squatted in front of her, eyes sparkling with interest. "Tell me some more."

Darcy couldn't remember any more. "We can make up our own. See the sun flashing off the ripples like eyes winking? Winking river. Or"—she pointed to the leaves—"they're telling each other secrets. Whispering leaves."

Blake leaned on his elbow. "My dad used to bring me here. I'd forgotten all about it. We floated bark boats."

Amy bounced up. "How? Show me."

Blake pushed to his feet and strode toward the trees. He showed Amy how to select bits and pieces of wood; then they went to the river and had boat races, Amy squealing with excitement.

Darcy found a piece of bark and joined the race, yelling and screaming as her boat crossed their arbitrary finish line ahead of the other two. "I win! I win!" She grabbed Amy's hands and danced around with her. Blake's boat had been last. She danced Amy up to Blake and chanted, "You lose. You lose."

Blake jammed his fists on his hips and gave her a mock scowl. "Nobody likes a poor winner. Besides, what kind of example are you setting for little Amy?"

"A fun one?"

Amy dropped Darcy's hands, crossed her arms over her chest in a militant stance, and glowered at Blake. "I'm not little. When are you going to stop treating me like a kid?" She stomped away.

Blake stared after Amy as if she'd developed two heads. "Where did that come from?"

Darcy whooped with laughter. Her little sister certainly had a good dose of moxie.

Blake's deep chuckle joined hers.

After that, they couldn't seem to stop laughing. They played a game of tag with Amy. Then they walked, three abreast, along the river. Amy broke away to pick up shiny stones.

"This was a real good idea," Blake murmured as they watched Amy filling her pockets with rocks. "I can't believe I haven't been here since Dad died. We used to come often."

"Maybe it's time to let yourself have some fun once in a while." He didn't answer, and she continued softly. "I understand life hasn't been easy for you. You've had to shoulder far too much responsibility far too young. But you can't let it keep you from enjoying life at the same time."

"I thought I was until you came along."

"Oh dear. That doesn't sound good."

"Believe me, it is." His stomach rumbled. "Did you bring enough food for me, or should I go home for lunch?"

"There's lots." She'd give up her own share if it meant he'd stay a bit longer.

They called to Amy and headed back to the blanket. Darcy divided the sandwiches and handed out boxes of juice. She was glad she'd baked cookies the night before and had generously filled a bag.

After they'd eaten, Amy sat at the edge of the river and tossed rocks into the water. Content with life, Darcy lay on her stomach next to Blake.

"A person could get used to living in the country," she said, then wondered where the thought had come from.

"I can't imagine living anywhere else," Blake murmured. "My great-great-grandfather, Cyril Thompson, came here before the government opened up the land for settlers. He had a thousand cows roaming freely. He built a log house for his wife and family."

"Sounds like Amy's story." She couldn't imagine roots going down four generations. The longest she'd ever lived in one place was the last three years in her own little apartment.

"My grandpa used to tell me all sorts of stories." Blake leaned on one elbow so he could look at Darcy. "I don't know how many of them were really true."

"Like what?"

"Well, he had this one wild story about a man who lived in the mountains. He used to point to a place where you could see a bit of valley and say, 'Right about there.' He said the man kidnapped a young woman right out of her own yard with the intention of forcing her to become his wife."

Darcy gasped. "Why would he do that? Did she get away?"

"Story goes he brought her back. I guess she wasn't too cooperative."

"Poor girl."

Blake chuckled. "Maybe poor man. But in the end they did marry. It seems the man had a scar on his face he thought made him ugly and figured the only way to get a wife was to force someone to marry him, but it seems the young lady saw past his scar to his heart."

"How romantic."

"Yes, indeed."

She narrowed her eyes and studied him. Was he mocking her? "Don't you believe in love?"

"Of course I do. I just don't think it has to be so dramatic. With my parents and with Rob and my mom, I saw it more as deep and steady. The kind of thing that's like a solid foundation."

Darcy studied the rippling water as unfamiliar longing washed through her. Blake knew where he belonged. And always had. He knew where he'd be at the end of his life. Right here with his children and grandchildren gathered around him. Darcy shook her head.

"What's the matter?" Blake asked.

"It's just so foreign to me. I can't imagine a place that's been in the family for generations. I can't even remember all the places I've lived." As to love that formed a foundation—well, she knew it existed. And she dreamed of the possibility in her own life, but she didn't have the calm assurance it was ordinary and expected. Not like Blake. For her it was a dream, and she'd learned long ago not to put too much hope in dreams. "Not everyone wants that sort of belonging. The very idea would give my mother hives. She liked moving on a regular basis. I think she found it exciting to look for a new place and welcomed the challenge of negotiating all the details."

"How about you?" His voice was low, serious, as if this were more than casual conversation.

She slid a quick glance at him, seeing the warmth in his chocolate-colored eyes. Then she forced her gaze back to the river.

"How do you feel about staying in one place?" His voice was soft.

She didn't answer right away. She was thinking of the house her father had left her. The idea still seemed impossible. She wanted to clutch at her ownership like a child refusing to let go of the penny needed to make a purchase. She didn't belong out here, even though she felt drawn to the place. And the people. Especially Amy. And, yes, Blake. But long ago she'd learned how disastrous it was to pin her hopes on one person, expecting him to provide her security. She'd learned to stand on her own feet and trust God for what she needed. She had a good, satisfying job back in Seattle where she knew what was expected of her. And she wasn't about to let any of her coworkers and friends down. She'd return. Run the half marathon and win it. And she'd resume her duties.

Blake got tired of waiting for her answer and dropped his chin to his hands. "I guess belonging doesn't appeal to everyone."

She didn't respond. How could she begin to explain the difference between them? The difference between knowing and dreaming.

Chapter 9

Darcy woke from a sound sleep and lay staring into the darkness. What wakened her? She strained into the silence. Usually she could hear the fridge or the clock on her bedside table. But the numbers on her clock had disappeared. She reached for the lamp and flicked it. Nothing. The power must be off. She shivered and snuggled deeper into her covers. And then she heard it. The roar and moan of the wind. A storm. Already the cold was enough to make her feet cramp. She supposed it would be a good idea to light a fire in the fireplace.

She gathered the bedclothes around her and padded into the living room, stumbling into the couch in the darkness. She'd seen a flashlight somewhere but didn't have a clue where and knew she'd never find it in the dark.

The fireplace was hard to miss, though. She stubbed her toe on the hearth and dropped her covers as she grabbed the offended member of her anatomy. The cold hit her like a blast, and she fumbled for the blankets.

She found the stack of wood to the right of the fireplace. A log rolled off and dropped on her foot. Darcy grunted, but this time she wasn't dropping her covers. She managed to open the fireplace screen and jab the log in.

Great. A fireplace and a log. But what she really needed was a fire. Which required matches. She patted her hips and chest as if she had pockets that might contain matches or lighter and giggled. Here she was doing the macarena alone and in the middle of a cold, dark night.

She edged her way to the couch and cuddled up under the blankets. It surely wasn't cold enough to pose any real threat, but something shivered across her neck and raced down her spine. She recognized the feeling as intense loneliness. She laid her head against the back of the couch. Suddenly she sat up. No way was she going to let it get to her. She marched back to her bedroom, bumping her shins on the corner of the coffee table and then banging her head into the door, but she only muttered under her breath. She pawed through her drawers and found a heavy sweater, pulled it over her head, then found jeans and warm socks. Reaching out until she found the bed, she sat down to pull them on. She toed her way into her shoes, giggling as she tried to put one on backward.

She found her way to the back door and pulled down a heavy coat from the hooks. She caught a hint of Blake's scent as she burrowed into it. It took a few minutes for the icy lining to grow warm.

She'd survive. As soon as morning came, she'd find matches and start a fire. It would be an adventure.

How were they managing up at the other house? Was someone making sure Amy was warm enough? She could imagine Amy curled against Blake's chest, warm and cherished. A long, slow ache filled her. Try as she might, she couldn't dismiss it as cold. Truth was, she felt shut out. Unwanted.

She stamped her feet to warm them. She wouldn't allow self-pity. She recited verses Mrs. R encouraged her "girls" to memorize. " 'For all have sinned and fall short of the glory of God'" might not be the most comforting passage. She mentally shifted to the psalms. Chapter 23. The shepherd psalm. " 'The Lord is my shepherd. . . .'" By the time she'd recited the whole passage, her fear and loneliness subsided. She would never be alone. She had God's comfort.

She edged toward the window, hoping for a glimpse of the house. Did she see a faint flash of light? She strained into the darkness. It had to be her imagination. That was one thing she shared with Amy—an all-too-vivid imagination. And blue eyes, though she doubted hers were as lively as Amy's. Plus a stubbornness that could cause others to grind their teeth.

She smiled into the unrelenting darkness. It was tons of fun to share similarities with a little sister.

She heard feet stamping on the wooden deck, the sound muffled by snow. Her city instincts kicked in, and she shrank back, fearing an intruder.

But she wasn't in the city. She was on the Bar T Ranch. And who would wander around in a blackout and a raging storm?

The door rattled as someone tried to open it.

"Darcy, open up! It's cold as the North Pole out here!"

"Blake?" she whispered. "I'm coming!" she called, not caring a bit that she cracked her knee twice in her rush to unlock the door.

Cold, like a blast from the Arctic, hit her in the face, and snow stung her eyes. Blake shone a light in her face, then shoved her aside and pushed the door closed.

He stamped his feet and brushed snow off his coat. "Are you okay?"

Little tickles of warmth, like the first cup of morning coffee, filled her. "You came out in this storm to check on me?" It was the cold making her voice so husky. Yeah. Like she believed that. She wanted to hug him for his concern. Except for his snow-covered coat. She stepped back from the cold coming off him. "I'm okay."

He again shone the light in her face. She closed her eyes until he lowered the beam over her. "I see you found my old coat." He chuckled. "I haven't worn that in ages. I outgrew it. Looks good on you, though."

From the glow of his flashlight, she could see his face in sharp planes, his wide smile, his hair hidden under a shaggy fur hat, and she giggled. "Has the wind blown us to Russia?"

He touched the hat. "You mean this? You like it?"

"Very aristocratic."

"Thank you." He bowed deeply. Then grew serious. "I wondered if you'd get a fire going."

"I'm not much of a Girl Scout. I wasn't prepared. And I couldn't find any matches." She patted her pockets again.

"The forecast is for the storm to last three days. No point in you trying to keep warm here. You might as well come up to the other house. We have a roaring fire in the fireplace. It's reasonably warm. Grab a few things, and I'll take you over. That way I can be sure you're okay." He pulled another flashlight out of his pocket. "While you do that, I'll crack open the taps so the water won't freeze."

She hurried to her room, humming as she threw some clothes and toiletries into a small bag. He cared enough to rescue her.

Blake was standing in the middle of the kitchen when she returned. She shone her light in his face. He turned aside to avoid the brightness.

"All ready?" he asked. At her nod he took her hand and pulled it through his arm. "Hang on, and whatever you do, don't let go. I wouldn't want to lose you out there."

She wouldn't want to get lost. And she certainly didn't mind keeping her arm tucked into his.

They stepped outside into a wall of snow and wind. She forgot everything but hanging on for dear life as they walked head-on into the storm. How did Blake know where to go? Fear made her stumble. What if they got lost? How long would they wander out in this wretched storm before they were buried in snow? Would they lie there until spring thawed out their lifeless bodies? *The Lord is my shepherd.*

Blake pulled her closer and forged ahead. She clung to him and trusted he knew the way.

The pressure of the wind stopped so suddenly she almost fell.

"We're at the house!" Blake shouted in her ear. "We're out of the wind here." She stumbled inside. He closed the door firmly after them. A battery-powered lamp provided a golden glow.

She slipped out of her coat, shook it before draping it on a hook. She pulled off her boots and stuck her feet in her slippers as he shrugged out of his coat.

"Come on. Let's get in where it's warm." He took her hand and drew her past the dark kitchen into the living room where a fire roared and crackled in the big stone fireplace. Amy slept on the love seat. Aunt Betty lay on one couch, her eyes closed.

Blake didn't drop her hand until they stood facing the fire; then he stretched his hands to the warmth.

Darcy did the same. "Fire," she murmured. "Man's greatest invention."

Blake looked around the room. "Everyone is safe and sound."

Darcy stared into the flames. Was that all it was for him? Taking care of responsibilities?

Blake reached over to the end of Amy's couch and picked up a stack of blankets and a pillow. "You might as well get comfortable. We're here for the night."

She glanced around the room. One couch and a recliner left.

"You take the couch," he said.

"I couldn't do that. I'll take the recliner."

"No, I need to keep an eye on the fire." He made a bed for her. "There you go."

She felt uncomfortable. "I'm not really tired."

"Would you like something warm to drink?"

"How—"

He lifted an old kettle off the hearth. "Fire. Man's greatest invention."

She grinned.

"Hot chocolate?" he asked.

"Sounds good."

He brought two mugs and instant drink powder from the kitchen. He pulled the couch around so it faced the fire, and they sat with their feet propped on the hearth.

"Maybe the pioneers didn't have it so bad." She sipped the hot, sweet drink. "This is kind of nice."

"It's inconvenient if it lasts three days."

"Could it really?"

"Been known to happen."

"Amy's snoring. She sounds like a kitten purring." She met Blake's gaze, and they chuckled.

Aunt Betty shifted on the other couch and groaned.

Darcy settled back against the couch. She stared into the fire. "This is like camping, only cozier. You know, with the couch and everything."

"Have you done a lot of camping?"

"I once went to a summer camp in a wilderness area. But I never learned to be Ranger Sue. The only way I can start a fire by rubbing two sticks together is if one of them is a match."

He chuckled. "So you failed the survival skills test?"

"I never even qualified for the test. They begged me to pretend I hadn't taken the course. They offered me a lifetime membership to the shoppers' club if I kept it a secret. I suppose you have all your Boy Scout badges?"

"Nope. Didn't even go. But I can change the oil in a tractor in record time. And I can find my way from point A to point B without a map."

"From what I hear that isn't so much a skill as a denial mechanism for men."

"You think I'd sooner wander around lost than ask for directions?"

"Would you?"

He got up, put wood on the fire, and made them more hot chocolate, then faced her, leaning back on his heels, backlit by the glow of the fire.

"I might not bother if it was just me, but I would never drag around Amy or someone I care about. For their sake I would certainly ask directions."

She couldn't see his eyes, but she suspected they were hard and determined. He took this protective business seriously.

He'd included Amy in his cared-for category. She wondered who else he'd include. Aunt Betty, for sure. Maybe her? After all, he'd come to rescue her from freezing to death. Okay, maybe that was a little too dramatic. But he'd cared enough to bring her to a warm place. Was it just responsibility? Or was it more? Like caring?

He sat beside her again, and the conversation returned to camping. He told of trips with his father and then later with Rob.

Darcy tried not to think how Blake enjoyed the father things with Rob she'd been denied. She no longer blamed Blake. But she was grateful when he switched the topic to something else. She loved listening to him. The way his voice filled with pride as he talked about belonging to a beef club and showing his first steer. She laughed when he told how his dad saved the day when his steer got loose and headed for home.

Suddenly he turned so he could look into her face. The flame caught in his eyes and seemed to go deeper, as if burning into his soul. "I just realized something. I haven't talked this much about my parents and Rob since—" His mouth pulled down at the corners as he stared at her. He blinked. "Well, I suppose since my dad died. I didn't want to talk about it because—" Again he paused and searched her face.

Darcy held his gaze steadily, wondering what he sought and if he would find it in her or be disappointed.

Chapter 10

Blake's smile deepened, and pleasure spilled through Darcy. "I guess I was afraid of my feelings. Losing the three most important people in your life is overwhelming. I don't know when my good memories of them became more powerful than the pain." He touched her cheek, and the warmth inside her rushed to that spot like iron filings to a magnet. "Thank you for helping me see that." He settled back, sighing. "I know I won't ever stop missing them, but there are so many good things to remember."

"Tell me more about Amy as a baby."

He chuckled. "She never lacked for attention with three doting adults, but Mom insisted she had to accept certain boundaries. She was right. That early teaching has made Amy a good kid."

"How did she handle losing both her parents?" She wanted to know if Amy blamed herself. Did she feel abandoned?

"In both cases we knew ahead of time, so Mom and Rob took care to prepare her. I guess it helped. She didn't quite grasp Mom's death, but when Rob died—" He broke off and rubbed the bridge of his nose.

Darcy reached for his hand. He turned his palm up and held on.

"She took it a lot harder. She cried for about three days. After the funeral she retreated to her room and refused to talk to anyone, but I heard her talking to her stuffed animals. I let her be. Then she seemed to be okay, but she has nightmares."

"It's an awful thing for a child her age to face." Darcy was doing her best not to let her own feelings get mixed up with her sister's. Darcy's loss was in the past. Gone. Forgotten. Forgiven. Erased by God's love. Yet at times still very much alive and full of sharp edges.

Her daddy had left because—Darcy always feared it was because of her. She hadn't been good enough, smart enough, happy enough. Her rational self said it wasn't the case. But that other side, the one that insisted on dreaming impossible dreams, still wondered quietly and insistently. *Why wasn't I good enough?*

"Amy knew she was loved." Her voice felt impossibly tight, a sure giveaway she was letting her emotions get out of hand. She hoped Blake wouldn't be able to tell.

He jerked away. "Amy is still loved." He sounded fierce. "She will always be loved."

"I didn't mean—" She'd only been thinking of her father. No. Truth was, she was only thinking about herself, and she was deeply remorseful. "I'm sorry. Of course she is. It's obvious how much you care about her. I do, too."

He stiffened.

If she hoped to avoid a confrontation on the subject, she needed to find a new topic real quick. "Do you often get storms like this in April?" she asked.

"Once in ten years is too often in my opinion. But they aren't unexpected. This is Montana. And we're close to the mountains. Three years ago we had a major storm in May." He went on to describe it, and she settled back, enjoying his stories and grateful to have sidestepped an argument about her role in Amy's life.

As Blake told about a storm that brought a tree down, destroying the house his grandfather had been raised in, Amy started to cry.

They both jerked to their feet and rushed to her. Darcy held back as Blake shook the little girl gently. "Amy, honey, wake up." He glanced over his shoulder to Darcy. "One of her nightmares." He scooped Amy into his arms, talking to her softly.

Darcy knew the minute Amy woke up. Her cry ended in a gasp. She stared into Blake's face and then, sobbing, buried her head against his shoulder. He carried her to the couch and sat rocking her and murmuring softly.

Darcy sat beside them, aching to ease Amy's pain, but all she could think to do was rub her sister's back and add her voice to Blake's.

After a few minutes Amy's sobs stopped. She spoke around hiccups. "I dreamed I was stuck in a hole. I kept calling and calling Daddy. He just stood there and didn't help me. Why wouldn't he help me?"

Blake held her close. "It was just a dream."

Darcy's eyes stung. Try telling a child his or her dreams didn't mean anything. She couldn't forget a similar dream. Only she was trapped in a box. And no one answered her cries. Her mother assured her the dream meant nothing. But at six Darcy had known it did. It meant nobody cared. She pushed the memory away. "Amy, honey. It's okay. It's your mind telling you how much you miss your daddy. He can't be here to help you anymore, but Blake is. If you need something, you call Blake."

"I'll be here for you," Blake said.

Amy nodded. "I miss Daddy."

"Of course you do." Blake cupped her head in his big hand and pressed her cheek to his chest. "I do, too."

Amy grabbed Darcy's hand. "Do you, too, Darcy?"

There was no way to explain she'd stopped missing him years ago. "Of course I do, sweetheart." Her throat clogged with tears. She missed him in her own way. But she didn't dare dredge up those feelings of abandonment. They were too vicious. *Please, God. Help me remember that You care. You are a Father to the fatherless.*

Amy fell asleep again, and Blake put her down and covered her. Darcy returned to the couch while Blake tended the fire. She must have fallen asleep because she woke when Blake got up to put more wood on the fire. She lay stretched out on the couch, a blanket over her. She sat up and peered over the back. Amy slept in the love seat.

"Go back to sleep," Blake murmured. "Everything is okay."

And, believing him, she lay down and slept.

◆

Blake struggled from his sleep and slipped from the recliner to put more wood on the fire. Amy hadn't wakened with another dream. Aunt Betty moved restlessly on the couch, coughing now and then. Darcy lay on her side, her dark hair loose around her face.

Everyone was safe from the storm.

Darcy sighed and shifted. For a moment he thought she looked at him; then the fire flared, and he could tell she slept. Even with her eyes closed, her resemblance to Amy was strong. But Darcy was even more like Rob than Amy. Why had there never been contact between them? There must be more than Darcy admitted or knew.

Aunt Betty coughed again and moaned. Darcy sat up and looked about her, confused. Then she yawned and stretched like a cat.

"Is it still storming?" she murmured, her voice thick with sleep.

"Yep."

Aunt Betty struggled to sit up. "My throat is very sore. Is there something hot to drink?" She swayed, moaned, and lay down again. "I'm sick."

Great, Blake thought. Do your best to take care of everyone, but there was so much you couldn't protect them from.

"I'll get you something," Darcy said, pushing to her feet. "What would you like?"

"Lemon tea," Aunt Betty croaked.

Gray light struggled through the windows as Darcy went to the kitchen to find the things she needed to meet Aunt Betty's request.

Blake headed after her but only made three steps before Amy woke, crying. "My throat hurts."

He turned back to comfort her. "You and Aunt Betty are sick."

Amy whimpered. "Where's Darcy?"

Darcy called from the other room. "I'm here! Would you like a nice hot drink?"

Amy tried to speak but grabbed her throat and nodded instead.

"That's affirmative!" Blake called. "There's lemonade mix on the lazy Susan! I'll fill the kettle!" He poured from the supply of bottled water and hung it over the fire to heat.

Together he and Darcy prepared hot drinks.

"What about food?" Darcy asked as they huddled side by side on the couch. "We'll need to eat."

"What can we do over the fireplace?" He promised himself he'd get a new generator the next time he went to town. He wouldn't leave himself or his family exposed to such hardship again. Family? Amy and Aunt Betty were his family now. And Darcy? He liked the idea of her being family, but she'd be gone once her days off were used up. What were the chances they'd see her again? Not very likely, if her past was any indication. He mentally pulled his family circle tight, leaving Darcy outside. He liked the woman, but he had no room in his life for a leaving kind of girl.

"If you have a big pot to hang where the kettle is, I could boil eggs for breakfast and make soup for later," Darcy said.

"Sounds like just what we need." He glanced at the two sick people behind him. When Darcy started to get up, he grabbed her hand and pulled her back down beside him. "Finish your tea first. There's nothing I can do for the cows until it's over. And I put out enough feed for the animals in the barn so that they're okay for now. We have all day."

He found a suitable pot. She boiled eggs while he toasted bread over the fire. They offered a nice breakfast to both Amy and Aunt Betty, who nibbled at their soft-boiled eggs, then pushed away the rest.

"I should feel guilty about being so hungry when they're sick," Blake murmured as he chowed down.

"But you don't." Darcy laughed. "And neither do I. I only hope I don't get what they have."

They finished and stacked the dirty dishes in the dishwasher. Darcy checked the two patients and passed out acetaminophen tablets. Both settled back and fell asleep.

Darcy filled the pot with a mixture of vegetables, tomato juice, and sausage, and left it to simmer over the fire. Delicious aromas made Blake's mouth water.

Darcy yawned and stretched. "Now what do we do?" She looked around the room. "I suppose I could sort another box of my father's papers."

Memories of Rob were the last thing he wanted crowding his mind. "How about looking at a photo album of Amy as a baby?"

Her eyes sparkled with interest. "I'd love to."

He found the album in the big chest under the window, and they sat close, the album balanced on both their knees. He took her through the first few years of Amy's life. A time filled with sweet, safe memories. "Life seemed so simple then. I knew Mom's heart wasn't strong, but it seemed she'd survived the pregnancy and delivery and regained her strength. I guess I didn't want to believe otherwise."

"Of course you didn't. Why let fears rob you of enjoying the present?"

"That's your philosophy, isn't it?"

She looked thoughtful a moment. "I suppose it is." She regarded him seriously. "What's yours?"

He looked at the fire. "I don't think I've ever thought about it, but I suppose I'd more likely want to hunker down and pull everything I cared about close to me and hang on."

She nodded slowly, as if she understood his statement. And if she did, she saw more clearly than he. "And shut out everything else to make sure it doesn't upset your little world."

"You make me sound like a selfish kid clutching his stash of toys to his chest and refusing to let anyone play with him."

"No. Not like that. Your world sounds nice to me. A safe, secure place. But that isn't my world. Never has been. So I've learned to look outside myself and enjoy the journey." She tipped her head, her blue eyes flashing a bright reflection from the fire. "I don't see you as being selfish so much as protective of both those you love and your own heart."

"I'm responsible for my family. It's not something I take lightly."

"I'd have to be blind not to see that. But I think you shut your heart against risks." She shrugged. "But what do I know? I'm playing armchair psychologist. You probably have a serious love interest I'm unaware of."

He laughed at that. "Depends on what you mean by love interest. Mrs. Shaw, one of our neighbors, has a lovely daughter she's handpicked to be my bride."

He leaned closer at the way Darcy's eyes darkened. Was she jealous?

"No doubt a very suitable match."

He delighted in the way her mouth puckered as she spoke. "Absolutely," he agreed.

Her frown deepened.

He couldn't resist stringing her along. "She's ranch-born and raised. Can ride and rope with the best of them. She's the one who always needles the calves in the spring." Seeing her startled look, he explained. "She gives the calves their vaccinations. She's quick and efficient. I couldn't ask for better. On top of that, she's a very good teacher right here in Blissdale."

"A truly remarkable woman." Darcy sounded anything but impressed.

"Only one problem."

She looked suitably shocked. "The woman has a flaw?"

He shrugged. "Probably not. But I guess I do. I can only see her as one of the guys. I'm just not interested in her as a woman." He didn't have room in his life for any more women. He turned his attention back to the photo album. "Here's Amy's third birthday party."

They bent together to study the people in the pictures. Did she linger longer on the ones with Rob in them? Was she beginning to see he was a good father to both Blake and Amy? Again that question—why not with Darcy? What had gone wrong?

The next page held a picture he'd forgotten. His mother holding Amy as she opened gifts. The look on his mother's face said so much. Sad yet full of love and pride. She must have known then that she wouldn't be around to see Amy grow up. How had she been able to sit through this party and smile at everyone? How had he been so blind he hadn't seen it coming?

Because he'd purposely chosen to ignore the signs. He wanted to protect himself from the pain of acknowledging her failing health. Maybe it wasn't such a bad way to be. Shut out pain. Don't give it a chance to linger. Don't even give it an opportunity to visit.

Darcy chuckled at the picture of Amy ripping open presents. Her arm pressed against his, warm and soft. Her hand brushed his as she turned a page. He could let himself get interested in this woman. Doing so meant doing exactly what he'd so firmly avoided for years—opening his heart to risk. Letting one more person into his world to be responsible for. And to face the chance of losing.

He wasn't prepared to do that. She'd be gone in a few more days, and he'd say good-bye without any cracks in his heart.

As the day grew long, Amy's temperature rose, and they kept busy sponging her. Aunt Betty, too, grew more miserable. She tried to get up to give her cat its needed shots but swayed so alarmingly Blake insisted she stay in bed. "We'll look after Missy."

Darcy held up her hands and grimaced. She turned away so Aunt Betty couldn't hear her and whispered, "You do it." So Blake gave the cat the needle.

Between caring for the sick humans and the cat, filling the kettle, making hot drinks, and serving soup, the day passed. Blake barely had time to look out the window and hoped his herd had found shelter and safety in some trees.

The gray light faded, and the room grew gloomy.

Amy and Aunt Betty refused to eat anything and settled into an uneasy sleep.

Blake and Darcy sat together on the couch as they enjoyed the last of the soup. The evening hours passed as they talked about growing up and school days.

He told Darcy he took all his schooling at Blissdale.

"The same school for twelve years? It's amazing. I went to at least that many schools."

"Why did you move so often?"

"Mom liked moving."

"You didn't mind?"

"I didn't know it wasn't normal until I was a teenager."

"Do you feel the same need to move all the time?"

"I haven't moved in three years if that means anything. I guess I could see moving if there was a need, but just to move? Nah. Not for me."

"Where's your mom now?"

Darcy laughed. "Now that's the funny thing. She met a guy in California. She used to go there almost every winter for the beaches. Anyway, they married a couple of years ago, and she lives there. Hasn't moved once since she married him. Of course, they go on lots of trips, so I suppose that meets her need."

Blake tried to fit Rob into this constant moving scenario and failed. "I can't see Rob liking that sort of thing. He could hardly bring himself to leave the ranch for any reason."

"You don't have to tell me."

"I'm sorry. I didn't mean to remind you."

She sighed. "Not to worry. Remember my philosophy—enjoy what God gives—the present. Besides, why is it you can't accept I lost my father years ago? Why do you want me to go over it all again? Why is it so important to you?"

He considered her question. "Partly because I think you're avoiding the past but also because I think it isn't fair to Rob's memory that you keep dismissing him as if he died a long time ago. There had to be something more to his not going back to see you."

She stared into his eyes, her own eyes flashing. "Like I was such a terribly bad kid he just had to get away from me. Or my mom was a mean drunk."

"It doesn't seem as if your mother was like that." He studied her features. The narrow chin. Was it quivering? He touched her cheek. Smooth as a spring breeze and kissed by the warmth of the fire. He caught a strand of hair that drifted across her cheek and tucked it behind her pretty little ear. Everything about her was so soft. "One thing I'm certain of, it wasn't because of you. You have a sweet, generous nature. You enjoy life and help others enjoy it, too." Too bad he wouldn't be enjoying it long term. "Perhaps Rob meant for you to come here and learn what he was like. Perhaps it's God's plan for you, as well."

She studied him soberly. "I never thought of it like that." She suddenly smiled, and the tension in his neck eased. "Thank you for reminding me that God is in control."

Chapter 11

Darcy woke next morning to the sun streaming across her face. She blinked, disoriented, then remembered where she was—sleeping on the couch in Blake's living room as they waited out the storm. Only the bright sunlight announced the storm had ended.

Aunt Betty coughed. Amy moaned. Darcy sat up and glanced over the back of the sofa. Blake sprawled out on the recliner, his arms hanging over the edges, his head tipped to one side. He'd have a sore neck when he woke. She could tuck her pillow under his head, but he'd wake up if she disturbed him. He needed his beauty sleep. Right. Like he needed the plague. He was the most handsome man she'd ever encountered. Those warm chocolate eyes seemed to treasure every word she said. *Whoa.* She jerked her thoughts back. Sure, he was good-looking and kind. But—

He sighed and turned toward her, and she forgot all her "buts." Last night something had shifted in her feelings toward him. And she knew the exact moment it happened—when he reminded her of God's hand in her life. She knew then, Blake was a man she could trust.

She slowly pushed aside her covers and eased to her feet, glancing at him, wishing he would waken and smile at her. Perhaps with his mind clouded with sleep he would let his guard down and see her for who she was.

Darcy stared into the glowing embers of the fire. Who was she, indeed? What a stupid thing to think. What you saw was what you got. Darcy. Nothing more. Nothing less. No pretense. She snickered softly. That's what came of too many late nights, sitting before a fire.

She pressed the heel of her hand to her forehead. She didn't dream. She just lived. Ignoring the deep ache behind her eyes, blaming it on the late night, she tiptoed over to Amy, touching her forehead to check for a fever. She didn't seem too warm. Tenderness filled her as she smiled down at her little sister. Her throat tightened. How did someone walk away from a child like this? Yet her father had walked away from her. And she would leave at the end of her two weeks. Not that she thought Amy would even notice Darcy's departure. She was surrounded by love and care.

"Is she okay?" Blake's whisper jarred through her thoughts. She jerked her gaze toward him. Yep. Eyes soft and filled with sleep-muffled thoughts. Her breath gave a little jerk at the way he smiled at her.

"Amy's okay?" he repeated.

She sucked in steadying air and scolded her imagination back to the corner. "I think her fever is gone."

He sat up and looked around. "The storm is over."

She smiled as he bounded from the chair and squinted out the window at the blinding sunlight. "Not as bad as it might have been."

She joined him. "It's beautiful." The landscape spread out like a clean white sheet, full of mounds of whipped cream with sharp peaks.

He grunted. "I guess I should be grateful for the moisture, but I'll just be glad if the cows and calves are safe."

Aunt Betty stirred and moaned.

Blake turned from the window. "How are you feeling?" he asked softly.

"Awful," she croaked.

Darcy hurried to make the older woman a hot drink and give her two acetaminophen tablets.

"Missy." She pointed toward the cat. Darcy hid her shudder.

"I'll do it." Blake gave the necessary shot.

He straightened, grinning as humming filled the room. "Power's on."

Soon the room filled with warmth from the furnace. Aunt Betty dragged herself from the couch. "I'm going to my bed. I don't want to be bothered until I'm over this." She shuffled to her room, mumbling, "I don't want to be bothered at all."

Amy sat up and rubbed her eyes. As soon as she saw the sunshine, she scrambled from under the covers and raced to the window for a glance, then shot for the back door. "I gotta check on my cats."

Blake caught her as she charged past. "You're not going out with that sore throat."

She struggled in his arms. "I got to see if the baby kittens are okay."

He carried her back to her tangled blankets. "I'll check on them. You have to stay inside until you're better."

"I'm better already."

"You're not going out today, and that's final."

Darcy turned to hide a smile as Amy dropped her crossed arms over her chest in a defiant gesture.

Already Blake headed for the door. "I'll have to shovel the snow."

Darcy made breakfast and coffee, glancing out often to watch Blake steadily tossing scoops of snow over his shoulder. She knew from the way the snow clung to the shovel and landed in lumps that it was heavy and wet, but he worked until he had the sidewalk and driveway cleared, then left the shovel in a snowbank and headed toward the barn.

A few minutes later he stomped into the house.

Amy raced toward him. "Are they okay?"

"All cats accounted for. I fed them and gave them water." Amy sighed loudly. Blake smiled across at Darcy. "I checked on your house. Everything's A-okay."

"I made breakfast." She loved cooking and often made meals for her friends, but there was something cozy and special about making it for Blake and Amy. *Stop playing house,* she warned herself.

"Great." He helped himself to the bacon and eggs. "Don't tell anyone I said so," he whispered to Amy, "but this is a nice break from Aunt Betty's cooking."

Amy nodded. "Darcy should cook for us all the time."

Darcy sent her little sister a suspicious look. Had Darcy's thoughts developed a neon sign over her head? She forced herself to keep her gaze on Amy, afraid her expression would reveal more than she wanted. She well knew the distinction between fantasy and reality. And would never make the mistake of confusing the two.

Blake sighed. "We can't keep her just to cook for us. Besides, she has to go back to Seattle in a few days."

"Aww," Amy protested. "Why don't you ask her to stay?"

Darcy stole a glimpse of Blake twitching uncomfortably at Amy's suggestions. Poor man. She'd have to rescue him. "It's not that easy, Amy."

"Why not?" she demanded. "Aren't you big enough to do what you want? When I get big I'll do what I want." Her scowl dared anyone to argue.

Darcy laughed. "I guess I'm not big enough yet. I still have to do things I don't want to."

Amy wasn't buying it. "I won't when I grow up."

Darcy finally allowed herself to look at Blake, seeing her amusement reflected in his eyes.

"Good luck, little sister," he said.

At least they didn't return to discussing Darcy's ability to stay. If she were asked. . .

She knew no one but Amy would ask.

Blake lingered over his coffee as Darcy put the dishes in the washer and turned it on. She wiped the table and dried her hands on a towel. "I guess I'd better get back to my house." There didn't seem any more excuse to hang about.

Blake set his cup down. "I have to go check on the herd."

"What about Amy?" Darcy asked. "Aunt Betty isn't going to be able to supervise her."

Amy did her "mad" routine—crossing her arms and jerking them across her chest. "I don't need Aunt Betty to look after me."

Blake appeared thoughtful. "Don't worry. Aunt Betty will hear her if she's into anything."

Darcy had her doubts. She'd seen enough of Amy wandering around on her own. Of course, she realized children needed less supervision on a ranch than in the city, but it still felt a little scary.

"I'll just hang around until you're back. I have one more box to sort out anyway."

Amy bounced forward. "Will you make lunch?"

"Do you want me to?" Darcy looked at Blake.

"I can't ask you to do that. It's not your job." But his eyes said yes.

Her smile came from a roped-off area behind her heart. "I don't mind. I like cooking." And they needed her. It filled her with intermingling thoughts of belonging, being appreciated, and a trickle of fear and caution against letting those feelings out to play.

Blake nodded. "If you're sure?"

"I am."

Amy whooped. "I want. . ." She paused. "I want. . ." She sent a blank look toward Blake. "What do I like?"

His eyes danced with mischief. "Macaroni and cheese?"

She crossed her arms. "Not macaroni and cheese." She leaned toward her brother. "Tell me what I like besides mashed potatoes and gravy and homemade soup." She smacked her lips.

Darcy laughed. "You hardly tasted the soup I made."

"Yes, I did. It was good."

Blake ruffled Amy's hair. "Why don't you let Darcy decide what she wants to make? I'm sure you'll like it."

Amy nodded so hard her hair tossed over her head. "I know I will."

Darcy decided she would spend time with Amy, showing her some girlish fun before she tackled the last box of papers.

As soon as Blake left, she ran a bubble bath. She scrubbed Amy's hair until it glistened like bottled sunshine and blew it dry, curling the ends into a sweet flip. She found a brand-new pair of green cords in the back of the closet. "Where did these come from?"

Amy shrugged. "I think someone gave them to me."

Darcy dug further and found a matching green sweater. "These are really cute. Why don't you put them on?"

As soon as Amy was dressed, Darcy led her to a mirror. Amy stared at her reflection. "I'm pretty, aren't I?"

Darcy hugged her hard. "You're beautiful."

Amy returned to the mirror, pirouetting and admiring herself. Darcy wondered if she'd created a vain monster. But Amy's gaze shifted to her pile of stuffed toys, and she skipped over to pick them up and talk to them as she arranged them on her bed.

"I'm going downstairs to the office. I'll be there if you need me." Amy was so engrossed in her make-believe that Darcy wondered if she even noticed her leave.

She didn't want to go back in the farm office. She felt as if her emotions had been dragged along on the storm's wind—battered and rearranged until she hardly knew what to think anymore. If she let herself, she could spin a whole imaginary world where she became an integral part of life on the ranch. A partner to Blake, him caring what she thought of various things. Really and truly joint guardians of Amy.

Enough make-believe. The sooner she finished the last box, the better.

She paused at the office door, listening to Amy's murmurs overhead. For two cents she'd go play with her little sister. But then this job would still be hanging over her. She might as well do it.

This box contained letters. She hoped they were all farm related, but it took her about five minutes to realize she couldn't be so lucky. There were letters from Blake's mom, Kathy, which she set aside for Blake to deal with. There were birthday cards from Kathy and Blake and various aunts and uncles. Again she set these aside for Blake. He might want to keep them for sentimental reasons.

She saw an envelope with her mother's writing on it and grabbed it. What would her mother have to say to the man who had abandoned both of them for ranch life? She pulled out a card and stared at a mountain scene, then flipped it open. It said only "new address" and gave a house and street number. Darcy didn't remember that address. She studied the postmark and did some math. She'd only been six at the time. Had her mother sent him a notice of every address change? If so, she should find the evidence in this box. She pulled out a stack of cards held with elastic. More address-change cards. She flipped through them. One every six months or so for several years, and then about fifteen years ago they ended. She tapped the stack with a fingertip. Odd. Had her mother stopped letting her father know when they moved? Why? Was this the reason he had never contacted her? But all he had to do was call information for a number. But when had her mother started getting an unlisted number? She couldn't remember. Only that she'd done so after an ex-boyfriend started to hassle her.

She tossed the stack in the garbage and continued to sort through the contents of the box. She pulled out an envelope with her own writing on it. Without looking, she knew it contained the invitation to her graduation. She'd sent two tickets, thinking how generous she was to include the second wife. She could still imagine the taste of the glue on the envelope as she'd licked it, her hands trembling. Would he come to share this important occasion with her? She'd clutched the reply envelope to her chest when it arrived and carried it to her room where she put it on the bedside table and stared at it for a long time before she could bring herself to open it.

The response was yes. She remembered how she'd kissed the official card with only a check mark by the word, as hot tears flooded her eyes.

But neither of them showed up. And she'd never spoken to him or contacted him again.

She pulled the two embossed invitations from the envelope and ran her fingers along the printing.

It was seven years ago. It no longer had any power to sting. *Please, God. Help me not to let those long-ago feelings return. I've given them to You. They can no longer hurt me.* But she couldn't keep back the pain of that day. Her throat closed off. Her eyes stung. He'd never called or offered an explanation. A tiny memory plucked at her thoughts. Hadn't Mom said he'd called? Something about his wife being very ill. But she'd shut her mind to the excuses. And refused the calls from him until they no longer came.

A mental abacus clicked in her brain.

Seven years ago.

Amy was six. That meant—was Kathy pregnant with her at the time? Blake had said they'd discovered her weak heart when she got pregnant. Was it the reason they hadn't come?

She shoved the invitation back in the envelope and tossed it in the garbage. She wouldn't allow herself this torture—looking for reasons. Hoping for something to explain her father's absence. Besides, it would explain only one event. Where had he been the previous twelve years? Why hadn't he called or visited or sent a card on her birthday?

Why was she letting herself get worked up about the past?

She dug further into the box. No more address-change notices. Nothing that gave her the slightest clue about what had taken her father so completely away from her.

Not that she was looking for it. She was only sorting old letters.

The box almost empty, she pulled out a folded letter and opened the three pages. She hadn't seen this dark bold scrawl before. She flipped the last page and read the signature. Rob Hagen. She lowered the pages and stared out the window, blinking from the glisten of the sun on snow. The eaves dripped. Blake's footprints filled with water.

She swallowed hard and looked at the pages in her hand. Her father had written this letter. Maybe it had been meant for her. She checked the first page. *Dear Kathy.*

What did she expect? A reasonable explanation?

The letter wasn't hers. She piled it with Blake's stuff.

A few more scraps of paper and the box was empty.

Darcy stood in front of the window, hugging her arms around her. Despite what she kept telling Blake, she'd been secretly clinging to the hope of something more. She hadn't found it.

Unless. . .

Chapter 12

She turned back to the desk.

No. The letter wasn't hers.

But Blake gave her permission to sort through everything and decide what to do with it.

She reached for the letter.

The first page described the business trip that took her father away from the ranch for a week. The second page asked about the ranch as if he couldn't wait for the week to end so he could get back and discover for himself.

The third page began, "Kathy, you asked me to be certain before I told you again that I love you. I am more certain than ever. And I hope to convince you when I get back, but in the meantime let me try to make you see just how much you mean to me. On the ranch I have found a peace and contentment I've never before known. I'd be the first to admit that something about the land calms me. The rolling hills, the sunshine at noon, the distant mountains like guardians—"

Darcy stopped reading to press her finger to the bridge of her nose. She, too, felt calmness and peace as she gazed at the landscape. She could understand how her father would feel pulled to it. She continued to read.

"And I love the ranch, the demands of the work, the pride I feel in knowing I had a part in bringing it back from the edge of bankruptcy."

Darcy smiled through the sheen of tears, proud to know her father had been so devoted to a good cause.

"But those are not the things that matter most. It is you who have helped me heal, enabled me to get past my anger to this place of peace. Your love has made me whole again. I resent each moment I am away from you. I want to be able to see your smile every morning, feel your arms around me every night, see you smile when I tell you day after day until we're both old and gray how much I love you. Kathy, you are everything to me. Without you I am empty and aimless. Thank you for loving me when I was unlovable, for showing me the way back to myself, for believing in me even when I didn't. For showing me that God loved me. I will never leave you."

Darcy sighed as she finished the letter. Had her father ever loved her mother like this? She tried to remember them together, but nothing came. Was she too young to have memories, or had she blocked them from her mind? She closed her eyes and breathed slowly, calming herself, letting herself go deep into her memories. She wasn't sure, but she thought she saw them arguing. Had her father run from a tumultuous relationship with her mother to this peaceful haven with Kathy?

If so, she could forgive him. At least for ending his first marriage.

She didn't know if she could forgive him for leaving her.

Forgiveness?

She spun around to the brightness of the window. She'd already forgiven him. It was over and done with. Yes, a little explanation would be nice, but forgiveness was unnecessary.

"Yes," the deep, calm voice within her said, *"you need to forgive him for abandoning you. And choosing Blake."*

What he did was unforgivable.

She leaned her head against the window frame, remembering something a friend shared from going to a series of workshops after her divorce. *"Unforgiveness is like drinking poison and expecting our enemy to die."*

But how could she let it go when there was no explanation? It was easier to cover it over and ignore it.

"It will never go away if you do that. You will always be haunted by feelings of unworthiness even though you know you are precious in God's sight."

Unworthiness. Where had that come from? This was getting way too weird. Besides, it was time to prepare lunch.

She hurried from the room as if chased by a hundred voices.

She made a Mexican chef salad for lunch.

Blake rushed in, soaked to the skin, and dashed upstairs to change before he ate. "This is good," he murmured. "Can you watch Amy this afternoon? I have to find the rest of my cows."

"What happened to them?"

"They moved with the storm. I expect I'll find them bunched up in some trees, but I won't be able to relax until I find them all safe and sound."

"Amy will be all right with me. Aunt Betty seems content to sleep."

"Thanks." And he was gone before she could offer him dessert. Which was fine because she only had ice cream and a can of fruit salad from the storeroom downstairs.

❖

All the cows and calves finally accounted for, Blake could go home, his mind at ease.

He hated leaving Darcy at the house all day. Not, he was honest enough to admit, because he didn't want her there, but because he wanted to be there with her.

He'd make it up to her with the new video Norma Shaw had given him a few days ago. A chick flick. No doubt she'd planned for him to ask her daughter, Jeannie, to watch it with him. But he didn't have the time and certainly not the inclination. The idea of watching it with Darcy, however, made him forget work.

He jerked the truck into park and jumped out. Halfway across the yard he smelled roast beef, and his taste buds urged him to pick up the pace. He forced himself to slow to a gentle stroll so he wouldn't race into the house, panting and drooling like a starved man.

Cinnamon and apple aromas joined the beef smell as he opened the door. Amy raced over. "I like roast beef and apple pie."

Blake swung her up in his arms. "Me, too, squirt."

He met Darcy's gaze across the kitchen and winked. "We're a shameless pair when it comes to food."

Her eyes darkened to stormy blue, and his heart took off like a cow headed for new pasture. He forced himself to wait until after they'd eaten and Amy had wandered away to ask the question burning in his brain. "Why don't you stay and watch a movie with me tonight?" At the startled look in her eyes, he added, "I owe you for watching Amy."

She frowned. "She's my sister, too. And I'm joint guardian."

What would it be like if she stayed? Blake pushed away the idea. It was stupid to set himself up to be hurt. All he wanted was an enjoyable evening with her. He smiled what he hoped was his more powerful smile. "A nice, quiet evening. . .just the two of us. It might be fun."

She squinted and tilted her head. "Is this a date?"

"Almost. A movie date at home. I might even be able to scare up some popcorn and old licorice."

She laughed. His heart did a quick two-step as mischief flashed across her eyes. "An action adventure with lots of killing?" she asked suspiciously.

"Nope. A chick flick." He named the movie. "Have you seen it?"

She shook her head and studied him through narrowed eyes. "You're asking me to watch a romantic comedy with you?"

He nodded.

She let out a long, deep sigh. "I've been wanting to see that movie." She glanced at her watch. "It's a date, but I want to have a shower and change my clothes." She wrinkled her nose as if she smelled bad.

He could tell her she didn't. "Go ahead while I put Amy to bed."

She spun around and headed for the door, pausing to grab the old coat off the hook and slide her feet into her boots. He watched her puddle through the slush to her house, her shoelaces trailing in the water, and then he called Amy and got her into bed.

He set up the movie, then made popcorn. He'd given himself several pep talks and warnings. *Be careful. Remember she'll be gone in a few days. Don't be begging for hurt and disappointment.* But surely he could enjoy an evening with her and still protect his emotions.

He knew the minute she opened the door. The soft gentle smell of spring rain wafted over him. A good clean scent.

He turned slowly. She stood uncertainly in the doorway, a fairy-tale princess in a luminescent pink shirt and white pants. Her dark hair shone as if it carried its own secret supply of diamonds. She wore it loose about her shoulders. "You look good," he murmured, his voice hoarse.

"So do you," she whispered, and he was glad he'd showered, shaved, and changed into black jeans and a black T-shirt. He reached for her hand and pulled her to his side as he led her into the living room. He'd pulled the love seat around to face the TV, and he settled her there.

"Can I offer you something to drink? Coffee, tea, a soft drink?"

"I'll have soda."

He opened two cans of soda, put the popcorn on the coffee table, and turned on the movie. It was the typical chick flick sort of thing with lots of girl-guy stuff, but she twisted her hands in her lap and sighed as if the plot didn't interest her.

Finally, he paused the movie. "What's wrong?"

"I keep thinking of something I found this afternoon."

He managed to mumble, "What?"

"A letter my father wrote to your mother."

"Something significant?" He could hardly resent this intrusion into their date. It was what he'd hoped for when he gave her the task.

She shrugged. "Maybe. I'll get it."

He stretched his arms across the back of the love seat and stared at the TV screen.

She brought a letter and handed it to him. "I probably shouldn't have read it, but I was curious."

"Not a problem." He skimmed the pages. "It sounds like Rob." He didn't know where she was going with this.

"You were right. I need some answers."

He could have pointed out it was a little late to be looking but held his tongue. "Did you find them in this?"

"Some clues. More clues here." She held up a bundle secured with a rubber band. "Address-change cards from my mother. The most recent is fifteen years ago."

216

His mental skills were good enough to do the math. "That's when Rob married Mom."

She nodded. "I know." She sat beside him, the cards in her lap. "If only. . ."

He pulled her close, and she rested against his shoulder, her fingers caressing the edges of the cards.

"I never realized how important it is for me to understand what happened. But I suppose it's too late."

He squeezed her shoulder, feeling her sadness, wishing he could ease it. "You could talk to Gene."

"The lawyer?"

"Maybe Rob said something to him."

She leaned forward, turning to grin at him. "Excellent idea. Why didn't I think of it?"

Because you need me. Out loud he said, "You probably would have." He almost wished he hadn't mentioned it because she sprang to her feet and crossed to the window, staring out into the dark. "I'll phone first thing in the morning and make an appointment." She headed for the door as if anxious to make the next day come faster.

He followed her. "I hope you find the answers you need."

"Thanks for the movie and the suggestion." Her eyes glowed with excitement. Unfortunately, he was pretty sure it was over visiting the lawyer, not over the evening she'd spent in Blake's company. But he was glad. He'd prayed she'd find the healing she needed.

◆

Darcy parked beside her house and sat staring out the window. Blake must have been watching for her return because he strode across the yard. She waited until he was beside her car before she climbed out.

"How'd it go?" he asked, searching her face.

She shrugged. "So-so."

"Well, what did he say?" He touched her chin tenderly. "Was it awful?"

"No. Just confusing. He said my father said I'd know what Amy needed." She searched Blake's eyes. "I don't understand. How can I know what she needs? I don't even know what I need."

Blake gave her a soft, understanding smile. "Maybe you know more than you realize." He touched her cheek.

She jerked away and instantly wished she hadn't. "Now you're going to talk in riddles, too?" She tried to pull mental armor around her. This whole business was turning into an emotional quagmire. "I was very angry with my father for a long time. I couldn't help wondering why he didn't care about me. What was wrong with me? It could have made me an angry, rebellious teenager if I hadn't been rescued by a very kind Christian lady. I just don't want to rake through all that stuff again. I don't want to derail my life, if you know what I mean."

"I'm sure he cared for you."

"Really?" She made no attempt to disguise her sarcasm. "And your proof for this theory is what?"

"I just know Rob. He was loyal and loving and—"

"To you. Do you know how that makes me feel? That he could love another man's son more than his own daughter?"

Blake jerked back as if she'd slapped him. "Maybe he just got tired of trying."

She recoiled. "As if I wasn't worth the effort?"

He reached for her. "No. I didn't mean it like that. I don't think that. You are a wonderful person, well worth knowing." He pulled her into his arms. At first she resisted his attempt to pull her close. But her need for comfort overcame her caution, and she let him cradle her to his chest. She could find peace in this man's arms. She'd seen how loyal and protective and caring he was.

"You know how I thought the world of Rob, but I confess he acted as if he had no past. Maybe he couldn't face whatever was back there. You have to see it was his failure, not yours, that kept you apart."

"It was my failure, too. I shut him out." His arm tightened around her as she shuddered. "I've never admitted it before, but I made it impossible for him to contact me after graduation."

He stroked her head and pressed his palm to her back.

Realizing they stood in the middle of the yard, she pulled away. "I just wish I could find some sort of closure."

"You will. You'll find a way. God will show you." He stroked her cheek. She grabbed his hand and clung to it.

She needed his reminder. Part of her wanted to drive away, push the whole thing into a dark corner, and forget about it entirely. But now that she'd cracked the door, there was no going back. She had to find peace with her past.

"I think I'll take Amy shopping in Blissdale."

"Good idea. I don't think Aunt Betty is ready to deal with her yet."

She found Amy, had her change into clean clothes, and did her hair.

"What are we going to buy?" Amy asked.

"Something new and pretty for you."

Amy looked interested. "Something pink?"

"Sounds about right."

Amy chatted all the way into town, pointing out neighbors and repeating everything she knew about them. As they neared the town, she showed Darcy her school. It was obvious she enjoyed her teacher and classmates.

The town had only two stores with children's clothing. Darcy let Amy choose several outfits and helped her try them on. She bought two pink outfits, some hair doodads, and a pair of glittering flip-flops Amy insisted on wearing. They had lunch at a little sandwich shop.

"Just like real ladies," Amy insisted.

Darcy laughed. Her little sister was a tomboy, raised in a man's world; yet she had deep feminine longings. Was that what her father meant when he said Darcy would know what Amy needed?

She didn't know. Perhaps she never would.

She knew only that she would miss Amy like crazy when she returned to Seattle. Their hours together had almost come to an end. Tomorrow Amy would return to school. The next day Darcy would leave.

Seeing a children's playground, she pulled over and spent an hour with Amy, storing up quality time and memories.

Finally, they had to call an end to the day and head back to the ranch. Darcy drove the length of the main street, then turned around.

Amy grew quiet as they passed the little white church. "Slow down," she said.

Darcy pulled to the curb. "What is it?"

Amy stared out the window. "That's the graveyard where Mommy and Daddy are. And Blake's daddy."

Darcy leaned over to look. A tidy little cemetery shaded by dark pines and poplars, in the pale green of early spring. "It looks nice." She studied the place with a deep ache.

"I go there to say good-bye. Sometimes we take flowers."

Darcy blinked. It was exactly what she needed. She'd take flowers and say good-bye. It would be her act of closure.

◆

The next morning Darcy delayed her trip to town until after nine so she could buy flowers. She ran an extra two miles in the morning just to deal with her nervous energy, pausing frequently to look around at the landscape. She loved the rolling hills, the fresh green of spring. She tipped her head and listened as a bird sang. A meadowlark. The prettiest sound she'd ever heard.

She lengthened her stride as she turned toward home, eager to head to town. It was silly, she knew, but this trip beckoned like a royal visit.

She bought a large bouquet in a heavy vase at the local florist and made her way to the cemetery. Suddenly, not wanting to face her task, she wandered up and down the rows, reading the headstones. And then there it was: ROBERT JOHN HAGEN. His date of birth, his date of death. In italics, *HE LIVED WELL AND*

LEFT TOO SOON. Blake must have picked out the inscription.

She set the vase on the cement pad under the headstone and knelt in the damp grass.

"Well, here I am," she whispered. Her words sighed away into soundlessness. She remained motionless, wondering what she expected. She rested in confidence that God would reveal it. Bits and pieces drifted through her mind. Her father's smile. His flashing eyes. She couldn't say if they were from her memories or from the photos she'd seen in Blake's album. Or even seeing Amy and recognizing his resemblance in her.

He said he'd found peace here. Something he wouldn't have found with Mom. She moved too often for anyone to have a chance to unpack, let alone settle down and enjoy the surroundings.

Her father and mother had been unsuited for each other. Her mother simply wandered away too often, too far.

Darcy delved down into her feelings. She'd felt totally betrayed when he failed to come to her graduation. Now she knew it was because Kathy was pregnant with Amy and struggling with her failing heart.

"I forgive you," she whispered. "I understand there were more important things. And thank you for putting Amy first. She's precious."

She sat back on her heels. Then he got cancer. From what Blake said, he deteriorated quickly. No doubt he poured all his energy into spending time with Amy, helping her cope. Blake said her father had tried to find Darcy. Couldn't. Ran out of time and energy. Blake had been angry about that.

"You did well," she whispered. "Amy is going to be okay."

Again she sat in silence. Birds serenaded from the trees. The whole place seemed bathed with peace.

Her father had found his peace here. He'd found love and acceptance. She was glad he'd found what he needed.

"Good-bye," she whispered. "I wish I'd forgiven you long ago so we could have enjoyed some time together. Thank you for giving me the house and making sure I got to meet Amy."

She paused. "And Blake. I understand why you loved him. He's so kind and steady."

Her father found what he needed here. So had she. She'd found her peace. She'd found a little sister. She'd found a man whom—

A man she could love?

She loved Blake. She let the idea slide through her, like a healing balm.

She chuckled softly. "Did you know this would happen?"

She arranged the flowers a little, then pushed to her feet. "I don't think I'll find the happy-ever-after life you did." Blake wanted no more emotional risks in his life. She understood that. It hurt to love, knowing you might lose the one you loved.

She stood in front of the headstone for a long time. Finally, sighing, she turned away. Tomorrow she had to head back to Seattle. But she wasn't walking away from everything she'd found here.

Chapter 13

Where's Amy?" Darcy asked Aunt Betty.

"Who knows? That child shouldn't be allowed to run helter-skelter all over the place. I keep telling Blake she should be confined to the house, or at least the yard. She has a very nice swing set and sandbox."

"I'll see if she's with her cats."

"That's another thing!" the older woman called after her. "Those cats are probably diseased! If she brings in something that infects Missy...!"

Darcy didn't hang about to see what Aunt Betty said. As far as Darcy was concerned, Aunt Betty's animal presented more of a disease risk than Amy's well-nourished, vigorous cats.

She found Amy in the supply room, singing to the baby kittens. Darcy settled down beside her.

For a while they talked about the kittens and how they'd grown. Amy told her what she'd named each of them.

"Amy," Darcy pulled her closer. "You remember I'm leaving tomorrow?"

Amy looked down, silent for a moment. "Do you have to go?"

" 'Fraid so. I have a job and responsibilities."

"I don't want you to go." Amy kept her face tipped down.

"I wish I didn't have to. But"—she squeezed Amy's little shoulders—"I promise I'll be back."

"Something might happen to you."

Darcy knew Amy had too much firsthand experience with loss to offer meaningless reassurances. Bad things did happen. "Amy, honey, it would have to be something really awful to keep me from coming back to see you."

Amy leaned her head against Darcy.

She had so many things she wanted to tell her; but her throat closed off, and for a moment she couldn't speak. She forced the tightness away. "I am so glad you're my little sister. I will see you every chance I get." She'd fly there for holidays. It was close enough that she could fly out for a weekend. "I want to know when you have something special going on. If it's on a weekend, I'll be here. And soon you'll be big enough to come and visit me. I'll take you to the ocean, and you can play in the water. We'll have lots of fun."

"I'll like the ocean, won't I?"

"Of course you will."

Amy faced Darcy, her lips quivering. "I'd sooner have you here every day than see the ocean."

Darcy pulled her little sister into her arms. "I'd like that, too." Hot tears coursed down her cheeks. If only she could stay. But she couldn't. She'd committed to the race. She had a job in Seattle. And she didn't belong here. Not in the way she wanted.

She spent the afternoon with Amy. She would have taken her home and cooked supper for her, but Aunt Betty already had macaroni bubbling on the stove.

"Time to get washed up," Aunt Betty told Amy. "Be sure to scrub really well. I don't want barn germs in here."

Amy wrinkled her nose, but at Darcy's warning look went to obey.

"Aunt Betty, would you tell Blake I'd like to see him after he's eaten?"

"Certainly."

She went home to prepare for the evening and to begin packing.

◆

By the time Blake arrived, she'd worked out the details of what she wanted to say.

She opened the door to his knock. He stood in the evening shadows, dressed in blue jeans and a navy plaid shirt, the sleeves rolled up to his elbows. He smiled, his dark eyes warm and watchful. She caught her breath as she acknowledged her love for him.

"You wanted to see me?"

The world seemed to hold still while she smiled at him. She would cherish this moment forever. "Come on in." She waved him toward the living room where she had put out icy drinks and fresh chocolate chip cookies. "Help yourself." She followed him and chose a chair facing him, knowing if she sat beside him on the couch as he expected, she would forget her carefully rehearsed words.

He took several cookies and bit into one. "Good."

"Thanks." She waited until he sipped his drink. "I'm leaving tomorrow." He put his glass down and studied her. "But I'm not relinquishing my joint guardianship of Amy." She'd never once agreed to, though she knew Blake expected she would. "I think she needs me. We can arrange for her to stay with me during her vacation time." She rushed on, ignoring the way his expression grew hard and set. She didn't want him to say anything until she was finished. "I've changed my mind about selling my house, too. I want to keep it so I can visit as often as I like." She took a deep breath and waited. It was the first time she'd belonged anywhere, and she wasn't going to give it up.

He continued to stare at her. She was sure she could smell rubber burning as he assessed her words. "Oka–a–ay," he finally managed. "I guess I'm not surprised. But are you sure it's the best thing for Amy?"

"Maybe this is what my father intended—that I would have input into Amy's life. I just know I can't walk away from her. I care too much about her." She tried not to think how much she cared about Blake. She didn't dare let her mind go there. Foolishly she'd fallen in love with him. But she wouldn't let it destroy her. She was an expert at pushing away things that hurt.

"You've certainly made her vacation memorable for her." He smiled. "And for me."

She nodded. "It's been fun." She mentally shut a few more doors against the pain she knew she would endure when she drove away. More than anything, she wanted to belong here. More than just owning the house. She wanted to be part of the fabric of his life. But she didn't belong. She never had, and she never would.

"I'm glad you're not going to walk away without a backward look."

She knew then he'd expected she would. Had perhaps even been counting on it. "I'm sorry I never tried to mend things with my father, but I can't change the past. I'm forever grateful he found what he needed here with you and your mother and Amy. I can't resent that."

"But you're going back?"

She nodded. "Tomorrow. I have to. The run and everything."

"Of course. Amy will miss you."

"I'll phone and write. And I'll be back every chance I get. I'd like it if she could spend part of her vacation time with me." He hadn't refused. Nor had he agreed. The last thing she wanted was a tug-of-war over custody arrangements.

"It won't be the same as having you here."

She pressed her lips together. She closed her eyes and forced a long, slow breath into her lungs. Somewhere she had to find the strength to leave. And the grace to do it without breaking down and upsetting everyone. *Lord, I trust You to help me.*

"We'll miss you."

"You mean Amy?"

He leaned forward, his eyes dark. "I mean me. *I* will miss you." He reached for her hands. "Who am I trying to fool? I love you. Marry me. It would be the ideal solution for Amy."

He loved her? How awfully convenient to discover he was in love just as she announced she intended to remain a part of Amy's life. How ironic he came up with this idea at the last minute. For a moment she seriously considered the offer. She could care for both Amy and Blake. She could see her sister every day. She could accept this very convenient offer and be a very convenient wife to a man she loved.

But she'd been shortchanging herself long enough. She was worthy of a heart-shattering, life-changing, world-altering love.

She withdrew her hands. "Blake, it's a very generous offer but one I have to refuse. I want to be more than a convenient solution to a problem." She stood, feeling an urgent need to put distance between them.

He rushed to her side. "Darcy, it's not like that."

She moved away. "I'm sure both you and Amy will settle into a nice little routine after I've gone, and you'll thank me for not taking you seriously."

He took a step toward her and then another.

She backed away until she ran into a wall.

He stopped, inches away, and studied her, his expression serious.

She could almost convince herself he looked sorrowful but knew she would only be transferring her own emotions.

"You've forgotten one small matter." He gently cupped her chin in his palm and slowly lowered his head.

When his lips touched hers, it was all she could do not to melt against him.

He lifted his head. "I love you."

"Funny you just discovered this."

He shrugged. "Call me slow. Or maybe cautious."

"It would be the best thing for Amy."

"Yes, it would."

"She'd never be torn between us."

"No, she wouldn't." His expression grew increasingly cautious.

She took a deep breath and found the strength she needed to push away from him. "Sorry. I'm not interested in a marriage of convenience."

"Me either." He stalked from the room, pausing at the door. "You're doing it again, Darcy."

"What am I doing?"

"You're pushing away love because you're afraid of getting hurt." He slowly closed the door behind him.

She sank to the couch. *No, Blake, I'm finally seeing that I'm worthy of real love, not just convenience.*

◆

That night she lay staring up at the ceiling, waiting in vain for sleep to come. If he loved her, why hadn't he said so earlier? Why now? It was just too coincidental.

Maybe he'd only discovered it. Her own discovery was new.

She stared into the darkness. Could it be. . . ? Was it possible? If he loved her, he would not let her leave tomorrow morning without trying again to convince her. She laughed softly in the darkness as she allowed herself to hope. To be loved by Blake. To be part of his life.

It was all she could do to remain in bed when she wanted to rush over, throw herself in his arms, and confess her own love.

Lord, is this why You brought me here? To heal the past, find a new beginning? If so, I thank You.

"I love you, Blake Thompson," she whispered into the dark.

◆

Blake sat in the office. What's a man to do? He finally comes to his senses and realizes his world revolves around a certain woman, and he tells her so only to have her refuse his offer. Generous. Convenient. Of course it was. But it was also honest.

He knew what to blame. Her honed defensiveness. She'd shut out her father. Afraid loving would mean rejection. She was doing the same with him. She couldn't let herself believe him. She was afraid to belong.

Well, she'd been wrong about her father. He *had* cared about her. He'd kept that old picture by his desk all those years.

He jerked upright so fast the chair creaked. He could prove her father loved her. Maybe that would make it possible for her to accept *his* love.

He opened the drawer where he'd dropped her picture days ago and smiled at her childish sweetness. He polished the frame on his shirtsleeve and set the picture in the middle of the desk.

Finally, smiling, he climbed the stairs and fell into bed. Sleep came quickly and easily.

The next morning he headed for her house as soon as the first rays of light trickled over the horizon. She was already throwing things into her car.

When she saw him coming, she straightened, cocked one hip against the trunk, and crossed her arms to wait. He broke his stride at the way her mouth turned up and her eyes brightened. All welcoming and sweet. Had she changed her mind?

He closed the distance between them and stood staring down at her, unable to speak for the explosion of hope inside him. She smiled with the brightness of the sun coming over the horizon.

"I had to catch you before you left." His voice felt thick and heavy.

"Some special reason?" She didn't act surprised at his presence or his words.

"Were you expecting me?"

She lowered her gaze. "I—I'm not sure."

"I have something to show you." He held out the picture.

She took it and studied it. "This is me. Where did you find it?"

"Your father always kept it by his desk."

"But I was in there and never saw it."

"I shoved it in the drawer when you came. I was a little angry at the time."

He gave her his best repentant smile.

"My father really kept it by his desk?"

"Always."

"And you never thought to tell me until now?"

He stepped back from the fierce look on her face.

She shook the picture at him. "You knew how much it would mean to me, but you never thought to tell me?"

This was not going the way he planned. "I forgot, but don't you see? You've always had a place here. A place in his heart. And now"—he held out his hands—"you have a place in my heart. Darcy, I love you."

She yanked open the car door and set the picture on the passenger seat. "One thing I've discovered here. I'm worth more than last-minute confessions and suddenly remembered revelations." She slid behind the steering wheel, slammed the door, and backed out of the yard, then paused and lowered her window. "I'll call Amy."

He managed to get in a few words before she closed the window and drove away. "Darcy, when are you going to stop running?"

◆

Running, running, running. The pavement pounding beneath her feet. Blood pulsating through her veins. Driving every thought from her head.

Blake. Amy. Her father. It all seemed so convoluted. Why had her father left her the house and named her joint guardian of Amy?

He thought she would know what Amy needed.

She didn't even know what *she* needed.

Faster. Faster. Run. Don't think.

It was what she did best. Run until she no longer remembered anything.

"When are you going to stop running?" She almost faltered as Blake's words echoed through her mind.

She picked up her pace again, every piston drive of her legs striking home a truth. She was running away. She'd done it before, shutting her father out of her life rather than chance being rejected. And she'd missed knowing him.

Blake said he loved her, but she hadn't even given him a chance. Instead, here she was, trying to run away from her thoughts.

She knew what Amy needed. As clearly as a message written in letters across the sky. Amy needed to know those who loved her would be with her day in and day out, rejoicing in her accomplishments, comforting her in times of disappointment.

Maybe it was time for Darcy to stop running from her fear of abandonment and feelings of being unworthy. Maybe it was time to take a risk. What was the worst thing that could happen? Blake might change his mind. Better to have loved and lost than never to have loved at all.

She chuckled, knowing how the girls in the office always changed that saying to "Better to have loved a short man than never to have loved a tall." Usually remarked when the CEO wandered the halls. A short man but incredibly handsome and a real sweetheart. All the girls were more than half in love with him.

As she rounded the corner and headed down the homestretch, she made up her mind. It was time to stop running and take a risk on the most important thing in her life—loving Blake.

She would quit her job and move to the ranch. She could either do contract work from home or get a job in Blissdale as an office manager. She might not get the same degree of responsibility she had now. That didn't matter. She could live on her savings for several months.

She would give her love for Blake a chance. And his love for her. Maybe he'd changed his mind. After all—

No, if he really loved her, he would welcome her back. No more running from her fears.

Darcy waved at Irene and pushed for one more burst of speed before she crossed the line.

Irene cheered. "Best time ever. You are going to take this race for sure, girl."

Darcy took the towel Irene offered and wiped her face as she paced in place, cooling off. "Two more days."

"I've never seen you work so hard. It's like you're trying to escape a horde of demons."

They headed for the showers. "Maybe I have been, but no more." She told Irene her plan. Her friend hugged her.

"Good for you. You deserve every bit of happiness you can find."

Chapter 14

Why'd you let her go?" Amy demanded.

Blake sighed. Amy had been difficult since Darcy left. Not that he could blame her for feeling out of sorts. His own patience had taken a beating these past few days. "She had to go. You know that."

"You could have stopped her. You could have made her stay."

"Honey, she's a grown-up. She has to decide to do things on her own." He'd known she would leave. From the beginning he'd expected it. After all, look at her record.

"She wanted to stay, but you wouldn't let her."

"No, Amy. That's not true."

Amy crossed her arms over her chest and glowered. "You said something to her. I know you did. You were mean."

"No, Amy. I asked her to stay, and she wouldn't."

"I don't believe you."

Amy stalked away. Blake considered following her, but he understood her need to blame someone or something for Darcy's departure. Who did he blame? Himself, Darcy, her past, her fears? Sighing deeply, he headed for the office, the only place he could find peace lately. He tried to convince himself it wasn't because he caught hints of her scent or imagined her standing at the window or sitting in the chair.

Amy was wrong. He'd tried to convince Darcy to stay. He'd said he loved her. What more could he do?

He could have told her sooner. Why did he wait until she was leaving so it looked just a little too convenient?

Because he'd been too busy trying to protect himself.

From what?

From risk. From hurt. He knew firsthand how much it hurt to lose a loved one. And in his mixed-up way of thinking he figured if he didn't let himself love someone, he wouldn't have to deal with that pain again. Trouble was, by protecting himself, he'd spoken too late; and he knew pain stronger, more intense, more mind-bending than the pain of losing Rob or his parents.

Because she wasn't gone—she was just out of reach.

Unless—

Lord, forgive me for being so blind. Help her to hear what I have to say. What I feel.

He overturned the chair as he sprang to his feet. "Aunt Betty! Amy!" he roared.

Aunt Betty called from the living room. "I'm in here."

He hurried into the room. "I'm going to Seattle to see Darcy."

That got her attention. She jerked her gaze from the TV. "So you've come to your senses finally?"

"What do you mean?"

"That girl loves you, and you let her go."

"I didn't—" Why was everyone blaming him? "She loves me? How do you know?"

She huffed. "I may be old, but even if I was half blind I could see it."

"She loves me?"

"Question is, do you love her?"

He grinned like a child being offered candy. "I do."

"Well, don't just stand there. Go find her and tell her." She turned back to the TV. "Are you taking Amy?"

"Taking me where?" Amy demanded.

"I'm going to see Darcy and try to persuade her to come back."

"I'm going, too." She pursed her lips.

He contemplated the idea. "It's a long drive, and I'm not going to waste time."

She didn't flinch. "I'm going, too. Darcy said she'd show me the ocean."

Blake hadn't thought what he would do when he got there past hugging Darcy and telling her he loved her until she was thoroughly convinced. But a little vacation sounded ideal. He'd arrange for someone to do the chores so he could get away.

He and Darcy could wander the beaches hand in hand, visit some special restaurants. He could see all her favorite places, go to church with her, see how she lived.

"I'm going," Amy said again, more forcefully. "You might mess up."

Blake laughed. "Six years old and you already think I can't handle things because I'm male."

"Me and Darcy are sisters." She said it vehemently. "We understand each other."

Chuckling, he swung her into his arms. "I'm sure you do. Yes, you can come. Let's go pack."

They were on the road in an hour. He figured if he drove straight through the night they'd get there in time to catch her race.

◆

Blake rubbed his stinging eyes as he fought the city traffic. He hated city driving. Stop. Start. Avoid the crazies trying to gain a fraction of a second by lane hopping. Only today, he was one of the crazies.

He glanced at his watch. They would never make it in time for the start of her race, but with a little luck they'd catch the end.

Traffic had been slowed to a crawl coming through the mountains, thanks to an accident. He'd prayed for God to open up a way for him and was grateful for getting through safely.

Amy struggled awake. Once she saw they were in the city, she sat up and strained to see everything. "Is this Seattle?"

"Yes, it is."

"Where's the ocean? Where's Darcy?"

"Haven't found either one yet."

"Why not?"

He sighed. She said it as if he'd been responsible for the delays. "We'll be there soon." He'd managed to track down the address of the race. It was only a few blocks away.

He jerked to a halt at a red light. Four more blocks to go. His knuckles whitened on the steering wheel. How long did this run take? He had no idea.

The light changed, and he edged forward, was cut off, and slammed on the brakes again. He struggled to keep his frustration under control.

He screeched the tires as soon as the way cleared. He came to a barricade. "This must be it." A few people hung about but not the crowd he'd expected. He drove around the block until he found a parking spot. "Come on, Amy. Hurry up."

She struggled a moment with her seat belt, then joined him. He locked the vehicle and strode toward the race route, practically dragging Amy along. He saw a knot of people ahead and hurried to them.

"Is the race over?"

A pretty young woman nodded. "You missed it."

"Who won?"

"Darcy Hagen. She blew away the competition."

Blake grinned. "Way to go. Where is she?"

The woman looked Blake up and down. "Who wants to know?"

Amy bounced up and down. "I'm her sister."

The woman turned her gaze toward Amy and smiled slowly. "You look like her." She looked again at Blake and studied him.

"Any idea where I can find her?" Blake asked.

She shrugged.

Now what? He pulled out his cell and called Darcy's home number. *No answer.* He didn't want to drive to her apartment if she was around the race route somewhere.

"Come on. Let's ask around." He asked several people if they knew where he could find Darcy Hagen. Some gave him blank stares.

Another woman looked him up and down before she said, "She left."

Amy tugged on his hand. "Blake, I'm hungry."

"Okay." They might as well grab something.

He found a fast-food joint and ordered egg burgers for them. While Amy used the washroom, he called Darcy's number again. Still no answer.

"Where's Darcy?" Amy demanded as she joined him, revitalized by her breakfast and bathroom break.

"Let's find her apartment and see if she's there."

He pored over the map, figuring how to get from the restaurant to her address. A few minutes later he found the place and knocked on the door. No answer.

A woman wearing pants too tight for her bulging figure and a man's plaid shirt yanked open a door down the hall. "You looking for Miss Hagen? You're too late. She checked out this morning."

"Checked out?"

"Yup. Didn't give me a month's notice like she's supposed to, but she gave me the money, so what do I care?" The woman shut the door.

"Blake. Where's Darcy?"

"Honey, I don't know." Had she run? Afraid to take a chance on a relationship? "I guess we might as well go home."

"I want to see Darcy."

"Me, too. But we'll have to wait for her to contact us." He clung to Amy's hand. This little girl would surely be enough to bring her back to them.

"Can we see the ocean?"

"Sure." No reason to rush back only to stare aimlessly out the window, wondering when Darcy would contact them.

◆

They spent two days in the city, then took their time on the return trip. Amy enjoyed herself, though Blake often caught a hint of sadness in her expression. "I miss Darcy," she confided every night as he prepared her for bed.

"I do, too, little sister. But she'll come back. I know she will." He had to believe it. And if she didn't, he would turn the world upside down until he found her. He would hire a private investigator. He would never stop looking. And when he found her, he would beg her to give him another chance. He would tell her every day, in every way he could, how much he loved her until she finally believed it.

It was midafternoon when they turned down the driveway to home.

Amy screeched.

Startled, Blake slammed on the brakes. "What's wrong?"

"Darcy! Darcy!" she squealed.

Blake followed her gaze. Darcy's car stood in the sunshine at the side of her house. A grin threatened to split his face in two. "She's been painting." The trim was bright pink.

He headed back to town.

"Where are you going? I want to see Darcy." Amy started to cry.

"Kid, you'll have to wait your turn. I get to see her first. And I'm going bearing gifts."

Amy slammed her crossed arms over her chest. "Why do you see her first? That's not fair."

"You already know she loves you. And she knows you love her. I want to convince her I love her, too."

Amy laughed. "I knew it. I just knew it."

"What exactly did you know?"

"That we would all be together, like a real family."

He hoped Amy was right.

He couldn't decide on flowers or candy, and in the end, with Amy offering her advice, he bought a large bouquet of mixed flowers. Roses just didn't seem right for Darcy, so he chose daisies and chrysanthemums and forget-me-nots. He bought a large heart-shaped box of chocolates, a wind catcher that twisted and danced, a lawn ornament of a girl smelling roses, and a coffee mug with the words LOVE MAKES THE WORLD GO ROUND written in large pink letters.

"I can't carry any more," he told Amy.

Amy allowed him to drop her off at their house without protest. She smiled and patted his arm. "Of course she loves you," she told him in a wise, grown-up voice.

"I hope you're right."

He drove to Darcy's house and parked beside her car. She turned from painting the trim around the kitchen window and, seeing who it was, put her brush on the paint tray and climbed down from the ladder.

She wore an old shirt of his he'd outgrown and left in the house. A slash of pink crossed her nose.

He grinned. His heart picked up speed. He slipped out of the truck and filled his arms with three of his gifts. "Welcome home. I brought you something."

"Thank you." She took the flowers, chocolates, and coffee mug, her expression uncertain. "Where were you?"

"I went to Seattle to convince you I truly love you. When I couldn't find you, we spent some time wandering around the city. We wanted to see your home."

"I decided to come back. No more running."

"You saved me from hunting you down."

She laughed. "Why would you do that?"

"Because I love you and I'm prepared to spend the rest of my life proving it."

She buried her nose in the flowers. "I should put these in water."

"Wait." He returned to the truck and took out his other two gifts. He put the lawn ornament beside the door and hooked the wind catcher on a nail by the window.

"What is all this?"

"I just want to show you how much I love you." He moved closer, admired her saucy little mouth, her fine eyebrows that arched upward in surprise, her big blue eyes watching, waiting. He touched the slash of pink on her nose. "I love you, Darcy Hagen. I need you. Not to take care of Amy but to fill the spot in my heart reserved for you. Nothing else matters to me as much as you. I'll sell the ranch if you don't want to live here. All that matters is we're together."

She pressed her fingers to his lips. "Don't you dare sell the ranch. I would never forgive you."

He caught her hand and kissed her fingertips. "I'm glad. I don't know any other life. Darcy, will you share my life with me? Please say yes and end my misery."

"Blake, I love you."

He cupped her face and kissed her gently. This kiss was different. It was two hearts becoming one.

He lifted his head to smile down at her. "You didn't answer my question."

A teasing light filled her eyes. "You haven't guessed? Blake, I will marry you. I will love you now and for always."

"Hurray!" Amy's shout pulled their gazes toward her, hiding around the corner of the house.

Blake shook his head and laughed. "You were supposed to wait."

"I couldn't."

"Come on." He and Darcy opened their arms to invite her into a three-cornered hug. For the first time in his life Blake felt complete and whole.

Epilogue

D arcy's mother helped her adjust her veil, pulling the shimmering material back from a satin comb tucked into Darcy's hair. Darcy had opted for having her face uncovered. "I don't want to miss one thing today."

"You're beautiful," her mother whispered before she took her husband's arm and let the usher walk her down the aisle.

Darcy stood at the back of the church, out of sight of the guests but where she could see them. She'd insisted they marry in the church Blake had attended all his life. Her friends had come from Seattle. Mrs. R sat right behind Darcy's mom. The rest of the guests were people who had known Blake forever and whom Darcy was learning to know. She'd been accepted into the community so quickly it amazed her. They'd welcomed her with invitations to dinner or coffee or quick chats when they met in town. They'd thrown a nice bridal shower. She'd been surprised when Blake informed her it was for both men and women. It had turned into a wonderful time of hearing stories about Blake she was certain he'd never have told her on his own.

She sighed deeply, her heart full to overflowing.

"What's wrong?" Amy asked.

Darcy turned her attention to her little sister. "Everything is perfect." She adjusted the pretty tiara in Amy's hair. Bright bits of rhinestone fell in narrow ribbons from the tiara like raindrops in the blond hair. She and Amy had shopped together for all the bridal finery. The more time she spent with the little girl, the more she grew to love her.

The same with Blake.

"Are you ready?" she asked Amy.

Amy nodded, her eyes bright with excitement.

"Then let's go." The girls held hands as they stepped through the doors to the sounds of the wedding march. Darcy faltered just a tiny bit as she found Blake's eyes and read his love. He'd opened his heart to her, filled her thoughts with his adoration, made up for all the years she'd wondered why she didn't measure up.

"You make everything worthwhile," he said often. "I will never stop thanking God for you. And thanking Rob for arranging for us to meet."

Blake made her feel whole and adored.

She and Amy reached the front of the church. As they had practiced, Amy stepped in front of them while Darcy and Blake joined their hands. And then everything else faded into the background as she turned to Blake, her heart so full of love and gratitude she wasn't sure how to control it. When she saw the same love and gratitude reflected in Blake's eyes, she silently promised she would spend the rest of her life pouring out her love for him.

And then they exchanged vows and kissed amid the applause and approval of friends, family, and neighbors.

As they made their way to sign the register, Blake whispered for her ears only, "Our life together has just begun. Just think how much better it will get with practice and with God's help."

Everlasting Love

Dedication

It would seem obvious that I dedicate this book to a couple that has exemplified enduring love. That would be my parents who were devoted to each other throughout life and are now enjoying the glories of heaven together.

But I want to give credit to another kind love—"Love is patient, love is kind." Many people have input into my book after it leaves my hands—people who check content, make sure I haven't had a character get into a car and end up in a truck, and correct my faulty grammar and punctuation. I want to give special credit to one such person: Debbie Cole, freelance copy editor with Heartsong Presents. She does a great job of showing me things I need to do to polish my story. Revisions and edits can be discouraging for the author, but Debbie manages to encourage me through the process. Debbie, thank you for everything you contribute and the spirit in which you do it.

Chapter 1

He'd said put him down for something.

He'd specifically mentioned ham or ice cream, but he sure didn't remember agreeing to this.

Steele Davis again read the note his secretary handed him. "Pastor Don says thanks for offering to help with the banquet. The planning committee is meeting at five at J'ava Moi, the café across the street."

No, he had definitely *not* offered to help plan the thing. Not that he couldn't do it. But with the café owner? No way. Something about her he found alarming, disturbing even.

He glanced out the window. There she was in the flesh—Holly Hope—serving a couple at one of her outside tables. Dispensing coffee, smiles, and eternal optimism, her wavy dark hair swinging about her shoulders as she danced her way back into the café.

The whole place screamed romantic nonsense. Practically made a man break into a cold sweat. He hadn't been raised to believe in such stuff, nor had his experience as a lawyer taught him to trust it.

He'd gone for an espresso a few months ago when she first opened her café. Uninvited, she'd told him all about her dreams for the place. "I want to give people a chance to nurture their love. That's why I've created a romantic little spot and named it J'ava Moi. It's a play on words. You know, 'would ya' have me?'"

Steele had been fascinated with the way her eyes flashed back and forth between amusement and determination as she talked. He'd also been more than a little awestruck at such a blatant, head-in-the-clouds attitude. As a lawyer, a dealer in realities, he'd felt the need to dispute her optimism. "Not everything can be fixed by flowers and candles."

"I think you'd have to agree it's hard to harbor bitterness while making romantic gestures."

He didn't agree the one canceled out the other and tried again to promote reason. "In my experience, romance doesn't last."

"Maybe because it's neglected." She'd challenged him with a steady look from her dark brown eyes.

To this day he couldn't explain why he didn't just walk away. Maybe it was her denial of facts that made him add, "How many couples do you think I see

239

every year who've vowed before God and man to love each other ' 'til death do them part' and who can now no longer stand the sight of each other? Personally, I will never be fool enough to let emotion overrule reason."

She'd considered him a full, tension-fraught moment then smiled.

The expression made him want to bite the edge off his china cup; it was the same sort of look opposing lawyers gave when they felt they'd argued better and smarter than he—all smug and self-assured.

"Sounds like you have some baggage to deal with," she said with calm assurance as if his life were her business. Which it wasn't.

He remembered clearly how he'd sputtered. He, a lawyer, paid to be good with his mouth, had been at a loss for words. He'd drained his cup, set it quietly on the table, and resorted to retreat.

He hadn't been back.

Didn't intend to ever return.

Did his best to avoid any contact with the overly cheerful Holly Hope at church.

He glanced again at the paper in his hand. Seems the discussion had been about a banquet as a fund-raiser for some charity. Anxious to get on with his plans for the day, he'd paid little attention to the whole thing—except to offer a food contribution. But if Holly planned it, he could count on lots of hearts and flowers. And if the menu board outside her café indicated her preference, there would be nothing but health food.

Someone needed to make sure she didn't go overboard with the romance nonsense. He checked his watch. Almost five. He had a few minutes before he had to be anywhere. He made up his mind. Steele to the rescue of any innocent man who'd be attending the banquet with a starry-eyed woman at his side.

Besides, how long would it take? He'd give a few suggestions, make sure everyone was on board with a practical plan, then step aside and let someone who *liked* doing this sort of thing take over.

He threw some documents into his briefcase and jogged down the stairs into the warm sunshine.

As he crossed the street, Holly glanced up from cleaning a table and looked startled. "I wasn't sure you'd come."

"Wouldn't miss it for the world." His sarcasm came easily. It'd always been his defense, and something about Holly put him on the defensive.

She straightened and studied him with a glint in her eyes that informed him she doubted he meant what he said. Then she nodded toward a table beside a large potted tree and sheltered by a long planter complete with trellis and drenched in pink flowers.

He shuddered and thought of pulling the table farther along the sidewalk to a place where a man could think.

"Can I bring you something? Espresso, wasn't it?"

How did she remember that? He was so surprised, he sat next to the flowers without protest and for the second time in his life was at a loss for words. All he could manage was a quick nod.

She went inside to get the coffee.

The place oozed romance—a trap to short-circuit a man's reason. He'd just proven it with his little mental lapse.

She returned with two cups and sat across from him. "I expect you'd like to get right to work."

He surely would. Not that he was desperate to get away or anything. He had his thoughts firmly under control. Now. "Shouldn't we wait for the others?"

She laughed.

A pleasant enough sound, but he didn't like the message it conveyed. As if he'd said something supremely foolish.

"We're it."

"The two of us? No way. The pastor said there was a committee."

"Yup. You and me."

He felt her look as much as saw it. Full of challenge. A dare. *Can you handle this, mister?* Of course he could. The sudden beading of sweat across his brow only proved the day was unseasonably warm.

She smiled and wriggled like some kind of overeager pup. "I'm so glad we decided to raise money for the AIDS orphans in Africa. The poor little things. Doesn't it make you want to adopt them all and give them a good home?"

"I doubt the kids would thank you for taking them from their own culture and their familiar world."

Her eager smile flattened. "I *know* that. But it doesn't stop me from wishing I could do more." She looked down and toyed with her cup.

His chest felt stiff at the way her enthusiasm had died. What was the matter with him? He wasn't usually so argumentative outside the courtroom.

He drew in a deep breath full of a jumble of scents—honey, cinnamon, and other spices he couldn't name. He couldn't tell if the smells came from the flowers, the cookies and muffins in the display case, or a combination of both.

He was thankful she spoke again, pulling him from considering the source of the intriguing aromas and back to the subject at hand.

"To start with, we need a theme. I thought something like 'For the love of—'"

He rolled his eyes.

She stopped. "You don't like that?" Again that long, considering look. "Am I sensing a problem here?"

"It isn't a Valentine banquet. If we must have a theme, let's make it something more appropriate like"—he did some quick mental gymnastics—" 'Aid for AIDS victims.'" He smiled, pleased he'd managed to come up with something in such a hurry. "It's simple and practical."

She tipped her head, a brittle gleam in her eyes. "It sounds like a newspaper headline. We need something a little catchier."

"What's wrong with newspaper headlines? They say things succinctly. No guessing as to what it's all about."

"Let's keep thinking about it. Maybe we'll come up with something better."

He knew what she really meant. Not something better—something *she* liked. He could see this was going to be about as much fun as stepping on a nail.

She nodded briskly. "Let's move on then. What about decorations?"

He gave a long, deliberate look around the place. "We could maybe skip the frilly and flowery. How about something—" Again he had to scramble for a substitute.

"You don't like the way I've decorated the café?"

Intuition was supposedly a woman's strength, but right now he had a sudden flash of understanding and knew he'd offended the woman.

"It's very pretty. Just a little too. . ." Pink. He glanced around. Apart from the flower cart, now almost empty, and the bank of pink to his right, there wasn't as much of the color as he pictured. In fact, he saw lots of green, some kind of tan color that probably had a fancy name, and black wrought iron furniture. "It's a little too"—he was stuck for words again—"romantic," he blurted.

"So you don't believe in love."

"Of course I do, but the biblical sort. Love is patient, kind, gentle, and forgiving—keeps no record of wrongs. As I see it, love is practical. It doesn't need all these trappings to be real."

She snorted. A very expressive sound, communicating quite effectively her disbelief. "So it's romance you object to." She favored him with a smile.

If her smile had been mocking, he would have known how to react, but it was full of sweet patience and slid right past his sarcasm and defensiveness. Left him speechless. Again. Not that she seemed to notice. She went right on as if intent on exploring the whole realm of psychology as per Steele Davis.

"That's a curious belief. I'm guessing it's more personal than dealing with angry couples seeking a divorce. Any chance you've been married?"

"Not me."

She struck out on that one.

"Your parents then? Are they divorced?"

"Nope." Strike two. "My parents have what I consider a very good marriage. It's not based on dreams. It's—"

"Practical?" She pulled her mouth down into a fierce frown. "A business arrangement maybe?"

"What's wrong with that?"

"Sounds cold and calculating."

"Not to me. It sounds sensible and lasting."

"And safe. But no risks, no glory."

He didn't like the way this conversation had headed south. How had she turned it from banquet plans to dissecting his parents' marriage and examining his motivation for disliking romance? Not caring for a whole lot of sentimentality didn't point to his having a deep, dark secret—just a long streak of practical. "About the decorations. . ."

"Not you. Not your parents."

"Maybe we could have something solid. Like—"

But she would not be sidetracked. He was beginning to think she'd missed her calling. She should have been a lawyer.

"A sibling then?"

Cold filled his insides. Cold, blue anger at her persistence, at being forced to admit, if only to himself, how Mike's divorce had hurt him. Hurt the whole family. He was still helping Mike clean up from it. Becky had practically destroyed them and could have destroyed the family business if Steele hadn't fought her every step of the way. Even so, it had cost them a bundle.

Steele and Mike had both sworn off women, but Bill, only twenty-four and six years younger than Steele, was unable to get past his hurt and anger at how Becky had treated them. He spent his time pursuing women only to dump them before they could dump him. Everyone in the family knew what he was doing, but they couldn't make Bill understand how irresponsible his behavior was.

It filled Steele with frustration to see his brothers trying to come to grips with their anger, though Steele preferred anger to the bouts of depression that so often gripped Mike.

Holly's smile faded. "I'm sorry. I didn't mean to hit a nerve. Let's get back to planning the banquet." She paused as if knowing he needed a minute to pull his thoughts back to the business at hand.

He wanted to resent her prodding more than he appreciated her insight and kindness, but it proved a difficult choice.

She seemed to know when he'd pushed away the intense emotion grabbing his throat. "Now about the decorations. I think we need to keep in mind this is a formal, dressy affair. People will expect something rather special. I thought a summer theme like a garden room. Banks of flowers and greenery. . ." She paused as if reading his mind.

Or maybe she simply saw the way his lips curled as he interrupted her. "I suppose lots and lots of pink flowers and pink and white balloons. You know a man could get some kind of fever with all that pink."

She narrowed her eyes as if to argue then suddenly chuckled.

The sound surprised him—a deep-throated trill like some kind of cheery songbird.

"But that's just what I had in mind—love fever."

He shuddered. "It's not something to joke about. There's nothing romantic or sensible about a couple with stars in their eyes and their brains out of gear." He'd seen over and over how it led to disaster.

She chuckled again.

And again he felt a sudden internal lurch at the sound. He shook his head to clear it, though the confusion seemed to originate from an unfamiliar place behind his heart. Something he was loath to admit even to himself.

She grew serious. "I say pink flowers, lots of greenery, maybe some streamers. We want to make it special."

"That's your idea of special, not mine." He glanced around the outdoor seating area and shot a pained look through the door to more flowers and fancy stuff.

Her brown eyes turned as cold as the soil on his grandfather's ranch in the dead of winter. "I'll have you know that many people, men and women alike, find my décor very relaxing, very romantic."

"Exactly. Could we skip romantic and go straight to something ordinary?"

She made an exasperated sound. "If people wanted ordinary, they would stay in their own backyards and save themselves the cost of a banquet. It has to be special somehow."

"Isn't that where the food comes in?"

"We also need entertainment, decorations, other things."

"Entertainment? Whoa." He glanced at his watch and saw his plans for a quick appearance disappear in a flash. "I thought the career group simply wanted to do something special for the summer."

"It's more than just something to do."

Remembering her impassioned argument at the meeting, wanting to turn the event into a fund-raiser, he guessed he couldn't blame her for sounding defensive any more than he could stop the sudden clenching of his gut at the idea of spending hours with this woman, arguing about minutia. He couldn't imagine how they'd work together. Her belief in romance grated against the facts he witnessed day after day. But with admirable determination, considering his long sigh of exasperation, she pushed on.

"I wanted to do something to benefit the AIDS victims. Something wonderful to get everyone involved."

"R–i–g–h–t." He waved around the empty café. "Let's get everyone involved. Oh, wait. You and I are everyone, and I didn't even offer to help plan the thing. I thought I could contribute something in the way of food or help set up." What had Pastor Don been thinking to assign him to help on a committee of two? He mentally shrugged. Likely the same as he—someone had to make sure this banquet didn't turn into a lovefest.

"So you're not behind this?"

"No." He backtracked as her hard look silently accused him of withholding food from a starving child. "I mean, yes, of course I'm behind it. I just hadn't planned to be in charge. Not that I mind helping. In fact I probably have a lot to contribute." *Yeah. Uh huh. Like what?* He hoped she didn't have the same thought.

"Really?" No mistaking the disbelief in her voice. "Then perhaps you'd like to be in charge of entertainment."

Then again maybe not. "I figure if you intend to hire a professional group of any sort, you should have done it months ago."

"No, if *you* want to hire a group. . .didn't we just agree you'd look after entertainment?"

"Holly, I did not agree to anything except bringing ice cream. But I'm here, and I can see you need help."

She snorted.

"I admit," he said, "I haven't given the whole thing a lot of thought." *None, in fact.* "But I'm prepared to do my part. Why don't I look after decorations and *you* arrange entertainment?"

She laughed out loud—the sound a mixture of horror and amusement that managed to scratch his nerve endings at the same time as it tickled the unfamiliar spot deep inside.

"I don't think so. I want this banquet to be memorable."

They stared at each other, his gaze, he suspected, as hard and unyielding as hers. He wanted nothing more than to hand the whole business over to her and let her do what she wanted. But his stubborn, practical side warned him he wouldn't be happy with himself or the results if he did. He owed it to the pastor, to the church members, and to the male populace as a whole to keep Holly from inflicting her sentimental notions on them.

"Very well," he conceded reluctantly. "We'll work together."

Boy, did she look happy about that. Yeah, right. She pulled her pretty pink lips down in the most daunting frown.

"That's an oxymoron if I ever heard one. You and I 'work together.' Why don't we just go to Pastor Don and ask him to replace you?"

"Why? It's not as if I don't have the brains to help plan a simple little banquet. We'll work together just fine." No way would he let anyone tell him he couldn't do it.

"You're sure? You won't just sneer at every one of my ideas and do your best to ruin the whole affair?"

He'd never been more certain he did *not* want to do something. Except maybe for the time he'd been forced to take dancing classes at school and had to dance with Penny, the prettiest girl in class. He'd broken out in hives every time her hand touched his. Come to think of it, this situation wasn't a lot different. He'd survived the Penny torture. And now he was all grown up—a lawyer who did not flinch at anything. "Why would I want to ruin things? I'll help. This will be the best banquet you've ever seen."

"Then we need to get down to work."

"Right. I'd say the most pressing is entertainment. When did you say the banquet will be?"

She gave a date less than two months away.

"Who can we possibly get at such short notice?"

She lifted her hand in an airy wave. "We don't have to hire entertainers. We could have a talent show."

He groaned. "I can just see it. Mr. Alaston reciting 'The Rime of the Ancient Mariner' and Grandma Moses singing 'Amazing Grace.'" Now that's memorable all right. But probably not the way you'd like it to be."

She laughed. "Her name is Mrs. Pocklington."

Funny, he'd never noticed before what a heartwarming laugh she had. Likely because he'd been so busy avoiding her.

She sobered, but her eyes continued to dance with amusement. "Then what do you suggest? I think it has to be local because of the time constraints; but also, the more people personally contribute, the more they will be invested in the whole purpose of this banquet—helping the orphans."

He glanced at his watch. "Hey, I've got to run." He had a six thirty appointment. "We'll need to continue this. I'll give it some thought, and we'll meet again."

"When? Or are you already changing your mind about helping?"

He stood and gave her a mocking grin. "Are you always so suspicious?"

She didn't answer, but the look she gave remained challenging. "When?"

"Tomorrow?" At her nod he tried to recall his appointments but couldn't. "I'll check my schedule and let you know what works."

"Of course." She sounded resigned, as if she expected him to be a no-show.

"I'm serious."

"Then I'll see you tomorrow."

He nodded and jogged toward his red SUV.

Halfway home it hit him. He'd just committed to spending time with a confirmed romantic. The same woman he'd spent several months avoiding because of her blatantly obvious sentimentality.

He groaned.

Hey, wait a minute, man. You survived Penny when you were thirteen; you can survive Holly when you're almost thirty.

Chapter 2

The next day, Holly pushed her planters out to the sidewalk and paused to sniff deeply of the scented purple pansies—sweet as new love. She gave a satisfied glance around. She loved her café. She had decorated it like a garden retreat, hoping to give it a bit of a European flair.

She aimed to provide coffee that made her customers sigh with contentment and sandwiches and snacks to rev up their taste buds, but she wanted to do even more. She wanted to give them hope, show them how to keep love thriving, and maybe show them a glimpse of God's great love.

Perhaps to some it sounded unrealistic, naive even.

Steele clearly thought along those lines.

She stole a glance toward the windows of his office. The first time he'd sauntered over for coffee shortly after she opened, she'd recognized him from church and asked where he worked. He'd pointed out his office windows. They had the kind of glass you couldn't see through from the outside. Not that she wanted to see him. What did it matter what he thought? Yet she felt a burning desire to prove him wrong about romance. But even more, whatever had happened that brought such sudden pain to his eyes yesterday, he needed to know the hurt could be healed. She realized she had pressed her hands to her chest, and immediately dropped them. His pain was not her pain.

She put the donation jar next to the cash register and paused to look at the pictures she'd glued to it. A great yawning sense of futility hit her as she touched the faces of the children—orphans in South Africa, their parents victims of the AIDS scourge. All her tips went into this jar as well as whatever people felt like donating. It was so little, but now with the proceeds from the banquet. . . *Lord, help it go well. Help us raise enough to repair the building.*

Her friend Heather worked with the orphans. In almost every e-mail, she mentioned the need to repair the building. It was impossible to keep the children, let alone the supplies, dry during the wet season. Holly had privately promised to raise enough money for the job before the next rainy season. She was counting on this banquet. She had her own plans for it—local involvement, special atmosphere, good food. She wouldn't let Steele's objections ruin it for her and, ultimately, the orphans.

The morning rush began, and she had little time to worry about Steele.

She and Annie, her morning assistant, kept busy right through the lunch hour. It finally slowed down midafternoon. She mixed up a fresh batch of muffins, a new recipe full of all sorts of nutritious things—sunflower seeds, grated orange, cranberries, and slivered almonds. As she slipped them into the oven, she heard someone enter and went to wait on her customer.

Steele. She faltered. Somehow, despite his assurance he'd help, she'd doubted he would return. But there he stood, eyeing the muffins and cookies in the display case.

"You have anything here but health food?"

She moved forward, smiling. Although her food wasn't technically health food, she often got that initial reaction. Her customers changed their minds after the first taste. "Just because it's healthy doesn't mean it tastes bad."

He looked unconvinced.

"My favorite is the sunshine muffin. Why don't you try one? I guarantee it won't kill you."

"Right. What you're saying is I'll survive. Now that sounds appealing. What does it have in it?"

She laughed at his look of uncertainty. "I can't tell you the exact ingredients, of course. That's one of my trade secrets. But it is moist and rich in flavor. May I get you one?"

Looking as if he'd agreed to being stabbed with a sword, he nodded. "And an espresso."

She filled the order and handed it to him.

He glanced about the café. There were only three other customers. "Can we talk?"

She hesitated. She'd been looking forward to a break and a chance to enjoy the sunshine and the scent of her flowers, but dealing with Steele's arguments would ruin her enjoyment of nature. She studied her donation jar. For the orphans, she reminded herself. "I can spare a few minutes. Why don't we sit outside?" She followed him with a coffee for herself.

He waited until she sat down before he bit into his muffin. Surprise, enjoyment, disbelief chased each other across his face.

She laughed until her eyes watered.

Finally he sighed. "This is good."

"Just like I said."

"You did."

She chose to ignore the surprise in his voice. "So have you had any more ideas for the banquet?"

He drank some coffee before he continued. "I've been thinking."

"Good. So have I. If you insist on helping, I can't stop you. After all, it's not my private thing. But I won't relent on what I consider the essentials."

"Yeah, I got that already. So here's my plan. We'll do some brainstorming. Each of us contributes until we find a plan we both agree on. It's the only way I can see this is going to work."

She groaned. "It's a great plan, Steele, but the banquet is supposed to be this summer. Not next century."

He slowly put his cup down and grinned. "Is it that bad?"

"I'm sure you've noticed we tend to disagree."

He suddenly leaned forward. "Seeing as it's for a good cause, I guess we'll just have to concentrate on the task at hand and forget our differences."

She met his gaze. She'd noticed his eyes the first day he wandered over full of doubt and curiosity. Unusual eyes, beautiful even, light hazel that subtly changed color, sometimes green, other times, like now, almost brown. She hoped the soft color meant he truly intended to get behind this project. On her part, she'd cooperate as much as possible. "We can try."

He looked surprised, as if expecting her to disagree, and then he laughed. "All right then."

She stared. His amusement was unexpected. Not only that, his laugh tickled up and down her spine, filled her chest with something she couldn't name. She might have called it shock, but it had a distinctly pleasant feel to it.

He glanced at his watch. "I'm out of time for now. When shall we do this brainstorming?"

"Why don't you come back here when you're finished at your office?" She'd even sweeten the offer with a promise of an early dinner. "We can eat and work at the same time."

He glanced at his empty plate where his healthy muffin had once sat. He looked doubtful. "I'm really not into health food."

She stuffed back annoyance at his blatant prejudice. Did he resist everything outside his normal experience? The man must live an extraordinarily boring life if he did. But sick of defending her food, her café, and her belief in love, she flicked her hand in a dismissive gesture. "Order something delivered if it makes you feel any better."

He didn't answer and had the decency to look uncomfortable, but she didn't give him a chance to provide any more excuses or arguments.

"What time should I expect you?" she asked.

He got to his feet. "I don't have any late appointments. Would five be okay?"

"Of course." She answered without giving herself a chance to think about it, because if she did, she'd be saying no. She had the uneasy feeling she'd regret working with him no matter how it turned out. She imagined continual arguments, more of his criticism of her belief in the value of romance, and, worst of all, more of that funny, happy, delicious feeling when he looked at her with surprise in his eyes. No, she could tell this wasn't going to turn out well.

She waited for him to cross the street then hurried in to stare at the little faces on the donation jar. She'd do whatever it took, even work with Steele. But she intended to be prepared.

"Annie, can you manage on your own for a few minutes? I'm going to dash home and pick up something."

◆

She was armed and ready when he appeared on the sidewalk. It was a lovely afternoon, so she'd taken her arsenal out to one of the outdoor tables. But he went past her into the café and stood in front of the display case.

"Did you order something to eat?"

He shot her a look, half grin, half grimace. "Decided to be brave and try something here." He checked out the remaining sandwiches.

The selection was pretty limited. Only two remained—a vegetarian and a wasabi roast beef. She chuckled at the way he tried to hide his distress.

"You wouldn't happen to have just a simple roast beef sandwich?"

"Wasabi is Japanese horseradish that usually accompanies sushi," she explained. "Be brave. Try it. If you don't like it, I'll refund your money."

Obviously not overjoyed at the prospect, he nodded. "Sure. I'll have it."

She pulled out the two remaining sandwiches—she'd eat the vegetarian—and poured them each a coffee. He offered to take the tray, but she shook her head and carried the food to one of the outside tables.

She waited until he bit into his sandwich, waited for him to decide if he liked it, grinned when his eyes widened and he sighed. "Good. Just like you said."

For a few minutes, they discussed the weather and made conversational noises. But as soon as he finished his sandwich, she pushed aside the rest of hers and pulled the papers toward her. "I want to show you something." She handed him the first page.

He stared at the picture Heather had sent of the ten-year-old girl. "What is this?"

"One of the orphans I want to help." She explained about Heather's work. As she talked, she handed him more pictures and repeated the stories Heather had told her. "Some of these children have cared for parents dying of the disease. Then they are alone trying to support themselves. Many of them have never had anyone teach them the skills they need to survive on their own."

"I've heard about the situation." He put the pictures aside. "You are showing me these for what purpose?"

She nodded. Should have known his lawyer brain would see through her ploy. "I hoped if you could put faces to the project, you'd understand why it's so important to me that this banquet succeed in a big way."

He had a way of studying her that seemed calculated to expose any pretense, but she had none. From the first, she'd been bluntly honest about her intention that this banquet must be special.

"You're saying it's more than entertainment for you and you want me to have the same commitment to a noble cause?"

She nodded, uncertain if he liked the idea or found it more of what he'd consider her idealistic, unrealistic romantic nonsense.

His eyes lightened to amber, and he smiled, filling his face with sudden agreement. "I'd say we both want the banquet to succeed. Our problem is in how each of us thinks is the best way to achieve that."

"Thank you. Now I've done some thinking. A banquet needs a number of things. I mentioned them before. Special decorations, good food, and entertainment. I want local entertainers because it gets people more personally involved and because we don't have time or money to bring in a group."

"You did mention theme yesterday."

"Right. Theme has a twofold purpose—it informs people of the cause and gives us something we can build everything else around."

"Aid for AIDS. That about covers it, I think."

She resisted the urge to roll her eyes. She'd done a lot of thinking about this and realized as a lawyer he needed facts, not feelings, to convince him. "It isn't quite the idea I want to convey. Makes it sound as if there will be a lot of pressure to give. We need something a little more upbeat."

He drummed his fingers on the table and looked into the distance. "Aid, aid, aid. How about band aid?"

This time she groaned. "Sure, and we'll drape tape and dressings all around for decoration."

He leaned forward. "Not that kind of band-aid. Hear me out while I think this through. Band—bands. Marching bands. Band AID. Band entertainment. By setting specifics for a talent show, we could eliminate Grandma Moses and that type of thing. There's a lot of talent in the church and community. Enough for several bands. We'll have a band playoff. Like that TV show, *American Idol.* The crowd votes one band out at a time until we have the new 'Band Idol.'"

She hadn't expected anything but arguments and opposition from him, but surprised as she was to admit it, this was a good idea. "What about decorations?" He'd made it clear he wanted nothing frilly, aka romantic.

"Bunting. Like an old-fashioned political rally. Lots and lots of red, white, and blue bunting."

She'd have never thought of it. "Did you spend the afternoon thinking about this?"

"Nope. Just came up with it. It's called brainstorming. You start throwing out ideas, think about words—"

She'd prayed for unity on this project. She'd prayed for God to bless the planning. This had to be a gift from Him. Even if He chose to send it through a man who openly mocked her on things she held near and dear. She gave a prayer of silent thanks and breathed in a request for strength to be cooperative. She smiled. "I like your ideas. We could keep the food in theme by serving red, white, and blue."

"No health food."

"Why not? We could do tofu with a red tomato sauce and a blueberry salad." She laughed at the shocked look on his face. "Steele, I'm kidding."

He let out a *whoof*. "Glad to hear that."

An hour later they'd come up with a menu they both agreed on—meat of some sort, baked potatoes, salads, desserts—Holly agreed to contact a caterer. She planned to suggest salads and desserts that would continue the theme. They'd drafted an announcement to go out to the various churches for the band competition. Steele had insisted he'd locate the material for decorations. Holly understood he didn't trust her not to turn it into something lovey-dovey.

Meggie, her afternoon assistant, poked her head out. "Shall I close up?"

Holly checked her watch, surprised at how the time had flown. "It's late. You run along. I'll close."

Steele got to his feet. "I think we have it organized for now, but I suppose we'll need to keep in touch as things develop."

"Right." She waited until he gathered his stuff before she started to pull things into the café.

He paused, dropped his briefcase on a chair, and grabbed the planter to push it inside.

"You don't need to help. It's my job. I can do it."

"I'm just being practical. If you hurt yourself, it leaves me to handle the banquet on my own." He grinned at her. "I'm not saying I couldn't do it, but. . ." He shrugged.

She thanked him, tipping her head down to hide the confusion his grin triggered in her. She was used to him as an adversary, not a friend. Having him act as if it mattered whether or not she needed help, even if only to protect her position as the other committee member, weakened her resistance to him. Now why that should matter, she couldn't say. It wasn't as if they were destined to become soul mates.

She chuckled at the idea, felt his curious look, and grinned at him. "You'd no doubt manage just fine."

Chapter 3

Steele tilted his chair back and let out a long, weary sigh.

It had been another of those mind-numbing, go-for-the-throat sessions. Despite both his mediation and the other lawyer's, it seemed the husband and wife were determined to do the most damage before they ended their marriage. This couple attended the same church he did, but it no longer shocked him to have believers come in for a divorce. Or maybe it did. But the vindictiveness left him shaking his head. If they felt the need to end their relationship, couldn't they do it calmly, efficiently?

He closed his eyes and rested his head on the back of his soft leather chair.

As a lawyer, he should take up something less draining—like defending serial killers.

Lethargy sucked at his bones. With a great effort, he opened his eyes and looked out the window, hoping to see some activity at the little café. He always got a chuckle out of watching Holly at work.

He'd spent far more time across the street in the past few weeks than in the entire six months she'd been there. They'd had to discuss all sorts of things to do with the banquet. How many guests could they expect? What was the upper limit? How many bands? Entry fees. Prizes. Choosing salads and desserts from the selection the caterer suggested.

Steele bolted to his feet. "I need a coffee," he muttered to himself and headed across the street. He chose an outside table against the window.

Holly hurried out with his usual espresso. Without waiting for an invitation, she pulled out the chair across from him and plunked herself down. "I saw the Bensons leaving your office." She mentioned the couple from church that had been in his office a few minutes ago.

He studied her over the top of his cup. "Have a chair."

Her startled laugh and faint blush made him smile. "Don't mind if I do," she said.

"I'm not the only office in the building."

"Maybe not, but not many people come out of the camera shop with murder in their eyes." She sat back, crossed her arms, and studied him.

He returned her look for look, attitude for attitude. She had her own peculiar ideas of how he should run his business. On several occasions he'd come close to being rude about her suggestions but instead restrained himself to pointing out it was a little late to hand out flowers by the time couples sought out lawyers. He got a kick from the way she always sprang to the defense of her romantic notions. He probably shouldn't enjoy teasing her as much as he did.

"Did you recommend a counselor to them?" she demanded.

He said nothing. After all, Mr. Benson was a client and entitled to his privacy even in downtown Missoula, Montana, where everyone seemed to know everyone else's business. But, no, he hadn't recommended counseling. He gave her a sad frown and shook his head. Maybe she'd give him one of her sunshine-drenched smiles if she thought he regretted the oversight. In his experience, though, people had to want to work things out. And if they didn't, trying to reason with them was futile.

She shifted her gaze away. He felt a momentary relief to be free of her concentrated study, but then she pinned him again, her eyes hard as ice. "It's just wrong."

He cocked one eyebrow. She'd never made any secret of what she thought about this part of his job. "Good coffee."

She served the perfect cup of coffee—hot enough to scald his tongue, strong enough to fuel jet planes.

That and the fact they had the banquet to plan were the only reasons he came here. Their worlds were light-years apart. Or perhaps, more accurately, their philosophies. She, a confirmed romantic; he, a practical lawyer who dealt with realities.

A tourist couple, complete with digital cameras they aimed indiscriminately, parked themselves at a table half-hidden by the potted flowers.

Holly spared him one more "how could you?" look that had as much impact as a slap with invisible paper, then rushed to wait on the couple.

"Welcome. And what brings you to Missoula?"

The couple admitted they were on their honeymoon. Steele sat back to listen to the conversation, smiling widely at Holly's predictable response. He'd seen her in action before.

"Congratulations." She selected three pink flowers from the cart she refilled every morning and handed them a card along with the tiny bouquet.

The young woman gushed over it. "How sweet. Did you paint this yourself?" She indicated the front of the card.

Holly laughed. "It's a hobby of mine. That and collecting sayings to include."

The new wife opened the card and read aloud, " 'How do I love thee? Let me count the ways. I love thee to the depth and breadth and height my soul can reach.' That's so special. Look, honey." She handed it to her husband.

He took the card, read it, and smiled adoringly at the young woman at his side before he lifted his gaze to Holly. "Do you do this for all your customers?"

"I believe in doing my part to keep love alive and well."

The newlyweds drank in each other's presence, and the woman whispered, "Our love is solid as a rock."

Steele studied their clasped hands, watched as the woman buried her nose in the bouquet, her gaze never leaving her husband, and felt a strange, empty hunger—a yawning ache deep inside.

Holly brought their coffee and left them to return to Steele. "Can I get you something to eat?"

He realized he'd forgotten to have lunch. No wonder he had such an empty feeling inside. "Do you have any of those roast beef sandwiches left?"

"Sure do."

Another reason he kept returning. The first time he'd read the name of the sandwich—wasabi roast beef—he'd grimaced. He'd studied the already-prepared sandwiches in the display case. And then she'd challenged him to try it. Her coffee-brown eyes seemed to dare him, and he wasn't about to turn down a dare, especially from a pretty young woman. From the first bite, he was hooked. The tender beef was sliced thin. The wasabi had enough zest to give the sandwich a delicious bite without clearing his sinuses. The sliced ripe tomato and crisp lettuce provided just the right amount of textural interest and coolness. It was the kind of sandwich that made him smile and lick his fingers when he finished.

Right now his mouth watered in anticipation.

She returned with the sandwich and a generous square of carrot cake spread with cream cheese frosting.

The young couple finished their coffee, called thanks, and wandered away, arm in arm. Steele wondered how much they saw of the sights of Missoula. They seldom took their gazes off each other.

"I love to see newlyweds," Holly said.

He picked up the sandwich and heard the wasabi and roast beef call his name, but he couldn't ignore her blind optimism. He hesitated a moment then said, "I wish them all the best, but the odds are against them, you know."

She sat down at his table again. "Steele, it's a pity you see only the disasters, but surely you've seen long-lasting marriages, full of romance."

He savored the flavor of his sandwich, too distracted by his hunger to think about her question.

"I know you said your parents have a practical relationship, but surely they have little romantic things they do."

He wiped his mouth and drank from the glass of water she'd provided. Finally, unable to avoid her probing gaze, he answered. "My parents aren't the least bit romantic." At her doubtful look, he added, "Unless you count running for parts for each other or changing the oil in one of the Cats." He chuckled at the way her eyes widened in surprise.

"A kitty cat?"

"No, a Caterpillar machine. Think tracks and lots of noise and bounce. As I said, my parents have a businesslike relationship. It works extremely well." He grinned as he watched her digest this information. Loved the way it shook her concept of marriage.

She blinked away the idea and shook her head as if his parents' marriage relationship didn't count. "I wish you could see my parents together. I think it would change your mind about romance."

He felt a flash of annoyance. Some people simply refused to accept any idea that didn't support their chosen belief. As a lawyer, he didn't have that luxury. Not that he'd allow such fuzzy thinking even if he drove a Cat D9 for a living. Time to change the subject.

"How many entries do you have for the band competition?"

"Four so far. How many are we going to accept?"

"Four? I never expected that many."

"O ye of little faith. From the beginning I've prayed for this to be a huge success."

"As if I didn't know that." She never let him forget it. "Hadn't we better limit it? Seems four is about all we can manage. We might have to change the voting thing. It's going to take too long to eliminate them one by one."

"Aww. I wanted to do the TV thing."

He checked for the telltale spark in her eyes, saw it, and knew she teased. "How about a three-round elimination?"

She shrugged. "If we can't vote them out one by one, I don't care how we do it."

He laughed. It hadn't taken him long to discover she had an irrepressible need to tease. One thing in her favor. About the only thing. Except maybe her dedication to a cause. He admired that in anyone.

Whoa, who's tallying points here? They were as opposite as day and night, as compatible as oil and water. The only thing they shared was the desire to make this banquet a success, each for their own reasons. She, because of her personal involvement with an African orphanage. He, because he didn't like to admit defeat in anything.

He headed back to his office a few minutes later, thankful they had the banquet plans well under way. They had no need to spend a lot of time together until last-minute jobs demanded attention.

◆

Holly stepped out of the back door of the café and locked up behind herself.

She headed down the alley toward historic East Pine Street, where she lived. She loved Missoula. Full of flowers and trees, it deserved its nickname as the Garden City. She'd loved it even before her first glimpse of the straw-colored hills crowned with emerald pines against a backdrop of smoky-blue mountains.

From when Holly was young, her grandmother had filled her vivid imagination with magical tales of a year spent in Missoula as nanny to a family who lived in one of the prestigious East Pine Street houses. Her grandmother told her of romantic walks along the river, picnics on the beautiful university campus. It was Nan's tales that had sent Holly from her home in Kalispell to Missoula, first to Montana U to get her business degree, then to buy the shop where she'd started her café—part of her dream come true. The other part of her dream had been achieved when she got an apartment in the historic Steigl complex.

She paused outside the building where she lived. She loved its genteel atmosphere with the brick exterior and the gentle arches on the first-story windows. She loved the leisurely, friendly feel of the city.

She climbed to her second-story apartment, grabbed her laptop, and headed for the chaise lounge on the balcony overlooking the street. She gave a satisfied sigh. Plans for the banquet were well in hand. Life was good. God was good.

She fired up her computer and started to type an e-mail.

Hey, Heather,

How's it goin', girl? Any more centipedes breaking into your mosquito netting? Please don't send me any more pictures of them. Ugh. I couldn't sleep for two days imagining one of them crawling over me. (Okay, it was only two minutes, but just the same—<shudder>)

I told you how I managed to sneak my colorful choice of salads under Steele's radar. All the man cared about was the portion size of the meat. He almost nixed the chicken in favor of steak, but the caterers don't do steak.

I want to do a slide show featuring you and your work. You don't have any objection, do you? Perhaps you can help me with it. Send me a bunch of pictures. Or I can sort through the ones you've already sent.

I have to tell you more about Steele. There's something below the surface of that man. He's a hard-nosed lawyer. He says he believes in a practical love and quotes scripture to substantiate his view. The man could argue the paint off a wall, but I'm not convinced. I know something's hurt him. Something to do with a sibling. I don't think I told you about his reaction when I suggested that very thing. I thought he was going to crack. Just like the first ice on a pond. Remember the way it crackled and snapped into ragged puzzle pieces? Anyway, that's the sort of reaction I got when I prodded a little too hard with Steele, kind of attacking his negative attitude toward romance. Something *has hurt the man real bad. I pray for his emotional healing. <long sigh> I'm not sure that would take care of his extreme practical nature, however.*

But back to the banquet. Just a couple more weeks. Everything is in place. I'm hoping we sell every ticket. I'm so excited. Wish you could be here in person. I miss you every day, but I know you're doing an important work.

BTW, how are the babies? Starting to grow yet? It still shocks me to think of someone's abandoning tiny twin girls by the side of the road. What a miracle they were found in time and taken to you. I pray for them every day and you, too, dear friend.

Lots of hugs and love and prayers,
Hol

Just as she hit SEND, the phone rang. She grabbed the cordless from the table beside her and answered it.

"Holly, how's my favorite girl?"

"Hi, Nan. How's my favorite grandmother?"

"Right as rain, child. Right as rain."

Holly settled back. A call from Nan always brightened her day. "You sound cheerful."

"Always am, aren't I?"

Holly chuckled. "You are. But you sound even more cheerful than usual. What's up?"

"I'm going to visit Missoula."

Holly pushed the laptop to the foot of the lounge chair and sat up. "It's about time." She'd tried for almost five years to get her grandmother to revisit the place of her youth, but she consistently refused, saying she didn't want to ruin her memories. "Why now, all of a sudden?"

Nan sucked in a breath that sounded quivery and uncertain to Holly.

"Something isn't wrong, is it?" What if Nan were sick, dying even, and had decided to visit Missoula while she still had the strength?

"Nothing's wrong. In fact, things might be just right."

Holly leaned over her knees, weak with relief. She wasn't ready to lose Nan. She was as close to her as she was to her parents. Nan had been a loving part of Holly's childhood even as she remained a loving force in her life today.

"Holly, I wonder if you aren't going to think me a silly old woman at what I'm going to do."

Holly smiled fondly. "I doubt it."

"You remember I told you what a wonderful time I had in Missoula when I first left home."

"Of course."

"What made it special was a young man I met. He was my first love."

"Grandpa?"

"No, dear. Your grandfather was after that."

Holly did some quick mental adjusting. She'd always assumed the man in the romantic stories was her grandfather. If not— "Then who was this wonderful man, and what happened to him?"

"Nothing. We just went our separate ways. But he phoned me the other day. He lost his wife a year or so ago, and now he wants to see me again. He suggested we meet in Missoula." Nan's voice fell to a whisper. "Where we met in the first place."

"Nan, how exciting. It's like a story."

"You don't think I'm being foolish?"

"It's romantic. They say you never forget your first love."

"Whoever 'they' are." Nan suddenly sounded all grandmotherly. "I'm sure we're different people after fifty years."

"I suppose. What do you plan to do?"

"He didn't say, but I…" She paused. "You'll really think I'm a silly old woman now." Again she hesitated, but when she spoke, her voice sounded strong. "I'd like to revisit as many places as possible. Do the things we did back then."

"Oh, Nan. That's so sweet. I don't think you're silly at all. I can help you."

"Holly, I'm scared."

"Nan." Her competent grandmother who had been a widow for twenty years, who changed her own oil, fixed flat tires, and had been known to fire up a chain saw to cut down a tree threatening her house, was afraid? "What's to be scared of?"

"What if I don't feel the same?" Holly strained to hear her words. "What if I do?"

"Don't you think you deserve the chance to find out either way? When are you coming? You'll stay with me, of course."

"Tomorrow. I'm so nervous."

"Don't be. By the way, does this old boyfriend have a name?"

"Henry Davis."

Holly pulled the phone away and stared at it. She must have misunderstood. She put the phone back to her ear. "Would you say that again?"

"Henry Davis, child. He says his grandson is a lawyer in Missoula. You might have heard of him. Steele Davis. Do you know him?"

Holly stared across the balustrade, saw the leaves on the trees, but felt as if she'd leapt off the railing into the wild blue sky.

"Holly, are you still there? Holly?"

"I'm here, Nan. Why didn't you tell me about Henry before?"

"I saw no need."

Holly tried to reconcile this new information with what she knew of Steele. Somehow she couldn't imagine romance in association with a relative of his. "I know Steele Davis. His office is across the street from my café."

"Well, well. Isn't that something? Why haven't you mentioned it?"

Holly laughed. "I didn't see the need."

Nan chuckled. "Seems we both have secrets."

"Nan, I'm not hiding anything." She didn't want Nan to get the wrong idea. "He's just someone I'm working with on the banquet." Nan knew of Holly's desire to raise funds for the orphanage.

"Still, small world."

Holly agreed, and they discussed it a little more then made arrangements for Nan to come to the café the next day. "I'll let Henry know. We can meet there. That way if he turns out to be a scoundrel, you can help me walk away. I hope he isn't. I have such fond memories of our time together."

A few minutes later, they said good-bye. Holly shook her head in wonder and caution. Steele's grandfather of all people. She could well guess Steele's reaction to this, but Holly intended to do what she could to help Nan recreate the summer of her youth. Even if this Henry Davis was at all like his grandson, Nan deserved to enjoy her memories. And if Mr. Davis was a kind old gentleman and treated Nan the way she remembered, then Holly would do everything in her power to help rekindle an old romance.

She lay back and smiled up at the blue sky.

Chapter 4

The phone rang. Steele's secretary had left already, so he grabbed it.

"Hi there, young man. How are you doing?" The familiar roar of his grandfather's voice boomed across the airwaves.

"Fine, Grandpops. Are you keeping out of trouble?"

"No fun in that now, is there?"

Steele leaned back and laughed. Pops always bragged about his wild escapades, half fiction, half wishful thinking and maybe—just maybe—a sliver of fact. Like Pops saying he'd caught a raging bull by tossing a rope out the truck window and wrapping the end around the steering wheel column. "Bull tried to charge the truck. Had to keep backing up to keep the grill between me and that red-eyed monster." There might have been a bit of truth in the story. After all, there was a grill the size and strength of a prison gate on the front of the truck Pops used to rattle around on his ranch. "Built tough to stop animals in their tracks," Pops liked to explain. But as to holding the bull single-handedly while driving defensively. . . Well, what could Steele say? It made a good story.

"I'm planning to spend a few days in Missoula."

That explained the call. Pops needed a favor. Not that he'd come right out and ask. He'd let you figure it out yourself. "You can stay with me," Steele said.

"Good. Are you prepared to put up with me for a week or two?"

Steele heard the note of caution in his grandfather's voice, and something else. Excitement maybe. "What are you up to?"

"Thought I'd go girling."

At the idea of his grandfather cruising the streets of Missoula trying to pick up "girls" his age, Steele laughed out loud. "Sure, Pops."

The old man grunted. "Maybe I can show you how it's done, and then you'll get off your duff and find a girl to marry. It's time you gave your father and mother some grandchildren. And me a great-grandchild while I'm still able to recognize him."

Whoa. The old man's slowing down—he used to jump right in there about marriage and kids. Took a whole minute this time.

"Three strapping young men," he'd say about Steele and his brothers. "And not one great-grandchild. Isn't it about time?" He'd look at each of them in turn, studying them like they'd neglected some important duty to the old man.

Good thing Steele and his brothers didn't take offense easily. They simply put it down to his crustiness and laughed it off.

Currently none of them was even married. Steele figured one failed marriage in the family was enough proof that some things were better left alone.

"Really, Grandpops, what's important enough to tear you away from the farm for a week?"

"Maybe two," Pops corrected. "It's kind of a reunion. Don't know if you're aware I spent a summer working in Missoula when I was a kid fresh out of school. Had a good time. Met some nice people. Plan to look some of them up. One in particular I was real fond of and hope to spend time with."

Steele contemplated his grandfather's words, tried to connect them with what he knew about the older man, and felt as if a link or two were missing. "Never knew you worked here. I always think of you on the farm."

"Yes, well, it's been my home forever, it seems. I plan to die here. But I think it could survive my absence for a week or two. You sure you're okay with my company that long?"

"I'm gone most of the day. You'll have the place to yourself." He thought of his grandfather's steadfast habit. "Only one request. No boots in the house."

The man grunted. "You expect me to walk around in my socks? A man could slip and fall doing that."

"Bring some good slippers. When will you be here?"

"Tomorrow. And get set for some serious girling." Pops sounded eager as a young pup released from a leash.

A picture of a wrinkled old woman, half deaf, smelling like liniment as she leered at Pops, brought a burst of laughter from Steele. "I doubt we'd be looking for the same sort of girls."

Pops grunted. "I expect you to find your own girl. I'll just show you how it's done."

Steele still chuckled as they said good-bye. "Girling." He chortled. The pictures flooding his mind would make a great comedy film.

◆

From his office the next morning, Steele watched Holly flitting about with her endless smile, dispensing pink flowers to everyone who sat at one of her tables. No more need to hang about the café. The banquet was organized. He'd succeeded in making sure it didn't turn all lovey-dovey and mushy. They'd have a good substantial meal, fun entertainment, and reasonable decorations. Yes, he'd done his job well. He could relax and let the rest of it fall together.

He stared at the pink flowers in the middle of each occupied table. For some reason just the sight of them made him tense. Maybe it was because they seemed to represent all the things he didn't believe in—romance, living in unrealistic dreams, expecting magic every day of a marriage. The only successful marriages he'd seen were based on something far more solid—shared interests, mutual benefit, a love like the Bible talked about.

He turned back to the papers on his desk. He had appointments and no time to muse over such foolishness.

Several hours later he glanced up again and saw Holly sitting alone at one of the tables, her laptop before her.

She looked toward his office. If he didn't know she couldn't see through the glass, he'd think their gazes had connected. He had a sudden desire for a good, strong cup of coffee and headed across the street.

"Annie," Holly called as she saw him approach. "Bring Steele his coffee." She nodded toward the chair opposite her, waited as if she expected him to have an announcement.

He mentally checked the to-do list for the banquet but couldn't think of anything he'd left undone.

Her expression grew quizzical. "I hear your grandfather is coming to town."

"Grandpops? Yeah. How would you know? You been tapping my phone line?"

She giggled. "As if I'd know how."

He fixed her with a demanding look. "How do you know he's coming?"

She sobered. "My grandmother told me."

He was missing something vital to understanding this conversation. "How would your grandmother know? Does she tap phone lines?"

She frowned in exasperation. "Surely you know they're meeting here this afternoon."

He knew how to keep his face expressionless, how to reveal nothing even when surprised. And her announcement certainly surprised him. Pops wasted no time with his "girling," but how did he start before he was even in town? No wonder he thought Steele and his brothers slow. To Steele's knowledge, none of them had picked up a woman before appearing on the scene.

Holly's expression went from suspicion to impatience. Her eyes grew dark.

Maybe he wasn't hiding his surprise as well as he thought. "He said he was going girling. I thought he was joking."

Her eyes darkened further, as if he'd said something nasty.

"My grandmother told me she and your grandfather were friends more than fifty years ago. In fact, they were boyfriend, girlfriend. Young love, Nan said. Said she'd never forgotten him. He tracked her down through the family she worked for here, and they want to meet again. See if they have that same old feeling."

He choked on a mouthful of coffee.

She jumped up, patted his back, and made soothing noises, though she patted a lot harder than he thought necessary; and when she spoke again, she sounded downright annoyed. "Why does it surprise you? You can't believe they might have enjoyed a little romance when they were young?"

"Pops? My grandpops? You must have the wrong grandfather. He never loved anyone but my grandmother."

She sat down again. Stared at him hard enough that he wondered if she saw his bones beneath his skin. "Nan said she was meeting a man named Henry Davis who was planning to stay with his grandson, Steele Davis, a lawyer in Missoula. Now I ask you, does that sound like someone else's grandfather?"

"No, it doesn't."

"Nan wants to recreate some of the events from back then."

He suddenly leaned forward, his eyes narrowing as he realized what she'd said. What kind of scheme had she and her grandmother cooked up? "She's doing what?"

"They're meeting here. Then they plan to visit some of the places they enjoyed when they were young." She seemed not to notice the way his mouth tightened but forged on with what he could only call belligerence. "Nan says they want to find out if the spark between them is still there. Isn't that cool? I can't think of anything more romantic than rediscovering an old love. Imagine. . .maybe they've loved each other all these years."

"That's disgusting. They both married someone else and raised a family. Besides, it was a half century ago. How can anyone in their right mind think they can turn the clock back?"

Her eyes flared. Dull red stained the tips of her ears. She sat as rigid and straight as the wall beside her. Just when he thought she would explode like an overinflated balloon, she let out a *whoosh* and spoke in slow, measured tones. "Look. I realize this doesn't fit into your view of love and romance."

She had that right.

"But I think they deserve to find out if there's still that spark, as Nan said. I intend to do everything I can to help them."

He snorted. "No doubt you'll give them your most private table and a pink carnation. Or will you give them a little bouquet because it's such a special occasion?" He felt a surge of victory when she ground out a sound of exasperation. He couldn't help a secret smile at the way her eyes flashed daggers.

"Maybe I'll buy them a dozen red roses."

"And give them a card full of sappy love sayings." His harsh tones said what he thought of *that* idea.

She pushed to her feet and lurched to his side. "Sappy? There is nothing sappy about love and romance."

He stilled the desire to put distance between them. "Romance is impractical."

Holly scowled at him.

He didn't much care for the way she breathed hard, curled and uncurled her fists. He stood, exhibiting no rush, though he couldn't wait to escape her presence. Pink flowers and sappy cards? And to think, not too many minutes ago he'd been imagining how pleasant it would be to visit Holly over coffee with no particular agenda between them. "I don't know what your grandmother has in mind, but I won't stand by and see my grandfather become a victim of some scheming woman."

She measured her words out one by one as if squeezing them past an asthma attack. "Make that two scheming women, because I intend to help her all I can."

He gave her a look meant to stop her before she could say anything more.

She ignored his silent warning. "You call yourself a lawyer, yet you ignore the facts. Number one, no one is forcing your grandfather to meet my grandmother. You might ask him who made the first contact. Two, I don't know about your grandfather, but my grandmother is perfectly capable of making her own choices. Nobody will coerce her into doing something she doesn't want to do."

Holly's arguments carried the ring of truth, but Steele didn't care. He had the incredible urge to bang his head against the nearest planter at Holly's blind belief in all this—he glanced around—flowery stuff.

He stalked away. Anger jabbed at him like a hot nail to his heart. Romance was one thing and pink flowers part of it. But turning her romantic notions toward his grandfather, aiding and abetting her desperate grandmother—no way. He would not, could not, in a million years stand by and let those women create a romantic trap to catch his poor grandfather. Sure, the man was strong physically. But he'd lost the love of his life recently. How often had Pops told Steele and his brothers that Grandma had saved him? "She came into my life when I was going through a tough time. I'd had my heart hurt. Thought I'd never be able to love again. Even wondered if life was worth living. Your grandmother changed all that. God bless her."

Maybe his grandfather thought he could replace Grandma and put an end to his mourning. But Pops had to understand it wasn't that easy.

Was Holly's grandmother the woman who'd broken Pops's heart? If so, Steele didn't intend to stand idly by and let it happen again.

How could he stop it? As Holly so angrily pointed out, their grandparents were capable of making their own choices.

Only one way he could think of to put a monkey wrench in this whole business. He'd stick close to Pops. Run interference on his behalf.

But Pops would not welcome such action.

Steele remembered Pops's invitation to go girling together. It provided the perfect setup. He'd let the old man think he'd taken up the offer. Maybe even let him think he was interested in Holly.

That ought to give him a chance to keep an eye on the proceedings. Holly had a head full of dreams, but Steele had the mind of a lawyer. He'd make sure Pops didn't get swept off his feet—willingly or unwillingly.

He intended to be ready. He canceled his afternoon appointments, shifted his chair so he could look up every minute for a quick study of the café, and pulled out some files to work on. Not that he accomplished anything with his thoughts jumping across the street to the pending meeting.

He saw several older ladies stop for coffee, but none lingered unusually long.

Around four o'clock he watched a slender woman with a floppy red hat stop at the café. Holly hurried out and hugged the woman, nudging the hat askew.

Had to be the scheming grandmother. "The eagle has landed," he muttered. Perfect timing for tea and crumpets. Though he'd never actually met a real-life crumpet.

Holly led the woman to a table.

Steele's eyes narrowed and his jaw clenched as he saw she'd arranged the planters to provide living walls around the table. Subtle? Not Holly. She might as well hang a flashing neon sign—OLD LOVES REKINDLED HERE—proclaiming her intention to see this poor old couple drowning in romance.

Well, not if he had anything to say about it. And he would.

Pops sauntered up, rolling on his cowboy boots with all the swagger of a man fifty years younger.

Steele groaned. Even without seeing his face, he could tell Pops was as eager as a young buck. An easy mark for two women. He'd probably be on one knee before Steele could intervene.

Holly glanced toward his office windows, a silent challenge. She might as well have waved a red flag or slapped him with a leather glove.

With a muttered warning, he charged down the stairs ready to duel.

❖

Holly took Nan a cup of rooibos tea. "It's so good to see you. I can hardly wait to share your favorite spots with you." She paused as Nan glanced past her. "Of course you might not be wanting *my* company."

"Nonsense, child. I'm too old to be all—what is it that movie says?— twitterpated about a man."

Holly hid a smile. Nan might believe she was too old to be excited, but she perched on the edge of her chair while her gaze darted past Holly.

Holly knew without turning the moment Mr. Davis stepped into view. Nan froze. Her cheeks stained a dull red. Holly lurched to Nan's side, fearing she would faint. Nan fluttered her hand, her eyes never shifting from the man on the sidewalk.

Slowly Holly turned, prepared to take a good, hard, impartial look at the man who after fifty years had the power to render Nan speechless. There might have been a spark back then, but who knows how the man had changed?

She tried to do a detached assessment. Tall and rangy. A full head of silver hair, eyes as hazel as Steele's. But at the look of wonder and longing and uncertainty in his eyes, Holly lost all ability to be critical. This man adored her nan. Nothing else mattered.

"Mr. Davis." She held out her hand. "I'm Holly Hope, Jean's granddaughter. Please have a chair. What can I bring you?"

The man pulled his gaze toward Holly. He held her hand between his and examined her closely. When he smiled, she felt as if she'd met his favor in some way. "You're very much like your grandmother when I first knew her. You have the same kind smile."

At that moment Holly blessed this man and silently prayed God would grant the older couple renewed love.

Mr. Davis turned his attention back to Nan and slowly crossed to the table. "Jean, I'd have known you anywhere." He took her hand and smiled into her eyes. "You're as beautiful as I remember."

At the look of shy pleasure in Nan's face, Holly pressed her lips together and widened her eyes to keep them from tearing.

The man chuckled as Nan ducked her head. "And just as shy."

Nan laughed. "And you, Henry, are just as full of nonsense as I recall. It's good to see you."

They smiled at each other.

"You going to stand all day or have a seat?" Nan asked.

Mr. Davis laughed heartily. "I see you've added a little vinegar to the mix." He sat in the chair across the tiny table.

"What will you have, Henry? Coffee, tea, or—"

Holly choked back a laugh at the bright color racing up Nan's face.

"You?" Mr. Davis finished. "How about two out of three? I'll have whatever she's having," he said, without taking his gaze off Nan.

Holly hurried to get a pot of tea and put a plate of mixed cookies before the pair. "There you go, Mr. Davis."

Nan smiled up at Holly, her eyes shining like bits of starlight. "Thank you, dear."

Holly winked and squeezed Nan's hand.

"Make it Henry," Mr. Davis said. "This looks delicious. Thank you." But Holly noted he didn't even look at what she'd placed before him.

She slipped away and joined Meggie behind the counter. "Here's hoping no one else comes for a while so they can enjoy some time alone together."

"Uh oh. You spoke too soon." Meggie nodded toward the door.

Steele headed across the street like a steamroller, ready to flatten everything in sight. Halfway across, he slowed, hesitated. If she wasn't mistaken, he sucked in a breath like a spent runner. Then he smiled and continued toward her, slow and easy, as if he had nothing more on his mind than a nice social visit.

Holly knew better. She'd seen the look in his eyes before he masked it. If ever a man was bent on putting an end to romance, Steele was that man. She met him at the edge of the sidewalk. "Come on inside, and I'll get you coffee." She grabbed his elbow and steered him toward the door.

He refused to be steered. "I saw Pops come here." He tried to edge around the planter blocking his view.

"He and my grandmother are having tea. Let's leave them alone for a few minutes."

He gave her a look of disbelief. "Pops would have a fit if he knew I was here and just ignored him. You're not busy. Why don't you join us?"

"Yes, why don't you two join us instead of muttering out there?" Nan called.

"Steele, get in here. I want to show off my grandson," Henry growled.

Steele grinned at Holly. "Care to say no?"

Holly rolled her eyes. "And incur Nan's wrath? I don't think so." But she didn't care for the gleam in Steele's eyes. He might have won this round, but only by default.

"Me either. Pops can still wield a big stick." He waved her ahead of him.

Meggie, a laugh in her voice, called from inside. "I'll bring you both a coffee."

Steele grabbed two chairs and shoved them up to the table. He sat beside his grandfather. Henry cupped his hand over the back of Steele's neck. "Jean, this is my grandson. His office is right across the street."

Holly felt two pairs of eyes swing from Steele to her, and then the older couple looked at each other, some silent message communicated.

"Jean and I have been talking," Henry said. "I'd like to reintroduce her to Missoula. A lot has changed in half a century."

Holly grinned at the way the older two smiled at each other. She glanced at Steele and saw a speculative look in his eyes. When he saw her watching, he smoothed away the tightness and smiled.

"I expect everything has changed," he said, his voice flat.

Holly wasn't fooled by his relaxed manner. She heard the warning in his voice, knew he had opposition on his mind. She narrowed her eyes and silently informed him she would not let him ruin this reunion. "Anything I can do to help, just ask."

"Actually," Nan said, "we'd like you to join us tomorrow."

"Not a problem." Tomorrow was Sunday, and she didn't open the café on Sundays. She'd enjoy spending part of the day with them if they didn't mind.

"Both of you," Henry added.

Holly met Steele's gaze and felt his tension in the way his smile tightened at the corners, the way his pupils narrowed.

"Sounds like a plan," he said.

A plan? Yeah, right. She could just imagine *his* plan. Did he figure to run interference? How? She jerked her chin just a fraction of an inch. Whatever he planned, she would be there to make sure the day went as Nan and Henry hoped.

"We met at church," Nan said. "We were both at loose ends, so we decided to spend the day together."

"We went on a picnic." Henry chuckled. "Kind of spontaneous. I think we had peanut butter sandwiches."

"I begged some cookies from my employers."

"Wasn't it the pastor who introduced us?"

Nan chuckled. "He probably felt sorry for us alone in the big city."

Henry slapped his thighs. "We want to go to church and then have a picnic. Just like that first day."

Holly sighed. "It sounds so romantic. But you don't need two other people with you."

Nan waved away her protests. "Nonsense. It will be fun to have a couple of young people along, won't it, Henry?"

"Can't think of anything better." He leaned toward Steele and lowered his voice to a gentle rumble. "I just might be able to teach this boy a thing or two."

Steele pushed back in his chair and cast a glance around as if hoping to escape.

Holly had never seen a man look so embarrassed and frightened at the same time, and she couldn't help but laugh.

He shot her a look full of sharp protest and warning.

She covered her mouth and tried to swallow her amusement. Her eyes stung with the effort.

"Pops," he managed to growl, "I don't need your help."

Henry shifted his gaze toward Holly. Her laugh died a sudden death at the look in the old man's eyes.

"Maybe you don't at that. You have a nice little gal here."

Holly gasped. "I'm not—"

Steele laughed. She resisted an urge to toss the rest of her coffee at him and drown the sound. "She's a little shy."

Henry nodded. "Just like her grandmother."

Holly sputtered. "That's not—" How dare Steele let Nan and Henry think there was something between them?

Steele leaned over and patted the back of her hand. "It's okay, Holly. We can go along with the grandparents and enjoy ourselves."

"Yes, dear. I'm sure you can." Nan gave her a warm smile.

Holly sent Steele a look she hoped would burn his mind like a splash of acid, then gave an unconcerned shrug. *Ohh, the man was impossible.*

He leaned back and smiled like a cat full of cream. "Of course if you're busy, I'm sure we can have fun without you."

As if she'd let him hang around the older couple alone. She could just imagine how he'd throw cold water on any romantic overtures.

"I'm not busy. I'll be glad to go along." Two could play this game. "I can prepare the meal. That is, if you don't object to something a little nicer than peanut butter sandwiches."

Henry gave a roaring laugh. "Little lady, I'd appreciate something a little nicer. How about you, Jean?"

"That would be fine."

"Great." Holly gave Steele a smile full of victory.

He nodded, his answering smile not revealing any hint of defeat.

"We should move along and make way for other customers," Nan said.

"Let me show you downtown Missoula," Steele's grandfather said.

Holly waited until the older couple was out of earshot before she confronted Steele. "I don't know what you're doing letting them assume we're such good friends. But I won't let you ruin this for them."

"Me?" He pressed his hand to his chest as if suffering a sudden pain. "I just want to join in the fun. Why would you think otherwise?"

She could not stop her eyes from squinting and her mouth from puckering. "You want me to believe you're not opposed to a romance between them?"

"Holly, Holly, Holly." He patted her shoulder in a grandfatherly gesture. "Let yourself enjoy the day without all that suspicion. After all, aren't you the purveyor of romance around here? Wouldn't want to ruin that, would we?"

"Ohh. You are up to something. I know it."

He slowly faced her. "I guess that gives me an advantage, because I *do* know what you're up to."

She stared at him. "Me?" His eyes narrowed and turned cold hazel. He suspected—that was crazy. "You really think Nan and I are out to get your grandfather? Open your eyes, Mr. Lawyerman. I don't think your grandfather needs any help from me."

She felt the heat of his anger burning from his eyes. They faced each other, taking measure, assessing the enemy. Suddenly she laughed. "Nope, I don't think he needs any help. It's going to be fun to sit back and watch." She jabbed her finger at him. "Pay attention. You just might learn a thing or two." She laughed again at the fury in his expression.

He jerked around and stalked back to his office.

"Meggie, give me a hand. I have to prepare a picnic for tomorrow." She chuckled. This was going to be a picnic to remember.

Chapter 5

Steele hurried home earlier than usual. It had taken all of thirty seconds of watching Pops at the café to realize the old man was ready for plucking. Almost begging for it, in fact. Steele's plan to be invited had succeeded. Both grandparents believed he and Holly had more than a passing interest in each other, but unfortunately his plan had its flaws. How could he keep an eye on Pops when he had office hours and commitments? He couldn't. So on to plan B—convince Pops he should forget this whole idea of reviving a fifty-year-old romance.

For some reason that now made no sense, Steele expected Pops to be home waiting for him. He wasn't and didn't show up until almost seven.

Pops grunted when Steele pointed at the cowboy boots. He grabbed a chair and sat down to tug them off then pulled rubber-soled slippers from a bag. "Had to go buy these."

"I saved you some dinner," Steele said, pointing to the congealing chicken and fries.

"I've eaten. And probably a good thing if that's all you have to offer." He shuddered. "Not so good for a man's arteries."

"So I heard."

"You're thirty in a few more months. Time to start taking care of yourself."

Steele tried to remember a single fat-free meal on the ranch and failed. "You still eat half a cow at every meal?"

Pops made a rude noise. "My beef is home-raised. The best you can find."

Steele shrugged and threw the leftovers in the garbage. He couldn't imagine what Pops had being doing since he'd last seen him, but how do you cross-examine your own grandparent? Someone who would as soon wrestle a cow as call your name? And then the old man beat him to the draw.

"You never told me about Holly. You been keeping secrets from an old man? That's not nice, you know."

Steele drew back and studied Pops to see if he was serious. Far as he could tell, he was. Steele shook his head. "You're one to talk. How long have you kept your secret romance hidden? Did Grandma know about Jean?"

Pops slapped his palms down on the counter with a resounding *thwack*. If Steele hadn't known how to keep his face and body under control, he would have cringed. He was almost certain his eyes would have given him away if Pops had cared to notice. He didn't.

"Now listen here, boy. I loved your grandmother. Never cheated on her in thought or deed. She was a good woman. Saved me from myself on more occasions than I care to remember."

"Jean is the woman who left you whipped and broken, isn't she?" He didn't need Pops's answer to know it was true. But perhaps reminding his grandfather would make him see how foolish this whole thing was.

"Boy, we aren't going to discuss things that aren't any of your business."

"Maybe I'm making it my business to see you don't buy yourself a heap of trouble. What makes you think it won't happen again?"

Pops grunted. "Seems I'm old enough to take care of myself."

"What is it you always say? 'No fool like an old fool'?"

"If you're suggesting I'm making a fool of myself—" Suddenly Pops chuckled. "Maybe I am at that. And I'm here to tell you, I don't mind a bit. Sometimes, young man, you need to give your emotions some freedom." He squinted hard at Steele.

Steele groaned. Here it came. The lecture on how he needed to get off his duff and charm some little gal into marrying him. Before Pops could deliver the message, Steele defended himself. "I don't intend to ever let my emotions rule my head."

"Well, then, there's your trouble. But I see the way you look at little Holly. Might be she's just the one to make you forget all your hard-and-fast rules."

Steele stuffed back his frustration. The old man was beyond reasoning with, which made it all the more necessary for Steele to run interference. Back to plan A. "Yeah, Pops. You could be right." Let Pops think Holly held an alluring interest for Steele. That way he could hope to be included in their outings, at least the evening ones—and wouldn't that be when all the lovey-dovey stuff took place? He'd just keep an eye on Pops and those two women. Make sure their feet remained on the ground as firmly as his own. Pops would explode like one of his angry bulls if he knew Steele intended to see this little holiday didn't turn into déjà vu all over again. Steele didn't intend to tell him.

Pops perched on one of the stools and leaned both elbows on the counter. "Now tell me about Holly. She seems like a nice girl. I can see, though, that you need some help in wooing her. My guess is she's the kind of gal that likes to be made to feel special."

Let Pops think he could help Steele, but frustration rose in his throat. This plan was going to prove a real challenge.

◆

Steele followed his grandfather into the pew. The old man slipped past Holly and sat on the other side beside Jean. That left Steele to sit beside Holly. Pops was anything but subtle, but not a problem. Let Pops think, let them all think, he joined them because he embraced this romantic stuff.

Holly glowed with some sort of inner excitement. She stole glances at him out of the corner of her eye, each time her eyes flashing light.

It made his skin itch. He rubbed his chin. She was up to something. He wished he knew what. Not that it mattered. He had his own agenda—to see that four pairs of feet remained planted in reality.

He'd sat close to her a few times in the past weeks as they worked on the banquet. He knew she didn't have the best singing voice in the world, but what she lacked in quality she made up for with enthusiasm. He admired that.

He settled back when the singing ended and the sermon began. He normally enjoyed this respite from the daily pressure of his work. Today was no different. Pastor Don challenged them all to reject competition with one another and seek to promote the peace of Christ. Steele applied it to factions based on denominational differences. No way did it have anything to do with this unspoken feud between him and Holly. Hardly a feud even. Just a slight dissimilarity in viewpoints. Besides, his motive was right. He only wanted to protect Pops.

It bothered him a tiny bit that he was misleading Pops about his interest in Holly. Not that she wasn't a nice enough young woman. Except for her sentimental belief in romance and flowers and—

A vision of pink flowers in a lattice-topped planter filled his mind. His insides twisted and knotted like the tea towels he'd pulled from the dryer last night. What was it with pink flowers? He dismissed the errant thought and concentrated on the closing remarks.

After the service, the four of them gathered on the sidewalk.

"Where is this picnic to take place?" Steele demanded.

"Down by the river," Holly answered as the other two wandered away. "The lunch is ready at the café. We can go that way."

"A walk. How nice." He put false enthusiasm into his voice and received a startled look from Holly.

She studied him a minute, as if wondering how sincere he was, then gave a quirk of her eyebrows, silently informing him she would accept his gesture as sincere as long as he lived up to it.

"Authentic," she said. "That's how Nan and Henry did it the first time."

He made sure she noticed how he rolled his eyes in disbelief. "We're going to have a little trouble making the river walk look like it did fifty years ago."

"Doesn't matter. Come on." She tucked her hand through his arm and headed him down the sidewalk.

What was with that? Was she trying to keep him away from Pops? But the older couple followed.

Holly's hand was warm and soft. He thought of sunshine and flowers—white ones, red ones, any color but pink. He would not think pink. As a lawyer, he knew he should question that idea, but instead he pushed it away.

They stopped to pick up a cooler and a big wicker basket at J'ava Moi.

"Couldn't you have given us each a brown bag?" he murmured as he hefted the cooler to his shoulder.

She smiled sweetly. "Wouldn't want to give the grandparents food poisoning now, would I?"

"So this chest is full of food on ice. And the basket?"

"Need dishes, don't we?"

"Not for sandwiches."

"We're going to have to hurry to catch up." Pops and Jean had gone ahead.

Steele waited for her to lock the café, then they strode after the older couple. But it was impossible to hurry with the awkward basket banging at Holly's shins.

He shifted the cooler to his other shoulder and grabbed the handle of the basket. "Give me that. We'll never catch them."

His hand brushed hers. Again he thought sunshine and flowers. This time he didn't picture any pink flowers, just pots of sweet purple ones, and found, to his surprise, he liked purple flowers. He grunted. *Steele, give your head a shake.* Sunday was no excuse to leave his brain in park. He stared at her hand as she refused to release the handle. "Come on, Holly. Be reasonable."

"Let's both carry it."

Let's not.

She took a step.

What could he do but grasp the basket between them, feeling the connection between their hands? Of course he felt a connection. After all, their fingers rubbed together. It would have been far more surprising if he hadn't felt it. Would have signaled his hand was numb or paralyzed. Nope. Wasn't his hand that was the problem—it was his brain. It was numb. He should have grabbed a coffee somewhere to jump start it.

Trouble was, the connection had nothing to do with the touch of her hand. It had everything to do with the sweet, crazy, mixed-up feeling he got around her. That strange yearning hollowness, or hunger, a longing—whatever it was—that grew more familiar each time they were together.

Pops would laugh himself sick if he knew how Steele was thinking. But no way would the old man find out, because as of this minute, Steele put an end to his mental detour.

They caught up to Pops and Jean as they reached Caras Park. Jean stopped and pressed her hand to her chest. "Oh, my. This is much different." She tilted

276

her head. "Do I hear 'Battle Hymn of the Republic'?"

"That's the carousel," Pops said, leading Jean in that direction.

Steele's stomach rumbled. His neck fired off a protest at the weight of the cooler on his shoulder. "Let's find a picnic table first." They found one close to a bunch of trees, next to the river walk. Wildflowers trailed along the pathway. The river tumbled past.

Holly opened the basket and pulled out a white cloth. She flipped it over the table.

Steele's stomach ached from hunger. Pops had insisted on a light breakfast of fruit and yogurt. A man could starve on such fare.

Holly lifted out four white china plates and silverware.

Silverware? Real, shiny silverware? This was a picnic not a banquet. Though he'd welcome banquet food. He'd imagined sandwiches, but now he pictured slabs of ham on the plates, mounds of potato and macaroni salads, and fresh buns slathered with butter. He swallowed hard. "Can I help?"

She put stemmed goblets at each place. "You can pour the drinks." She handed him a long-necked bottle of sparkling apple juice.

He shook his head as he unwrapped the lid, screwed it off, and filled the goblets. No need to wonder what Holly's plans were for the day—romance at its best, or worst, but Pops didn't need any encouragement. "I thought the idea was to recreate the events of yesteryear. Wouldn't water have been more appropriate?"

Holly only laughed. "I bet they wished they had something special back then, so why not give it to them now?"

He had lots of reasons. Reality, practicality, safety, protecting Pops. But Jean and Pops, who had gone to the pathway to look out on the river, saw the table set and hurried back before he could give her even one bit of rationale.

"Holly, this is beautiful. Makes me feel special." Nan hugged her granddaughter. "Thank you."

Pops grinned like a silly pup. "Looks a lot better than our first picnic."

"I guess it's not the same," Steele said. *Nothing's the same—can't you all see that?* It was silly to think they could bring back the past.

"It's better. Lots of things about the present are better than the past." Pops smiled at Jean as he spoke.

Steele clenched down on his jaw so hard it would take concerted effort to release it. Pops was so vulnerable. So eager to be hurt again.

Jean looked starry-eyed and mellow. But Steele wasn't ready to believe this whole business was above suspicion.

"Did you bring your camera?" Jean asked Holly. "Can you take a picture of us? I always wished I had some pictures of that summer."

"Hang on a minute." Holly pulled a foil-covered bundle from the basket and unwrapped it to reveal a plant covered in pink flowers.

Steele's jaw tightened even more. He couldn't tear his gaze from the pink as a churn of emotions flooded through him, staining every thought, burning away everything but the taste of anger. He hated pink flowers. He didn't realize he'd spoken the words aloud until he felt three people stare at him in surprise.

"Boy," Pops said, "that's downright rude of you. Holly, they're beautiful."

Steele closed his eyes and tried to blot from his mind the sight of those flowers. He sucked in sanity, glanced at Holly. Her eager expression no longer existed. Instead she looked hurt, offended. She blinked rapidly, as if the wind had blown something into her eyes. His insides gave another vicious twist. "It's nothing personal, Holly. I'm sorry I said anything."

Holly nodded, but her smile seemed stiff and unnatural. "Apology accepted." She ducked her head and refused to look at him.

He could hardly blame her. Even though it wasn't anything to do with her, he understood he'd managed to attack something near and dear to her. He hadn't meant to hurt her and didn't care for the way it made him feel all prunelike inside. Somehow he had to make it up to her.

He headed in her direction intending to—

Pops pulled Jean to his side. "Now take our picture."

Holly turned on her camera and took a couple of exposures.

Steele stopped, filled with confusion at the sight of Pops and Jean with their arms around each other, smiling into each other's faces with such—

Steele shook his head. They were old friends, enjoying memories of the past. There could be nothing more. They'd both married others, raised families, lived whole lives without once seeing each other. No way could they fall in love so easily. Unless they were desperate. Which was not a good way to be around love.

And Holly smiling and encouraging them? He wanted to put an end to this whole scene. No. He wanted to be part of it instead of outside it. How could he want such differing things at the same time? What was going on inside his head? Whatever it was felt unfamiliar and scary. He needed to eat before his brain grew any fuzzier. But everyone else seemed more interested in pictures.

"This one is perfect." Holly handed the camera to Jean.

Jean blushed to the roots of her hair. "I look like a star-struck kid."

"You're beautiful when you blush," Pops said. "I remember that about you."

"Oh, you." She fluttered her hands and turned to Holly. "Now you and Steele."

All Steele's efforts to get his thoughts squared away failed. He backed up. He could not be part of this. . .this. . .

Holly shook her head. "Uh-uh. This is *your* picnic."

"Come on, boy. Get over here," Pops roared.

No way did Steele want to pose behind that bunch of pink flowers. He looked at Holly and saw a reflection of his horror. He blinked. What did she have to be so antagonistic about? Apart from the pink flower comment, he'd been nothing but charming. She must have a problem of some sort that had nothing to do with him.

Her resistance made him change his mind. He could handle this. It was only a posed picture. It meant nothing. "Sure, why not?" He took a step toward the table, focused on the pink flowers, and paused.

"Oh, give it up." Holly plucked the plant off the table and set it on the ground. "Just for this picture—then it goes back."

She showed Jean how to use the camera then joined him behind the table.

Pops groaned. "Show a little affection. Put your arm around her. Stop looking like you've got a toothache. Come on, Holly. Show him how much you care."

Holly laughed. "Yes, Henry." And she put her arm around Steele's waist and pinched him.

He jumped. "Hey." He glowered down at her.

She smiled up as sweet as honey on morning toast. "Smile, Steele." She dropped her voice to a low whisper. "Even if it kills you, or I'll pinch you again. You are not going to ruin Nan's special day with hating pink flowers and grumbling about everything nice."

He bared his teeth. "How's this?"

"Most attractive." She smiled toward her grandmother.

"All done," Jean announced. "Want to see?"

Holly glanced at the picture so quickly he knew she couldn't have seen it.

He did the same. "Can we eat now? I'm starved."

"I'll get right at it." She put the flowers back on the table and opened the cooler.

He wasn't fooled by the false cheerfulness of her voice. Beneath the polite words, he heard anger. Well, he was doing his best. She should at least give him credit for trying.

She pulled out a tray of finger food—tiny cubes of cheese on toothpicks, grape-sized tomatoes, slices of cucumber, baby carrots, and coils of deli meat.

His hunger grabbed at his gut. He could clean off that whole tray and not fill a quarter of his empty stomach. He waited for the good stuff.

Out came a plastic-covered silver plate with tiny little sandwiches—crusts cut off, cookie-cutter, fancy shapes.

There had to be more to eat than that, or he would starve.

Another plate. This one piled high with a tower of little tarts with some sort of yellowish brown filling. "What are those?" He hadn't meant to sound so harsh, but he was desperately hungry.

"Individual quiches." She shot him a venomous look. "And don't bother telling me real men don't eat quiche."

"Never crossed my mind." He wondered what she'd say if he ate the entire stack. He watched and waited for her to pull out more food—the good stuff. The real stuff.

She waved at the grandparents, who had gone to look at some of the flowers.

That was it? He looked longingly toward the street, knowing fast food was only a few blocks away. Knowing if he went for it, Pops would skin him alive and nail his hide to the outside of his barn. Pops had threatened to do so many times in the past. Steele had never doubted he could do it. He no longer thought he would, but a wise man never played with fire.

He hid a sudden grin. He could imagine Pops's reaction to this fine fare. "A man has to eat something substantial if he expects to handle a good day of work." Maybe Pops would end the meal with a trip to one of the fast-food places. Steele considered which ones were closest. His vehicle was back at the church. He could jog back for it and return in less than fifteen minutes. Right now he didn't care where they went so long as he got some real food.

Pops and Jean sat side by side, leaving Steele to sit beside Holly. Pops held out his hands. "Let's pray."

Steele bowed his head and concentrated on Pops's big, work-rough hand on one side and tried not to think of how Holly's small, cool hand on the other side sent a queer mingling of anger and longing through him. If he wasn't starving, he'd be able to think better. He wouldn't have this confusion. He never heard a word of his grandfather's grace and only realized "amen" had been said when Pops dropped his hand.

He forced himself to release Holly's hand when she tugged.

"I wish I could have done something this special that first day," Pops said as he checked out the picnic fare.

Yeah, right. They would have starved to death, and then he, Steele, would have a different grandfather. Or maybe never been born.

Jean chuckled. "I don't remember caring what we ate. It was just nice to have someone to share a day off with." She helped herself to the finger food as Holly passed it.

"I know Nan had a job as a nanny, but what brought you to Missoula?" Holly asked Pops as she shuffled the trays in his direction.

Steele restrained himself from grabbing the food and stuffing his mouth. When the trays finally reached him, he took half of what was left, knowing he'd still be hungry when it was gone. He wrapped cucumber and tomatoes in the meat as Pops answered Holly's question.

"I grew up on a ranch an hour away. A struggling, dirt-poor ranch where a man—or a boy—could work from daylight to dark and never catch up. Where about all you got as reward for the hard labor was more of the same. My father and I had words. I came to Missoula to earn some money and gain some freedom. I was pretty good with motors and found a job in a garage. I thought I had it made."

His mouth full of food, Steele stared at Pops. A dirt-poor ranch? He chewed enough to get the vegetables down. "The ranch isn't poor."

"Not now. I've put in fifty years getting it where it is. But back then—" He shrugged.

"What took you back to the ranch?" Holly asked.

Steele watched Jean, her fork poised halfway to her mouth. He had the feeling she wanted to know Pops's answer more than Holly.

"My father was injured. I knew if I didn't go back home, the ranch would be gone."

Jean lowered her fork to her plate. "I always wondered what happened. Why didn't you tell me?"

Pops toyed with the food before him. "I couldn't face you again. I had nothing to offer you."

"Don't you think I should have had a chance to decide that?"

Pops sent Steele and Holly an apologetic look then turned to take Jean's hands. "Jean, you had such big dreams. You planned to get a nanny job in Europe and see the world. I faced nothing but hard work and poor wages."

Nan patted Pops's cheek. "I was hurt that you left without a word. I always figured you'd found someone you preferred and didn't know how to tell me."

"Nothing like that."

The four of them turned back to the food. Steele ate half a dozen of the little sandwiches, finding them full of some sort of tasty filling. He didn't dare ask what it was. And the quiches? Whoever said real men didn't eat quiche had not tasted Holly's. After Jean and Pops had both declined any more, Steele eyed the remaining stack.

"Help yourself," Holly invited, correctly interpreting his hungry look.

Eight quiches later, he discovered the hollowness of hunger had disappeared.

She reached into the cooler and pulled out a tray of fresh fruit, more cheese, and a plate stacked with muffins. Then she pulled thermos bottles of coffee from the picnic basket.

"Nan, did you meet Grandfather after Henry left?" Holly asked.

"No, dear. I actually went home a few weeks later." She smiled gently at Pops. "It wasn't the same anymore." She turned back to Holly. "Your grandfather was an old friend. We just seemed to fit together after that. He was good to me. I've missed him these past twenty years."

Holly turned to Henry. "And your wife? How did you meet her?"

"She came to care for an elderly lady in the community. At the time I was kind of a mess. Fighting hard to satisfy my father, trying to keep the ranch from disaster. Alma was sweet and kind and understanding. She pointed me back to trusting God."

Steele figured it was time they all stopped flirting with the allure of this whole setup and got back to trusting God before Pops ended up in another emotional mess. But right now he was too busy enjoying his coffee and the satisfaction of a good feed to think of how to express his thoughts without inviting further wrath from the old man.

Chapter 6

Holly sighed her satisfaction that both Nan and Henry had enjoyed their long years of marriage. She sighed again at the sorrow of their lost first love.

Nan seemed to read her thoughts and reached over to pat her hand. "We were just kids. I don't suppose either of us knew what we wanted."

Henry nodded. "I felt obligated to help my father. I knew the ranch was at risk. Didn't see how I could possibly ask a woman to give up her dreams to share nothing, and that's all I had."

"I know what I want." Holly was a few years older than Nan would have been at the time, but her dreams of a magical love to last forever hadn't changed since she was a small child.

Nan smiled gently. "You might discover your wants change when you're faced with reality. I know mine did. All my fine dreams of travel didn't mean a thing when I was so lonely my heart hurt."

"I'm glad you found someone to fill that loneliness." Henry pushed to his feet. "Shall we clean up then wander around a bit?"

Holly waved them away. "You show Nan the sights while Steele and I put stuff away."

"We'll do that." Henry took Nan's arm, and they headed toward the carousel.

Steele grunted and stared after them.

"I think they've found love again," Holly said.

"Or maybe they're so lonely they'll jump at any chance to share their lives with someone."

"No. I think they loved each other when they were kids. They lost that or maybe walked away from it. They've spent most of their lives loving someone else, but now they've found each other again and rediscovered the love of their youth." One look at his face and she knew he didn't believe it. "And if it's simply loneliness, what would be so wrong with that?"

"Nothing as long as they both understand the game rules." He pointed at the remains of the picnic. "Either way, isn't this romantic setup just a little too blatant?"

"What's with you and pink flowers?"

"I just don't like them."

"So you said. Why?"

"Does there have to be a reason?"

"It seems odd to hate them just because they're pink."

He stared at the flowers and shuddered.

She'd guess he didn't know how his eyes had grown stark. Something had caused this reaction to the flowers even if he didn't care to admit it. She'd be willing to put his dislike of romantic "trappings" down to the same cause. "Maybe you should get counseling."

He bolted to his feet. "If that isn't the stupidest thing I've heard in a long time. Just because I don't like pink flowers, you think I'm crazy."

She shrugged. "No one said you were crazy, but you have to admit it's a weird hang-up. And closely connected to your fear of romantic things, I'm guessing."

"Wow. No need for me to see a shrink. I'll just consult Miss Holly Hopes-for-the-Best. Funny you don't see any association between the divorces I witness in my office and my caution about candlelight and flowers. You want to see a long-lasting marriage—you give me a couple with common interests, shared ideals, even a business arrangement."

She nodded occasionally as she piled up the used dishes and stowed everything away. She wrapped the pink flowers in foil and put them in the basket. "They're gone. Do you feel better?"

"No. Yes."

She laughed, earning her a black look from the confused lawyer. "Steele, I think our grandparents are going to prove you wrong about romantic love." She turned to watch them. Henry bent and plucked a flower and tucked it behind Nan's ear. "Isn't that sweet?"

She didn't have to look at Steele to know his face would be thunderous.

"What my grandfather didn't tell you—" Steele's voice grated with disapproval. "He turned into an angry, bitter young man after he left Missoula. I don't know how many times I heard him credit my grandmother with saving him from destruction. He gave her flowers for every special occasion and for no reason whatsoever. My mom always said it was a waste of good money. She figured he could have had a fortune to invest by the end of each year with what he spent on them."

"This is your mother—your father's business partner?" She dripped sarcasm from every word. No doubt he could have reached out and scooped up handfuls of it. Of course, all sorts of marriages worked, but his parents' sounded cold as the inside of a fridge.

"Yes. And I might point out they've been married almost thirty-two years. Happily."

"That's nice. It's no doubt where you learned romance has no place in a relationship."

"I'm sure it's nothing to do with what I see in my office."

"Oh, wait. There was something about a sibling, wasn't there?"

He grabbed the tablecloth and folded it precisely. He handed it to her to put in the basket. "Any coffee left?"

"Subject closed. Got it. A pink flower phobia and a taboo subject. Interesting dynamics going on here." She refilled his cup with some of her fine Arabica coffee, poured a little more into her own, and sat down.

He glowered at her a minute then sat beside her. "Everything seems to be in order for the banquet."

"Yup. Looking good. Unless something comes up, we don't have anything to do until that weekend. I've put up a poster for helpers to set up."

"Lots of takers, I suppose. Like the hoards that wanted to serve on the planning committee."

His wry humor tickled her. She laughed and placed a playful punch on his shoulder. "You and I did fine together, didn't we?"

The look he gave her made her laugh again.

"Surprised, aren't you?"

He blinked and then laughed. "Yeah, I guess I am at that. We not only did fine, but it was kind of fun. At times."

"Ohh." She pressed her palm to her chest in mock gratitude. "Faint praise from the practical lawyer. I can't believe it."

He shifted his gaze away then returned it to her, his eyes light green, a slightly embarrassed look pulling at the corners of his mouth. "I'm having trouble believing it myself."

She looked at him with eyes that saw him with new insight, to a hurting heart, a doubting mind, and other things too fragile and new to name. She felt him studying her with the same intensity, wondered what he saw as his gaze probed past the outside layer she presented to the public. His eyes darkened; his gaze reached toward her soul. She held her breath, waited for his approval, waited...

A tune intruded. She blinked and turned to locate her cell phone in the basket. "It's Mom. I'd better take the call. Sorry." She hit the TALK button. Sorry to lose the moment before she knew his response; disappointed because she'd hoped for his approval. She knew something was wrong with that thought, but before she could examine it, she said, "Hello, Mom."

"Hi. What are you doing?"

"Mom, you wouldn't believe it. I just had a picnic with Nan and a man she knew fifty years ago. It's so romantic." She turned her back to Steele so she didn't have to bear the desperate way he rolled his eyes and pretended to gag. She told her mother all about it, enjoyed her mother's excited response, then asked, "How are you guys doing?"

"Great. We have a honeymoon couple coming tonight and a famous actor on Monday."

"Oh, fun. Where's Dad?"

"Making sure the flowers and lawn are perfect."

She ended the call a few minutes later. "My mom. She and Dad own a resort in the Kalispell area. They often have famous guests." She named the actor who had booked. "And honeymooners. Mom likes to go all out for them."

Steele looked bored. "Let me guess. This is where you get all your ideas about romance." He sighed. "I know the track record on actors' marriages isn't good. It would be interesting to see how many of your 'honeymooners' are still together a year or two later."

She waved her hand at him. "Don't knock romance. Despite your doubts, it usually works."

He met her look again. She felt the same deep-throated tug. And then he gave a brisk nod, and the moment disappeared. "I have no interest in a relationship based on such nonsense. I hope to marry someday, but it will be because of mutual, practical interests."

Holly jerked her gaze away and prayed he hadn't seen the disappointment flashing through her. She immediately scolded herself. Sure, she and Steele enjoyed planning the banquet together more than either of them had anticipated. Sure, she enjoyed his ironic sense of humor and liked the open affection between him and Henry. None of that provided reason for wishing he could be more romantic. And she had no interest in a "practical" relationship.

◆

For the next few days, Holly saw little of Nan and even less of Henry as they spent their days exploring the city. Nan fell into bed exhausted so early every evening Holly barely had time to discover what the couple had done. As for Steele, he had all but disappeared. Of course, they had no need to meet. The banquet required nothing more of them for now, the grandparents kept busy, and Holly had to work. As did Steele. She caught glimpses of him entering the building across the street.

She sighed. Why should she feel so lonely? Nothing had changed. With a start, she realized something had—she had. Like it or not, she'd gotten used to Steele running over for coffee once or twice a day. She missed his company, which was as corny as an old country-and-western song. All they did when they were together was argue.

Yes, she missed him even though she kept busy serving guests, giving them pink flowers and hand-painted cards.

She looked at the cart, with many of the flowers already dispensed. What could have happened to Steele to make him hate pink flowers?

At the sound of approaching footsteps, she turned. "Steele." She stopped at the husky sound of her voice, took a deep breath, and tried again. "Hi." Still a little airy but not too revealing, she hoped. Like what was she afraid to reveal— surprise, pleasure? Yes, both.

"Annie," she called into the shop. "Could you bring an espresso for Steele and a mocha for me, please?"

They headed toward the table against the window. She'd taken to putting the planter full of purple pansies next to this table.

"How have you been?" she asked.

"Good. Busy."

They made a few more conversational comments. She wondered if he'd come for a particular reason, or had he missed their visits?

He bent over the purple blossoms. "They smell good."

Her insides felt like a drink of sweet coffee at his appreciation of the flowers. She was glad she had moved them here and shifted the pink ones away.

"I love their scent." She leaned over and breathed deeply of the dark pansies.

What was she thinking? Her face was inches from Steele's. She was certain the blaze of her embarrassment lit her face as if she'd hidden votive candles in her cheeks. She pulled back slowly, grasped the cup Annie placed before her, and studied the contents. She lifted the cup to her mouth then set it back without taking a drink. No way could she swallow. Her throat constricted as though it were being squeezed by a fist.

He sat up straight. Took a drink. Shifted. Rolled his head as if his neck hurt.

She cleared her throat with a little cough. "You don't mind purple flowers?"

"No. I know. It's strange. I should see a shrink."

She couldn't tell if he meant to be cross with her for her suggestion, so she stole a glance at him.

He grinned. "Of course, it might be cheaper simply to avoid pink flowers."

At the teasing look in his eyes, her throat closed again. For a minute she thought she might suffocate as she struggled to suck in air. She'd always known he was handsome, with dark blond hair that dipped over his forehead in a beguiling wave, a strong chin with the slightest hint of a dimple in the center, and eyes she'd admired from first glance. But she'd never before felt the full potency of his look.

Her eyes stung with a queasy mingle of embarrassment and acute aware-ness. She shifted away, instantly regretted breaking the contact, and reversed her gaze.

"Marty and the Mice canceled," he said.

The real reason for his visit? Why should she be so disappointed? She wasn't. If anything, it was a relief to be released from her dreadful awareness.

"Marty and the Mice?" She chuckled. "I was so looking forward to the explanation behind that name for a band. We had a couple of bands we turned down when we decided to limit it to four. Can one of them fill in at the last minute?"

"I'll call and see. It would be nice to have the four since we have it set up for that."

"Good thing we didn't print the programs."

"My idea, as I recall."

"Yes, Mr. Practical. You were right on this one."

He quirked one eyebrow as if to suggest he'd been right more often than that if she cared to notice.

"Okay, you've been right a couple of times."

"All right then." He grinned at her, and she told herself it was foolish to feel so pleased. "I'm liking this. Care to be more specific?"

"Let me think." She tilted her chin as if giving it serious thought. "No."

She put the brakes on silly emotions. "I suppose we should finalize the judging forms." They had agreed to eliminate the bands by means of judges rather than the audience.

"We had several criteria—audience appreciation, creativity of presentation, musical ability. Anything else?"

"It's all about having fun. Only thing I might suggest is to rate the criteria in order of importance."

He chuckled. "Like audience appreciation is more important than musical ability."

"Exactly. So let's make sure the judges know that."

"We could weigh each point differently."

"Huh?"

"Sure. Audience appreciation has a value of, say, ten, and the judges rate it one to ten. Creativity in presentation, a value of eight; musical ability, five. So a band that is a real crowd pleaser could get a ten, an eight, and maybe a two for ability."

"Steele, I hate to admit it, but that's a real good idea."

He sat up straighter and looked pleased with himself. "Practical has its upside."

"Yeah. I guess so." She thought of the presentation she and Heather had prepared. "Heather has been so helpful with the slide show. It's really a portrait of her work over there."

"I'm glad it's going well. I'm sure you and Heather have done a good job. It was a great idea." He held his thumb up in a salute of approval. His smile filled his eyes with such kindness she ached inside.

They talked some more about the upcoming banquet, laughing at the names the bands had given themselves.

"I'm excited about the whole thing," she said. "My prayer is that it goes so well we raise enough money for the new roof."

"Let's join our prayers in asking for that." He reached for her hands across the table.

They'd prayed for the success of the banquet in the past, but never before had she felt such unity of purpose. She let him take her hands and focused her thoughts on the purpose of the banquet—the orphans in Africa.

Steele prayed. "Heavenly Father, God of all mercy and grace, the giver of good gifts, we ask You to touch this banquet and the entertainment with Your power and blessing so, in turn, the little kids in Africa might be blessed and especially that they might learn of Your love through our gifts." He stopped.

Holly wanted to pray out loud, too, but fought to squeeze words past the thickness in her brain—part gratitude, part surprise, and complete confusion. This was Steele Davis, she informed her muddled brain. Logical, practical, scared to death of pink flowers and romance—not the kind of man she should be feeling so confused about.

She sucked in air, laden with the scent of purple pansies and espresso coffee, and forced her throat to work. "Dear Lord, help things to go so well our expectations will be exceeded. Help Heather as she cares for so many children, so many needs. May we be able to provide the funds to fix the roof before next rainy season. Thank You. Amen."

Steele squeezed her fingers gently. "It's in God's very capable hands."

All her serious self-talk vanished like an e-mail lost in cyberspace at the way he looked so content and sure of God's control. It gave her a dizzying sense of something so good and strong and attractive about him. She gently extracted her hands before she totally lost her equilibrium. "Care for another coffee?"

He studied his empty cup as he seemed to consider the question.

Of course, he would have appointments. He didn't have time to linger over coffee any more than she did. But, surprisingly, only two customers had shown up in a half hour or more, and they had opted to sit inside. Annie had no trouble coping with their needs. Holly shifted, prepared to retract her offer, plead work.

"Sure, I could use another."

"Annie, refills, please," Holly called.

Suddenly she could think of nothing to say to this man. Which was stupid, considering they each had a grandparent on the loose. "So what are the grandparents up to? Nan falls into bed practically as soon as she gets home."

"Pops does the same. When I ask what he's been doing, he says walking and talking or having coffee and talking. I think they've gone to the museum and a couple of galleries."

"I hope Nan isn't wearing herself out. Mom and Dad would hold me personally responsible if she made herself sick."

"Has she said anything about what she and Pops are talking about?"

Holly sat back and studied Steele, saw the glint of determination in his eyes. "If I said they were talking marriage, would you try to dissuade them?"

His gaze grew darker, harder. "I might."

She laughed. "Then it's a good thing I'm not going to say that."

He leaned forward, his look so intense she squirmed and tried to look away. "Because you don't want me to know or because Jean hasn't said anything?"

She stuck out her chin. He didn't intimidate her. At least not very much. "Yes."

He scowled. "Yes what?"

"Yes, sir?"

He laughed. "You forgot to salute."

"Oh yeah. Sorry." She touched two fingers to her forehead. "Sir."

"Do I get the feeling you won't tell me if you don't want to?"

"Yup. You got it."

"You can't blame me for worrying about Pops. He's—"

"Vulnerable. I know. You've said it before." She suddenly felt sorry for the concern in his eyes. "But Nan hasn't said anything to me. She's come back a few times looking a little troubled. I'm not sure what that's all about." She leaned forward and tapped her finger on the table directly in front of Steele. "I don't want to see Nan hurt, either."

He searched her eyes as if looking for something.

She held his gaze, letting him see and feel the slight shift of dynamics between them. She couldn't say exactly what it meant, didn't want to think about it too deeply at this time. She only knew the change felt good and right and scary and dangerous.

He smiled. "Does that mean romance isn't necessarily the answer for our grandparents?"

She laughed. "Romance is not the problem. It's a good way to explore relationships. It satisfies the need for affirmation in each of us. But I admit there has to be more than that. I want Nan to be romanced, but I also want her to be comfortable with the realities of a relationship with your grandfather."

He leaned back, held up his thumb in another salute. "Right on." Suddenly he jerked forward, grabbed her hands, and gave her a look so intense it made her eyes water. "Tell me, Holly Hope, have I had any influence in making you admit the need for practicality?"

She tore her gaze from his, studied their united hands, wondered at the myriad of emotions springing from that simple touch—amusement, hope, affirmation.

Affirmation? He was no romantic, but there was something solid about him that felt good and right.

She pulled her thoughts back to his question. "I'm not saying anything."

He chuckled. "On the grounds it might incriminate you?"

She tried unsuccessfully to stop her laugh from escaping. "Something like that."

"So we both agree we need to make sure our grandparents keep their feet firmly on the ground? I've been thinking it's time I encourage Pops to go back to the ranch. Put an end to this romantic foray. Why don't you see if you can convince Jean to go home?"

She jerked back. "I will do no such thing. I don't want Nan hurt, but I am fully behind her if she wants to pursue her interest in Henry. No way would I do anything to come between them. That's their decision to make." She huffed hard, mad at herself as much as at Steele. How could she even think he'd changed or things between them had changed? He was as stubborn, as practical to the point of cruelness, as unappealing as ever. And if she felt just a twinge of regret at having to admit she'd hoped otherwise, she could blame no one but herself and her eternal romantic optimism.

"I will help my grandmother any way I can. They both deserve the chance to recreate this special time from their youth, and if it leads to something in their declining years, I'll be thrilled."

Steele pushed back and got to his feet. "I see you aren't prepared to be reasonable about this. The way I see it, Pops is too vulnerable. He needs someone to run interference, make sure he thinks with his head and not his heart. Your grandmother has had twenty years to plan this. Pops—"

She jumped to her feet, fighting an incredible urge to do the man bodily harm. It didn't bother her a bit that he outweighed her by fifty pounds or more and his lean body showed the effects of all the time he spent in physical activity. "Stop right there." She pressed her fingertip to his chest. "If you accuse my grandmother of scheming, I won't be responsible for what I do."

His eyes flashed that pale color again. And then he laughed. "What are you going to do? Hit me?"

She dropped her hands to her side and uncurled her fists. "Of course not."

"Good. Because I prefer to use my head"—he leaned forward—"to using either my heart or my fists." He stalked away before she could calm her anger enough to answer.

She searched frantically for the perfect retort as he widened the distance between them. "You stay away from my grandmother."

She slammed the heel of her hand into her forehead. That was really a clincher all right. Aaggh. Why could she never think of what she wanted to say when she was upset? No doubt she'd think of the perfect thing about two in the morning.

Not that it mattered. They were as far apart as the north from the south on how their grandparents should conduct their relationship. As they were on so many things. She grabbed the empty cups and headed inside to do something useful. She refused to allow herself even a hint of regret at the way things had gone south with the speed of a rocket ship.

Suddenly she laughed.

"What's so funny?" Annie asked. "Didn't I just see you and Steele practically ready to kill each other?"

"He thinks he should interfere with Nan and Henry's romance. I was just thinking what Nan would say to anyone poking his nose in her business. I hope Steele tries it, though I feel sorry for him if he does."

Chapter 7

Steele dropped to his chair, turned it away from the window, and stared at the bright geometric framed print on his wall. He felt as fractured as all those triangles and squares. He'd always liked the picture, even though it made no sense—no pattern, no reason for the arrangement.

His gaze fixed on a bright spot of purple. A tiny square in the midst of large orange, red, and green shapes. The same color as the flowers in the planter at J'ava Moi.

Why had she rearranged the planters so he didn't have to sit beside pink flowers? More important, why did he sniff the flowers and act all lovey-dovey? He grunted and felt an incredible disgust at himself. That was why he didn't believe in romance. It got a man all confused just when he needed to have his wits about him. And if it could happen to him, a lawyer, practiced in rational thought, a man who didn't believe in such foolishness in the first place, he could only imagine how the whole business of recreating scenes of first love could make it impossible for Pops to think straight.

As he'd said to Holly, the best thing would be for Pops and Jean to go back home and think about this whole business without the confusing trappings of picnics and flowers and late evenings. He chuckled. Eight o'clock didn't qualify as late in his books, but it seemed to in his grandfather's.

He rubbed his chest where Holly had planted her finger. He knew a flash of regret that she'd shifted from starry-eyed to combative so quickly. Which further proved how all those trappings could confuse a man. Sure, she was a beautiful woman, with her wavy brown hair and expressive brown eyes. He snorted. Looks were only skin deep, after all.

He pushed to his feet, strode over to stare at the purple square on the picture, then turned and without conscious thought crossed to the window to look down at the outdoor tables and flowers. He located the planter full of pink ones and shuddered. No way was he going to let himself get tangled up by such foolishness.

◆

Pops unlocked the door and walked into the apartment. Steele pointed at his boots, and the older man gave a long-suffering sigh, backed up, and grabbed his slippers. "Sissy footwear," he muttered and made a great show of tiptoeing into the living room in his slippers.

293

"Whatcha been doing? You and Jean."

"We've been out and about."

"Yeah. Doing what?"

Pops fixed him with a hard look. "You cross-examining me?"

Steele shrugged. "Just trying to show a little interest."

Pops headed for the fridge. "You ever fix a meal? There's nothing in here but junk food." He pulled out a leftover piece of pizza with two fingertips and dropped it into the garbage.

"There goes dinner," Steele said, laughing at the way Pops wrinkled his nose.

"I haven't eaten," Pops said. "And I don't want to go out."

"I'll order in. What do you like—Chinese or pizza?"

"A man could die of all this high-fat junk. I want a plain old meal—meat and potatoes and lots of veggies."

Steele joined Pops at the fridge, pulled open the freezer side, and dug out a package of sirloin steak. The plastic had cracked. The meat had streaks of freezer burn. "Here you go."

Pops drew back and refused to touch the meat. "That's disgusting. Grab your boots, boy. We're going shopping."

"I thought you were too tired to go out."

"Lesser of two evils." He looked at the steaks and shuddered. "I would have brought meat from home if I'd known this was the best you had to offer."

Steele shoved the steak back in the freezer and closed the door. "Something eating at you, Pops?"

"Just my hunger."

An hour later they returned with bags of groceries, enough to feed a small army, Steele figured. He hoped it didn't hint at Pops planning an extended stay. "You'll be headed back to the ranch soon, I suppose." He kept his attention on the potatoes he scrubbed.

"You telling me it's time to move on? 'Cause if you are, there're lots of motels in town."

Steele dried the potatoes, wrapped them in foil, and stuck them in the oven before he faced Pops. "You've been acting like a cow with a nail in her cud all evening. You want to tell me what's going on, or am I expected to shut up and ignore your snipes?"

Pops's expression grew stubborn, then he sighed and pulled himself up on a stool. "It's Jean."

Steele nodded. He'd seen this coming. The old guy was going to get hurt all over again.

"I want to marry her. I should never have walked away from her fifty years ago, though I don't regret a minute of my time with your grandmother. It's just that Jean and I have"—he waggled his hands—"something. A connection I can't explain. She makes me feel good about myself. She does thoughtful little things." He must have seen the skepticism in Steele's face. "Yeah, I know you'll mock, but she does romantic things. Your grandmother never did. I bought flowers and gifts. Your grandmother was far more practical, but it makes a person feel special to be the recipient, you know."

Steele didn't, but he wasn't going to say so. Nor was he going to acknowledge the hollow echo deep inside him as he remembered Holly saying something similar. "So what's the problem?"

"There are many things to consider—money, property. . ." He sighed deeply. "So many choices and decisions. It gives me a headache just thinking of it. Maybe I'm too old for this sort of nonsense."

Maybe Pops had begun to discover things on his own. "Pops, why complicate your life? Why not go home and enjoy what you've worked so hard to build?"

"A man gets lonely."

Steele thought of all the lonely, unhappily married men he'd seen. "Pops, a man can be married and still be lonelier than he imagined."

"You are far too cynical for a young man. I'm not afraid I'd be lonely if I married Jean. I just don't care for all the decisions that need to be made."

"Maybe it's time to forget this business." He kept his voice soft, almost pleading. *Please, Pops, go home before you get hurt. Before you buy yourself a whole set of problems you don't want to deal with.*

"No. Avoiding problems is never a way to solve them. Jean and I have some decisions to make, and it's time to make them." He slapped his palm on the counter. The harsh noise caused Steele to jump. "I know what I'm going to do. Jean and I took a long drive once. Out toward Anaconda on the Pintler scenic route. We looped around to Deer Lodge and returned. Had a really good time as I recall. I'm going to take her on that trip, and we're going to deal with things."

Steele could imagine them confined to a small vehicle for hours with nothing to do but talk. "I'll tell you what. I'll drive. That way you and Jean can concentrate on the scenery."

Pops's eyes lit up. "Good idea. We can sit in the back, and I can hold her hand."

Steele resisted the urge to roll his eyes. Great. He thought he'd make it impossible for them to scheme in private; Pops saw it as an opportunity to cuddle in the back. Sometimes he couldn't believe they shared the same genes. Steele had obviously inherited more of his mother's genes than his father's.

As he plotted how to nip this little problem in the bud, he washed lettuce for a salad then went to the balcony and turned on the barbecue to grill steaks.

◆

Saturday morning dawned as bright and clear as only a Montana day could, promising never-ending sunshine.

Pops had shaved twice and slicked his hair down too many times for Steele to count. He headed for the door a half dozen times as Steele drank his second cup of coffee. Finally he jerked on his boots. "Come on, boy. What's holding you up? There's a lot to see and do before the day is out."

Steele gathered up his keys. "Pops, hold your horses."

But the older man hurried outside and stood by the SUV as Steele locked the apartment.

"I'll ride shotgun until we pick up the ladies."

Steele pulled himself behind the wheel before he answered. "You mean Jean." His gut warned him he couldn't be so fortunate.

"Holly's coming, too. No point in you being alone." Pops leered at him. "You pay attention, boy, and I'll show you how to win a woman's heart."

Steele's stomach did a strange little bounce—rising in a rocket launch arc at the idea of Holly at his side all day then plummeting with a mingling of dread and nervousness. He wanted nothing to distract him from being Pops's voice of reason throughout the day. Somehow he felt certain Holly's presence would prove exactly that—a distraction.

Steele gripped the steering wheel. Holly hadn't been part of the plan, but he could deal with it. He'd had worse surprises. Like the time he'd fallen off his horse and rolled to the bottom of a hill, scaring a porcupine. He'd found his feet faster than lightning and backed away from the angry little creature.

"Boy, stop your daydreaming and let's get moving."

His knuckles white, Steele drove away, heading downtown to historic East Pine Street.

Holly and Jean—holding a single purple daisy of some sort—waited on the sidewalk. Pops obviously wasn't the only eager one this morning.

Pops jumped out and opened the back door for Jean. She handed him the flower.

"What's this?"

"I remembered you asked the florist about gerbera daisies the other day. You said how bold they were. So I bought you one."

Pops took the flower, his gaze never leaving Jean's face. He brushed his knuckles against her cheek. "Thank you."

No mistaking the huskiness in Pops's voice. These little gestures made him feel special, he'd said. But as Steele watched the older man stand rooted to the sidewalk, he figured such nonsense only mucked up the old man's reasoning. It wasn't until Holly opened the passenger-side door that Pops and Jean seemed to remember they weren't the only two people in the world.

Holly climbed in beside Steele. "Good morning."

He nodded. "Morning."

She studied him. Her smile faded. "How nice of you to offer to take Nan and Henry on this trip."

Steele heard the warning in her voice, knew she suspected him of ulterior motives, and ignored her.

"Nan is excited. She hasn't been back in fifty years."

"I expect things will have changed." What he meant, what he wanted to say, was, *Holly, get real. Only fools and romantics think you can recreate something fifty years after the fact.* Pops wasn't the same man, and Jean was certainly not the young, innocent woman of fifty years ago.

"So you've mentioned a time or two." She snapped open a map. "This should be fun."

He didn't miss the emphasis on "should" any more than he mistook her subtle warning.

They locked gazes and did silent battle for a moment. He sensed her drawing a mental line in the dust.

"Come on, boy," Pops boomed. "Time's a-getting away."

Steele tipped his chin in silent acceptance of her challenge. "Should be quite a day," he murmured, pulling away from the curb and heading out of town.

Jean settled back. "The country is just as pretty as I remember it. Rolling hills like draped fabric. Each fold growing more and more gray in the distance. Never have seen anything prettier."

Steele had to wonder where she'd spent the past half century. "Where's home for you?"

"Seattle. Tom and I bought a house there shortly after we married."

"Which," Holly murmured, "is now worth a fortune."

"Point taken." It didn't negate all the other obstacles to a relationship between the older pair.

"I remember we stopped often to look at the sprawling vistas," Jean said.

Steele kept up a steady speed. After all, as Pops had said numerous times already, they had a lot of miles to cover.

"Nan, we'll stop at the next pullout." Holly said her grandmother's name, but Steele knew she spoke to him.

"Oh, don't bother for me. I know Steele wants to get—"

"Exactly where are you going in such a hurry?" Pops demanded.

Steele lifted his hand off the wheel in a sign of defeat. "Who was chomping at the bit not more than forty-five minutes ago?"

"I wanted to start the trip, not hurry and end it. You gonna be like this, and I'll wish I'd brought my own vehicle. Jean wants to stop and admire the scenery. What's wrong with that?"

The air inside the SUV grew heavy with combined disapproval from the others. Steele gave a grin that felt too small for his mouth. "My misunderstanding. I thought we had a destination." He saw a turnout and pulled over. The others piled out of the vehicle and gathered at the edge of the road to admire the deep valley before them.

"It's beautiful," Jean said, turning to smile sweetly at Pops. Poor old Pops practically melted like hot butter right on the spot.

Steele stood beside the vehicle, arms crossed over his chest, a feeling of frustrated fury tightening his lungs.

Holly pulled herself away from the view and came to his side. "Steele, what's wrong?"

"Nothing." Except he didn't want Pops hurt.

"Glad to hear that. Would it kill you to show it?"

He relaxed his arms, leaned back on his heels, and forced a smile to his lips.

A few minutes later, they were on their way. The two in the back talked softly. Steele strained to hear what they said. Holly, consciously or not, ran interference. "I brought a map. It's got all sorts of information. Did you know the Number One highway is the oldest paved road in Montana?"

He grunted. Didn't know. And wondered why he should care.

They reached Philipsburg, according to Holly's running commentary, the liveliest ghost town in the West. "Twice the town has won the award for the prettiest painted place."

"My, it's changed since we were here," Jean said, peering out the side window. "It's very pretty, isn't it?"

"Look." Pops pointed past Jean's shoulder. "There's a little courtyard and some tables. We can get coffee there."

Steele pulled to the curb before anyone could suggest stopping.

"What a pretty spot," Jean said. "Holly, just think what you could do if you had that much outdoor space. Look at the pots of flowers and trees. And the artwork."

Holly pressed her nose to the side window. "It's lovely."

"Henry." Jean's voice was as round as the daisy on the seat between the two. "I do believe we stopped at this very spot. I don't remember the patio; but I recall a bench beneath the sign on that building, and I remember you telling me about the silver mines and the manganese needed in World War One." She clasped her hands together in front of her chest. "We had such a good time. We sat right there"—she pointed to the place—"for a long time and discussed so many things—our faith, our families, our dreams. We prayed together for God to lead us regarding our future." Her voice grew husky. "I believe this is a sign—remembering how we asked God to direct us. I've been praying to know how we should proceed." She sent a shy smile to Holly, including Steele. "Henry has asked me to marry him. I've hesitated because there are so many things to consider. It's not like being young and having nothing to think about but the future."

Steele had done his best to restrain his frustration at the flowers, the impractical dreams, the purposeful disregard for facts, but Jean's sudden revelation grabbed at his throat. Suddenly he could keep quiet no longer. "Enjoy coffee. Enjoy the town. Buy some little souvenir if you like. But don't let flowers and faded memories cloud your thinking. Jean's right. You both need to hesitate and get your feet back on the ground before you make any big decisions you could regret later."

Silence filled the vehicle. He knew they all stared at him, but he pulled the keys from the ignition and grabbed the door handle.

"Steele, you're out of line." Pops's voice growled his anger. "Jean, you'll have to forgive him. He has no business speaking that way. Boy, you're far too much like your mother. Don't get me wrong. She's a good woman, but she sees no value in anything but work. I'm sure she'd stomp a flower if it crossed her path."

His gut burning, Steele wrenched the door open and strode away.

He didn't realize Holly had followed him until she grabbed his elbow. Still, he didn't slow his steps until she edged around him and blocked his way. "Steele, what gives you the right to speak to my grandmother like that? Or your grandfather, for that matter. What is wrong with you?"

He saw the brick walls of the building beside him. Saw a sign. Read the words without knowing what they said. "Nothing. I'm worried about my grandfather. I don't want to see him hurt."

"Aren't they entitled to make their own choices? They're not exactly senile."

"Don't you think they should take some time and think about what they're doing? A break. Go home." He said the words woodenly, not thinking them, not feeling them, simply repeating them from the arguments he'd provided himself for days.

"Steele, I get the feeling this isn't about Nan and Henry. It's about you. What are you running from?"

There were no flowers in sight. Just brick and board. Yet he had the same stupid, nameless, suffocating feeling he got when he saw pink flowers. He shuddered.

She maneuvered him toward a bench at the edge of the sidewalk and nudged him toward the wooden seat. He sat.

"Something's bothering you. What is it?" Like a soft spring breeze, her voice pulled at his thoughts. But how could he tell her something he didn't understand? Pops's words echoed inside his head, tangling with his own confused thoughts.

Work. Practical. *Stomp*—why did he shudder at the word? Flowers. Pink flowers. A thought tugged at the edges of his mind. A little boy kneeling, tears on his cheeks. Was he the boy? No way. He'd never been a crybaby.

"What's wrong?" Holly asked again.

"I don't know." He looked at her and resisted an urge to catch the strands of hair blowing across her cheek and tuck them back.

"Is it what Henry said about your mother?"

"No. Mom is very practical. She operates a Cat. Pushes dirt around."

Holly touched the back of his hand. "Tell me about your parents."

"Not much to say. They met when Mom asked for a job with the construction company. Threatened to sue Dad if he refused because she was a woman. He says she pestered him until he finally said okay. Said the same about getting married. She pestered him into it. Not that he doesn't adore her. I always think of them with Dad's arm around her waist standing at the side of a construction project discussing the work. They have a great relationship." He felt he had to make sure she knew that.

"So you think every relationship should be as practical?"

"Yes. No. I don't know." What was there about this woman that turned his brain to powder?

Her hand still rested on his, and he grew aware of its gentle weight. The boiling turmoil of a few minutes ago settled into a simmer, and he slowly relaxed.

"Seems to me all kinds of relationships work. It's not up to us to judge, so long as they do work," she said.

"Are you talking about Pops and Jean?"

"Partly. I don't think they need us to tell them how to run their lives. In fact, I hope I can learn something from them."

"Uh-huh." A noise meant to be noncommittal. He jerked to his feet. "I'm going to poke around the shops." It beat thinking about the crying young boy and how it related to Pops and Jean. If indeed it did, which seemed highly unlikely. He stood and waited for Holly. "Want to come along?"

"I might want to buy flowers or something frilly."

"I might want to buy a different map."

She chuckled. "One with nothing but the miles and the names of the towns, I suppose."

"You must have read my mind."

She came to his side and nudged him with her shoulder, causing him to stumble. He grabbed her hand and pulled her to his side to stop her from repeating it. She swung their joined hands as they marched along the street. Holly browsed through gift shops and boutiques while Steele picked up a colorful brochure describing the historic buildings. He found the history fascinating. They passed Pops and Nan several times, and each time he felt a pang that he wasn't fulfilling his goal and keeping them from discussing marriage. He blinked. Had that been his goal? He thought he only wanted to make sure they didn't make foolish decisions. When had marriage become the foolish thing he worried about?

Holly must have felt his start of surprise. "What's up with you? You're acting so strange today."

"That's hardly flattering."

"You're the guy who likes his feet planted on terra firma. I would think flattery would be an insult."

"Flattery is an insult because it's insincere." He grabbed her hand and pulled her from the store. "We'd better continue this journey." He'd better get himself sorted out before he lost his way.

They rounded up Pops and Jean and headed down the road. Everyone was quiet as they drove. Steele blamed himself and his out-of-line comments about their relationship. He couldn't ignore the tension.

"Pops, I'm sorry I spoke out of turn."

"Boy, I'm sorry if I insulted your mother."

"You didn't. Did you?"

"Didn't mean to."

"Okay then. Now tell me what you want to do next."

"Lunch," three voices chorused.

Determined to make up for his earlier behavior, Steele repeated the historical information about Philipsburg. They passed Georgetown Lake, and he scoured his mind to remember everything he could about the lake. "At one time special trains came to the lake from Butte with chairs on open gondola cars." He rattled on about the mountains, the mines, the forest service, and even remembered to mention the huge elk herds of the area. Anything to keep from thinking about the little boy with the tear-stained face, pink flowers, and Jean and Pops. They seemed to be connected, which made no sense whatsoever.

At one point he glanced in his mirror, saw Jean, her eyes closed, her head resting on Pops's shoulder. He'd put her to sleep. Given her a reason to nestle against Pops. Hardly his intention.

He instantly shut up.

They pulled in at Anaconda, where the main street seemed to disappear into the foot of a mountain. Pops insisted they have a "real" meal, and they stopped at a steak joint.

"Great tour guide," Pops said as they waited for their meal. "Had no idea you knew so much about the area."

Steele nodded. "I read a lot."

"Talk a lot, too," Holly murmured, low so the other two didn't hear, then turned to include Jean and Pops. "Sure surprised me when he spouted all that information."

Jean chuckled. "I slept through most of it. Sorry."

Steele was thankful the steak arrived at that point, and he gave it his total attention. He didn't need anyone to point out how strange he'd been acting. From rude to talkative. He wished he knew what was wrong with him.

When Holly excused herself later to visit the ladies' room, he slipped away, saying he needed to check the oil in the SUV. He popped the hood and pulled out the dipstick. Of course it didn't need oil. He'd checked it last night. Had it changed a week ago. But he needed *his* dipstick checked. This whole day had gone from bad to worse, and it was only half over. He felt Holly's presence like something under his skin even before she spoke.

"Everything okay?"

No. He'd never felt less okay. She meant the SUV, of course. "Yup."

"I shouldn't have said that about you talking too much. I'm sorry. I realize you're doing your best to entertain Nan and Henry. It's very thoughtful of you."

He straightened, turned to stare at her. A compliment? Her approval slid along his senses like sweet perfume. This time he did tuck back those wandering lengths of hair. His fingers lingered on her smooth cheek. "You're beautiful." He couldn't believe he'd said the words aloud. "Sorry."

She caught his hand before he could jerk back. "Don't be sorry. I don't mind hearing compliments once in a while. Thank you."

Her eyes filled with something soft and inviting.

He curled his fingers around hers and felt her face beneath his knuckles. He studied her smiling lips and thought about kissing her.

Then the confusion of the day centered down on this woman. They fought like cats and dogs, and yet here he was longing to kiss her. He needed a checkup from the neck up.

She saw his sudden silent withdrawal and slipped away.

He turned to close the hood, wondering if he should slam his head between the pieces of metal. He couldn't remember ever feeling so torqued up inside.

"Next stop Deer Lodge," Pops said, holding the back door open for Jean.

"What's there?" Steele directed his question to Pops, but it was Holly he watched as she scooted to the passenger seat and snapped the map open. He'd offended her somehow. He just wasn't sure how or what to do about it.

"Auto museum, old Montana prison, cowboy collectibles, gun collection," Holly read from the map.

"We want to see the old autos," Pops said. "Even though we're probably older than lots of them."

"We'll have to be careful, or they'll want to keep us in the museum," Jean said, and the two of them chuckled like a couple of Laurel and Hardy movie nuts.

Holly sent them a wide smile, and Steele let himself relax. "I'd like to see the prison." Surely a visit to such a cold, cruel place would put him firmly back on his feet.

Chapter 8

Holly put on her sunglasses and adjusted her seatbelt. For a moment at the side of the vehicle, she'd thought Steele meant to kiss her. She tried to analyze her feelings.

Disappointment? A little, she admitted. She couldn't deny she felt drawn to him in ways defying reason. And not just today. Somehow, the more time they spent together, the more her feelings toward him shifted.

A touch of concern? That, too. All day she'd sensed a tension about him, as if he were fighting himself. It made her ache to hug him and tell him whatever bothered him could be fixed if not by talking then certainly by prayer. And she didn't mean the kind of chatter that had him talking nonstop for over an hour as if he feared silence. He'd gone out of his way to entertain them for the last part of the morning, which was cute and charming.

And wary? For sure. He was a man who confessed he despised the things she considered important. The man hated pink flowers. What was with that?

Yet she had hoped he'd kiss her. Felt certain he would. Then something happened to change his mind. She gave a deprecating smile. Probably the man remembered her penchant for romance, and it scared him.

Not that she intended to let it ruin her day. Nan and Henry were having a good time, and that made everything else less important.

They headed down the highway to more adventure. She expected the older couple to be tired, wanting to nap after the heavy lunch, but the food seemed to have energized them. Henry was a good storyteller and soon had them laughing at his tales of cow wrestling, bull stomping, and calf busting on the ranch. A time or two Holly wondered at the complete accuracy of his stories. They seemed a little too big to be real. She stole a glance at Steele. He met her look, grinned, and rolled his eyes.

She choked back laughter. And suddenly the road seemed smoother. All too soon they arrived at the museum site.

"You two antiques can look at the old cars," Steele said. "I'm going to visit the prison. Holly, you want to come with me?"

She was surprised and touched that he would arrange for Nan and Henry to wander off by themselves and quickly agreed to stay with Steele. She watched the older couple head into the auto museum, holding hands and nudging each other, laughing at secret jokes. "How nice of you to give them this time alone."

He grinned and looked pleased.

She patted his shoulder. "I'm beginning to think you're a romantic after all."

Instantly his face settled into hard lines.

There was something to be said for knowing when to keep her mouth shut. This would have been one of those times. One thing this man did not want to be called was romantic. But she wouldn't let one slip ruin the rest of the day and grabbed the brochure for a self-guided tour of the prison. "Lead on. Let's see where the bad guys were sent."

"This is my sort of museum." He snagged the brochure from her and took her hand.

She almost tripped at the doorway. Maybe she was wrong. Could be the man knew more about romance than he let on, because holding hands as he read from the brochure seemed to her to be pretty romantic.

"No running water or sewer when it was first built," he read. "Just two buckets. One for sewage and another for water. Sounds appealing."

"Not."

They laughed, their gazes locking for a heartbeat. She turned away first.

They read and joked and laughed around the perimeter of the prison. The sun shone down, and the reason for the buildings seemed far removed from them until they stepped into the cellblocks and Steele read stories of some of the inmates. By the time they got to the "hole"—a dark, cement room—Holly could no longer smile, and Steele had grown quiet. They backed out and stared around the prison yard.

"It's so bleak," Holly murmured.

"Utilitarian," Steele insisted. He grabbed her hand and bolted out the exit into the open air.

Holly laughed. "That's a tour I'll remember for a long time."

"I should never have suggested it."

"Why not?"

He caught a strand of hair between his fingers and examined it. "You belong in sunshine and flowers." His expression grew bleak, and he sank to the nearby bench and buried his face in his hands.

"It's only an old jail. We can be thankful times have changed."

"It's not the jail." His voice was muffled.

"Then what?"

"I don't know." He sounded angry.

She sat beside him and put her hand lightly on his shoulders. She wished she could do more, but the man had to find his own way to whatever truth he needed. She prayed God would help him and felt compelled to let Steele know her concern. "Dear God, help Steele deal with whatever is bothering him."

"I keep seeing this little boy in my mind."

"Who is the little boy?"

"I think it might be me."

"Why does it bother you to see him?"

He jerked his head up and stared away. "Because he's crying. He shouldn't be crying."

She felt the harshness of his pain like scraping her fingertips over the rough cement in the prison behind them.

"He's just a little boy, isn't he? Don't little boys cry?"

"Not over dumb things." He jerked to his feet and strode away, swung around, and returned. He stood in front of her, his fists clenched.

She raised her gaze to his face, saw desperation quickly replaced with fury. Slowly she rose. "What were you crying about?"

"Nothing." He snapped around to stare at the museum door. "I don't remember."

Holly went to his side, touched his arm. "I'm sure the little boy didn't think it was dumb. Aren't the child's opinions valid?"

She felt him stiffen, felt a sort of expectant surprise, as if he held his breath. She knew her words hit a nerve and prayed he would face whatever it was he kept denying. Her heart squeezed as she thought of the crying child that was Steele. It pained her to think of him hurting. Suddenly she realized whatever had caused him to cry back then still bothered him today. *Oh God, pour Your healing into his heart. Comfort that little boy who is now this man.* She wished she could see his expression, but the sunshine off the windows they faced allowed her only a flash.

She pressed the side of her finger against her upper lip to stop the stinging in her nose. She wanted to comfort him, show him love. She slipped her arm around his waist and hugged gently, fearing he would resist her touch, but he allowed her to hold him.

A sigh whooshed from his depths. He relaxed inch by inch as she held him. "Sometimes," she whispered, "hurting boys just need a hug."

He dropped his arm across her shoulders. "Thank you."

The air seemed awash with silvery light, which settled around her heart and lungs like a fine necklace draped around her neck. She pressed her cheek against his arm. He wore a short-sleeved, button-front shirt in soft cotton. She'd noticed how the pale tan color made his eyes glow with amber highlights. Now she noted the warmth of the material caressing her cheek like a sun-laden day at the lake. A shadow fell across the window, and she saw their reflection and gasped. Here they were hugging each other in full view of God and everyone—it was the *everyone* she worried about. What would people think? The warmth in her cheeks intensified, and she put several inches between them even as Steele jerked his arm from across her shoulders and backed away.

Nan and Henry stepped out of the museum.

One look at her grandmother's grin and twinkling eyes and Holly knew Nan had been one of the spectators.

"Good to see you learning from my example," Henry boomed as he draped his arm across Nan's shoulders. He pulled her close and whispered in a voice that could be heard for a block, "Might be hope for these two after all."

Holly didn't dare glance at Steele. She feared his expression would be thunderous.

"You ready to head home?" Steele asked, his voice revealing nothing. He grabbed Holly's hand and headed for the vehicle.

She stole a look then. It might be wishful thinking, but he looked pretty pleased with life. She laughed soft and low in the back of her throat. This feeling of unity with him might be short lived, but she wasn't about to waste it by wondering when he'd shift back into his practical, no-nonsense, lawyer mode.

He opened the door and held her elbow as he guided her to the front seat. She gave him a smile no doubt as full of happiness as her heart, which had developed this strange, alarming ability to do a Snoopy dance.

"Thank you," she said as she settled on the soft leather seat of the SUV. She met his gaze, overflowing with something so tender and fragile she feared taking a breath would shatter it.

"Hey, you two," Henry growled. "I thought we were going home."

Steele glanced at his grandfather, effectively releasing Holly from the uncertain tension.

As they headed back down the highway toward Missoula, Holly tried to sort out what had just happened and how she felt about it. She tried to be rational and failed. She could think of nothing but gratitude. Something had taken place in Steele's heart, some sort of healing, and in that moment he'd reached for her and smiled his favor. She wanted to hug herself with the joy of it.

The bubbling feeling of it couldn't be contained. She had to find an outlet. A victory dance couldn't be performed in the confines of the vehicle. A *rah-rah* cheer would scare the others. Silly grinning out the side window wasn't entirely satisfying. Talk was the only release available at this moment.

She shifted so she could see into the backseat. "Henry, did Nan tell you about the banquet Steele and I are planning? It's next week." She didn't wait for his answer but rushed on with details of the orphans, the bands, and the decorations. Both grandparents laughed as she described the argument about what form the decorations should take.

"I'm actually eager to see how the red, white, and blue theme will play out."

Steele laughed. "Still doubtful?"

"Not a bit."

He pulled his gaze briefly from the road, his glance rife with meaning.

She knew neither of them meant the decorations alone.

"Do we have volunteers to help set up?" he asked, his attention back on his driving.

"So far it's just you and me."

Another quick glance. Another silent message. He grinned with unusual warmth, as if the idea of the two of them pleased him. Of course, it might be wishful thinking on her part.

"I'll do some recruiting Sunday." His tone informed her people would be agreeing to help.

"Are there still tickets available? Jean, why don't we go? Sounds like fun and a cause I'd like to support."

Holly couldn't think of anyone she'd sooner have there than Nan and Henry. And about a hundred others.

◆

"It looks great," Holly said. The red, white, and blue bunting hung from a stage created to look like a bandstand. Streamers hung from the ceiling. The patriotic theme carried through to the napkins on the table and the floral centerpieces.

"I didn't realize it would be so much work."

"Good thing you got so many people to 'volunteer.'" A dozen people, mostly young men, had appeared to set out tables and chairs and help put up streamers. They'd done their part and left. Only Steele and Holly remained to take care of last-minute details.

"I can hardly wait," Holly said. "I sent Heather an e-mail reminding her tomorrow is the big day. Do you have an estimate of the income yet?"

"We still have a few bills to pay, so I won't know for sure until tomorrow." He touched Holly's chin. "Don't look so worried. It looks like the orphanage will be able to repair the entire roof. Why don't we put out a donation box in case people want to donate more?"

His touch crowded her mind, made her think of a flower-filled arbor, long walks in the moonlight, staring up into the stars and dreaming mutual dreams. She pulled her thoughts back to center. "Wouldn't it be wonderful if we raised enough for the orphanage to expand? Heather is always telling me how crowded they are. She says they need more space but never have enough funds."

He trailed his finger along her cheek, filling her with such longing she feared it showed in her eyes.

"You are the most generous person I know," he said. "I can't think of anyone else who would pour themselves into an event the way you have to help children you've never even met."

His undeserved words pleased her. "You've worked as hard as I have."

He chuckled, bringing her curious gaze up to his eyes. He looked at her with dark intensity, searching deep into her soul. Her smile faded as, equally intent, she sought beyond his eyes into what this moment meant.

"I didn't start out caring about orphans. It was only a job assigned to me."

Her smile returned at his confession. Since their public hug outside the old prison, she'd been aware of a change in him, a softening, a gentleness she had only rare glimpses of in the past.

Somewhere in the distance a phone chirped. Hers.

Neither of them moved. He trailed his finger back along her cheek and across her chin, pausing there. She caught her breath, waited as he studied her mouth.

The chirping stopped.

He lowered his head and—

The phone rang again.

He pulled back. "Someone wants you."

She nodded, choking back disappointment. She located the phone near the door, tucked into her bag, and flicked it on without checking the caller ID.

"Hello." Her voice sounded as tense as she felt.

"Hi, honey, did I interrupt you?"

"No, Dad. I was at the far end of the banquet hall. How are you?"

Her father didn't answer. "Dad?" Nothing. She pulled the phone away to make sure it hadn't shut down. Nope. All systems bright and cheerful. She pressed the phone back to her ear. "Dad, are you there?"

"Holly, I have some bad news."

Her knees seemed to disappear. She grabbed at the wall, eased herself down to the bench. "Mom?" she whispered.

"She's gone."

"Gone? What happened?" She imagined an accident on the mountain roads. She always warned Mom she drove too fast.

"She didn't say. Just packed her bag and said it was over."

"She's not dead?"

"Feels like she is. She left me, Holly. She left me."

Holly sucked in air. Mom was alive. That was good news. She'd left Dad. That was bad news. Holly stared at the pine-board floor as she tried to take it in. "Mom can't have left you. You guys have a good marriage."

"I thought so, but I guess she didn't."

Holly tried to make sense of her dad's announcement. "Maybe she's just upset at something. Go talk to her."

"I don't know where she is. I haven't heard from her since she left. It's been a week. Has she called you?"

"Not in days."

"You'll let me know if you find out where she is?"

"Of course."

Her father said good-bye and broke the connection.

Holly leaned over her knees and moaned.

Steele found her like that, sat beside her, and put his arm around her. "Holly, what's wrong?" He rubbed her shoulder.

She turned into his arms and buried her face against his chest. Shudders racked her body. She did not cry. She felt nothing but shock.

"Who was on the phone?" Steele probed gently.

"My dad. Mom's left him."

Steele rubbed her back, stroked her hair. "I'm sorry. Perhaps it's temporary."

She pretended she didn't hear the doubt, the resignation in his voice. She understood he'd seen too many marriages go down the tubes to be convinced of his words, but she didn't want to deal with the reality of his viewpoint. Right now she just wanted the comfort of his arms.

"I've always believed in forever marriages because of them. They've had problems and dealt with them. They share the same joys and hopes and dreams. How could this happen?"

She was thankful he didn't spout meaningless platitudes.

"How will I tell Nan?"

"I don't know. Must you?"

"If she finds out I knew and didn't tell her, she'll never forgive me." He smelled good, felt warm and strong. "I don't know what to do," she wailed.

"Would you like me to pray?"

"Oh, please." She pushed herself off his chest. It hardly seemed appropriate to be thinking of the way he smelled and felt while talking to God.

He took her hand and bowed his head. "Heavenly Father, this is not good news. We ask You to work things out according to Your will."

He made it sound as if things could end in more than one way. She didn't like that idea. But he'd asked for God's will. God created marriage to last a lifetime. His will would surely be for Mom and Dad to get back together.

"Thank you," she whispered. "I have to believe this is only a bump in the road."

He cupped her cheek and turned her to face him. "Keep believing. Keep trusting. It's what you do best. It's one of the things I like about you."

And before she could do more than blink at his admission he liked something, anything, about her, before she could think to ask what other things he liked, he lowered his head and kissed her. She sighed and forgot everything she should wonder about. Forgot everything but how right this felt.

He lifted his head and smiled at her as he searched her eyes. Whatever he saw there, his smile widened, and he kissed her again then reluctantly, it seemed to her, pulled her gently to her feet and led her toward the door. "It's time to go home."

She made a protesting noise, and he chuckled, the sound strangely hypnotic.

"We've never really discussed this, but"—he paused—"do you have an escort to the banquet?"

Never really discussed it? More like never mentioned it. She knew she wouldn't have time to be a proper date, so she'd planned to go alone. "No," she said. "No one."

"Then may I be your official escort?"

She laughed, a sound of pure joy that found its way from some unfamiliar place behind her heart. The idea of being Steele's date made her momentarily forget her dad's announcement. "I'd like that."

He dropped her off at her apartment. As she climbed the steps, she tried to cling to the feeling of security when he'd held her, the oneness expressed by his kiss. But by the time she turned her key in the lock, the pleasure and wonder of it had been consumed by worry about her parents. Nan had already gone to bed. Holly tiptoed into the living room and dialed Mom's cell phone, receiving a message the customer was out of area. *Mom, where are you? What's going on?* She left a message begging her mother to call.

❖

When the phone jangled the next morning, she dove for it. Recognizing her mother's hello, Holly sank to the couch in relief. "Mom, where are you?" She repeated her silent words of the night before. "Dad phoned me. What's going on?"

"I had to leave." In faltering tones, her mother told her story. "A man stayed at the resort. A good-looking man with a quick smile. He paid me compliments. Made me feel special. You know how romantic I am. How I like those little gestures."

"Guess I inherited that from you."

"Well, I'm going to tell you, there's nothing romantic about being unfaithful."

Holly's stomach clenched. The air blasted out of her as if someone had stomped on her chest. "Mom, you didn't—" She couldn't think it, let alone say it. "Say you didn't."

"It never went that far."

"Thank God. Where are you?" Mom gave the name of a friend.

"Dad's really worried. He wants to call you."

"I can't talk to him."

"Why not? You two have always talked about everything."

"What I did was wrong. Besides, this is only a symptom of a faltering marriage. I just feel like there's no magic left."

"Walking away from Dad is wrong. Didn't you always tell me two wrongs don't make a right? Mom, at least talk to him."

"I will on one condition—you promise not to tell him what I told you about. . .well, you know what."

"I'll leave that up to you."

They said tearful good-byes. As soon as the connection ended, Holly dialed her father's number and told him to call her mother.

"Did she say what was wrong?"

"You need to ask her. Dad, send her flowers. Make her feel special. That's all she needs."

"I have to go. I have to call your mother."

Holly said good-bye. She leaned back into the cushions and groaned.

Nan sat at the table listening to every word. "What's going on?"

"Mom left Dad. She doesn't seem happy in their marriage anymore. She said the magic was gone."

Nan tsked. "Your mother always did think with her heart rather than her head."

Holly knew she was like her mother in that way. She liked romance, feeling special. She liked the charm and enchantment of flowers and cards, the concrete evidence of love. "Isn't that an okay thing?"

"Child, the head should always rule the heart."

"I don't understand."

"Feelings are great. God created us with emotions. But feelings should always be guided by facts. Sometimes I don't feel like God loves me. Does that change His love? No. So instead of believing my weak emotions, I trust His love. A man and woman marry, usually with hearts overflowing with emotional love. Do you suppose that impassioned feeling lasts day after day?" She chuckled, though Holly failed to see anything amusing. "Believe me, it would be exhausting if it did. But while the feelings wax and wane, the commitment is consistent. Feelings are subject to facts."

Holly considered Nan's words as she made coffee and toasted bagels for breakfast. "But, Nan, doesn't love need to be fed to survive?"

She felt Nan's quiet study of her before her grandmother added, "Love is many things. People need different aspects of it at different times in their lives."

Holly left a short time later, Nan's words replaying in her mind. She couldn't imagine what Mom needed at this time of her life except for Dad to show his love in romantic ways. She was grateful she was too busy most of the day to fret about it and had to hurry home early to prepare for the banquet, leaving Meggie to end the day on her own.

Chapter 9

Steele looked at the corsage in his hand—a white orchid to be worn around the wrist. Pops's idea. Just as it was his grandfather's idea for them to travel separately tonight. He insisted he'd pick up Jean, and then Steele could come for Holly. Steele snorted. Good thing Pops was too old for Holly. They would have been soul mates—both so romantic.

He climbed the steps and knocked at the door. Holly pulled it open. He felt his chin dangling. With great effort, he clanged his mouth shut.

Her dress skimmed over her like spun silver. She'd pulled her hair into a bouncing creation on top of her head. Tiny curls cascaded from it down her neck and in front of her ears. He reached out and tugged one curl and laughed as it sprang back into place. She'd done something with her eyes so they looked bigger, darker, more full of love and trust, though he wondered if he didn't detect a hint of worry. No doubt concern about her parents' marital problems.

"You're beautiful." One word for the way she looked? He needed the whole dictionary, and even that would be inadequate.

"You're looking mighty fine yourself." She touched his tie, straightening it. Her fingers brushed his chin, practically stalling his heart.

"For me?" She nodded toward the corsage box.

"Hope it's all right."

She opened it and slipped the flower over her wrist. "Perfect. Thank you." She placed a quick kiss on his chin. A butterfly kiss that echoed inside his stomach and multiplied a thousand times. If one small flower could fill her eyes with pleasure and make her react this way, he just might reconsider his feelings about flowers and romance.

He crooked his elbow and let a surge of pleasure fill his chest as she placed her hand on his arm. He led her down the stairs and into his vehicle.

She sighed as he climbed behind the steering wheel.

He didn't like the sound. Had he forgotten something? "What's wrong?"

"I don't feel much like partying. Not with Mom and Dad split up." She turned to face him, her expression worried. "Mom called." She shook her head. "I don't know what's going on with her. I wish I could tell you about it, but it's Mom's story."

He paused, grateful his fingers were on the keys in the ignition because he felt an incredible urge to pull her into his arms and comfort her as she had comforted him at the museum. Her touch and her words had eased the tension accompanying the memory of that crying little boy. He found he could let it go.

Slowly, trying to plan what to say and do, he reached for her hand and held it. "Holly, if there's anything I can do. . . ?"

She turned her hand, twined her fingers through his. "Thank you for offering. Let's go have a good time."

He promised himself he would do everything he could to ensure she enjoyed the evening. She deserved a reward for all her hard work and dedication.

The minute they stepped into the hall, several people rushed up to them demanding Holly's attention.

"The coffeepot isn't working." "One of the judges called in sick." "Did you want—?"

Steele steered her through the questions. "Give her a chance to get in the door." He guided her to the head table. "I'll send someone to replace the judge," he murmured. "You explain the score sheets. I'll deal with the rest." He put the coffeepot on another outlet so it didn't blow the breaker. He made several flyby decisions then returned to Holly's side.

She brushed his hand. "Thank you, Steele. That was sweet."

Her touch filled his veins with warmth. He leaned over, intending to tell her again how beautiful she was, but Pastor Don showed up at Holly's side. He'd agreed to emcee the event and flipped through his notes. "It's time to start."

As he moved to the mike, Holly grabbed Steele's hand.

"It's going to be great," he said and led her to their places at the table. He could hardly wait until she discovered his surprise contribution.

Pastor Don welcomed everyone. "To get us all focusing on the real purpose of the evening, I ask you to sit back and enjoy a brief presentation."

The lights dimmed, and the slide show Holly and her friend had prepared began. COME AND JOIN THE BAND OF LOVE scrolled across the screen then pictures that faded and blended—crying babies, wide-eyed toddlers. For a minute Steele wondered if they were going to be inundated with pictures so sad that none of them would be able to eat. And then the music changed slightly, growing more upbeat. LOVE IS—and pictures of people touching others, handing out food and water, washing feet; staff hugging and comforting children, playing games with them, teaching them to read. The music gained another beat. Children sang in rollicking African melodies. A children's choir appeared on the screen, and then the pictures focused on boys and girls playing various rhythm instruments. The words SHARE YOUR LOVE—JOIN THE BAND scrolled across the screen. The pictures faded, and from the murky background came a picture of a beautiful African girl, about ten, he'd guess, her nose buried in a white flower, her eyes reaching out to the audience.

The screen faded to black.

Steele welcomed the moment before the lights came up again, giving him a chance to blink back the sudden sting in his eyes.

He felt the emotional silence around him and then an outburst of applause and cheers. "That was a great presentation. You and Heather did that?"

"I'm afraid neither of us can take credit. Her parents were over visiting, and when her father heard what we wanted, he took on the project. He's a hobby photographer. He did a great job, didn't he?"

"Excellent." He suspected some of the images would haunt him for a long time.

Pastor Don rose and prayed, asking for a blessing on the food and for the needs of the children to be met.

The food was excellent. Even the salads, Holly pointed out, matched the red, white, and blue theme. As the caterers cleaned up the main course and prepared to serve dessert, tea, and coffee, Steele got up to explain the band competition.

The bands, despite their funny names, were excellent. Finally Freddie and the Bent Fenders won with their crowd-pleasing combination of bluegrass and classic rock, combined with a touch of standup comic.

Holly grinned at him. "That was fun."

Steele nodded. "The music was great, too."

She blinked, glancing at their clasped hands, and color rose in her cheeks. He held on when she tried to pull away.

"I enjoyed the evening," she whispered. "Much more than I thought I would."

He hoped he'd been part of the reason. He had gone out of his way to make her laugh. Enjoyed teasing the little curls hanging down her neck.

Pastor Don took the mike again. "I think we all agree it's been a great evening." Cheers and applause. "Let's hope we've contributed to putting a new roof on the orphanage." More applause. "And we've had fun." Cheers and whistles. Freddie's drummer accompanied with a clash of cymbals. "Two people have put in an incredible amount of work to see that this evening was a success. Holly Hope and Steele Davis, come on up here." There was a loud drum roll.

Steele felt Holly twitch under his fingers. He pulled her to her feet and smiled encouragement as she glanced at him. Amid clapping and cheering, they walked to the front to stand by Pastor Don.

Pastor Don waited for the noise to die down.

"It began with the vision of one person." Someone handed him a bouquet of red roses, and he placed it in Holly's arms. "Holly, thank you for all your hard work. Thank you for caring about the work in Africa and for sharing your concern. I think all of us will now share a bit of your vision."

Steele's heart swelled with a mixture of pride and wonder and amazement as Holly beamed at the audience. She leaned over to speak into the mike. "Thank you all for coming. Thank you for your generosity, but it was Steele who made sure you had chicken and not tofu, who decided the program would be more than a talent show. And wasn't it great?" More cheers and clapping and a drum roll. "Steele deserves the credit for taking care of all sorts of practical things I wouldn't have thought of. The sound system, the stage, even the coffee."

They might have been the only two people in the room at that moment as she smiled and nodded at him, her eyes dark, brimming over with emotion.

She'd just admitted she admired his practical side—the part she'd dismissed only a few weeks ago as unromantic—and by the way her eyes shone with gratitude and acknowledgment, he had to wonder if she realized love was so much more than flowers. He glanced at the orchid on her wrist. He'd noticed how often she admired it during the evening, each time smiling at him in a way that seemed full of promise, and he had to admit flowers served a purpose, too.

She pulled a red rose from the bouquet and tucked it into his lapel. "Thank you, Steele. You've been marvelous." The way she smiled at him made him dream she meant more than his practical help.

He thanked Holly and the audience. "I expect you were all moved by the plight of these children and by the heroic measures of the people trying to care for them. When Holly and I began to plan this banquet, I'd heard about the many thousands of children being left without adults in their lives. I'm sure you had, too. But Holly made me see it as more than statistics, more than a sad newspaper story. She's been praying this banquet would raise enough money for the roof, but there are so many needs. She made me care so much that I canvassed the downtown businesses, and I'm pleased to present her with"—he reached into his inside pocket and pulled out the check—"a check for five thousand dollars, thanks to the generosity of the good people of Missoula."

Tears filled Holly's eyes. She swallowed hard. And in front of Pastor Don and the whole audience, she kissed his cheek. "Thank you," she whispered then turned to the audience. Still whispering, not realizing they couldn't hear her, she said, "Thank you all."

Steele pulled her to his side. "She says thanks."

More laughter and clapping followed.

People began to leave. Pops and Jean found them and congratulated them on a good job before the older pair left. The caterers cleaned up. And then they were the only ones there.

He pulled her into his arms. "Holly, you did it. You raised enough money for the roof and more. You must be happy."

She touched his cheek. "We did it, Steele. I can't believe you did that on your own." Her brown gaze locked with his, filled with gentleness and something else. She searched his eyes, into the depths of his heart. He waited for her to see him as he was, to remember his practical nature, so different from her own, and pull back. Instead she let her gaze roam over his face like the touch of morning sun. He needed no more invitation and bent to meet her lips, as sweet and accepting as the woman herself.

His phone buzzed.

She withdrew.

He pulled her back, ignoring the sound, but whoever it was didn't hang up. The sound went on and on.

He grabbed the phone from his pocket, checked the display. Mike. "I'd better get this."

She nodded and turned away.

He wanted to reach for her, pull her back, explain it was only a pause. Instead he took the call. "Hey, Mike. What's up?"

"Man, where are you? It doesn't matter. I can't take any more."

Steele tensed at the desperate sound in Mike's voice. "What are you talking about?"

"Today is my wedding anniversary."

Steele pressed the heel of his hand to his forehead. He'd forgotten. He'd been so busy letting Holly and her romantic notions affect his thinking that he'd forgotten his own brother. This romance stuff was a land mine to a man's reason.

◆

Holly moved away, keeping her back to Steele so he wouldn't see her frustration and disappointment. *Don't be silly, Holly.* The evening had exceeded expectations. Only this wasn't about the evening. This was about Steele and her. He'd kissed her. And she'd welcomed it. Enjoyed it even. Something had shifted between them. She couldn't say when it had occurred or what it meant—only that it felt both fragile and strong at the same time.

She wandered past the bare tables. The banquet had gone well. Steele had been attentive and charming. She touched the orchid on her wrist. Flowers even. The man was changing. Did he realize it? She'd hoped they'd have some private time to enjoy the aftereffects of the banquet, the glow of success, and talk about what was happening between them. Would it end now that they had no compelling reason to be together? She hoped not. She had grown to be genuinely fond of him. She huffed. Fond? What kind of word was that? Not the sort to describe the fledgling, demanding emotions within her chest.

She realized Steele had ended his conversation and was heading toward her. She trailed her finger across a nametag left behind on the table as she waited and wondered if he would pick up where they'd left off.

"Sorry about that. It was Mike. My brother."

She nodded, still not able to face him.

"I forgot today would have been his anniversary."

She heard something in his voice. Something she'd never heard before except for hints when she mentioned siblings. She turned and saw the harsh lines around his eyes. "I take it Mike was married."

"For a few years. And now divorced. That woman practically destroyed him. She might succeed yet." As he talked, he gathered her things and handed them to her. "He's talking real stupid. I have to find him and calm him down."

She'd never heard so much emotion in his voice nor seen so much pain in his eyes. "I'm going with you." She knew he'd argue. Knew he didn't want anyone to see him vulnerable. "I'll keep you company on the drive."

He hesitated then headed for the door. "I don't expect I'll have time to entertain you."

She ignored his blunt words, knew he was worried about his brother, felt grateful he hadn't dismissed her, hadn't insisted on taking her home.

They headed out of town and were soon on the highway. "I let music and flowers make me forget what really matters. If something happens to Mike—"

They arrived at a construction site, piles of dirt pushed up into hills. They bounced along a rugged trail. Steele seemed to know where he was going. They arrived at some trailers. Steele shone his headlights at one, jumped out, and raced to the door. He wrenched it open and hit the inside lights. "Mike!" he roared. He disappeared inside, returned in a few minutes, and bolted back to the SUV. "He's been living on the site, but he isn't in there."

He was about to jerk the vehicle into gear when he stopped. "Do you hear that?"

Holly heard nothing but the SUV's engine.

Steele cut the motor and stepped out. "He's over there." He jumped back under the wheel, restarted the motor, and spun away with no regard for the rough ground.

The sound he'd heard soon grew audible to Holly. A deep-throated roar of a big machine. Steele pulled to a halt beside a huge yellow Cat. "Stay here," he murmured.

Like she had a choice. No way would she go out and wander around in this dark moonscape. But before she could answer, he was gone.

She hunkered down to wait. Sometime later, the roar of the big motor ended. She waited, but still Steele did not return. She leaned her head back and closed her eyes.

◆

"Holly, wake up."

For a moment she thought she must be dreaming. Why else would she hear Steele's voice calling her from sleep? Then she felt the seat belt digging into her neck, the tingle in her legs from being crammed against the door, Steele's hand heavy on her shoulder as he shook her awake.

She sat there a moment, hesitant to drag herself back to reality.

"Holly?"

She could feel his breath on her cheek. "I'm awake." His hands were firm on her shoulders, a patch of warmth against her chilled body. She shivered. "I'm cold."

He pulled off his tuxedo jacket and wrapped it around her.

Still half asleep, she sighed. "Warm. Smells like you. Good."

He chuckled. "Holly, are you really awake?"

She yawned. "Getting there." She yawned again. "Is Mike okay?"

"Yeah, I guess so, but I don't think he should be alone right now. Can you drive the SUV and follow us?"

"Anywhere you want." Oh, my. She sounded like she meant the words as part of wedding vows or something.

"Just to my parents' house." His voice rang with amusement, which filled her with a sensation of enjoyment.

"Are you sure you're awake?" he asked. "Maybe you'd better get out and walk around for a minute."

She stepped outside, the cool air jolting her brain closer to alert. But she didn't intend to take one more step than required on the rough ground and, clutching the SUV, edged around to the driver's side.

Steele held the door open, touched the back of her neck as she climbed in, then leaned in to speak to her. "I really appreciate this."

She nodded and started the motor. He strode over to a half-ton truck. As he drove away, she followed, gritting her teeth against the bouncing of the vehicle on the rough ground.

They reached a gravel road, much less rough, and she settled back. Realizing the jacket still hung around her shoulders, Holly breathed in his masculine scent. She wondered if he used an aftershave, or was the hint of ocean breezes and pine trees uniquely his?

He pulled to a halt in front of a house with wide cement steps. She stopped behind him. He hurried around to open the passenger door and wave his brother out. She got her first glimpse of Mike. He was as tall as Steele and as muscular. In the headlights, she saw he had the same angular facial structure. Lights came on inside the house, then the yard flooded with light. The door jerked open, and a man and woman hurried out. Steele's parents. His father looked like a younger version of Henry, and his mother—she tried to guess what the woman would look like not pulled suddenly from her sleep. She wore pajamas. Seemed rather squarish built, her hair as short as her husband's. In the harsh lights, she seemed almost masculine. Holly wondered if it was a true evaluation or her own prejudice at the way Steele described his mother as practical and businesslike.

Steele spoke briefly to them before they went to Mike and on either side of him led him toward the house. Steele hurried back to the SUV.

She climbed out to switch sides so he could take the wheel. "Do you want to stay? Because if you do, I could sleep in this or go back to Missoula and return for you in the morning."

"He'll be all right now. But thank you for the offer." He touched her cheek. "You've been very patient. Thank you."

His fingers lingered, making it hard for her to think. "What are friends for?"

"Friends? I guess that's progress from being pretty much on the opposite side of things." He stepped aside so she could hurry around to the other door.

She welcomed the cool air on her face and hoped it would clear her brain. Friends? Was that what she wanted? She shook her head, sucked in a deep breath at the longing that filled her. She had to be suffering from sleep deprivation. *Please, God, help me be sensible.* She smirked at her choice of words. She, the confirmed romantic, praying for sense—*my, how things have changed.*

She climbed in beside Steele, and they headed back to the city.

"Mike and I had a long talk." Steele spoke slowly, as if sorting out his thoughts. "He's a little turned off by love and marriage and all that kind of stuff. I guess we were all raised to think it was foolish. Mom has no use for anything like flowers and what she calls romantic nonsense. You remember the little boy I told you about?"

"The one that is you?"

"Yeah. Me. I remember why I was crying."

She sensed he'd remembered something profoundly significant, and hardly dared breathe. She wanted to say something supportive but feared to drive him back into denial. Instead she prayed for wisdom to know when to speak and when to listen and for Steele—healing for this distant pain.

"It's all about pink flowers, which probably doesn't surprise you."

Actually it did, but all she said was, "Tell me about the pink flowers."

They came to the first traffic light. He turned right into an empty parking lot and pulled to a stop. He reached out and took her hand.

"Mom and Dad often took us along to their work sites. We played while they worked. I remember how I liked this new place. We weren't allowed to go into a few old buildings, but we had lots of other places to explore. We spent hours of fun there. I found an old garden. I remember the grass had grown into the plants. I had to push aside the tall blades to see the flowers that seemed to me to be hiding as if they had a secret. There was a whole row of pink flowers. I have no idea what they were. I just knew they were beautiful and, I thought, special. I decided to pick them. I thought I'd give them to Mom and she'd like them. But she rode her Cat toward me, waved me away, and plowed them all down. I tried to stop her. When she saw me waving, she stopped long enough to tell me to stay back. I sat at the edge of the field and cried."

He stared straight ahead. His voice grew hoarse. His hand tightened.

She welcomed the way it made her fingers press together. It hurt ever so slightly. Made her feel she shared his pain. And she continued to pray that God would lead him through this. She knew the memory carried far more pain than he would likely admit. She guessed he'd never shared this before. Perhaps never allowed himself to remember it. She felt as privileged as if he had picked all those pink flowers and brought them to her. She didn't dare move for fear of making him pull back into himself, and yet her arms ached to comfort the little boy Steele had been. But would the child—clothed in the body of a man taught to be manly—know how to accept such a gesture?

A car passed on the street, the sound muted and lonely. The headlights sliced across the tree at the edge of the parking lot. The leaves, gray and colorless in the night, fluttered like birds in a courting dance, seeking to gain attention and approval from their desired one. She pressed her lips together. *Oh, Steele, if only I could kiss away your hurt and make it all better.*

Where had his mother been when he needed hugging? Why had she denied her child this basic motherly duty? Wouldn't most mothers consider it a privilege? For a moment she allowed herself the luxury of anger at Steele's mother. Then she pictured the way the woman had taken Mike's arm and led him into the house. She knew she cared and showed it in her own way.

"When she found me crying, she said flowers didn't matter. And men didn't cry. I don't know how many times we were told men don't cry. Tonight Mike cried. And I realized Mom was wrong. Men can cry."

She sensed he struggled with something momentous and squeezed his hand, hoping he felt her support.

"I remember telling Mom that Grandpops liked flowers. He was always buying them for Grandma. She said Pops acted foolish sometimes. Said no man should make a fool of himself over a woman."

He paused. His fingers twitched against her palm.

"That's why I don't want Pops marrying Jean. I'm afraid he's making a fool of himself over a woman."

Suddenly so many things were clear to Holly. "Steele, I think you and Mike made a very important discovery tonight. Several of them, in fact. You realize men can have and express deep emotions." As she spoke, she prayed for the right words to help Steele.

"Mike is all man."

"Exactly. And I'll bet he found the tears healing. Sometimes, maybe, to deny something inside us that God has put there is to tell God He made a mistake. And it robs us of being all God intended."

She shifted so she could watch his face and saw a play of emotions—doubt, stubborn refusal, acceptance, confusion. She thought of that little boy who had been Steele. "I think you have a very tender heart that you've been taught to deny. A little boy who likes pink flowers is the man who would rather pretend he hates them than have to face the hurt of that moment."

"I admit it. My feelings were hurt by Mom's remarks. I guess I got used to it. She loves me. Loves us all. But she thinks only tough feelings are masculine enough for her boys." He turned to face her, lifting his arm over the back of the seat to rest across her shoulders.

She tried not to miss the touch of their hands, the connection that had communicated his feelings even better than his words.

"It's all confusing, and I don't like the feeling. I want things to be sorted out. Cut and dried."

"Sometimes we have to take one step at a time, in faith, knowing God loves us and will show us what is best for us."

He cupped her cheek. "I wonder. What is best for us?"

"Us?" She could hardly get the word out past the sudden spasm of her lungs.

"A little surprising, maybe, but don't you think there's something between us? Something we should explore?"

Her lungs continued to draw inward as if guarding her surprise, her joy at his sudden realization and her own blaring truth. She loved this man who had just revealed a touching tenderness. Her love had been growing secretly day by day as he did sweet things for her that he would no doubt have called practical. She'd seen bits of romance in him, too, which served as rich nutrients to her emerging love. She forced her mouth to work. "I think there is definitely something that should be explored."

She leaned toward him, feeling so many things at once—a sorrow for the sad little boy, anger at the many years Steele had denied his real feelings, needing romance as much as she. Knowing gave her the boldness to touch his cheek with her fingertips. His whiskers were rough beneath her hand. "Steele, you're a man with deep emotions both tough and tender. And they make you very appealing."

He needed no more invitation to pull her close and kiss her. She felt the answer of a lifetime of need and longing in this man who had admitted to hating pink flowers just because he liked them so much.

Chapter 10

The next couple of weeks were a delicious exploration of their relationship. They spent long hours walking and talking. Steele started showing up each day at closing time to help her push the planters and tables away. He took her to dinner and surprised her by choosing the most romantic place in town. On her part, Holly slipped over every day with a flower in a vase. She carefully avoided pink ones, sensing he still had some work to do in coming to grips with his feelings about them and all they signified for him. She knew he was changing but didn't want to push it. But she rejoiced to see him open up more and more about his feelings.

Nan and Henry had gone home.

"Are you two getting married?" Holly asked as Nan prepared to leave.

"We love each other, but we want to take our time. Not too much time, mind you. We aren't getting any younger. But there are some matters to take care of. Practical things."

Holly laughed as she told Steele. "There you go. Romantic and practical together."

There remained only one thing that stole from her happiness—her parents' continuing separation.

"Mom," she said, "Dad's trying hard. He's doing all the little things you like. Why don't you give him a chance?"

Her mother would only say, "I've gone too far to come back."

When Holly discussed it with Nan by phone, she voiced her confusion. "I don't understand. Dad's being romantic. Why isn't Mom accepting that?"

"Sometimes love needs more," Nan said. "Something else, like forgiveness."

"I'm sure Dad forgives her. After all, it wasn't like she committed the big sin."

"Maybe your mother needs to forgive herself. We will continue to pray for God to reach her heart and show her she's forgiven simply by confessing."

"She has to believe it. This can't be the end of their marriage."

But despite the bad, and the good, life went on.

She glanced up from giving a middle-aged couple a pink carnation and a card with the inscription by Martin Luther, "There is no more lovely, friendly, and charming relationship, communion, or company than a good marriage." She saw a man enter the building across the street. "No way," she muttered.

"Excuse me," the man at the table said.

"I'm sorry. I thought I saw my father go into that building." Out of loneliness, Holly supposed, her father had come to town to visit her.

"Then I expect he'll come over and have coffee with you when he's conducted his business."

"Of course." She moved away, putting a planter between herself and her customers, and stared across the street. Dad had met Steele on two occasions and voiced his admiration of him, but what business would he have over there? The light bounced off the dark glass of the windows of Steele's office. *No way.* But her insides froze into sharp, icy spears.

She pretended to be busy pruning the flowers and picking off dead leaves. Several times she washed the tables that allowed her a view of the street. Mostly she neglected her work for the next hour as she watched for her father to reappear. As the minutes ticked by, the icy spears melted with the dreaded suspicion that Dad would have only one reason to see Steele. She thought of the business he conducted there: divorce by request. But surely he wouldn't do that in this case. He'd send her father to a counselor, advise him to reconsider. Anything else was unthinkable. Yet, she knew it was part of his job. He only offered what any lawyer would. Still, she developed a slow simmer as she waited.

The minute her father stepped into view, she darted across the street, and barely missed being hit by a car.

"Dad!" she called.

He stopped, looked about as if wishing he could avoid this meeting.

"What were you doing in there?" She edged him toward the café as she talked. She'd serve him coffee with her inquisition, but she'd find out the truth.

"I spoke to Steele."

"About what?"

Dad sighed. "I guess you deserve the truth. I asked him to give your mother a speedy divorce."

She was thankful they had made it across the street, because Holly grabbed his arm and jerked him to a stop. "Dad, you can't be serious. You can't walk away from thirty years of marriage. Win her back. Romance her."

"Don't you think I've tried? It's not enough. I'm not enough. My love isn't enough. It's not fair for me to keep her tied to me when she's moved on in her heart."

Holly swallowed hard against the sudden nausea in her throat. "No way. You can't divorce. I won't let you." This couldn't be happening. Not to her parents. She believed in everlasting love. Hadn't they taught her love was for a lifetime? This was Steele's fault. "What did Steele say?" She ground out the words.

"He said I had a lot of things to take care of to ensure this didn't turn into a dirty fight. I told him I didn't care. Split everything down the middle. She deserves it. But it's a little hard to split a resort down the middle. One of us will have to buy out the other, I suppose. Or sell it to a third party."

Somehow Holly made her legs work and managed to sit down on a chair that felt as if someone had filled the seat with tiny tacks. She squeezed her knees together to stop her legs from shaking. "How can you even say that? It's my home."

Her father rubbed at his eyes. Peripherally, she noted how red rimmed they were, how he seemed to have aged twenty years. She forced herself to speak calmly, rationally, even though she could barely put together a coherent sentence.

"Dad, I can't believe there isn't some way to work things out. I'll talk to Mom again. Maybe if I invite her here, you could visit her."

"Honey, you can try. But don't be surprised if she refuses. I think she's having too much fun on her own."

"No, I think she's scared and alone and afraid to admit it. She keeps saying that what she did is so wrong, she's stepped beyond going back."

"I've tried to tell her it isn't so, but she doesn't hear me." The way he downed his coffee made her wonder that he didn't set his tongue on fire. Then he bolted to his feet. "I have to go. Steele insisted I make a list of all our assets."

Steele did, did he? He was actually encouraging her father in this? She struggled to her feet, waited for her legs to steady, then marched across the street and up the stairs to his office.

◆

Steele watched her head in his direction. Knew she'd be coming. But Glenn had asked for advice, and Steele couldn't refuse it. The man had too much to lose. Not just his marriage, which was devastating to everyone involved, but also his whole life's work and perhaps his retirement fund unless he had some good counsel to guide him through this. Not that Glenn cared. "Give it all to her," he'd said.

But one thing Steele had learned—when people were the most vulnerable, they made the worst choices and lived to regret them. They needed someone with a cool business head. That's where he came in.

Would Holly see this as part of his job, or would she take it personally?

She barged through the door before his secretary could end her message warning him, preparing him. He'd been preparing himself for the last twenty minutes, since Glenn left the office.

One look at her face, and he answered his own question. She would take it personally.

"How could you?" She breathed hard.

"Holly, have a chair. Let's talk reasonably."

"I don't want to sit." She leaned over the desk, eyeing him with all the feeling she'd give a bug crawling across her table. "You had the nerve to advise my father about a divorce? My father. This isn't someone coming in off the street, strangers or people who sit at the far side of the church. These are my parents. This affects me."

"I realize that. Which is why I want to make sure your father gets good advice and has some sound direction."

"Good advice? Did that include suggestions as to how he could mend things with my mother? The name of a good counselor?"

"Holly, that's not my expertise."

"Well, apparently my expertise doesn't include thinking you might have changed. How can I have anything to do with a man who is helping my father divorce my mother?" She took a step backward. "You don't believe in love."

"I believe in a love based on practical things, a love built on a solid foundation."

"I'm sorry. That's not the sort of love I need." She spun on her heel and left the room.

"Holly." He hurried after her, but she either didn't hear him or didn't care.

He returned to his office and stared out the window, watching as she returned to the café. She turned once to glower up at his windows then disappeared inside.

So that was that. Why should he be disappointed? Or surprised? He knew all that romance and lovey-dovey stuff didn't last. Had known it since he was knee-high to a grasshopper, as Pops would say. So why did he feel this terrible tightness in his chest, a stinging in his eyes?

Besides, who had said anything about love? Certainly not him.

Who was he kidding? No words had been spoken, but he knew without voicing the thought what was in his mind. And he'd thought Holly's, as well.

He spun around and pulled out a stack of files. Men didn't cry. They worked.

By the end of the day, he was forced to admit that working got his desk cleared but didn't drive away the thought of Holly just a few steps away.

He stood at the windows, saw the empty flower cart. The day had almost ended. He could bury himself in work, but what would that get him? A clean desk. A harried secretary? Of course, he could always hire a second secretary, but that wouldn't solve what really bothered him.

He didn't want to lose Holly and this growing depth of feeling between them. He understood her anger and fear at her father's decision, but whether he came to Steele or went elsewhere, it shouldn't affect Holly and Steele's relationship. Surely she'd had time to realize that. He glanced at his watch. She'd soon be closing up. Indeed, she had already started carrying chairs inside.

He hurried out of his office and reached the café in time to grab the last two chairs from the sidewalk and carry them indoors.

They almost collided as she came through the door. "What are you doing here? Didn't I make it clear how angry I am with you?"

"You were pretty clear about it."

She stomped away.

"Your parents' problems aren't my fault, and you'd realize that if you gave yourself a chance." He pushed the planters inside and helped her drag in the tables. He waited until they'd done the chore before he poured them each a cup of coffee and led her to a table. "Holly, didn't you say at the banquet that you appreciated my practical help?"

"I did, and thank you for helping put the furniture inside."

He didn't want thanks. He wanted acknowledgment of what worked between them. "I've learned a lot from you. I might even be able to enjoy pink flowers now. Doesn't that mean anything to you?"

Her eyes softened. "I'm glad you are facing up to who you are—a blend of tough and tender."

He hoped for her to see the possibilities. But the corners of her mouth drew into tight lines, and he knew he had a long fight on his hands if he were to convince her.

She held her cup so tightly, her knuckles whitened. "But it isn't enough. There has to be more."

"What more? We could have a solid relationship built on mutual interests."

She rolled her eyes. "You sound like marriage is a contract."

"It is. A legal contract between a man and a woman."

"It's more than that. It's an emotional relationship."

"Granted. I thought we were achieving that." He fought his years of pushing away every soft and tender feeling, of hating romance, of scorning silly gestures. His parents didn't say the words of love. He'd learned, supposed, they weren't necessary. Knew the feeling without the words or acknowledgment. Now, when he wanted to say them, all those years of practicing not saying them stood in the way. He pushed through the habits, the teaching, the practice, and, yes, the fear. He found his way to the surface by focusing on Holly's face, seeing her sad, hurt eyes, remembering her sweetness and generosity. Surely she'd believe him if he brought the words out of the secret place inside him, the place that housed the scared little boy, the child crying over the pink flowers. "Holly, I think I might love you." He'd said it. Breathed the words that meant so much once spoken. It gave him a sudden rush of triumph, as if he'd reached the top of a steep slope and gained a view beyond words.

"Steele, I think I love you, too. That only makes this harder." She settled her gaze on the center of the table. "I don't know if it's enough. I don't want to end up like my mother—needing something for so long, so badly, that I ruin a marriage, a relationship, a family, and maybe even myself. I have to know that what we have is enough to satisfy me. I'm not sure it is." She pushed from the table, took their empty cups, and carried them to the sink behind the counter. "I have to be sure," she murmured before she turned on the water.

He followed her as far as the counter, leaned his elbows on it, and watched, waited, hoping for more. Hoping, he realized with such clarity he glanced overhead to see if she had somehow remotely flipped the lights on, that she'd do what she did best—believe in romance, fill his unfamiliar attempts with her bubbly optimism. Where were her verses and quotes of love now, when he was the one needing them?

Or was it she needing them? He knew no special verses, or he would offer them. *Love is. . .* He couldn't even remember the verses from the Bible he'd memorized in Sunday school.

She turned and faced him. "Steele, I need time to think. I need to work things out. Until I do, I think it's best if we don't see each other. Except when we can't avoid it like church, across the street. That sort of thing."

He searched her eyes, hoping for hesitation, regret, a change of heart. But her gaze had closed against him. He saw nothing but determined brown eyes.

"I'm sorry," she whispered. "I wish things could be different."

She turned away, returning to the hot water in the sink.

He backed out of the café and onto the sidewalk, where he stood staring about him, unable to think where to go next. Finally, with no destination in mind except to put his heart back the way it was before Holly had interfered, he strode down the street.

◆

Over the next few days, he buried himself in work, putting in longer hours than ever before. He dealt with a number of files he'd been neglecting, closed others with a few notes and the last bill.

He even agreed to represent the hotel across the street in dealing with a zoning bylaw. He usually avoided these meaningless legal wranglings. It kept him busy but was still boring enough to make his eyes water with stifled yawns.

On Saturday he persuaded Mike to go hiking with him in the mountains. Holly's parents owned a resort in the mountains. He wondered what it was like. From Glenn's list of assets, he guessed it was more than a couple of cabins and a gas station. And hadn't Holly mentioned movie stars staying there?

He increased his pace. Who needed to think about Holly? The sun was bright. The sky blue. The air pure. What else did a man need?

"Steele," Mike called. "Wait for me."

He realized he was panting from exertion. His legs quivered. He must be getting out of shape. He sat down and waited for Mike to join him.

"Trying to set a world record?" his brother demanded.

"Just working off energy."

Mike snorted. "Never seen you so angry."

"I'm not angry." He kept his voice supremely calm.

"Yeah. Tell that to someone who might believe you. Wouldn't have anything to do with Holly? I hear tell you two are on the outs."

"We found we want different things in life."

"Care to talk about it?"

"Let me think." He pushed to his feet. "No." He rushed up the trail, not caring that Mike was left behind. He reached the summit and sat down to enjoy the view. *Enjoy*, he ordered himself. As far as a man could see, not a sign of another human. Could make a man feel mighty lonely if he was given to such emotional nonsense. Steele wasn't. It was a wonderful view. Worth the climb.

Mike caught up and plunked down on the ground beside Steele, panting hard. "You can't outrun your feelings, you know."

"Who's running? Not me." He forced himself to remain seated, calmly looking out over the scene.

"For a smart lawyer, you can be mighty dumb."

Steele didn't answer. Lately he'd been feeling dumb all right. Why had he let Holly sweet-talk him into thinking they had something in common? Why had he shared that stupid story about crying over pink flowers? Mom was right. Flowers were silly, and a man could make a fool of himself over a woman. He didn't have to look farther than the mirror to know the truth of that statement.

◆

His days blended into a steady stream of work. He allowed himself to think of nothing else. He avoided the windows of his office, but unbidden his gaze went to the spot on his desk where Holly had daily put a flower in a tiny crystal vase. He did not miss the flower. And he'd get used to not seeing her.

The phone rang, and he answered it.

"Hi there, young man. How are you doing?"

"Fine, Grandpops. Are you keeping out of trouble?"

"No fun in that now, is there?"

Steele leaned back, trying to remember how this exchange used to amuse him.

"How's that little Holly girl?"

"Fine."

"That's not the way I hear it. Jean says she's moping."

"She's worried about her parents' marriage." He ignored Pops's grunt of disbelief. If Holly had any other reason to be unhappy, it was not his doing. It was hers. She'd been the one to close the door between them.

"So how are things with you and Jean?" Surefire way to get Pops to leave him alone.

"Couldn't be better." He chuckled heartily. "The old sweetie has agreed to marry me."

Steele stilled his objections, knowing they were based on something from his childhood. "Glad for both of you."

"There's lots to consider for an old pair like us. We've both been to see our lawyers and signed papers and stuff. But I want to make sure I've done it all right. That's where having a lawyer in the family comes in handy. We signed prenups keeping all the inheritances in each family as they should be. I set up a fund for her in case something should happen to me. She didn't much care for that. Said she had plenty of her own to live on."

After a few minutes, Steele admitted Grandpops had taken care of everything in a very efficient manner. "Here I was afraid you'd let all that romantic nonsense and memories of being young and fancy-free affect your good sense."

"Boy, it's possible to have both romance and practicality. Maybe that's what you need to learn. Seems all my girling lessons failed to take on you. You're not such a good student."

Steele ignored the undeserved jibe. "Maybe you're not such a good teacher."

"Whatever you did to that little gal, it's time you swallowed your pride and fixed it."

Sounded easy coming from Pops's mouth.

"Steele, you have what that girl needs. Now go convince her of it. By the way, Jean and I are planning an engagement party for next Saturday. We decided to have it in Missoula as sort of a central place. We expect all the family to be in attendance."

It wasn't even offered as an invite. It was an order if he'd ever heard one, and no one ignored his grandfather's orders unless they wanted to deal with an irate old man.

"I'll be there to congratulate you both."

He stared at the phone long after he'd hung up, Pops's words circling in his head. *You have what that girl needs.* How could Pops think such a thing? Holly wasn't convinced. Steele sure wasn't.

Go convince her.

First he had to convince himself.

Chapter 11

When Nan asked to stay with Holly and wanted her to help plan the engagement party, Holly had mixed feelings. She couldn't get enthused about all the flowers and candles, but she couldn't refuse Nan. Any more than her parents would be able to. Whether they wanted to see each other or not, she doubted either would have a sufficient excuse to miss the party. Nan might accept an absence if one of them were in ICU, but she could think of nothing short of that her grandmother would consider reason enough to miss this event.

Even though Holly understood she would have to face Steele, which filled her heart with a queer mixture of anticipation and dread, she looked forward to the chance to see her parents together in the same room. This might be the answer to her prayers as a way to get her parents back together.

When they each protested they couldn't come, Holly just laughed. "I'll let you explain that to Nan yourself." Neither of them had pursued the topic further.

The best part of the whole thing, though, was working with Nan. She saw a side of her grandmother she'd never before seen. An efficient, hard-driving side that rented a hall in Missoula and saw things got done according to her wishes and on her time schedule.

And now the day of the party had arrived. Holly and Nan planned to spend the afternoon preparing.

"Where do you want the flowers?" Holly asked.

"Everywhere. I want the whole room to breathe perfume."

"That would explain the scented candles in this box. Sure hope no one is allergic to scents."

"If anyone complains, we'll put the candles out. So what's happening between you and Steele?"

"Nothing, Nan. I told you. We just don't fit together."

Nan put a large bouquet in the center of the head table then turned and took Holly's hands. "Child, do you love him?"

Holly nodded. "Unwisely, yes."

Nan chuckled softly. "When is love wise?"

"I have been praying I can forget him." Saying the words felt like acid on her soul.

"Holly, sweetie, are you sure that's what you want? Or are you just afraid to take a risk? Look at Henry and me and see what happens when you're afraid of risks."

"But look at Mom and Dad. They married, and they discovered they couldn't get what they needed in a marriage."

"I admit your parents are going through a rough time, but I know they'll be okay. And maybe marriage isn't about getting what we need as much as it is about loving someone enough to see they get what they need. Meeting their emotional needs becomes our emotional need."

Nan's statement made Holly realize how small and selfish her desires were. And yet. . .

Nan continued. "Love is so many things. It's being romantic; it's being practical. It's speaking kind words. It's forgiving the unkind ones. It's changing the baby, fixing a tire, mowing the lawn, holding hands, holding a basin while someone is sick. People need different things at different times, and that's what real love is. Doing what the person you love needs at the moment."

Tears stung Holly's eyes. "Nan, that is beautiful. You should make it your wedding vows."

"Maybe I will, but right now I want to know, do you love Steele enough to meet his needs? If not, maybe you don't love him enough."

Nan turned back to the flowers and left Holly to consider her words. How much did she love Steele? Enough to be practical? She smiled, thinking of how she'd learned to be just that in the past few weeks. In little ways she'd hardly noticed—fixing Steele his favorite sandwich, applying a bandage when he scraped his knuckles bringing in a table. She'd seen it as romantic, but it was practical, too.

How could she be sure? She didn't want to end up like so many couples, visiting lawyers, begging for a divorce. Or stuck in a relationship that left her empty and unsatisfied.

Could she trust a man who would help her parents get a divorce?

She had to know what was right. She didn't want to make a mistake. Too many people could be hurt. She'd seen how devastated her father was by his marriage problems. She knew her mother's pain, had listened to her cry and been powerless to do anything. *Dear God, please help my parents find a way back together, and show me what's best for me.*

◆

Nan was beautiful in a beige suit with a corsage of red, red roses pinned to her jacket. Beside her, in his black suit with a red rose boutonniere, Henry looked as handsome and proud as a gold medal winner on a podium.

Holly held her father's arm. "Don't they look nice together?"

Dad nodded. "I'm glad for my mother. I just wish. . ."

"Me, too."

"Is your mother coming?"

"She said she was. Nan ordered it, you know. Don't think that leaves much room for excuses."

They chuckled together, sharing the knowledge that family members didn't disobey a directive from Grandmother Hope.

But Holly wondered if Mom would show. She allowed herself a glance around the room, telling herself she was only checking to see if Mom had slipped in. But it wasn't Mom her gaze sought. It was Steele.

He wore a casual gray blazer and dark pants. His white shirt lay open at the neck, emphasizing his summer tan. His hair had lightened. He must be spending time outdoors.

She was glad. He should enjoy the lovely weather.

He turned. Their gazes collided.

Even from this distance, she jolted from the demanding power in his eyes. Her knees began to wilt like yesterday's flowers. She loved him. She ached to be able to give him what he needed. But she was her mother's daughter in so many ways. She would walk away right now rather than risk hurting Steele farther down the road, as her mother was hurting her father with her hunger for romance.

Steele pulled a rose from the bouquet in front of him and lifted it to her.

She jerked away. What did that gesture mean? Was he saying she must be happy to see all these flowers and feel the romance that filled the room as much as the scent of candles and roses? She was happy, but not for the flowers and scents. Rather she was happy for the love Nan and Henry had rediscovered. She'd have been just as happy in a tiny hall without a decoration or flower in sight or huddled around the kitchen table if it allowed her to share this moment.

She saw a movement at the doorway. "Dad, Mom just came in."

"Holly, she looks lost and scared." He took a step toward her, stopped. "She doesn't want to see me." He turned back to Holly, his face so filled with sorrow that she grabbed his shoulders and hugged him.

His words strangled, he said, "Go to your mother and make sure she's all right."

She studied his face, saw the tears on his cheeks. "Oh, Dad. This is just so wrong."

"I wish your mother agreed." He tried to smile but failed miserably.

Holly glanced over his shoulder to her mother, wanted to go to her, but didn't want to abandon her father. "Will you be okay if I leave?"

"I'll never be okay again." He gave her a little shove. "Go to her."

Holly crossed the room, felt Steele's gaze as she passed him, but carefully avoided glancing in his direction.

"Mom, I'm glad you made it." She hugged her mother and felt the tension in her, which made Holly hold her gently for fear of breaking something. Her mother had lost weight. Her eyes lacked their usual sparkle, and yet she was still beautiful in her royal blue dress.

"I shouldn't have come. I don't belong here."

"Of course you do. You're part of the family."

"Things have changed."

Holly held back the words crowding her mind. *Yes, Mom, they have. And you're the only one who can put them back together.* "Mom, I wish you'd give Dad a chance."

"Let's not talk about that. I'm finding it hard enough to stay here without having to face my guilt."

Holly couldn't let it go. "Mom, didn't you teach me there is a remedy for guilt?"

Mom turned her startled gaze toward Holly.

"You said there is nothing God can't forgive. Nothing. I remember how you emphasized that word."

Mom's surprised expression turned into stubbornness. "It's not that easy. Sin has a consequence."

"For which, if I remember the Bible correctly, Jesus died. Again it was you who taught me the words in John 8:36." She grinned triumphantly. "See, I even remember where it's found." She was rewarded with a fleeting smile from her mother. " 'So if the Son sets you free, you will be free indeed.' " Her voice fell to a hoarse whisper. "I remember the day you taught me that verse. I had done something really bad, and I was miserable about it. We were visiting Nan, and I had stolen raspberries from the neighbor's bushes. I was so filled with guilt. It was you who said I had done wrong and I needed to apologize for it. You said one must always do what they could to make up for wrongdoings. You went with me to speak to the neighbor." She wrapped her arm around her mother's thin waist. "I don't remember what she said, but I remember as clearly as if it were today what you said. 'Use this as a lesson to never repeat the sin, but move on from here knowing God has forgiven you.' "

Her mother shuddered twice, as if holding back sobs.

"Mom, maybe you should follow your own advice."

She turned to Holly, her eyes watery. "If only—"

At the front of the hall, Henry cleared his throat. "Folks!" he roared and instantly had everyone's attention.

Holly held her mother's elbow. "What?" She wanted to know what Mom had been about to say.

Mom shook her head and turned her gaze toward the front of the room, where Henry and Nan stood.

Holly swallowed her disappointment. *If only what? Why couldn't Henry have waited two more minutes?* She sucked in a deep breath. It was a start. *Lord, help Mom be willing to believe in Your forgiveness.*

Henry held up his hand. "I expect you all know why you're here, but allow me to do the honors." He reached for Nan's hand and pulled her to his side. "Jean has generously agreed to marry this old goat of a man. She has given me joy I never expected to have again. We haven't set a date yet, but it will be soon. We haven't near enough time left to enjoy each other."

People laughed.

"Now that our two families are to be joined, I think we need to make introductions."

Mom jerked as if she'd been jump started with electric paddles. She stepped away from Holly and darted a glance to the door.

"I have to leave," she whispered.

"Not until you are introduced as my mother." Holly grabbed her hand and refused to release her.

Henry called Steele's parents up. "My son and daughter-in-law, John and Justine."

Holly studied the couple. The man wore jeans and a button-front, open-necked, denim shirt. He had the rugged appearance of a man who worked out-doors, made his living doing physical work.

Steele's mother wore black jeans and a shirt much like her husband's in a softer shade of blue. She shared a similar rugged appearance. But the look they gave each other spoke of mutual love and care.

Nan kissed each of them on the cheek then turned to her son. "Glenn." She held out one hand to Holly's father. "Karen." She held out the other to Holly's mom.

Holly urged her mother forward, one painfully slow step at a time. She stood back as soon as Nan took Mom's hand. Her grandmother quirked her eyebrow, and Holly knew Mom would not be escaping Nan's firm grasp until Nan decided it was time.

"My son and daughter-in-law," Nan announced.

Henry kissed Mom on the cheek and shook hands with Dad. "You did a fine job of raising Jean," he said. Everyone but Mom laughed.

Steele's parents shook hands with Holly's parents.

"My grandsons," Henry boomed. "Mike, Steele, and Billy-boy."

Holly chuckled as a young man groaned. Apparently Bill didn't care for his grandfather's nickname. She smiled at Mike, skipped past Steele, and smiled at Bill as he took his place in the family lineup.

"Three strapping young men and none of them married. Can you believe it? Where did I fail?"

More laughter. Holly giggled as the three young men groaned.

Nan beckoned to Holly. "My one and only grandchild."

Holly moved to stand at her mother's side, took her hand, let her squeeze as hard as she wanted.

Nan smiled at Henry. "I'm dreaming of a whole bunch of great-grandchildren."

He chortled. "At the rate this bunch of ours is going, you might have a long wait."

Holly wouldn't look at Steele to see his reaction to all this good-natured teasing. Just a quick glimpse to see if he found it amusing or annoying.

A jolt raced through her when their gazes connected. She felt Mom glance at her, aware of the way Holly had jerked. She couldn't tear her gaze away from Steele's to assure Mom everything was okay.

A sudden, terrible, lovely truth filled her.

Not only did she love him, but he'd given her everything she needed. Maybe he'd get over his pink phobia. Maybe he wouldn't. It didn't matter. She knew his tender side. Had felt his pain at rejecting his inner needs. Knew he ached for the words and gestures she would willingly give.

Mom squeezed her hand hard enough to make her fingers hurt.

Holly knew how much she and her mother were alike. Would she hurt Steele with her needs and demands? It was a risk she couldn't take. But how could she live without him? Again she prayed for wisdom and guidance.

Henry spoke. "I want you all to be friends. Now help yourself to coffee and tea. Enjoy the cakes and sandwiches. Most of all, enjoy visiting."

Mom broke free and with stiff dignity walked to the back of the room.

Holly grabbed coffee and snacks, hurried after her, and persuaded her to sit. She knew the strain was taking its toll and feared her mother would faint.

As she sat beside her, she watched Steele and her dad talking. Was he counseling her father about a divorce? She wanted to trust Steele, but this aspect of his work bothered her. She did not believe divorce was the answer for troubled marriages.

Mike approached her, and she rose to speak to him.

"You're the girl who came with Steele to rescue me a few weeks ago. Thank you."

"I didn't do anything." She studied him. Liked his loose-limbed casualness. "How are you doing?"

"Better. I guess each day gets a little better, though it will never be the same as before, if you know what I mean."

"I can only understand from my perspective." Experiencing the idea of divorce through her parents hurt bad enough. She couldn't imagine Mike's pain. Or how he dealt with it.

She shifted to check on Mom. She wasn't there. She stood near the door, talking to Steele. First Dad and now Mom. This then was God's direction. She couldn't trust a man who counseled her parents about divorce. How dare he?

Mom nodded at whatever he said and moved away.

"Excuse me." She left Mike in midsentence and headed for Steele. He must have seen the anger on her face, for he backed away at her approach.

"I do not want my parents to divorce," she spat out. "Don't be telling them the best way to do it."

He gave a smug smile. "Hello, Holly, how are you? Nice get-together for the grandparents. I hope they'll be very happy."

She faltered. "Steele, why do you have to make it possible for people to get a divorce?"

"I am not responsible for marriage breakdown."

"I know that."

"I see my job being to protect people when they're too vulnerable to make sound choices. They have to live with their decisions long after the papers are signed. And there are often children to consider."

She hesitated. He made it sound so logical. But it was personal when it came to her parents. Too confused to know what to say, she turned, saw her mother across the room, and went to join her.

"Do you know what Steele just offered me—us?" Mom said, sounding surprised, almost hopeful.

"No." She didn't want to know. She didn't want to deal with this aspect of Steele. Yes, it was his work. But it hurt her somewhere deep inside to think of his helping people end their marriages. Marriages, he pointed out, that were already over. Suddenly she had an insight into his thinking. His concern was protecting the people involved. She gave a little laugh.

Mom sent her a startled look. "What's so funny?"

"Sorry, Mom. I was thinking of something else." Maybe she could live with this part of his work if she just kept in mind how he'd explained it. "What did Steele say to you?"

"He said he thought what your father and I had was too precious to throw away. He offered to pay for some marriage counseling and a weekend in a resort near Seattle. He said if we both felt the same way afterward, he would then help us with the divorce and property settlement."

Holly massaged her chest as if she could stop the pain by the action. She'd been so wrong about Steele. She grabbed her mother's arms. "You're going to take him up on his offer, aren't you?"

Mom sniffed. "I don't know."

Holly continued to rub her chest. "I've made a really stupid mistake." She told how she'd misjudged Steele.

"It was an understandable mistake. Forgive yourself," Mom said.

"It's not easy, is it?"

Doubt returned to her mother's eyes.

"I'll tell you what. I'll forgive myself if you forgive yourself."

Mom allowed hope to enter her eyes then shook her head. Suddenly she smiled, taking ten years off her face. "I guess I have to practice what I preach. I think you and I are a lot alike. Holly, honey, we can't afford to overlook the love that's right under our noses." Mom patted Holly's arm. "Now if you'll excuse me, I am going to talk to your father. Steele's right. We need to give our marriage another chance."

Holly watched Mom through a haze of tears. She dashed them away so she could see the love and relief on Dad's face when Mom spoke to him. *Thank You, Lord. Thank You.*

Maybe being her mother's daughter wasn't something to fear but to embrace.

Her father gave Holly a thumbs-up sign.

It was a beginning. A new beginning for them.

She looked around for Steele and found him standing with his brothers. She gathered up her courage and headed in his direction, but before she crossed the room, the three of them hurried outside. She rushed after them and reached the door in time to see them drive away in Steele's SUV.

For a long time, she stared after them.

She had no one but herself to blame that he couldn't wait to get away from her. She'd hurt him so many times. She vowed she'd never hurt him again. *With Your help, God.* She wanted to share his joys, halve his sorrows, but never again hurt him. His mother had done so in the past through her own strong character. Out of ignorance, Holly was sure. But Holly wanted to spend the rest of her life nurturing his gentle side while enjoying his practical side.

She remembered Nan's words. "It's about loving someone enough to see they get what they need. Meeting their emotional needs becomes our emotional need."

She smiled into the now-empty street, seeing Steele's gestures—filling her coffee cup, pushing in the planters. A unique combination of romantic and practical.

"The boys left, did they?"

Holly turned to acknowledge Steele's mother. "Yes."

The woman studied her openly. "So our families are to be united."

Holly felt hot embarrassment rush up her neck, thinking the woman read her thoughts, startled to realize she'd been thinking marriage to Steele. Then her mind kicked into gear. "Nan and Henry. Yes."

"Henry is a nice man."

"Nan's a nice woman."

"I'm sure she is, or he wouldn't be marrying her."

Their conversation felt like a duel of words. She welcomed the relief when the woman looked down the street again.

"Steele is like Henry." She sounded more exasperated than proud. "A strange combination of hardness and softness. I never did know how to handle him. Now the other two, they're not so complicated. Give them some good hard work, and they're happy."

Although the other woman sounded frustrated, her words filled Holly with growing assurance that Steele was exactly the sort of man she needed and wanted.

But how to make up for all her mistakes and prove to him what was in her heart, buried for a time beneath doubts and fears?

Steele's father joined them, draping his arm across his wife's shoulders. "What are the boys up to?"

Mrs. Davis smiled. "They've gone to pick up something for Grandpops."

Holly excused herself and returned to the party although she felt little party spirit. Even the return of Steele and his brothers didn't give her cause to celebrate. They delivered a parcel to the front. Henry quietly presented it to Nan. She unwrapped it and laughed then threw her arms around Henry's neck.

Henry held the gift for all to see. Holly's eyes blurred when she saw it was a painting of Henry and Nan together at the picnic she and Steele had gone on with them. Henry must have had it painted from the photo Holly had taken that day. And it would explain why Henry had begged it off her and made her promise not to mention it to Nan.

Afterward, the three brothers moved around the room as a unit, making it impossible for her to apologize to Steele. She overheard him tell his mother he and his brothers planned to spend the weekend hiking in the mountains.

She'd have to wait until his return to speak to him.

◆

Steele returned from a vigorous weekend. His brothers might be into physical work on a daily basis, but he had left them panting and begging him to slow down.

Mike had waited until they huddled around the fireplace roasting wieners and burning marshmallows before he started his free analysis of Steele's psyche. "You can't get away from your feelings, man. Take it from someone who knows."

"Sounds to me like you're about to make excuses for not being able to keep up. Maybe your age is starting to show." He loved to rub in the fact Mike was a year older. "So what's your excuse, Billy-boy?"

The youngest brother laughed. "Leave me out of this argument. Trouble with you two is you let yourself care too much about one woman. Take me. I know how to enjoy them without getting all tangled up inside."

Mike understood too much of how Steele was feeling, though Steele would never give him the satisfaction of admitting it. He'd spent two days trying to drive Holly from his thoughts with physical exercise, but sore muscles were all he'd managed to achieve.

She'd made it clear at the engagement party that she would never trust him. She hadn't even given him a chance to explain. Later, he'd avoided her. Didn't want to hear any more accusations. He just wanted to forget her.

But Mike was right. There seemed no way to run from his feelings. Feelings he didn't intend to validate by naming.

◆

Steele sat behind his desk staring at the pile of work before him. His secretary knocked. "Delivery for you, Steele." She placed a parcel on his desk and retreated.

He turned the package around with little interest. He hadn't ordered anything and didn't much care for unsolicited freebies. But it beat tackling the files on his desk, so he ripped it open. Inside sat a foil-wrapped parcel and an envelope.

He slid his thumbnail under the flap of the envelope and pulled out a card. His thoughts stalled as he saw a construction scene with piles of dirt and rough ground with a big yellow Cat in the back. Right dead center in the foreground sat a tiny green wrought-iron bistro table and two people with their hands clasped. The man, his back showing, wore a suit and a bright yellow hard hat. No mistaking the caricature of the woman. A mass of waves, big brown eyes. Really big. Surrounding the table, cutting them off from the construction scene, banks and banks of purple flowers.

He traced his fingertip over the flowers, rested it on the face of the woman. A smile tugged at his heart, crept to his mouth. Holly—sweet, romantic and idealistic—had sent him a card she'd painted. He wasn't sure what it meant except it promised better things ahead.

He flipped open the card and read the verse inside, penned in precise calligraphy:

Love is a many splendored thing.
It is different for different people,
Different things at different times.

Beneath it she had written, *Steele, I'm sorry. Can you give me another chance?*

Men don't cry. They don't get all mushy about flowers and cards. He'd been told so all his life. Yet he'd never believed it. Not really. And he certainly didn't at this moment as his vision blurred. He knew what this card meant. It was more than an apology. It was an invitation. Acceptance. By putting the flowers and table in the center of a construction site, she'd informed him that their very different viewpoints worked together in a way unique to them.

He hurried over to the windows and stared down at the café, hoping to see her giving out flowers and optimism. He wasn't disappointed. She bent toward a couple at a table tucked between two planter dividers, placing a pink flower in the center of the table and then spun away, her hair cascading about her shoulders as she turned. In his mind, he heard her laughing.

He grabbed the phone and made arrangements for a special delivery. Only then did he reach for the unopened gift and pulled out a tiny crystal vase. It held a purple gerbera daisy in water. How had it managed not to spill? He tipped it slightly. It wasn't water, just some kind of gel that looked like water. He laughed out loud and put the vase in the center front of his desk where he sat and stared at it.

The clock moved toward closing time with agonizing slowness. Finally the hour arrived, and he hurried across the street, carrying the card and gift with him.

She saw him, stopped, and waited, her eyes almost as wide as on the card. He sensed her uncertainty in the way she squeezed the tea towel in her hands until her knuckles looked like a row of white marbles.

"Thanks for the gift." He held out the vase. "And a very nice card."

"You like them?" Her voice quavered uncertainly.

He longed to ease her concerns but knew it wasn't as simple as pulling her into his arms and kissing her. They had to resolve some of the issues between them. "I do. Especially the card. Did you mean to show us working things out?"

She nodded. "Is it possible?"

He turned her toward a table and called for Meggie to bring them coffee. "I think it's very possible. What we are is a little bit romantic, a little bit practical. We have our own unique blend. A balance maybe."

"Nan said we balanced each other." Holly chuckled. "She seemed to think that was a good thing."

He traced the line of her jaw with his finger, paused to play with a strand of hair, letting himself love everything about this woman from her wavy hair, to her uncertain smile, to her romantic idealism. "Holly, for the first time since I was a little kid, I feel satisfied about who I am. I've been hiding my true feelings about a lot of things behind my defense of practical. But the closer I get to you, the more comfortable I am acknowledging who I really am and what I want."

Her eyes filled with the light of a thousand stars. "That's wonderful. I'm glad." She pressed her hand over his, capturing it against her cheek. "In you I've found what I need and want. I've found solidness that allows me to trust as much as I dream. I trust you. I know I haven't exactly shown it, but I've been afraid." She turned and placed a kiss in his palm.

Her confession puzzled him. "What are you afraid of?"

She lifted a shy look to him. "Hurting you like Mom hurt Dad. I don't know that I can be all you need."

His words scratched from a throat that tightened at her confession. "No one has ever cared about what I need like you do. Holly, we'll both make mistakes. Only God is perfect. As long as we stay close to Him, He'll enable us to overcome our weaknesses, to grow and to forgive each other and ourselves when we need it."

"I like that," she whispered.

He forced himself to ignore the way she looked at him, all kissable and eager. "Holly, I've done some serious soul searching about what I believe—really believe—about love and marriage. Not just the words but where the rubber meets the road. Right in my office. I still want to help people so they don't make momentous mistakes at a time when they are thinking with their emotions. But in the future, I'll only act to protect a marriage."

Tears spilled from her eyes.

He grabbed a napkin and dabbed at them, his heart ready to burst from the pain of making her cry. "I thought you'd be happy about it."

"I am. These are happy tears."

"Whew. You scared me."

"Steele Davis, you are a generous and kind man. I'm so proud to know you."

At that moment, the delivery van pulled up. Two men got out carrying armloads of pink carnations. They filled Holly's arms and her lap. Several times they returned to the van for more flowers. They piled them on the table, arranged vases of them on the floor around Holly, and put more on the adjoining table.

Steele handed them a tip, grinning at Holly's surprise.

"What is this?"

"I'm setting the scene." Every pain of rejected, denied emotions of his past was washed away by the look in her darkening eyes, full of expectant trust. He would spend the rest of his life fulfilling that trust if she'd let him.

He went to her side, fell to one knee, and took her hand. "Holly Hope, I love you. I want to spend the rest of my life doing my best to make you happy. Will you marry me and let me do that?"

"I love you, Steele Davis. I'd be honored to marry you. And I promise to spend the rest of my life doing my best to satisfy your needs."

Ignoring the pink flowers that almost buried her, he cupped her head and kissed her with a heart full of love and gratitude.

When he finally released her, her cheeks glowed the color of the flowers. Her eyes glistened with some sort of inner joy.

She gave a long look around. "Pink flowers?"

He nodded. "Can't think of a better way to say 'I love you.'"

Epilogue

Holly's mother smiled as she adjusted Holly's veil. "You're the most beautiful bride."

Nan chuckled. "What does that make me?"

Holly and Mom laughed and shared a special glance of understanding. "You're beautiful, too," they chorused. Indeed, Nan, in a slim-fitting, pink silk suit, glowed like a summer sky just as the sun teased at the horizon. Holly knew the glow had nothing to do with the color of Nan's suit. It came from inside. She knew because her own insides glowed so warm she thought her heart would spontaneously combust.

Mom hurried to peek through the doors. For the seven hundredth time. As if she were the one getting married. "Isn't it time to begin? When's the organist going to start our song?"

Nan and Holly smiled at each other at Mom's impatience.

"You're sure you don't mind sharing your day with an old lady?" Nan asked, marring her serenity with a tiny frown.

"Not one bit. I'm glad we decided to do this together," Holly whispered, her throat tightening. "It makes the day even more special."

The music changed.

"About time," Mom grumbled. She backed from the door. "Do I look okay?"

"Mom, you're beautiful." She wore a frothy dress in pale blue. She'd gained back the weight she'd lost. "You could pass for my sister. Now go."

Mom drew in a deep breath and marched down the aisle.

Nan was next. She never faltered. Never hesitated. Didn't even glance back at Holly.

And then it was Holly's turn. Dad joined her. "You ready, my sweet daughter?"

"Are you ready, my handsome father?"

He grinned. "Let's do this."

Holly stepped into the church, forced herself to look at Mom waiting at the front, Nan and Henry beside her, and then allowed herself to meet Steele's gaze. After that, nothing else mattered. If not for Dad's steadying arm, she would have raced to Steele's side.

"Who giveth this woman?" Pastor Don asked.

Dad handed her to Steele then took his place beside Mom.

Pastor Don addressed the gathered friends and family.

"Today we are witnesses of a unique ceremony. The marriage of Steele and Holly. The marriage of their grandparents. And the renewal of vows between Holly's parents. A blessed occasion, indeed."

Mom and Dad renewed their vows. Holly had promised herself she wouldn't cry, and she succeeded, though it took a few deep breaths. Steele squeezed her hand. She knew he understood her emotion at seeing her parents recommit to each other. She had him to thank for helping them.

Then Nan and Henry exchanged vows. Holly pressed her lips together and widened her eyes. She would not cry on her wedding day no matter how touched she was by the deep, open love between the older couple.

And then it was their turn. She turned to face Steele and almost lost control of her tears when she saw how his eyes glistened. She loved him all the more for his tender side.

They promised to love each other until death. Then the three couples moved to sign the register, Mom and Dad witnessing both marriages.

She glanced about. Love was truly a unique thing for each couple. The grandparents, a blend of romance and practicality. Her parents, a love based on hope and forgiveness. Steele's parents, their love so practical, yet for them exactly what they needed and wanted.

She glanced up at Steele, her new husband. Their love was a blend of all of the above. It would change and grow as they did.

The pastor asked the congregation to stand as he prayed.

"Lord, bless these unions with enduring marriages and everlasting love. Amen."

The six people at the front echoed with a resounding "Amen."

A Letter to Our Readers

Dear Readers:

In order that we might better contribute to your reading enjoyment, we would appreciate your taking a few minutes to respond to the following questions. When completed, please return to the following: Fiction Editor, Barbour Publishing, Inc., P.O. Box 719, Uhrichsville, OH 44683.

1. Did you enjoy reading *Montana Weddings* by Linda Ford?
   ❑ Very much—I would like to see more books like this.
   ❑ Moderately—I would have enjoyed it more if _____
   _____
   _____

2. What influenced your decision to purchase this book?
   (Check those that apply.)
   ❑ Cover   ❑ Back cover copy   ❑ Title   ❑ Price
   ❑ Friends   ❑ Publicity   ❑ Other

3. Which story was your favorite?
   ❑ *Cry of My Heart*   ❑ *Everlasting Love*
   ❑ *Darcy's Inheritance*

4. Please check your age range:
   ❑ Under 18   ❑ 18–24   ❑ 25–34
   ❑ 35–45   ❑ 46–55   ❑ Over 55

5. How many hours per week do you read? _____

Name _____

Occupation _____

Address _____

City _____ State _____ Zip _____

E-mail _____

If you enjoyed

MONTANA
Weddings

then read

New Mexico
Weddings

Family Is the Tie that Binds in Three Romances

Family Circle, Family Ties, Family Reunion
by Janet Lee Barton
